THE REVELATIONS OF PRESTON BLACK

RAW DOG
SCREAMING
PRESS

Published by Raw Dog Screaming Press
Bowie, MD

First Edition

Cover: Brad Vetter, BradVetterDesigns.com
Book Design: Jennifer Barnes

Printed in the United States of America

ISBN: 978-1-935738-48-0
Library of Congress Control Number: 2013940314

www.RawDogScreaming.com

This book is for my mom, Sandra.

HOLDING HANDS WITH THE DEVIL

Kill Every Sparrow, Friday, March 15, 7:30, The Orpheum Theater, Bardstown Road, Louisville.

If you skipped Foster the People's show to sneak into the Bonnaroo Music and Arts Festival's 'That Tent' back in June, you know that Kill Every Sparrow is a raw new talent that combines musical intricacy with atom bomb fury. And you understand that their foray into the iTunes Top 100 this summer was no fluke, making some wonder if the whispered stories they've heard about West Virginia's Katy Stefanic and Preston Black are true.

Kill Every Sparrow arrives in Louisville hot off a series of summer festival appearances and a string of sold-out East Coast club shows. But most fans know their story really starts with the EP LIVE AT THE STINK released by Blacksnake Recordings back in May. That night saw a bar band guitarist musically reborn as one half of this indie/revivalist/punk duet during a show some eyewitnesses described as "surreal." The concert's pivotal moment appears on the EP's final track, the eponymous "The Sad Ballad of Preston Black," when the singer challenges the devil with the line, "If I don't have a soul to steal then we sure as hell don't have a deal."

It's a line he hasn't sung since.

From the moment she walks across that stage, you know Katy Stefanic is the kind of girl you could fall in love with. Though romantically involved, but not married, the pair play off each other like they have been attached at the hip for twenty years, instantaneously responding to frequent and impulsive key and tempo changes. Call me jaded, but watching Stefanic and Black work the aural space over the crowd mesmerizes me in a way only more seasoned acts have been able to do nowadays. Except for the random, "Marry me, Katy," (or "Preston, call me,") the crowd remained stone silent during ballads and soft instrumentals. Even more curious was the way the audience responded to the mix of old time throw-down melodies and punk-fast tempos with fists in the air and good old-fashioned foot stomping. And when the lights came up for the first encore the frenzied crowd responded like Joe Strummer himself had decided to join them for a song or two.

I had a chance to talk to Stefanic and Black after their show in D.C. last Saturday and asked them about their relationship and how it affected their musical development. Preston sat contentedly, letting his beloved do most of the talking.

With a wide smile, she folded her hands over her knee and explained, "Sharing music with somebody is a lot like sharing a bed. After a while you start to know when something's building, when things are going to sour, when the temperature's going to change with a look."

Preston added, "It's like *yinz* and *y'all*. Same language, just different ways of saying things. What the audience hears is where we meet in the middle."

When I ask Preston to talk about 'the song' he gets quiet. After a thoughtful moment, he says, "You ever hear that story about Zeppelin and the sharks? That supposedly didn't happen either. I think that night at The Stink served as a way—my way, at least—of being resurrected into music. Basically a way for me to make the statement, 'This is what we're going to do and this is how we're going to do it.' It's like that. Did I go down to the crossroads and make a deal with the devil?" He looks at Katy, then adds, "Did Robert Johnson?"

I remind Preston that a reporter from the Virginia Tech Collegiate Times quotes him as saying he, "...spent too much time down at the crossroads..." and, "...the devil tried to get to him by hurting his brother and killing his drummer, Stu..." in an interview from last October.

At that point Katy takes over. "Preston said a lot of things while swept up in that early hype. Some of us aren't used to having everything we say recorded for posterity."

When I mention that some of his fans have bought into the whole '...freed himself from the devil's clutches' mythos Preston regains his composure. He laughs and says, "The audience hears what it hears."

Tickets for Friday's show are available online or by calling The Orpheum Theater's box office.

BODY OF MISSING NORTH CAROLINA HIKER
FOUND IN TENNESSEE RIVER

Huntsville Times, Sunday, March 17

The search for a missing Asheville, North Carolina hiker ended tragically Saturday along the Tennessee River just north of Guntersville, Alabama.

Family members told the Marshall County Sheriff's Office that they had not heard from their daughter, Savannah Trucks, since she called from a Rite Aid in East Ellijay, Georgia, before beginning an Appalachian Trail through-hike from Springer Mountain in mid-February. Her mother, Shirley Trucks, said that Savannah had been harassed by a man and a woman in a white van while she waited for her ride to the trailhead. Authorities began searching for Savannah on March 13 after she missed a pre-arranged meeting with her family in Fontana Lake, North Carolina, to resupply.

A pair of Albertville fishermen notified authorities after spotting the victim in an arm of Guntersville Lake near Buck's Pocket State Park Saturday morning, where EMS personnel recovered her body. The Sheriff's Office spokesman said that an autopsy from the Marshall County Coroner's Office wouldn't be ready for a few days, but he believed that drowning did not cause her death, noting the presence of extensive bruising on her forearms and wrists, which are consistent with a more violent crime. "This is going to be a very, very horrendous act. I am convinced of that after having observed the body. A young lady's death is always a terrible thing, but a young lady who dies under extreme violence is the absolute worst," he told reporters.

"She's a very outgoing and a kind individual," Bill Trucks said from North Carolina before his daughter was found. "She's got a heart of gold."

THE FIRST REVELATION OF PRESTON BLACK

CHAPTER ONE

Raindrops and fireflies, autumn lightning splashed across the sky,
While down here it's still July.
City's dark except for the cars, and high above I see the same stars
That we wished on twenty years ago.
The alarm clock is set, and even though it isn't tomorrow yet,
I see something I don't want to forget,
And stay up all night watching you.

"Anniversary Song" Music and Lyrics by Katy Stefanic and Preston Black

Nobody wants to fight. You're stupid if you do. Or an asshole.

When you pull yourself up out of the dirt the last thing you want to do is talk about it. You want to go home, clean yourself up and have a drink or five. The drinking isn't to loosen your lips. It's to knock you out, so you can go to bed without thinking about it.

If you're good, or smart, you can let weeks and months go by without ever discussing it. The people around you will always know you got your ass handed to you, and if they love you they don't ever bring it up. Eventually, it stings a little less each time you drive by the place where the ass-kicking happened. The blood stains come out of your shirt. Then a year goes by, and you're the only one who still remembers it. Which is fine. Ain't a thing wrong with it.

Then you're rolling out of a new town, feeling about as sad as rolling into a new town makes you happy. You come over a bridge or through a tunnel and catch that first glimpse of a new skyline or the first few notes of the local alt rock or college radio station and feel like all the TV dinners and frat house basements were worth it. You know a new city means possibilities, new food and new accents. Tamales in Austin and real Carolina barbeque in Lexington. You bump into some of the coolest people you'll ever meet in Boulder, Colorado, and laugh, because you'd never even heard of the place before July. Having a worldview shaped by one small town in north-central West Virginia makes seeing places like Charlotte and Tempe feel about as exciting as seeing Liverpool itself. You hadn't taken a single picture since that photography class back in high school and you just took that class because you heard you could get high in the dark room. But since last summer you've taken at least ten thousand because you don't want to forget a single second of this.

And coming into Louisville felt no different. All morning we talked about fried pickles and burgoo and ribs, and how good food could make you feel safe and warm, almost like being in your own bed. Getting to share it with your two best friends—the woman that I loved and my brother—made me wonder what I'd done to deserve it all. The only thing I could think about as we loaded our gear and got ready to roll out was all the stuff I wanted to see and do next time we came back.

And how that asshole reporter from that shitty little alternative newspaper crapped all over everything bringing that fucking devil thing back up.

Katy leaned over the steering wheel. "We got problems."

The protestors swarmed past the club's security guys to block the alley. The assorted men, women, and children looked like the kind of people who spent a lot of time oppressing pleasure. The type of people who'd protest a soldier's funeral because somewhere down the line a burning bush told them to. Mostly women wearing skirts down to their ankles and long hair piled high on top of their heads. Women with faces that never even wore smiles, let alone lipstick.

They shook their brightly colored hand-painted signs at us.

DEATH PENALTY FOR WITCHES.

NOT BLESSED JUST CURSED.

DEAL WITH THE DEVIL? BURN IN HELL.

Before Katy could react I reached over and locked her door. "Get ready to drive."

But she fixated on a sign that said *GOD HATES WITCHES* for a long moment. Her lips parted, like she'd try to reason with each and every one of them single-handedly given the chance. "Run them over, you mean?"

"Jesus, no, Katy. You want to end up in a Kentucky state pen?" Pauly climbed out of the van's sliding side door and stomped his cigarette into the concrete. Pauly leaned against the passenger-side door and said, "Drive real slow and don't stop until you hit the street."

Four bikers wearing leather and club colors spread themselves across the alley, trying to make themselves look bigger in the van's headlights. Katy flicked the high beams, forcing their tall shadows onto the brick buildings on the other side of Bardstown Road. The chains they wore shined in the halogen lamps, sparkling like disco balls.

"Shit, Katy," I said. "Look."

Tattooed across the bikers' jawlines and shaved heads were vertical rows of small squiggles. They looked like words, disjointed verses in black ink. Warnings, curses, poetry… I couldn't make them out from this distance. The biker with his arms exposed had the same markings there too—all the way down to his wrist. Like somebody had drawn all over him with a black Sharpie.

I said, "You think I should call the police?"

"You can give it a shot," Pauly said, "Just don't leave me, okay?"

I said, "Where you going?"

"Roll your window up." He slammed the side door shut and disappeared into the darkness.

Katy drove her palm into the steering wheel. The horn echoed off both sides of the narrow alley.

I didn't even ask if they'd seen the needle tracks covering the women's hands. Tiny black and blue marks pocked the skin from their elbows to their wrists. Like my dad had on his arms. "Fucking hypocrite junkies," I said.

As the van drifted ahead the protestors screamed louder and shook their signs harder. Katy checked the door locks again to make sure.

Women and children shouted, "*God hates witches. You hate God.*" They locked arms, forming a wall between us and the road. The chilly Kentucky air let their frosty breath hang over their heads for a moment before being eaten up by the streetlights.

"Preston…who are these people?" She rolled down her window like she wanted to have some kind of dialog with them. The brakes squealed as she brought the van to a halt.

I rolled down my window a few inches and yelled, "I don't know what kind of issues you all are dealing with—"

One of the bikers stepped out of formation and strode toward me like a cop at a traffic stop. He stood a head taller than me and wore a sleeveless denim vest over a black T-shirt. He ran his hand along his scalp. I half expected the black ink on his head to smudge. The other bikers followed a few steps behind him. They stopped right in front of the van and pounded the hood.

I jammed my hand under the seat and grabbed the only thing I could find. A long plastic window scraper with a brush along one side. I shook it at the biker and said, "What the fuck do you need?"

"Just a word, my friend," he said as he hooked a thumb into his belt. His other hand went to his back pocket. "Step on out of the van so we can talk."

"Well, send an email and get the hell out of the way."

"Hell is what I'm talking about." His Southern accent didn't sound like anything I'd heard in Kentucky. Sounded more like the kids in Austin. He took a small metal rod from his back pocket. "Jesus died for your sins, you know? Least you could do is cut the blasphemy."

"Last time I checked, I can believe whatever I want. You got something you want to say to me? That's your problem, not mine. Now why don't you move along?" Fear made my voice waver.

"Step out of the van." With a snap of his wrist the metal rod became a long metal bar. "Tell you what. Let's talk about the Lord for a spell and I'll spare your fingers."

"What are you doing, Katy? Just go," I yelled, waving her ahead. "I'm calling the cops because you got no right, man. No right at all."

Katy let the van drift forward as she laid on the horn. A chorus of shouts rang through the protestors. A woman screamed, "We got young ones here!"

I dug for my phone without ever once taking my eyes off him. But instead of making eye contact, I stared at the scrawl all over his bare skin, over his scalp and neck and cheeks and jaw.

Off to the left side of the van one of the women screamed so loud I thought she'd been run over. The biker spun to face the street, swinging the retractable baton out in front of him. The mob jerked out of their trance in unison and retreated to Bardstown Road as two, then three, then four of the women shielded their faces with their arms and signs. My first reaction was to push Katy to the floor, but I caught movement in the side view mirror and turned around.

Pauly emerged from the darkness behind the van grinning like a jack-o'-lantern, working a stream of cold water from a hose like a fireman putting out a house fire. Back and forth again and again, mercilessly dousing their faces and clothes. Pauly's very own Bible-thumper wet T-shirt contest.

"Come get some, bitches." Pauly laughed and held the hose between his legs like he was pissing on them. I hadn't seen him laugh so much since we left Philly. "This one's for Pipeline."

"Go, Katy. Take your foot off the brake and go." I leaned over and hit the horn.

Some of the protestors shielded themselves with their signs, wet poster board crumpled in their hands. The rest dispersed, their unified chants broke down into a loud murmur of personalized curses. The biker with the baton beat on the hood in an attempt to regain his ground, but Katy nosed the van ahead like an old pro. The rest banged on the side and tried rocking it, but we were already out on the street.

Pauly came around the back of the van and walked beside the sliding door, still dousing the protestors.

"He's going to get us killed," Katy said. "Get him in here."

"Katy, watch the road. How's it going to look if you take out a little kid?"

"Preston!"

I turned as the biker swung his baton. It hit the door with a loud crack that left a heavy dent. He'd meant to break my arm or jaw. Definitely not a love tap.

"You self-righteous prick." Pauly hit him in the face with a blast from his hose. "I'm a fucking kill you!"

I said, "C'mon, Pauly. Get in," as I reached back to open the door behind me. I felt bad for squashing his fun. Like I was the one who had to tell him he'd gotten too old for trick-or-treat or whatever.

"This might be a good fucking gig after all," Pauly climbed onto the bench seat and slid the door shut, smiling like he'd just won free Subway for a year. He turned to the crowd and flipped them off with both hands. He waggled his fingers back and forth and said, "Fuck off."

Once Katy got out of the alley she hit the gas. Two of the bikers followed on foot, banging the trailer with their batons.

I turned to watch them fall behind us. The women and kids huddled together, shivering in the chill. One man stood calmly apart from the crowd. A young guy with a full beard and close-cropped blond hair. He wore a fine grey jacket and vest with jeans and a white button-down. He maintained eye contact with me until we got to the end of the block. I'd seen him before, in Morgantown, from a distance. Like a ghost, or a face in the crowd. It wasn't only the way he looked. The way he dressed and carried himself struck a chord of familiarity with me. He knew me, too.

"What do you think, Pres?" Pauly tried to light a cigarette but his hands were shaking too bad. "Still got it?"

"Yeah, Pauly. You're not going to tell your sponsor about this, are you?" I watched the bearded guy until he faded into the darkness.

"No way. What happens in the van in a dark alley in Kentucky does not come back to the Mountain State with me."

"You're going to hell for that, you know?" Katy said with a smile. She made a right turn on red and we passed the front of the old theater. I watched it, trying to remember every single thing that happened behind those doors before Katy built up even more speed.

Pauly said, "I know," folded his hands behind his head and lay down in the back seat.

"Nobody on earth except for Katy Stefanic ever ate at a Waffle House because they wanted to." Pauly's anger came out a little at a time, like bees from a hive on a summer morning. "Don't act like this happened accidentally either. The way I see it, I'm driving, doing the sound, playing bass on a few songs, and playing security with those Westboro Baptist wannabes. How am I not getting more of a say in where we eat?"

"Don't act like you cast a tiebreaker with your one vote." Katy tossed him the keys and bounded around the van. She waited for me to slide out of the passenger seat. "And I drove tonight."

"Did we vote?" Pauly took a cigarette out of the pack and slid it behind his ear. "Pres, did you vote for this? Just because we're in the South don't mean we have to eat at every Waffle House we see. What about a pizza? We'll order when we get to our hotel."

I had my mouth open to say something, but Katy struck fast, like a cat. "Because it's going to be on the interstate and we're going to get stuck at a Krystal because you know there's no such thing as good pizza along an interstate."

"Better than white gravy," Pauly said.

I'd been asleep. Waking up in the Waffle House parking lot surprised me about as much as waking up on Mick's floor would've. Which was to say it didn't surprise me at all. My legs still weren't totally beneath me. I leaned against the van and yawned while Katy weaseled a hug and a kiss out of me. Even I-65 was quiet except for a stray semi here and there. In this part of the world people went to bed early. I said, "No, Pauly, I didn't vote. I wouldn't mind if we skipped all this and found a hotel to be totally honest. Don't put me in the middle."

"Driver votes twice anyway. You know the rules by now, Pallini. Took me two cheese steaks to figure out your system. You'll eat good in Nashville." She grabbed my hand and pulled me toward the yellow-and-black-checked interior of the only thing keeping me from getting a full seven hours tonight. "I promise."

"Hear that, Pallini?" As I held the door for him, I caught a whiff of bacon, maple syrup and floor cleaner. "Besides, you got a week off while we hit the studio. Then when we see you in Atlanta you're going to be hugging all over us, like, 'Man, I missed you guys so much… What would I ever do without you in my life?' So savor the moment, brother. Enjoy your waffles."

While Pauly followed Katy to an ice-cold, rock hard booth, the jukebox sucked me over like some kind of musical black hole. By now I knew to totally disregard the Waffle House songs in the first row, like Mary Welch Rogers's "Waffle House Thank You."

From the booth Katy asked if I wanted 'savory' or 'sweet.'

"Savory. Thanks, *chicita*," I said without thinking. I ran through the rows of songs, putting together a little playlist in my head. Most people didn't realize it, but song order played as important a role as song choice. "No Beatles?"

"Pres, give it a break, will you? There's a whole 'nother world of music out there waiting to be discovered." Pauly's head swiveled, looking for the young waitress while he mentally subtracted dimes off her potential tip for making him wait.

"Jackson" came through the shitty speakers first. I looked at Katy and smiled but she rolled her eyes. I said, "You're hotter than a pepper sprout, you know that, my love?"

She smiled an acknowledgement. "Haven't heard that one yet."

"Any requests?"

"Yeah," Pauly said. "Sit down so we can eat."

So I spent the rest of my quarters playing "In Memory of Elizabeth Reed," some Hank Williams, Kris Kristofferson, and Deana Carter. Then to throw everybody off I played two more from 'back in the day' for Katy—Reba's "The Night the Lights Went Out In Georgia" and No Doubt's version of "It's My Life."

I spun, looking for the restroom. The night manager pointed off to the right and I had to shuffle all the way to the end of the counter before I could see the door. The thing I loved most about Waffle Houses was how they crammed two thousand square feet of interior into a thousand square foot exterior. I knocked on the door twice then pushed it open with my foot.

The condom dispenser had Bible verses written on it. I read them while the hot water ran. When I saw steam I lowered my face to the sink and sucked up as much as I could. Going from the warm stage to the cold street played havoc with my sinuses. I tried to blow mucus out of my throat and ears, then squirted soap onto my hands, lathered up real good and scrubbed my face. It felt so nice to get rid of the funk in my eyes and the little bit of old sweat that clung to my hairline.

I pulled a long strip of paper towels out of the dispenser and patted my skin and hair dry, then used it to pull the door open. Before stepping out of the bathroom I checked my phone. Nothing except Twitter updates and mentions.

As soon as I came around the corner I saw my Arnold Palmer waiting for me. Katy and Pauly had been fighting about something. Probably money.

Pauly pointed at my crotch and said, "Kennywood's open."

I checked my zipper and gave him the classic, "So funny I forgot to laugh," then sat down and said, "What's going on here?"

"Nothing," Pauly said. "Nothing at all."

Katy bit her lip. I knew a lie when I heard one.

I said, "Well, somebody had better start talking."

She said, "The theater had all kinds of returns when these Holy Roller nutjobs showed up in town this week. And they refunded a bunch of tickets today."

"Whatever," I said, disgusted. "What about merch?"

She shook her head.

"So we didn't sell anything? Stickers?"

"Preston, we're covering our expenses." I tried to say something else but she cut me off. Her worry fell away, like she finally remembered that she was Katy Stefanic and she sure as hell didn't get bothered by stuff like this. "Look, this is our first disappointing night. No big deal. Spring break happened last week and Easter's coming up. Plus it's the tournament and both Louisville and UK are still in it. You know how Morgantown gets when WVU is playing basketball this late in the season. I don't know, Preston, but it's no reason to panic. Because you're going to get Pauly all fired up and next thing I know I'm dealing with two crybabies the whole way to Nashville instead of one."

"So we're supposed to suck it up? Can the label help us out? With getting our money, I mean?"

Katy sipped her tea.

Pauly didn't say anything either, but he hadn't done much to hide the fact that this last leg of the tour had worn him out. The miles didn't hurt so much as the hours. I didn't ask him to burn vacation days to shuttle me and Katy around. He volunteered. Said we couldn't afford union labor. And he probably did save us thousands of dollars. But I felt like he regretted it. Or resented it. He still walked with a limp from the accident last winter, and I cringed whenever I saw him popping ibuprofen like Tic Tacs.

"Forget about it, okay?" Katy kissed me on the cheek.

"Yeah."

The waitress set my food on the table as I tried to let go of my anger. I patted Katy on the knee and smiled. "Okay."

My order never changed unless I wanted sweet instead of savory, and as the smell of smothered, covered, diced and topped hash browns hit my nose I found myself wishing I'd gotten waffles and bacon instead.

Pauly didn't say a word as the waitress set his plate down.

"T-bone?" She said the 'T' so it rhymed with 'hay.'

Pauly nodded.

I said, "Don't hear you complaining anymore."

"I'm not," Pauly said with a big smile.

They both dug in. Having just awoken, I wasn't as hungry, and took the opportunity to break down the show like we always did once we were back on the road. I believed the analysis made us play better, gave us a sense of what worked and what didn't. "What do you guys think about what went down tonight?"

"Preston…" Katy put her fork down. "Not now, okay? Don't talk like somebody who left the mountains just to climb more mountains."

Not the response I expected.

"These whack jobs show up and basically take money from our pockets. What else is there to discuss? Until tonight this had been a pretty fun trip." Pauly put a big bite of steak into his mouth and said, "Look where we're at, brother. Imagine somebody from New York down here. They'd want to know where to get their passport stamped. It ain't a big deal."

"That's not really what I meant. I hoped we could talk about the music," I said. "Besides, we didn't have any problems like this in Florida."

"Well, Florida ain't exactly the South. More like the biggest island in the Caribbean. Last July I got lost in Miami hauling a load of furniture and I had to find a translator before I could get directions. Got stuck at this *bodega*. Ate like seven ham sandwiches, no lie." Still chewing, Pauly said, "Heard the blond guy we saw back in Louisville grew up preaching. One of the guys hanging out by the soundboard said he got all kinds of videos on YouTube, speaking in front of big churches. Said he was on the Today Show with Katie Couric when he was six or seven."

Nobody talked while the jukebox skipped to the next song. Like we had to observe the silence too. As soon as "Strawberry Wine" came on Katy chimed in, saying, "The man's name is Elijah Clay Hicks. He's a nut."

When Katy said the name I flinched. I knew that I knew him, and until she said the name I couldn't figure out how.

"Jamie had me out on the festival circuit as a kid. Those things are like bug zappers for attracting the type of people that speak in tongues and blow up abortion clinics. Hicks's daddy had a big old revival tent where folks would writhe on the ground and handle serpents as part of a network of churches all over Appalachia. Supposedly they hid fugitives from the law, moving them from place to place like some kind of fundamentalist Underground Railroad. That's how they never arrested anybody for those bombings in Atlanta." She paused while she poured more honey into her tea. "The club manager said Hicks and his group showed up in town on Wednesday. They went to some of the student organizations and campus ministries at U of L and to a few of the big mega-churches spreading all this stuff about Preston and the devil. I figure they just cost us a lot of the last minute sales we might've gotten. It's not a big deal."

"What about Hicks? You know him?"

"Hicks believed proximity made us a likely couple. Like I should have been queen of his little road show. He pursued me so aggressively I stopped going to festivals with Jamie."

"So you have a history?"

"Preston. Don't. Hicks and I never shared a pop let alone a moment, although we could've made a nice life off those collection plates of his. Hicks is the only preacher I know whose mission work in New York City includes trips to Barneys. And I've told you everything you need to know about my past romantic endeavors. Which is everything. If I left anything out it's because I'd forgotten. That's it. "

"I'm sorry." I stood corrected and took a bite of my hash browns. To deflect attention from my insinuation, I said, "So they take that song literally? And that's why they were all up in our business? Don't tell me they've got nothing better to do."

"They think the earth was created in four thousand years, why wouldn't they believe you when you sing 'tried to make the devil a deal, but the devil said I didn't have a soul to steal?'" She set her knife and fork down like she couldn't eat with this kind of talk buzzing around the table like horseflies.

"Because it's a fucking song, that's why. There isn't a real stairway to heaven either. Sergeant Pepper isn't a real guy." I gulped down the rest of my tea. "You think it's over?"

"We'll see what happens tonight. Having next week off might make them lose interest. Unless they find out where we're recording. I don't know." She poured maple syrup onto her waffle and cut herself off a few more squares. "We have Nashville then Atlanta then we go home. We have lives to live—they don't. Those people are dying so slowly they don't even know they're dying. Like *Tamagotchis*. Remember those? They eat and go to the bathroom and die and we can do two more shows with or without them. Okay? It'll be Easter and we'll get to see everybody and Rachel will make you breakfast and you can drink all day long with my pap. I'm looking forward to that more than I would a week in Paris or a million dollars."

I shook my head.

"Preston…the only reason we're here is to do what we're meant to do."

"Yeah. Fine. But I have to say this and then I'll be done for the night—maybe this is what I meant when I told you guys the hellhounds are catching up to me."

"Preston, jeez—"

Pauly cut her off, "You got to stop with that shit. Move on, bro."

I said, "Berry Oakley told his wife he had hellhounds on his trail the week before he died. Tell me that ain't coincidence. Besides, how can I let it go? You walk with a limp you'll never get rid of. Stu's gone—"

"You think the devil did that?" Pauly's voice got real loud. He pounded the table so hard the silverware jumped. "Am I supposed to sit here and believe your situation caused my accident? I fell off the wagon, man. Stu'd just died. A freak accident. There ain't nothing mysterious about it at all. Katy said she never even saw the woman you're talking about and she played at The Stink with you that night. Get out of your head, man. Live in reality."

"You told Pauly you didn't see her?" My face burned.

Katy looked at Pauly like she would've stabbed him with her fork if she could've gotten away with it. She turned to me and said, "I told you I didn't want you opening with that song because you're perpetuating this whole thing in your head. Robert Johnson had hellhounds on his tail, not you."

"Trail," I corrected her.

"Whatever, Preston. You have to learn to separate who you are on stage from who you are with Pauly and me. I know you feel like you have an image to maintain, but trying to live up to it is stressing you out. You can't be two different people. Most of us have a hard enough time being one. Your drinking is borderline out of hand and the not being able to sleep is from the anxiety of touring and writing. Not hellhounds."

"You know," I said, pushing my plate away, "I had people tonight wanting to grab a drink with me after the show. And I wanted to join them. They paid money to see us and I feel like I let them down."

I raised my finger to let them know I had more to say because if I didn't either one of them would've jumped in. "And I've never been subjected to as much scrutiny and ridicule as I have been since last March. I never had people call me 'fraud' or 'carpetbagger' until the record came out. Accusing me of being disingenuous. Accusing me of 'riding my student's coattails' or 'appropriating Appalachian culture.' You know that all those statements are from reviewers, right?"

"Bloggers, Preston. Big difference. Remember that. And I told you to stay off Twitter, didn't I?"

"Doesn't matter. When we were playing Motley Crüe covers at Squares or The Stink we never got this kind of shit."

"No," Pauly said. "It sucked even worse. People fucked with us all the time. They threw shit and heckled us. Playing at China Palace #1 and having people tell us to shut-up because we were giving them indigestion. Playing down at the riverfront— remember that? You said, 'What do you want to hear for an encore?' and that guy yelled, 'You. Drowning.' It ain't all exactly how you remembered, Preston."

I held up my hands and tried to wave him off. "You can't compare because we weren't playing our own songs. My songs. Anymore I don't know if I can even trust what people are telling me. When the record came out I got a hundred phone calls from people wanting to buy me a drink and asking if I wanted to hear their demo. People from high school who wouldn't look at me twice if they saw me walking up Pleasant after leaving Mick's. So I understand that the hellhounds on my trail aren't really hellhounds. Believe it or not I'm not stupid. But when I sing that song I'm thinking about the fact that my life isn't my own and things are happening in a way I can't quite control. Can you give me that? Please."

"Preston, how much control do you think any of us have over our own lives?" Katy took my hand and put it onto her lap. She ran her little fingers down mine, calming me while she talked. "I didn't start living until I gave up on the sure thing. Until I decided to dream this dream with you the world felt like a very dark place. Sometimes I feel like I'm flying. Sometimes I feel like I can look down on all those people who are too afraid to follow their dreams and I want to reach out to them. But I know if I reach out to too many, they'll just pull me right back into the darkness."

She rested her head on my shoulder. "It's been a phenomenal year and it's winding down. Think about how excited you got when you heard we could book studio time in Muscle Shoals or when you heard Hatch Show Print could print posters for the show tonight. You're here. We're doing it. And it's really hard right now because we're at the end of the first part of this long trip. People are going to talk and criticize. But fans are going to still come out and adore everything we do. I bet you could talk to a hundred people and thirty will hate The Beatles. So you can't worry about stuff like that."

"Yeah. I got you. No more 'Hellhounds on My Trail.'"

"Every time you close a door or burn a bridge you're pushing yourself toward something greater." She sat up, then faced me. "Besides, not everybody gets to fall in love with their best friend."

As a peace offering, Pauly said, "You guys should go back to opening with 'Strawberry Fields.'"

"Feels like it's time to move forward, doesn't it?" Katy stood up and kissed the top of my head. "You guys pay, and we'll leave when I get back."

I watched her walk to the bathroom. I could watch her walk just about anywhere.

Pauly said, "She's right. Your dreams are coming true, even if you don't totally see it. Muscle Shoals? Skynard and the Allmans? You kidding me?"

"You need to join us, man. I don't know why you won't. I used to stay up all night dreaming about this kind of stuff with you right there. This is for you too. You busted your hump as much as me or Stu or anybody."

"No, Pres. You booked the gigs and found money to advertise and buy strings and a new PA. You taught me the bass lines for all our new songs. You kept gas in the Jeep. Don't think for a second I feel like I'm missing out on something. You guys deserve this, and I'm more than happy doing what I'm doing now. Driving. Being on stage for three or four songs. I'm very happy and I'm very happy for you." He waved for more sweet tea and said, "I have to hit an A.A. meeting anyway. Then I'm going to see a buddy of mine near the Tennessee River in Versailles before heading home to take care of bills and wash clothes. We're going to fish for a day or two."

I said, "One song so you get an album credit?"

"My sponsor says I can't."

"How's that different than joining us onstage?"

"My sponsor says I can't get in the frame of mind that I can make a living doing this. Driving the truck pays the bills and keeps me insured. It's a real nice living."

"Yeah, I got you." I set my phone on the table and checked for texts again. But Pauly looked at me like he knew and I hurried up and put my phone right back in my pocket. My face must've gotten red because my cheeks felt warm.

"Still waiting for John Lennon to get back to you?" He didn't look at me when he said it. He swirled the ice around the bottom of his glass over and over again. "You and this devil shit. Look at where it's gotten you with these church people. Is this really what you want your career to be?"

"I don't believe you." My heart fell. I reeled to find a way to defend myself. "Somebody ran you off the road and put you in the hospital. I remember that night like it was last night."

He threw his knife and fork onto his plate and pushed it all to the clean part of the table. "Yeah, and my BAC was twice the legal limit when it happened. I practically had more vodka in me than blood. And the car was covered in salt and ash. It could've been red under all that crud for all I know."

"What about how I paid for Mick's Caddy? You know I didn't have that kind of money." I tried to monitor my words while the waitress came over to clear the plates. I didn't want her knowing my business, and the fact that I didn't want her knowing planted a tiny seed of doubt into my head.

"Want me to call Mick and ask him? Let all that go. The devil? Hellhounds? Same shit, different year. Except this time you're going to bring Katy down with you. Checking your phone for texts from John Lennon and Joe Strummer? C'mon, man."

"I can't believe I ever told you any of that." And it was true. I felt like an asshole for opening up to him about those things. "I only told you because I've never kept anything from you. I thought it could make things right after everything that happened."

"Well, you need help. When you snap from all the shit in your head at least somebody will be able to tell the doctors what you had flowing through your brain before you went over the edge." He pulled thirty bucks out of his wallet and set it on the table. "I got dinner tonight."

I studied his face for a long time. Finally I smiled and said, "Fuck off, Pauly."

CHAPTER TWO

A thousand rocks to make a road, and still I go alone,
A thousand more to build a bridge, a union made of stone,
A thousand more to raise a dam, though the river wants to be free,
A thousand more has the mountain, and the mountain will always be.

"Small Stones" Music and Lyrics by Katy Stefanic and Preston Black

"Katy, you sure I'm not dead?"

Everywhere I looked there were guitars. Suspended above doorways. Painted onto buildings. Onto doors and windows. Instead of honking horns and grumbling busses I heard music. In the air I smelled bourbon and BBQ.

"What makes you think you'd end up in heaven, Preston Black?" The bright light streaming down from the robin's-egg-blue sky suited her. Her skin glowed prettier than it ever did beneath a spotlight.

It felt as if God created a town where people like Katy and me were queens and kings. Instead of a hardware store, Broadway had Gruhn Guitars where I could just pop in and buy a bottleneck slide any old time I felt like it. Instead of a pharmacy, there was Ernest Tubbs' Record Shop, a hole in the wall selling legacy and tradition as a cure-all to whatever ailed a weary soul. Where Morgantown had clubs with well drinks and wet T-shirts contests, Nashville had The Stage on Broadway and Layla's Bluegrass Inn and Tootsie's Orchid Lounge and Legends Corner, where folks could step up to a bar with real music and dreams on tap. Instead of churches they had the Ryman. If man had ever created a more suitable place for talking to God, I'd never seen it. I'm sure Nashville had more than a few real churches scattered around, but they were right to hide their faces from The Ryman.

And instead of a newspaper, they had Hatch Show Print to tell the folks all about the most important comings and goings in town. An honest-to-God letterpress where people spread ink onto rollers and pulled levers by hand. The walls were covered with the likes of Patsy Cline, Hank Williams, Johnny Cash, Muse, Wilco, Bill Monroe and His Bluegrass Boys, Mumford and Sons, B. B. King, John Legend, and on and on and on. Posters hung everywhere—I couldn't see an inch of bare wall that hadn't been covered. Even the bit beneath a set of stairs that angled up to the ceiling had posters tacked to it. On the opposite side were shelves absolutely drooping with the weight of thousands of plates from artists long-forgotten to radio and TV. Posters hung to dry on clothes lines strung from shelf to shelf. No matter where I turned I saw The Avett Brothers or Willie Nelson from the corner of my eye. Every breath I took filled me with that magical air, and I knew that my voice would sound better than it ever had, if only for a show or two, from having breathed all this in.

"Doesn't it feel like we belong here?" I lifted the carton of posters off the floor and tucked it under my arm. Our posters. Posters that had been printed especially for little old Katy and me.

"The universe knows when you want something. And whether what you want is good or bad, the universe is going to give it to you." She carefully placed my Hatch Show Print stickers into the little Gruhn Guitar bag with my picks and new bottleneck slide. She bent over to scratch the belly of one of the shop cats—a chubby little orange guy with bright green eyes.

I held the door open for her and turned, hoping to catch Brad or Jim's eye just to give them one last little wave or a thank you, but they were back at the presses. Back to work.

Down the street I saw our shiny white rental van, our home for the last few weeks. My feet wouldn't move though. "Should I tell Pauly to come up and see?"

"We'll be back, Pres." She grabbed my hand and pulled me down the sidewalk.

As soon as Pauly looked up I let go of Katy's hand and slid a poster out to show him. He reached across to unlock the door, and I passed it over to him before setting the rest in the back.

While I got in, Pauly studied it and even sniffed the ink like when the teacher passed out fresh Dittos back in elementary school. He said, "Pretty good, I guess," and nothing more.

"Brad said they used the same type for that Johnny Cash." I pointed at the iconic poster displayed in the shop's window as I pulled the door shut. "But they use it in a bunch of others too, of course. Looks nice, huh?"

"Looks real nice, bro." He reached over and turned the radio off.

24

I felt like Pauly could've acted a little more excited even if he had to fake it. If I would've known he'd poop all over my parade I would've kept my mouth shut. So I bit my lip for a second, decided not to let him bring me down, and said, "We'll put some on the merch table and what we don't move tonight we'll sell online. You should've come in with us. Brad gave us a tour and showed us how to set type and everything."

"Wish I could've been there," Pauly said in a tone flatter than a buckwheat cake. He looked over his shoulder then studied his mirror before pulling onto the street. He got up a little speed, looked over to his right, and said, "So that's where Margaritaville's at? Thought Buffett lived in Key West."

Since I didn't know whether or not he was being serious, I ignored the comment. "How did the A.A. meeting go, anyway?"

"Pretty good, I guess."

And I'd always have that discussion as my parting memory of Broadway. A little part of me ached to stay and it pissed me off that I had to cater to Pauly's whims all because he was doing us a solid. I vowed right then and there to never have to owe anybody ever again. Maybe the road had worn me down a bit, but I decided if I couldn't afford somebody, I didn't need them. I'd drive the van, do our own sound. We could sell merch online for all I cared. The knot in my belly killed what remained of our morning in Nashville.

"I went and filled up too. Gas is outrageous anymore." Pauly drifted left, depriving me of a last good look at The Ryman. "Sometimes it's tough feeling good about going to meetings on the road because you don't know anybody. One of the old-timers talked about gratitude and how you express it through action. I never heard that before and kind of liked it."

"That's great, man." His apathy ate at me and I tried real hard not to say anything, especially after all that crap in Louisville.

He inhaled, like he had something else to say, then released his breath without saying anything. Riding in silence suited me just fine. I looked for the river and the stadium where the Titans played, but Pauly's driving disoriented me.

Once we hit the interstate, Pauly said, "There's something else I wanted to talk about more than anything." He cracked his window in anticipation of lighting a smoke. "I mentioned the incident at the show last night when I shared. They knew who I meant. It's not Westboro Baptist. They said this group's real militant, which we knew."

Pauly drove on, letting the news hang for a minute or two. "They call themselves Circuit Riders. The leader is a guy named Zebadiah Boggs. They are big in Tennessee.

They mainly run in Alabama, Georgia and up through Kentucky to West Virginia. Boggs used to be a Texas lawman before he got reprimanded for using traffic stops as opportunities to witness. So he enlisted in the Army after the attack on the American embassy in Kenya in 1998, figuring he'd have a chance to kill Muslims. But he got into too much trouble and got something called a 'Big Chicken Dinner' for bad conduct. Bad conduct discharge? Guess that makes sense. Anyway, he's supposedly trying to convert or kill ten thousand heathens. Homeland Security calls them a legit domestic terror threat."

"Shit."

"Yeah, it ain't good, bro. His right-hand man rode with the Pagans for years before becoming a government snitch. Albert Gallatin Ashby—A.G. for short. He got busted up in Rocky Point for helping distribute coke and oxy. Got saved in prison. Boggs picks his guys based on tests of Biblical faith. Like how the Bloods and Crips have to shoot somebody in broad daylight or whatever? Boggs is into stoning big time. They have to murder a witch or an adulterer or some other kind of non-believer."

Katy spoke up for the first time. "Did he say witch specifically?"

Pauly nodded.

"Hypocrite," she said. "Doesn't he know that Leviticus specifically prohibits tattooing?"

"I don't know, Katy. Sorry." He looked in the rearview when he spoke to her. "You can ask him when you see him."

"Maybe we can get them to change a bunch of water into wine tonight?" I tried to blow off the severity of the threat by making light. But Pauly's words had heft.

"I'm just saying they're legit. They are the ones responsible for sending those nail bombs to all those abortion clinics a few years back. Then Hicks's church sheltered the fugitive on its property while the manhunt was on. Like Katy said, his old man has camps and farms and warehouses in all these old towns down here. The guy that told me this used to be a federal agent. Said they're very slippery."

"Well, they can protest and pray all they want because eventually that's going to be more publicity for us. Especially if the media paints us as an underdog. Just wait." I cracked my window and watched the rest of Nashville fly by. Cars and trucks filled with people that got to call this place home. I could see me and Katy living here one day. "Where we headed? I want to get back to the club and forget about this shit."

"Can't go back to the club yet. Going to take you guys to lunch. Prince's Hot Chicken. Saw it on the Food Network."

Katy piped up. "Oh, no. I can't eat anything hot and get phlegmy before tonight. What else is there?"

"You can get mild, your worship."

I smiled because Pauly did his best Han Solo impersonation. Trying to lighten the mood.

"Take me back to the club then and we'll order something," she said. "You wanted pizza, right? So bad you couldn't stop talking about it all night."

"We're already on this side of town so let me at least run by and pick up some for myself." Pauly stammered a bit when he said it, and that gave him away. And he knew that I knew.

I said, "What is it? No fucking around."

Pauly checked his mirrors, crossed an empty lane of traffic and rolled his window down. He raised his voice over the road noise and wind. "Can't go back to the venue. Not right now anyway."

Katy looked way more agitated than I felt, and said, "Why not?"

"When I dropped the trailer off the manager said they got a bomb threat." With an apologetic shrug he popped a cigarette into his mouth, lit it and inhaled deeply. "I guess technically you guys got the bomb threat."

He blew smoke out of the window and took another deep drag. He held it, exhaled it then threw the cigarette onto the highway. He rolled the window up, shook his head like he didn't really want to say more, and muttered, "The bomb squad has its dogs there now."

I hid my face in the clean white towel.

They were all still back there, no matter what I did. I could hear them. Over the faint hum of my in-ear monitor—IEM—I could hear people from the audience headed to the bar, out to the street to smoke. They were bored. And I felt like a coward for letting Katy hang out there by herself while I regrouped. Smoke from some real kind bud floated up to the stage. I closed my eyes and inhaled as much as I could.

Pauly's voice buzzed to life in my IEM. "You're getting slaughtered."

Laughing, I adjusted the earpiece to make like I couldn't hear him. I found him off in the back behind the mixing board and mouthed, "You want to join us."

He laughed into my IEM and turned his little desk lamp off.

So I shrugged, pointed at my amp, then my earpiece and pointed down. I twisted the old Fender Twin's volume up to about seven and a half to really juice the tubes.

Hot static dripped onto the floor like melting wax. I let my Tele feedback for a second before stepping right back to the mic.

"A minor," I said to Katy, before busting out an angry pentatonic riff, rocking a steady-chugging low G that I hammered onto A over and over again. Some of the guys in the crowd recognized "Whipping Post" immediately. "Hold back for a few measures though."

She didn't like the improv. And I knew I'd hear about it later. But we were losing these guys, fast. Probably all the extra security on the way in. The cops on horseback. People loved having their shit searched before a concert. Waiting in line for an extra forty minutes. *Fuck those protesting pricks out front.* I let the crowd talk for a minute, letting word get around.

Just wait, I thought, smiling, making eye contact with the fans right up front, *I'm about to turn this motherfucker right on its ear.*

I stepped up to the mic. In my head I rewrote "Rocky Top" for tonight's crowd. I sang the verse in a monotone that mirrored the staccato bursts of noise from my amp. For a second I could've sworn somebody tossed firecrackers into the crowd the way they got to their feet and smiled.

Katy raised the bow to her strings and I told her to hold, then gestured for the crowd to take the chorus. They belted out the lines just like they did for a Vols game, and ended with a burst of rapturous applause.

Katy took over with a wail from her fiddle that they could've heard all the way back into Kentucky. Maybe even all the way back to West Virginia. She wiggled her head as her little fingers arpeggiated along her fingerboard, working that black Mod mini dress she picked up at that vintage shop on Carson Street back in Pittsburgh. The silver bracelets dangling below her rolled-up sleeves reflected the light like a million little stars. Her purple nails danced across the fingerboard like butterflies hopping from flower to flower. She hacked at the strings with her little bow in long, swooping arcs.

I turned the guitar's volume down and flipped the switch to the neck pickup. Tearing through the rhythm like I singlehandedly bore responsibility for every heartbeat in the room. Like, the instant I stopped, every one of us would keel over and die. "One more time," I said.

Katy built her music brick-by-brick as I maintained that steady driving rhythm. One brick for the assholes after the show last night, and another for the same assholes standing out in front of the club today. One brick for the unkind words they said, another for their signs. A brick for their beliefs and their lies. A brick for all the fans who turned around and went home after seeing their sidewalk sideshow.

And in one giant swoop my little Katy kicked the wall right over. The crowd ate it up, swaying and dancing with their eyes closed and fists in the air.

I leaned right into the mic and sang my own version of "Whipping Post" as Katy mirrored my rhythm with the throaty drone of her fiddle. Some of the older fans sang the original lyrics. The one who didn't know the song watched and danced. For the last line in the verse I thought about the protestors out front and sang, "And there's the devil, right in there with them, she's just wearing a new disguise."

Katy smiled. This was fucking fun. I pulled my glass Coricidin bottle out of my back pocket and slid it over my ring finger, coaxing my Tele to squeal and scream an accent to Katy's rhythm throughout the next few lines. I couldn't play slide to save my life and supported the melody instead of trying to sound anything at all like what Duane Allman played. My noise sounded more like the slide on Lennon's "Number 9 Dream"—little droning glissandos to maintain the illusion of structure. I smiled and bobbed as I sang the rest of the verse, building a head of steam with each note I played. Jacking up the volume and intensity.

At the chorus, I stood on my toes and screamed the line, but didn't finish with my throat. I jammed my Tele's volume all the way back up and broke out a high note that came from way past my frets, almost past the neck pickup. The crowd kept singing so I ripped into the pentatonics thinking about Duane's last ride through those shady, winding Georgia hills. Past live oaks dripping with Spanish moss with warm wind in his hair like he knew he'd never see a tomorrow. I let the notes pile up in the amp, held them there for a second like holding a hit from a joint before releasing them into the room in giant bursts that shook dust from the rafters.

When I opened my eyes to take the next verse I looked for the smiles and nods of approval from the audience. Especially from the older guys, the ones who'd been to enough shows to know we were earning our cash money tonight. The ones who'd seen The Stones or Clapton in the seventies or Van Halen in the eighties. I wanted to make eye contact and let them know that I appreciated their approval. That I needed to make them happy, not the kids. But they weren't looking at me. None of them. Instead they all watched something in the back of the room.

In my earpiece Pauly kept saying, "We got trouble. We got trouble."

The bright lights of the lobby poured over the heads of the people in the last few rows. The house lights came up, and Katy stopped playing. As much as I didn't want to, I stopped too. Pauly got off his chair and ran down the aisle to the edge of the stage. I yanked my IEM out of my ear, reached out a hand, and pulled him onto the stage with us.

Pauly reacted to the sight of the four Circuit Riders pushing through the audience by grabbing the wooden stool I'd set my water bottles and capo on. He leveled that stool out in front of him like some kind of blue-collar lion tamer. It took another minute for my eyes to adjust to the light, but as soon as I saw all that black leather and ink pressing toward us I pulled the cord from my Tele and set it into its stand. Then I pushed Katy behind me and grabbed my mic stand. When the first Circuit Rider got to the stage I could see the words on his face and shaved head. As soon as he put his hand on the laminated wood floor I stomped his fingers with the heel of my boot.

He pulled his hand away like he'd touched a hot stove. He didn't make a sound as he shook his fingers out. Pauly swung the stool at him.

In the time it took to blink, Zebadiah Boggs jumped onto the stage and charged right at me. I lifted the mic stand and jabbed it at him, catching him right in the face with its weighted base. Blood spurted from his nose and he reeled into the crowd, knocking some fans onto their asses. The rest spread, giving him a wide berth.

Boggs struggled to his feet, shouting, "I want them both!"

His companion lunged for the stage again, but Pauly kept him back with the wooden stool. His face grew red and he kept shouting, "You fucking pussy. You ain't nothing."

A low whine of feedback built in my amp, and when I backed over to it to shut it off I pulled Katy right along with me. In the aisle a pair of cops squared off against one of the intruders. Being outnumbered at least two-to-one didn't stop the biker from reaching for his retractable baton. He was short and built like a fifty-gallon barrel. Had to be A.G. Ashby, Boggs's right-hand man. Both cops drew their weapons.

The fourth biker came from the cover of the crowd and got one of the cops in a headlock. Seeing the change in momentum, Boggs broke for the stage again. More police officers came in from the lobby, but I knew they wouldn't get down here in time to do anything. I pulled Katy toward the green room.

Out of the corner of my eye I saw Pauly get Boggs's crony in the neck and shoulder with his wooden stool. Pauly smiled and whooped as the guy hit the hardwood floor. "Stay down, you son of a bitch."

The man didn't even twitch. I swear to God I thought Pauly killed him.

Boggs watched his guy go down and switched direction. He bore down on Pauly like the poor kid had slept with his mama or something. Blood dripped down Boggs's face and onto his chest. Both of his eyes had purpled a bit from where I'd hit him. I said, "Katy, stay right here," and went back onto the stage.

Pauly hit Boggs once in the jaw with the stool and retreated a few steps, and Boggs moved forward totally unfazed. Boggs took a swing and Pauly ducked, then ran at him with his head down, pushing Boggs right to me. I grabbed Katy's mic stand and pulled it tight around Boggs's neck.

He fell backward, landing on me, knocking the wind out of me. Pauly kicked him a few times. Boggs was wiry, the muscles in his arms felt like steel cables. He twisted and bucked but I knew if I let go of the mic stand, or even thought of it, I'd wake up in a hospital.

Katy yelled my name and I looked for her to try to tell her I felt fine, but couldn't angle my head back far enough. By then a few guys from the audience had joined us on stage and were doing their best to help Pauly and me out. They pulled Boggs off me and held him to the ground.

"Are you fucking kidding me?" I got to my knees and tried to get my head straight. Pauly helped me to my feet. But my hands shook and my knees wobbled, so I stood there for a second, using the mic stand for support. As soon as I got my breath I lifted it, held it right over the shiny part of Boggs's skull. Right over Romans 1:18, *"They are full of every type of evil, greed and wickedness, full of jealousy, murder, discord, deceit and malice..."*

I could barely keep my grip. The rage made me see spots. "Who are you to disrupt our little gig, man? We didn't do a thing to you."

"Sir," a voice behind me said. "Please put the weapon down."

I didn't respond, because I didn't consider the mic stand to be a weapon. A police officer stepped in front of me and twisted it right out of my hands. "Please step away."

Pauly put his arm around me and led me away from Boggs. I turned to find Katy and held her. She shook her head. I gave her a little kiss. The fans that had jumped onstage to help me and Pauly lingered around us protectively.

I whispered, "This is going to blow up all over YouTube and Twitter."

More cops came through the front of the house and from the fire exits. They swept through the room, down the aisles, full of purpose. Beams from their flashlights went row-by-row looking for stragglers, but from what I had seen, Boggs's guys weren't the type to hide. Having said that, it startled me just a bit when a pair of police officers came in through the stage door from the alley behind the club.

One of them said, "Who does the rental van belong to?"

Me and Katy and Pauly all raised our hands.

"Well, one of you is going to have to step outside with me."

It took a while to get everything sorted out. Most of the remaining audience lurked near the stage while the police took statements. Some sat in the first few rows, yawning, sleeping until they had to talk to the authorities. In the process Katy and me learned how stalking was a Class A Misdemeanor in Tennessee, unless the act occurred within seven years of a prior conviction, in which case it was a Class E Felony. The officer said that it might even turn out to be aggravated stalking, and warned us that anybody charged with stalking or aggravated stalking would be eligible to post bail and be released until the trial.

None of that made Katy very happy, even though the officer countered by saying any threat against an occupied building could ultimately be considered terrorism, but she didn't hear anything after he'd said 'released until the trial.'

While all this went down, Pauly tried to get a representative from the rental agency to come out and help deal with the damage to the van and trailer. During the ruckus somebody slashed the tires and smashed the windows and the agency wanted to wait until morning to sort it out. Pauly argued tenaciously and finally arranged for a rental car so me and Katy could head down to Alabama while he sorted out the stuff with the van before joining us in a day or two. A few fans helped us load as much as we could into the rental. Amps, instrument cases, and mic stands so we could record, suitcases, and some of the merch. I appreciated everything Pauly had done to help so far and didn't want to stick him with having to load everything back into the trailer by himself.

The transition left us with a quiet moment. I pulled Katy into a dark hallway backstage. The night had taken its toll on her. When I held her she slumped into me, like she could barely muster the energy to remain standing.

"Hey," I said, pulling her head to my shoulder, where I soaked in the scent of her Chanel Mademoiselle. "You're a star, right? I'm not talking about what you do on stage. I'm talking about what you do for me. You are the Sun. You give me the energy I need to live."

"When does a star rest?" I couldn't see her face in the dark. I could only feel her warm breath on my cheek. "It doesn't, Pres. It either fades out or explodes. There's no in-between."

"Well, if this isn't fun for you we'll make it fun. Or give it up."

"Do I get to choose?"

"We get to try." I pulled her back toward the dimly lit stage.

The police had left. The thirty or forty people still hanging around drifted toward the lobby or rested across rows of seats. Trying to make the best of a bad situation, I called them back down and told them to get comfortable, figuring we could thank them with a song or two. Most plopped down along the edge of the stage with their feet dangling down, so Katy and I placed ourselves on a pair of stools and faced the stage.

We kicked-off with a cover we hadn't touched since last spring—"(Nice Dream)." Hearing Katy singing Radiohead reminded me of being in Morgantown with her, and how those days ended up being some of the most important in my whole life. We followed up with "(What's So Funny 'Bout) Peace, Love and Understanding" and "In My Life."

We joked with the audience and told a few stories. I had Pauly tell them about how Stu hazed Delt pledges despite the fact he wasn't even a student, let alone a frat brother. I talked a little bit about my trip down to the Currence's farm with Jamie and then going down to Elkins with Katy and Jamie later that summer and they wanted to know all about Jamie. Katy gave me a little look like I'd opened up too much so I said Jamie was a real good friend and left it at that.

And I could see what Katy had meant, because then somebody asked about the devil and the song and if we'd play it. I remembered what the little old lady said about "The Sad Ballad of Preston Black" the morning I met Jamie. *"That song hain't of no account and you can honor my hospitality by not asking no more about it."*

Ignoring the request, we played them our version of Arcade Fire's "Suburban War" and finished the night with an abbreviated version of our set list. Harmonizing with Katy on an a cappella "If I Fell" as an encore became my personal highlight. We always practiced it in the car—Katy doing the Paul part and me doing the John part—but never sang it in public. The song had become our little secret, our way of telling each other that everything would be fine. And after tonight, we all needed a little assurance.

Nobody wanted to leave. After so much chaos we all felt safe in our little nest. But we'd played right up to the curfew and couldn't afford a fine. So we signed posters and took a few pictures as a way of thanking everybody and saying our goodbyes. One of the tapers recorded the whole thing, from beginning to end, and mentioned the possibility of making the recording available commercially. He asked if I wanted him to sit on it for a while and I told him to put it out there.

Saying goodbye to Pauly hurt the most. The last few weeks really changed things between us. Like, I felt like I really had a brother again. And over the last few days our relationship had been reinvented altogether. He'd become the friend I'd always wanted him to be. We dropped him off at his hotel, helped him with his bags, and left Nashville on a bit of a high. Like we'd squeaked by with a win after all was said and done.

But on the drive to Muscle Shoals a sense of defeat finally settled in. The first blow came when I saw a billboard that said IMAGINE NO RELIGION? SO DID HE.

"Look at that," I said, thinking it meant everything would be okay.

"That's Stalin," Katy replied. The tone of her voice confused me. She should've been more excited. "The man on the billboard is Joseph Stalin."

The name rang a bell, but I only knew that he was a historical figure.

"Depending on who's counting, he killed somewhere between five and fifty-five million people. It's not what you think, Preston." She shook her head. "I always wanted to believe. Now I'm tired of trying."

"I'm sorry." I cracked my window and let fresh air in. "I thought our trip to Alabama would be a little more like *Smokey and the Bandit*. So far it's been more like *Children of the Corn*."

With a deep breath, she forced a change of demeanor. She cheered herself right up and went to work on cheering me up too. "And after the Atlanta show when we're on our way home you won't be able to stop talking about it." She grabbed my hand and placed it on her lap.

I didn't want her to sleep and kept talking as a way to keep her awake, but eventually she stopped responding. The interstate felt lonely enough, so far from lights and anybody I knew. She happened to be my only friend at the moment.

When I saw a billboard that said WHOREMONGERS AND ALL LIARS SHALL HAVE THEIR PART IN THE LAKE OF FIRE. REVELATION: 2:18 I knew we'd never beat these people. Not when they had God on their side.

I could handle the billboards and the protestors. They were real because other people had seen them too. Reality never kept me up at night.

But everything changed at a little gas station just over the Alabama line. My head had grown heavier and I needed Mountain Dew so I didn't run us into a ditch before we got to the hotel. I filled the tank. The bright fluorescent lights only called attention to the fact that nobody else was around. Jerry Reed's "When You're Hot, You're Hot" trickled out of the tinny speakers above the gas pumps. Moths and gnats circled endlessly and Katy never once stirred, so I locked up the car and walked through the lonely parking lot.

I started peeing at the same time Little Feat's "Oh, Atlanta" ended. I washed my face, went out to stare at the beef jerky and Zapp's potato chips before deciding I didn't need the heartburn and bought my Mountain Dew. While paying, I watched Katy. And on the way back to the car I heard something that stopped me dead in my tracks. I really, really had to listen to make sure I heard what I thought I heard.

My tongue stuck to the roof of my mouth.

Young Johnny Cash.

My hands shook. "Katy!"

Not Rick Rubin's version of Johnny Cash.

I heard Sam Phillips's Johnny Cash.

"Katy!" I yelled. I needed her to hear it too.

I spun, trying to get a fix on a speaker.

Luther Perkins's Tele picked out a twangy run while Johnny sang, "...*got them hellhounds on his trail. Preston Black got them hellhounds on his trail...*"

"Katy!" I threw my pop at the car. It hit the window with a thud and bounced onto the concrete. She didn't move.

As I stepped on the trashcan next to the closest pump, I heard, "*If you want to shake them hounds off your tail, the first stop's the crossroads, the second stop's hell. Preston Black got them hellhounds on his trail.*"

I went to the car and banged the hood. "Hey, get up."

I pulled my keys out, opened the driver's side door and gave Katy a shake. "You have to hear this. Get up."

When I heard Johnny's voice again I yelled one last time. "Katy!"

"What?" She stretched, but didn't open her eyes.

"Listen." I climbed onto the hood, balancing myself on my tiptoes to get my ears closer to the speakers, yet somehow I still couldn't hear. I stepped over the windshield and onto the roof.

"Preston! Get down."

"Quiet."

I craned my ear as high as I could in time to catch Johnny sing the last verse. "*Preston Black, you got to be born again. Preston Black you got to be born again. Let the water wash your sins away, before you let the devil have his say, Preston Black, it's time to be born again.*"

The passenger side door opened. Katy stood and wiped her eyes with the back of her hand. She looked up at me, squinted at the bright lights, and said, "What is wrong with you, boy?"

CHAPTER THREE

Breathing just to breathe, when you're with me,
Swimming in your smile, while I watch you read,
Laughing for a while as we sip our tea,
You know it ain't my style just to let you sleep.

"Summer Sleep" Music and Lyrics by Katy Stefanic and Preston Black

Waking up in Alabama didn't come as easy as waking up in Tennessee had. I always preferred the noise of living in the city to wide open spaces. To my ears, the cars going by sounded like waves at the beach. The only other thing I heard last night was a train that took an hour to pass.

With Katy curled up next to me though, I could sleep anywhere. And I loved waking her up. She ripped blankets away from me, stole pillows in the middle of the night, kicked me, talked in her sleep and got up to pee every forty minutes.

But she made the nightmares stop.

She gave me a reason to count blessings when I closed my eyes.

And she gave off heat like a sleeping housecat.

I pushed her hair off her shoulder and leaned over her, watching the soft curve of her cheek catch the little bit of sunlight that streamed through the heavy drapes. Her sleeping eyes were like little quarter moons. I kissed her neck and ran my fingertips across the warm, soft skin between her hip and her belly. I loved waking her up.

She rolled toward me and nuzzled her head into the nook beneath my chin. I listened for her breathing to change, or some other sign that she might be awake. When I didn't hear anything I fell onto my back and figured I had no choice but to go back to sleep myself. But her hand, which had moved slowly from my thigh, to my waist, to my pajama bottoms' drawstring stirred, at least. She said, "You're mean, you know that?"

"I know," I said, as I kissed her neck and shoulder, just above the spot where she'd been shot last summer.

She kicked blankets away as I rolled onto her and slid a vintage Dead Letter Office T-shirt up over her belly and breasts, over her uplifted arms. The way she looked at me like I could never let her down or hurt her scared me to no end. Every single time. That look stripped me of my confidence, broke through the shell I wore to protect myself from the stones and arrows. Almost like I had to be a little self-conscious, like I had to remember my sad past, my quiet self, before she could kiss my lips.

She slid my bottoms over my thighs, past my knees and over my ankles while she kissed my collarbone and neck. The way her warm, soft skin felt against mine reminded me that the bright sunlight on the other side of the window could be taken as a sign things didn't have to always get worse before they got better. The way the soft skin on the inside of her thigh felt against my hips reminded me that I'd never have to be cold again.

In that moment everything changed, just like it always did, every single time. When we came together, I returned to a home I never knew, to a family I didn't grow up with. She turned her head and smiled, an invitation to kiss the soft skin behind her ear where tiny little hairs tickled my cheek. For one fleeting moment I caught a glimpse of who I'd been before we'd met and it reminded me that I am the man I am today because I don't ever want her eyes to see me as the broken person I used to be. I died and came back from the dead for her. Her touch, the way she whispered my name and laughed at my jokes, the way she held my hand and finished my sentences. The way she arched her back like she couldn't get close enough to me. The way she pulled me into her...

Her touch reminded me that the next time I died, would be forever.

I loved waking her up.

I finally figured out something was wrong at breakfast. Katy couldn't enjoy her pancakes, even with the butter pecan syrup, making me feel guilty for enjoying mine as much as I did. The way the butter coated my tongue as I rolled it against the roof of my mouth and the feeling of warmth and fullness they gave me, and how she—for the first time ever—didn't feel the same, worried me a little.

I'd finished reading all the little hand-painted signs that said stuff like, "*Do unto others, and share a slice of pie!*" and "*Fresh Joe all day long!*" Above the shelves of water glasses and coffee cups the walls had faded where the early morning sunlight hit day after day.

This morning she wore blue jeans and a little blue button-down shirt covered with tiny white birds beneath a fake leather jacket. I loved that she was beautiful, no matter what she wore, and that she used to smile whenever I looked at her. I'd spent the rest of the morning trying to get her to smile again.

After I'd finished eating she finally broke her silence with a sigh. She said, "I didn't go to school with anybody who interested me even a little bit. I had friends who never read books and never wanted to talk about anything meaningful. Except I couldn't ever grumble because I still wanted them all to like me. Always too smart for my own good." She took her little silver barrette out of her hair, set it on the counter, and said, "Do you know what that's like? Being smart enough to know something is wrong with you socially and not having the courage to fix it?"

Before I could come up with the answer she'd hoped to hear, she asked, "How did they know, Pres?" and I didn't have to wonder anymore. "Their posters were pretty specific, right? I never did a thing to any of them and they hate me."

I said, "I don't know," to buy a little time to think. When the guy at the counter next to me tore into his biscuits and cheesy grits my belly rumbled with hunger. "It's the song. It's a stupid thing to base a career on. And all the cops before the show didn't help, did they?"

I watched the pie spin in the carousel as I talked. Banana creams and key limes, topped with meringues and maraschino cherries. They looked so perfect in that glass case I figured they could only be plastic. But we were being cautious with our per diem so I tried to forget about dessert. I said, "I don't like cops on horseback anyway. It's like the horse is judging you too."

"No, Preston. It's not your song or the cops. The term 'witch' is pretty specific." She ripped open two more packets of sugar and shook them into her coffee. "Those memories are like knives. Pap said Curtis Lewis spent so much of his time on the witness stand blabbing about magic and witches that the judge almost bought the insanity plea his lawyer had pushed for."

"Well, the signs were nonspecific even though it may have seemed like they were directed at you. Like 'heathen' or 'heretic.' Just nonspecific terms they use to describe anybody who doesn't believe exactly what they do. John Lennon got death threats down here when he said The Beatles were bigger than God even though he spoke metaphorically, more or less." I gave her knee a squeeze. "It's the devil stuff, I'm telling you. Tipper Gore and the PMRC. This is ground zero for all that shit. Playing records backward and blaming Ozzy for your kid killing himself and doing drugs."

The old cook flipped sausage patties and hummed gospel tunes. His white shirt and apron and pants looked like they'd never seen a spot of grease.

"It's going to pass. Look at last night. Some of those people are going to talk about last night forever. And that's how we grow an audience. I know because I did it once back in Morgantown." I connected the dots in the flecks of mica in the countertop while I talked. "A small audience, but we did it the way we're doing it now. It's a skill and we can apply it where and whenever we like. Last night felt totally magical. You can't plan for stuff like that."

"Well, Morgantown's one of the few places I know where high BAC is more respectable than a high GPA. So from now on, don't start any more stories by telling me what the kids in Morgantown do."

I put my arm over her shoulder and pulled her over to me and kissed her on the forehead. "Okay, then. Pearl Jam at Penn State in 2003. Eddie decided that night they'd play the longest show they ever played. In the third encore Eddie said he was drinking the best bottle of wine he'd had all year and wasn't leaving until he'd polished it off. Magic. The people had no way of knowing that when they bought their tickets. And think of all the people who could've gotten tickets, or had tickets and didn't go. They talk."

She nodded.

"And look at Stevie Nicks. Being a witch hasn't hurt her."

She rolled her eyes.

"C'mon. We got this, *chicita*. The hardest part was finding each other." I grabbed her hand. "We need to have fun today."

"One last thing though," she took a deep breath. "That was supposed to be a secret—my secret. And nobody outside of my family was ever supposed to know."

"Well, you can keep a secret for so long. Then you're the only one who remembers it. Then you find out it's not a secret at all. It's something totally new. Like a resentment or regret." I stood and put my jacket on. "Look at it like this—what's crazier—what your family believes? Or what those people think your family believes? Nobody's taking these fanatics seriously. And you have your roots. Believe it or not, your family, and what they believe, means something."

"Roots are important, but they don't let you move on. Seeds are just as important, but nobody ever talks about seeds." She looped a thin blue scarf around her neck and gently knotted it.

"So, me and you are seeds?" I pulled her chair out for her.

"Kind of. You're a nut." Her smile told me everything was good for the moment.

We paid up and got back into our rental car and drove. The bright sun forced us to find our sunglasses at the bottom of our bags. And the warm air let us roll the windows down a bit. Redbuds bloomed everywhere and the smell reminded me of home. The scent of green grass instead of brown, of flowers blooming somewhere, made the air smell sweet in a way I couldn't fully grasp. I'd had a destination in mind when I started driving. A surprise for Katy. The sweetness in the air was a bonus.

And even though I thought I knew the way I still had to ask at a gas station after a few minutes of going in circles. As soon as I got myself oriented I ran back to the car, turned it around and went back the way we came. I scrolled through my iPod to look for a specific album, because this moment needed a soundtrack. "East Avalon," I said at the turn I'd missed.

"This is what you wanted to show me?" She didn't try to hide her lack of excitement.

I set the iPod on the dashboard and slowed down because I didn't know what side of the road to look on. As soon as I saw it I drifted onto the shoulder. "FAME Studios."

Katy didn't say anything. I knew she wouldn't be as excited as me, but I didn't expect her to be downright disappointed.

"This is where Duane Allman camped in the parking lot and taught Wilson Pickett 'Hey Jude' to break into the business. Music history. He knew the world needed him like he needed the world." Nothing I said would change her mind so I toned down my excitement. "I'm sorry. I really thought you'd be into this."

She shrugged.

"I guess you don't want to go to Muscle Shoals Sound and see where The Stones recorded 'Wild Horses' and 'Brown Sugar?'" I imagined us taking pictures and listening to music while we hung out, soaking up the magic before we hit the studio ourselves.

"It's my day off, Pres." She put her hand on my knee and looked me right in the eye. "No music. No songs. I don't want to have to think about anything. Not today."

"What do you want to do then?"

"Honestly, make a decision. Even a mall or something. I don't want to have to think about anything at all. I'll take over again tomorrow." She handed her coffee to me and said, "Drink the rest."

Gulping it down gave me an excuse to keep my mouth shut. I'd let her have this after all that had happened, but I couldn't help wondering if she'd feel this same way when we saw Abbey Road for the first time. I scrolled down to an Allman Brothers bootleg. *The Warehouse, New Orleans, Louisiana, March 20, 1971.* I hit the gas and said, "Skydog's guitar sounds just like a banshee tangled in barbed wire screaming to be set free."

The studio faded in my rearview mirror.

I drove without consulting her. Choosing random roads that spiraled out and away from the city, quietly trying to find Jackson Highway so I could see Muscle Shoals Sound even though I knew I couldn't do so without her catching on to my plan. When I got to the main drag I picked a direction and went, and once we weren't stopping at stoplights every thirty yards the world looked a lot different. The Alabama countryside put on her first shades of green. Pink and white blooms on the trees were a far cry from the grey we left in the northeast a week ago. Roadkill meant the critters were starting to stumble out of their holes. They didn't care that Punxsutawney Phil said we had six more weeks of winter left.

"Thanks for taking care of me," she finally said as we were totally free of suburbia. "Lately the road feels like home, the truck stops and hotels. But it's not home."

"Well, with you I'm never lost, never hungry. Never wanting. Maybe that's why you feel that way?" I put my arm around her. "But you deserve more."

"All you have to do is love me. That's the only thing I need."

After an awkward delay, I said, "Not really sure your mom would agree with you." I shook my head and went on, talking just to talk. Never knowing when to shut up. "I think I'm a bit of a letdown in her eyes."

"Preston, do you have any idea how hurt she'd be if she heard you ever say something like that?" She got angry and pulled away from me. "My mother never expected me—not for a second—to go out and find a man to take care of me. If you think that's who I am then we have so much more to discuss."

"That's not how I meant it, Katy. You know that, right?"

"Then you should've said what you meant."

"In my head I think about what Ben would've done to those people last night. Maybe I feel like I'm not aggressive enough. Just forget about it, okay?"

"No, it's in the air now. We can't roll the windows back up like it never happened. If we're going to take this to the next level we're going to have to get some things straight. You know why I never wanted a serious relationship? Because my dad was an asshole. My mom didn't need somebody to protect her and she certainly didn't sit around all day waiting for some guy to swoop in and save her." She crossed her arms and stared out the window. "One of the first guys I ever got close to was Dante Fiorelli—a forestry major from New Jersey. I told you about him. He thought he knew how to take care of me. Every week he'd drag me up to Dolly Sods to backpack—never mind that the mountain sat in my backyard. Or that we'd spent three or four nights at week down at Wamsley's talking to Jeremy or Chip about bikes. Henry and Ben antagonized him relentlessly because they didn't respect him. After I broke it off with Dante I went for a bookish guy. A quiet European Lit major who could only express emotion as a reference to a novel or character. Needless to say, it didn't last very long, and I knew I had to raise my standards higher if I was ever going to really fall in love. Then I met you."

She smiled, even though I didn't really get it.

"Well, we have an amazing thing here and I don't want to change any of it. I hope you feel the same way."

She sighed. "You know, boys are like singles—they just want to get to the point and move on. Like every situation is another problem to be solved. Girls are like albums, they want to spend time in your thoughts. They want you to see them as a whole, not as a collection of pieces." Her tone grew angry again and I couldn't quite figure out why. She closed her eyes and let her head fall back against the headrest. "We're not going to go steady forever, I hope."

"Look, in my thoughts I'm able to give you the house you deserve. Nice things. But what if this is temporary and we have to scrounge for money after this bubble bursts? That's what I'm afraid of. That one day I'll be back to a nine-to-five and all we'll have is the stories of our time on the road."

"Well, soon enough you'll see that what matters most is being together. Not the shows or the fans. Besides, do you think my opinion of you changes based on what you do for a living? Or that my mom's does? I know that you and Pauly had a hard time growing up, and I'm not sure I could ever walk in your shoes, but think about being up on the mountain at that farm. We have our fair share of alcohol and food and laughs but six months before all that I buried my kid cousin. Crops fail and animals get sick. It's a different way of life, but we don't change our opinions of somebody based on circumstances beyond their control. The river floods. Springs go bad or dry up. It's nobody's fault—everybody pitches in and makes it right. That's what you'd be a part of. A support group that extends far and wide. What would Jamie say if he heard you talking like this?"

"I know."

She knew that would get me. And she was right. "It scares me to think it isn't going to last forever. Your people can be pretty intimidating, you know that? They have all these memories and shared experiences. I never get the inside jokes."

"Preston. Are you worried about being an outsider? Because there's not an event on God's green earth any more *inside* than burying Odelia Lewis and Lucinda Tasso in a mine shaft above the Blackwater. Can you imagine coming into the family not being a part of that? Consider that your initiation and let it be. I have cousins and aunts who don't know what happened because they weren't there. My pap and grandma respect the fact that you would've died for me given a chance. And you pulled a trigger for me. What else is there? Really? You have their love and respect."

But she kept going like she never had any intention of letting me jump in. "Jamie came to our first show. You don't think Ben would've wanted to be there if he would've known? Or my mom and Chloey? They came out to Philly just to see us and followed us up to New York City. You think Jamie wouldn't have dropped everything to be there if he could've?"

"I get it, Katy. I know where you're coming from." After a long minute, I said, "Well, what about Pauly? I can't leave him all by himself."

"You know Pauly will be my brother as long as you love me." She put her hand on my shoulder. "But you know he's going to fall in love and get married too, right?"

Emotion made me say things I didn't want to say. Things I'd been afraid to say. Clichéd things. "Katy, I'm never going to let anything happen to you. You know that, right?"

"I appreciate that, Preston. I really do. But stuff happens and I know you'll do everything you can."

"No. No way." I got a little mad now. "I'm never going to let anything happen to you. I promise."

We stayed at Cloudland Canyon for as long as we were able to without making the long drive back to Muscle Shoals feel like some sort of overnight epic. After the last two days we didn't need any drama, and this little side trip suited us perfectly. We walked through the blooming dogwoods and talked about everything but music and I realized I had no idea how badly she needed a day off. As much as I hated to admit it, I needed time off too.

The mountains reminded Katy of West Virginia, except the dogwoods were blooming way too early and there were pines instead of hemlocks and the smell seemed a little off. "Earthier," she said. "This is rockier than Blackwater Canyon. And there's only a stream at the bottom instead of a river."

I smiled knowing I'd accidentally given her the one thing she needed the most. Her homesickness manifested itself as nonstop chatter about her mom and Chloey. Counting down the days until we could sleep in our own bed made us feel like little kids counting down the days until Christmas.

We stood at an overlook for a real long time watching clouds move in from the west and not saying anything. Lightning struck the rolling Alabama hills, and I worried a little about driving back through the rain. Fog rolled up from the stream on the valley floor as the temperature cooled. She shivered, so I took off my coat and wrapped her in it.

She laughed when I tied the ends of the sleeves together like a strait jacket. I kissed her neck then set her up on the railing while she struggled and laughed. She wrapped her legs around me and leaned back over the drop, saying, "Save me, Preston! My hero."

And I got a little embarrassed because I thought she might have been giving me a hard time about what I'd said in the car this morning, about not ever letting anything happen to her. But when I told her to be quiet she said, "You know how to shut me up."

I kissed her and she closed her eyes. She slid off the rail. I caught her and lowered her gently to the deck while she kissed me back. Her hand drifted up to my cheek and lingered there. I'll never forget the way she looked at me when she finally let me go. Like she tried to look past my skin and hair. Like she was testing me with her eyes, trying to figure out what I hid behind my smile. Like my name was a lie, and that I had to tell her the truth before we could go on.

The way she looked at me, a little scared and vulnerable filled me with words I'd never said before. Made me dizzy. And before I knew it my face got warm and I lowered my knee to the cold ground. I'd never planned this moment and worried a little about not having any kind of ring to give her, but I knew that whatever I said would be the right thing. I grabbed her hand and rested my cheek on her palm. "Katy Stefanic," I said. But before I could say anything else she pulled her hand away and walked toward the car.

Still on my knees, I leaned against the rail and watched the mist rise from the canyon. Lightning split the distance, and I couldn't hear the thunder.

When I stood, I saw her headed toward the bathroom and wondered how I could've fucked that up. It took a lot to convince myself that she hadn't rejected me. At least it didn't feel like a rejection. I knew the timing just could've been better, and figuring that out on my own without being reactionary or angry made me a little stronger. Meant I'd grown up. I knew she loved me.

The minute I got back to the car the rain fell in buckets. I drove toward the bathroom and got as close to the door as I could so she could stay dry. But she took her good old time coming back out. I remained patient, because in the past being hotheaded never worked out for me. I turned on the radio—"I'm So Lonesome I Could Cry" by Hank Williams. I turned the station and got Skynyrd. "Simple Man."

After hearing Conway Twitty and Loretta Lynn's "Louisiana Woman, Mississippi Man" and Alabama's "Feels So Right" she appeared in the doorway. She paused, looking a bit relieved that she didn't have to sprint across the parking lot. When she finally scooted her way over to the car I reached over and opened the door for her. She sat down but didn't shut the door and I panicked, like she'd try to escape or something. Only after she started talking did I realize she just wanted the interior light on so I could see her face.

"Yes," she said. "Definitely yes a thousand times. But I don't want this to be the moment. Not on the road when we're both worn out and not thinking straight, okay? Take your time and we'll make it count. But you know it's 'yes' or you wouldn't have ever asked." She rested her head on my shoulder and her hand on my thigh.

For the longest time we sat there without moving. Right in front of the bathrooms with the *Door Ajar* chime dinging into the night. When she finally sat up, she looked at me and said, "Preston, I love you."

"I know." I smiled. "I love you, Katy."

"How much?" she said as she pulled the door shut and clicked her seatbelt.

I circled out of the parking lot.

It took her finally saying, "I'm waiting," for me to realize she wasn't being rhetorical.

I laughed and said the first thing that popped into my mind. "More than words."

"No, Preston. Before we go to bed tonight I want something better than 'more than words.'" She changed the station. "I want the words."

So we left the park to return to the small hotel room, our home for the next week. The last room before the last room in Atlanta. The last bed before the last bed before heading back to the sleepy Morgantown apartment we shared. And I drove knowing her words meant something.

Just outside Huntsville, between Curley and Woodley, we stopped for dinner at a large truck diner. Just past the *International Harvester* hats and books on tape and windshield wash fluid we found a place making catfish sandwiches on white bread, with sides of greens and black-eyed peas and dirty rice. They had brisket on the menu and I had to assume it was for real because I could smell the hickory smoke coming from the back. I would've been happy with cornbread and a few sides, but ended up with country fried steak and white gravy with biscuits and green beans with ham hock and sweet potato casserole. More food than I could ever want or need.

Katy smiled as she ate her sweet potato casserole. Eating made her happy, and I totally understood it. Comfort. That feeling that your mom is going to pop around a corner any second now with juice and cookies.

"I owe you a dessert," I said, wanting to prolong the good feelings. I could've spent all night here, with her.

"Yeah. I think it's time for pecan pie. We've been in the South long enough, right? Long enough to build up immunity. Pecan pie and butter pecan ice cream. I wonder if that's even a thing? If not it should be." She stood up. "I have to pee. Order it so it's waiting for me when I get back."

With that, she sauntered over to the bathroom. Leaving wood-paneled romance for the bright lights of hand driers and liquid soap.

I ordered her pie and played with the silver barrette she'd left on the table. Out of curiosity, I picked up her phone and saw that we hadn't texted each other since October. Meaning that since last fall, we'd spent almost every waking minute together.

While I waited I thought of the words she'd challenged me to come up with earlier. I tried to think poetically and lyrically. Romantically at first, then more straightforward. In metaphor and scientifically. I approached it as John Lennon would, with a bit of clever wit, then as Paul, all gooey and straightforward. I thought about it in terms of Southern symbolism—warm nights and magnolias and peanuts. I thought about it as a Mountaineer, imagining my love for her in terms of wide mountains and deep, dark forests.

"I love you more than…"

It didn't matter that I seemed lost before I'd met her, or that my heart only beat half as strong, or my days were all nights until she came into my life.

"I love you like…"

And the funny thing was it didn't matter. And I knew exactly what I'd say as soon as she sat back down and dug into her pecan pie with butter pecan ice cream. I knew that I loved her like only I could. Like only Preston Black could. A love greater than my love for The Beatles or The Clash. Greater than my love for Pink Floyd's *Dogs* or *Yankee Hotel Foxtrot*. I loved her more than my Tele. More than music, which she knew was like air and blood to me. That my life was just quarter notes and tempos without sound until I met her.

Her ice cream melted as I waited, excited that I finally had something to tell her. I laid her fork and napkin on the paper placemat next to her phone and purse. The texture of the ice cream scoop softened as it melted, ridges turned into soft curves that caught the light and dribbled over the sharp edges of the pie and onto the plate where it pooled.

While I watched, the puddle deepened one drop at a time. Bits of pecan emerged from the ice cream on top of the pie as it melted. Eventually it overflowed, and a tiny drip fell onto the table without making a sound.

I knew she wasn't coming back.

I interrupted our waitress as she counted out her tips and asked her if she'd seen the girl who'd been sitting with me. When she explained that she hadn't, I asked if she could go into the bathroom and look. She hesitated and I knew that the seconds mattered. And I dialed 911 before I even heard the bathroom door open back up.

"Brown hair just past her shoulders, blue eyes. Fair skin. Wearing a white short-sleeved shirt with a pattern of little navy blue birds and tiny buttons. I mean blue with white birds. I always had a hard time getting the buttons with my clumsy fingers. Um, a few silver bracelets on her left wrist, and a silver band on her right ring finger. And jeans and brown heels. Like, light brown. Brown like a baseball glove. And she had on a little fake brown leather jacket with a green army-looking jacket over top of it because she was cold."

The dispatcher asked me to clarify.

"My jacket, because of the cold air. And I had toothpicks in the right pocket and a receipt from a Waffle House in Warren, Kentucky."

The dispatcher asked about medical conditions.

"None. Like, sometimes her blood sugar gets low when she's hungry and gets a little irritable, but nothing serious."

And even when I hung up I kept describing her. I wanted to call back and tell them all the things I'd thought of since I'd gotten off the phone.

I'd been in the parking lot and in the women's restroom and all through the trucks in the lot. Talked to the drivers and attendants and they were all helpful but nobody saw her. I called the cops back and told them I talked to everybody here and they said they were still sending somebody out and I told them to start looking for motorcycles. When the highway patrol showed up I told them everything I told the lady on the phone. I went on and on about the Circuit Riders and Boggs and the attack in the venue. I told them all about Elijah Clay Hicks and how he came to The Met the night I talked to Mikey Kovachick about the show at The Stink, and how Hicks went by 'Clay' back then. I sent them pictures of Katy from my phone and let them look through her purse and I told them about the canyon and the rain and the hotel back in Muscle Shoals. When they left they told me I needed to get back to my hotel and sleep and to call Missing Persons in the morning, but I called as soon as the police left and told them everything I told the cops and the 911 dispatcher. But I didn't leave. Not when a chance remained that she could be here.

Then I called Pauly and he told me I had to call Katy's mom. But I couldn't. So I called Jamie to see what he'd say but he didn't answer.

So I called Katy's cousin, Ben. He was in Florida and said he'd be here in the morning. He'd call Rachel, he said.

"No, man. I have to do it."

And when I called her I cried and kept waiting for her to be angry. I told her I did everything I could, and she thanked me. I told her Ben left Florida to help as soon as I called.

Then I posted it to Twitter and Facebook. Ten minutes later I posted it again and begged for RTs and shares.

When I'd finally run out of options, I could only sit there. The waitress brought me coffee until she went home, then another waitress kept bringing me coffee until me and the waitress and the other employees were the only ones left. The new waitress's shift had begun after it all went down and she wasn't as sympathetic to my situation.

And the new waitress finally stopped bringing me coffee in the small hours of the night. Between two and four. Around the time I saw Barry Oakley paying for a fill-up and Ronnie Van Zant and Steve Gaines buying six packs. At three June Carter went into the ladies room and I didn't see her come out either. When old Sylvester Weaver himself sat down at the counter and ordered a few scoops of orange pineapple ice cream to go with his coffee I knew it was time to leave the diner and walk the lot. All the trucks were sleeping. I went back into the truck stop side and wandered through the aisles of maps and Advil. The bright lights were the only things keeping me from breaking down and losing it altogether. Somewhere amongst the pork rinds and sunflower seeds I finally said, "She's gone."

I returned to the diner and laid myself down in the booth, but did not sleep. Not with the sound of steel guitars and two-part harmony dripping down from the overhead speakers. I tried pulling my shirt over my face and lying with my head on the table. It felt empty, like a sky with no stars. I didn't know whether I felt sad, or some new thing I'd never experienced before.

The wooden booth creaked and I knew I wasn't alone. I jerked myself into a sitting position. Duane Allman sat across from me, sipping iced tea. He shook the sugar dispenser, but the humidity made the sugar clump. When he smiled his sideburns rose like they'd just seen a snake. He said, "What're you going to do to shake them hounds?"

"I don't know."

"Well, what did Johnny tell you to do?"

It took a while to catch on, but I knew who he meant even if I didn't want to say it out loud. "He said to go to the crossroads."

"Sounds like a plan." Duane smiled. "You're going to need some kind of help finding her, baybrah," before standing and disappearing into the glare of the grocery lights, with his iced tea still in hand.

CHAPTER FOUR

At the end of the hall is the room where you used to live,
And now the door's wide open.
The voices coming out make no sense to my ears,
I think they just might be echoes.

"Landlord" Music and Lyrics by Preston Black and Katy Stefanic

The knocking went on forever.

I heard it first in my dream. I remembered being a little surprised when the noise continued long after I opened my eyes. Too bad I couldn't keep them open.

"Let me in, man."

When I tried to get up I rolled onto a large wet spot where the rest of my Woodford Reserve had spilled onto the bed. That I drank Woodford and not Jim Beam somehow made my binge classier, even if the smell made me sick. "Yeah," I said, my voice little more than a rumble in my throat, "…like it's the fucking smell making me sick."

Splinters of dull pain rippled through my skull when I moved. I could only sit on the edge of the bed. I knew if I wanted Pauly to stop knocking I had to make it all the way to the door. "Coming," I said, but I knew he couldn't hear.

I slid into a standing position and shuffled over as the wall fell toward me. As soon as I turned the handle Pauly stepped in and ripped the drapes aside and filled the little water glasses with apple juice he picked up at a gas station. "Drink them," he said, then went into the bathroom and ran the hot water.

I shook my head and tried to say something to explain what'd happened last night. But the words got caught in my throat like wet leaves in a storm drain.

"No, Preston. Get your ass moving and clean yourself off. C'mon, man. Get your shit together." He grabbed my wrist and pulled me up from the edge of the bed. "Take your clothes off."

"I'll take my clothes off, but I ain't dancing for you."

I started to unbutton my shirt and he shoved the apple juice at me and said, "You need to hydrate, man. Preston, I'm not fucking around here. Get your shit together."

"I know, Pauly. I know." My head swam in the pool of bourbon that continued to slosh even after I'd stopped. I tripped on my pant leg and stumbled into Pauly. "I'm going to get her back, man. Watch me. I'll cut my way through the fucking South if I have to. Just sitting along the interstate with a gun shooting every motorcycle I see."

"You have got to sober the fuck up. I have shit to tell you and I can't tell you when you're like this. So drink the fucking juice, get in the fucking shower and get that fucking stink off you. You got all kinds of missed calls and I'm going to take care of those while you get your shit together."

"Tell me first. What you heard."

He shook his head.

"Fucking tell me."

"Drink this and I'll tell you." He handed me a glass. "It ain't the Circuit Riders."

Pauly sat down in the chair at the little desk.

I took off my shirt and dropped it onto the floor and he went on.

"Heard over the radio the Circuit Riders escaped custody this morning. So they didn't do it. Boggs spent yesterday in jail." He poured himself some juice and sipped while he talked. "They suspect the guy Katy mentioned—Elijah Clay Hicks. He has this cult over where Alabama and Georgia meet Tennessee. Like she said, this guy had been preaching since he was two or three. There's videos of him on YouTube shouting into the microphone, faith healing and all that. He's the leader of the group. All the protestors at the shows were with him."

"You think he did it?"

"That's who the cops are looking at according to the chatter I heard over the radio. But if the cops get a warrant and show up they're never going to find anything. I guess this group's property holdings are pretty extensive. They're like gypsies. They have all these camps and stuff. Old farms. People let them live on their property. Going to take a miracle to find her. Hicks got word out that you're a false prophet because you claim to have freed yourself from the devil's grasp. They see the people who show up at your shows as your flock."

"What about Katy?"

"They never said anything about her. But they stone adulterers. What do you think they're going to do to a supposed witch? The guy I got most of this from has a sister-in-law who had a third cousin disappear with these people a few years back. His wife is always checking message boards for her whereabouts. That's how he knew so much. He recognized your name as soon as I said it."

"Do you know where he lives? Like, if he's close could that be a place to start looking?"

"He's from South Carolina. Sorry, bro."

I let my pants fall to the floor and kicked them onto my shirt. "This is what I meant by hellhounds, Pauly. This bad luck that's never going to leave me be. Just like my fucking shadow—following me around forever."

"You need to shake this stupid devil supernatural bullshit. I'm tired of you using all this as a source of your woes."

I finished my last glass of apple juice. "You have to admit, shit is fucked-up despite all the good stuff's been happening. Like every dollar I earn costs me a pint of blood. You can say what you want, but my life wasn't like this before Dani and the record. Don't tell me it was, like that shit the other night about being heckled by fans. You know that for as bad as things got they never got this bad. Black cats and broken mirrors bad."

I talked as I looked for more juice to drink. "Katy's gone like I drug her into all this blackness with me. Like she's paying a price now too. We would've been better off winning the lottery because it's all luck anyway. It'd be some other band on that stage if it wasn't us. I'm stupid to think hard work had anything to do with it. Stupid to think I'd change as a person just because more people knew my name. Stupid to think all the things that made me a shitty person before would go away once I got a record out there."

"Get all this out of your system now. A little purge every now and then is good for the soul. When you get out of the shower your head's going to hurt, but it had better be in a healthier place. We got work to do."

I stepped into the bathroom and shut the door. Steam filled the space and coated the mirror and window. It filled my lungs and throat, which had grown a little scratchy from all the booze. When I started to sweat I could smell the bourbon coming out of my pores. The hot water turned my skin pink. I folded my arms against the cold tile and rested my head on them.

Johnny Cash said I had to let the water wash my sins away, but so far it'd only made me wet. But I continued to let it run over me and down the drain for a long time. Pulling me out of the alcoholic haze that got me through the rest of last night. I kept telling myself that Katy wasn't gone. That I'd find her. I said it so many times that it ran through my mind like a chord long after it had been struck.

I wanted to punch the wall but didn't need a broken wrist.

I wanted to hang my head and continue feeling bad for myself, but Pauly was right. We had work to do. I shut the water off, stepped onto the cold tile.

Pauly was talking to somebody, so I crept out of the bathroom cautiously.

"You remember to wash both your faces?" Katy's cousin, Ben Collins, put his hand on my neck and pulled me toward him until our foreheads touched. His hair was still Army short but he'd been letting his beard grow. "We'll get her, Pres. Pauly's been on the phone since I got here. And I'm already making calls. Got a buddy in the Bureau. We're all over this shit."

"Sorry for not being out here to meet you and introduce you guys." Seeing Ben made me really happy. He'd shed a lot of the anger he usually carried with him, which meant the PTSD meds from the VA were working. His change in demeanor would've made Katy really happy.

"You mean my brother from another mother? It's all good. Right now you don't know whether to shit or go blind. At least Pauly wasn't naked as a jay bird when I met him."

I wrapped a towel around my waist and stepped into the room. The air conditioning gave me an immediate chill. As I got dry clothes out of my suitcase I noticed all Katy's things sitting there exactly as they were when we left for breakfast yesterday morning.

"Over here, Pres," Pauly said, snapping me out of the moment. "We've been on the phone with Missing Persons and we put that shit all over Facebook and Twitter. Ellie at the label is going to contact the media down here and over in Atlanta, and back in Pittsburgh, D.C. and Charleston. Ben's going to meet with his guy from the FBI and see if ATF can get involved and I'm going to talk to lawyers and see if we can start the process of getting some kind of warrant for those religious fucks and their little freak show so we can move as soon as we find them. Got three numbers already, one of these suits had dealings with the church before. Civil lawsuit for a lady who'd escaped. Said they'd brainwashed her and everything."

So I asked again, "What can I do?"

"You're a little too sorry to work right now. Rest up." Ben had been trying to plug his laptop in, but couldn't get his arm behind the desk. His face grew redder. In a fit of anger he jerked the desk away from the wall, spilling deodorant and phone chargers and cups and Katy's makeup all over the place. He tried to regain his composure as his computer booted. "Just keep your head. Let us do what we can. If we can't get anywhere today legally we're going to find this place and go up ourselves tomorrow."

When I woke up Pauly and Ben were gone. Pauly'd taken the keys to my rental and I searched all over for the key to the van. But they didn't even leave me a room key. I picked up my phone and called Pauly. As it rang I saw the note he left. *Meeting with lawyer in Huntsville. Back by 5.* The call went to voicemail anyway.

I shook with rage and kept telling myself to stop with the pointless anger. No need to go through all that again. The time for being mad had passed. I needed to act. Sitting around waiting for the phone to ring wasn't going to get Katy back. I needed to know that even after we covered the entire planet there was always going to be one more place left for me to look, one more plan of action to take.

Maybe he had good intentions, leaving me here like this. But he'd made a mistake by not including me. I had to be involved, doing something instead of sitting on my hands. My skill set was limited, and I could only think of one thing I could do that they couldn't.

When Katy disappeared, the hellhounds became as real as radio. I tried to remember what Johnny Cash told me that night at the gas station. I closed my eyes but the words weren't coming. I fought to push all the other songs and emotions away. I had to stop thinking about Katy. After a long moment it came to me.

First stop's the crossroads, the second stop's hell. I got dressed, even if I didn't know where to start looking.

"Have to see what Robert Johnson saw."

Zeppelin and the Stones had left me some pretty good clues. They didn't exactly mark the spot with a big red X, but they got me close. I was headed to Mississippi. Rosedale or Clarksdale. Somewhere near Highway 49. I pulled my boots on and put on my jacket and dropped my phone in one pocket and dropped Katy's into the other. Right before I left I wrote a note for Pauly on the back of the note he left me. *Mississippi. Back tomorrow.*

In the hotel lobby I found Clarksdale on a map easy enough. But there were a hundred possible crossroads along Highway 49. I wanted to ask the girl at the desk if she knew anything about this, but she was studying psychology out of a book that contained more highlighted pink squiggles than words. I asked if I could take the map and she said, "Yup."

In the shelter of the carport I studied it. Looking for clues. A warm breeze made it difficult to hold the map still.

Another Zeppelin tune? "No."

Johnny Cash? Allmans? Beatles? "No."

Then I saw it on the map right outside Clarksdale.

"Highway 61." Running into Highway 49, plain as day. "Dylan."

Shoving the map into my pocket, I ran across the parking lot and slowly picked my way across the four-lane divided highway. I hopped a Jersey barrier while dodging cars, then ran through a Krystal parking lot and down an embankment, over old shopping buggies, rusted trash cans and broken bottles to a set of railroad tracks. A muddy wind blew from the west, bringing dense, moist air with it, like a breath from the Mississippi itself. I turned toward the setting sun and oncoming rain and started walking. Gravel cobbles and creosote-soaked rail ties made the going slow. Then an eastbound train rounded the bend and I stepped off to the side to wait while its whistle reminded me I wasn't supposed to be here. I ignored it, pulled my collar up, and kept going.

Ten minutes later another eastbound train came and I wondered if I'd been following the wrong set of tracks and took a moment to get my head together. All around me, the city gave way to an old industrial park. The rotting steel buildings reminded me of home, which I took as a positive sign. With the red dog and coal ash crunching beneath my feet and my eyes closed, it felt just like walking along the tracks after school, hoping somebody would save me before I actually had to set foot in the front door. Jeff for a guitar lesson. Therese for a quick walk around the baseball fields, which meant making out and a hand job usually. Stu with a J and an idea for a new song.

The old steel skeletons rattled in the wind, loose metal banged against unseen support railings, bird cries echoed through their wasted frames. And as soon as I got used to seeing them, they were gone, devoured by suburban neighborhoods and middle schools. Not exactly the kind of place to begin an adventure. Even the pre-fab plastic churches lacked the magical feelings the big brick churches back home radiated.

Another eastbound train cleared me off the tracks, activating a new wave of doubt. I started accepting the idea that I'd based this whole plan on the assumption that I wasn't kidding myself. That I had been operating under the influence of total sanity for the last few days. As far as I could tell, nobody ever considered me totally sane after everything that happened last year. The sky grew darker and I started to think maybe I wasn't even fit to be with a woman like her.

I knew my mood would make it easier for me to make dangerous decisions. I wasn't John Lennon or Joe Strummer. I was Preston-fucking-Black and sometimes I thought dumb thoughts. There were a hundred million people out there who could tell you that I could've done a lot better than ask Robert Johnson for help getting my girl back.

I wasn't one of them.

With the city a few miles behind me the houses all started to look the same. Like the same cookie cutter had been used row after row. The rails split from two to four, to eight lines and behind me the steady chug of a locomotive grew. I stepped over the tracks, trying to anticipate which ones this train would take. Red lights mounted on a scaffold high above cast a hellish glow onto me. Puffs of steam from air brakes always came from the wrong direction and I reminded myself that the hotel only sat a few miles away. I kept telling myself that I was wrong, and that I just made the wrong decision because I wasn't quite ready to lead yet. Being a follower was my best bet. And if I just called Ben I could sleep back at the hotel and let them work on getting Katy back. I'd crossed through the gates of misunderstanding a long time ago—before the Currence farm, before kicking the shit out of my old man in front of the Evansdale Towers, before the record.

And nobody believed any of that either.

As I kicked a hunk of limestone along the tracks, a westbound train, the first of the night, came into the rail yard. It slowed and rested on the tracks ahead, breathing heavily like a napping bulldog. Guys with flashlights inspected the undercarriage, and as soon as they passed I knew I could board one of the empties. The smell reminded me of the county fair and the grease they used for the rides. The double Ferris wheel spinning through the night, glowing like a fortress made of stars. When you're little, that's the pinnacle. Your mom watches you on the carousel but you're watching the double Ferris wheel. Then you have a strip of tickets to share with your brother and you're talking him out of the bumper cars and into the Round-Up. Then you get a girlfriend and you're on the double Ferris wheel trying to spit on people or harass the flunkies pulling the levers. You start going to the fair to score weed or girls. To drink in the parking lot. Then it's your band on the small stage playing Stone Temple Pilots wondering how you get back onto the carousel.

And that's why I hopped on the fucking train. Not because I thought Ben or Pauly were right. But because I knew I was. For once, I knew my plan was the plan. She was my girl, the only girl I ever truly loved and I'd bleed all over Alabama and Mississippi to get her back.

The engine released a sharp whistle blast and drifted forward. The cars inched ahead until each one caught the next car's connection with a bang. Bang after bang until the last one, faintly banging at the end of the line. I knew we'd be moving.

The sky turned green with the eastbound storm. Lightning flashed at the extreme edge of flat cotton fields. The sky never looked blue or black—it was always green with scattered bits of slate floating down like broken butterfly wings. The color of an old bruise. When lightning flashed, black clouds jumped out of the sky and returned just as fast. Thunder followed, rattling the cars, shaking the very rails themselves. The sky didn't look like the kind of sky that forgave.

It looked like the kind of sky that pushed rivers into basements. The kind of sky that carried away cars and mothers coming home from work. The kind of sky that gave newscasters something to talk about the next day when they rolled through your neighborhood in their news vans, talking about how this used to be the school and that was the church. My ears popped as the pressure dropped. All across the flat countryside dogs barked at the sky. The cars bucked and jumped along the tracks.

I didn't see any lights from houses or cars or grocery stores or hotels. Just the light from the sky, the green light that let me see a thousand miles before fading back into the clouds. And I couldn't compose songs or apologies or even think of what I'd say if I ever saw Katy again because the lightning stole my words from my throat. I knew this was one of those times to sit and watch and stay out of the way.

When the rain came it didn't come from the sky. It came from across the fields in horizontal bands that got me wet from the bottom up. I shivered in the green light and decided I'd made a mistake. That I wanted off the train and I'd call Pauly to come pick me up as soon as I figured out the name of the town I ended up in. That I'd gotten in over my head again. That all my words about being sad and mopey were just words that I couldn't control as much as I controlled breathing or my heartbeat.

And I supposed that was why I was doing this. Knowing she was gone left me with few options. I had to go to Mississippi. I knew Johnny Cash wouldn't steer me wrong.

Under flashes of white and green light the landscape opened up into vast muddy cotton fields waiting to be planted. Shotgun shacks shook in the violent wind. The flooded lowlands reflected the white and green lightshow like an old black and white TV shut off before going to bed. That was how I knew I was in Mississippi, a landscape described by Led Zeppelin and Johnny Cash and Elvis. Like, my bones knew even if my head didn't. I couldn't think of a better place, or better night, to seek the help from another plane. The way I felt on that train, alone, like no part of me touched any other living thing was a feeling I carried until I met Katy—the one voice out of thousands that connected with me. And when I responded, she acknowledged.

Last summer, while her shoulder healed after that shit with the Lewises, she led me into the mountains above her pap's house with a blanket and a packed lunch. We took our time strolling through ferns that smelled like peaches and fields where butterflies were too fat and lazy to even fly away when we passed by. Clumps of trees broke up the wide meadows. The wind blew warm air from the valleys on the other side. I spent a lot of time worrying we'd get lost, but never said anything because I trusted Katy. Tree trunks got thicker and farther apart. The little plants that grew between them slowly disappeared into deep beds of pine needles and dry leaves. The limbs were so dense I thought we'd need a flashlight to get back. And just when I felt like I needed to say something the sunlight streamed in on golden ribbons, and we were standing on a ledge of white rocks looking over hundreds of square miles.

When the sun set I said we needed to get home before it got dark and she said we weren't going back. That the show hadn't started. And when the first stars appeared I got scared. Venus cut through the darkness. I kept hearing animal noises from the trees behind us. But her reassuring demeanor calmed me. And I knew I could never be scared or lonely with her. I knew she'd do everything in her power to get me through.

Tonight I was scared. I had to get myself through to get her back.

The train slowed and I got off the first time I saw streetlights. I sloshed across the muddy fields toward a truck stop. My Docs were covered in heavy clay but the rain fell so hard it barely mattered. I took shelter beneath the awning that covered the gas pumps and let the water drip off me. An old man filled up his tank and I asked if Lula was nearby. He took off his Mississippi State Bulldogs cap, and in a slow voice, said it took about an hour to get there. I asked if he had plans to head out that way and he shook his head.

And I asked every person that came through. An hour wasted on truck drivers and young married couples trying to wrangle their kids into car seats. I finally went inside and asked the attendant if he knew anybody who could help me. But he said he could help customers only, so I bought some boiled peanuts and he said he didn't know anybody heading out that way.

Now angry, I went back outside. He didn't realize that Katy could die and that I didn't have time to fuck around.

An old maroon Ford Taurus driven by a pair of teenage boys pulled in next. The driver had on a *Master of Puppets* T-shirt. The other had on a red flannel and an Atlanta Braves cap. Pantera blasted out of their car speakers. I went over and said, "You guys think you can give me a lift?"

The one in the Braves cap spit a brown stream of snuff spit into a Mountain Dew bottle and said, "No, man. Give yourself a lift."

Before his partner could get a word in, I said, "I'll fill up your tank and buy you booze."

They didn't even have to discuss it.

And that was how I made my way from that gas station in Oxford to the intersection of Highway 49 and Highway 61 near the Barbee Cemetery, just outside Lula.

Ray and Vance were more than content to wait in the car once they found out what I meant to get into. Besides, they had booze now. They backed onto a gravel road that ended a few yards into a fallow field and shut out their headlights. To make sure they didn't split I took the keys and told them to start drinking. Didn't make me much of a role model, but they weren't exactly brain surgeon candidates and I figured they knew their way around a case of Coors Light. Way I saw it I was keeping an eye on them. Keeping them out of trouble. Or my version of trouble. The air had warmed since the rain stopped so I left my jacket in the car. As soon as I shut the car door and started walking, Ray yelled, "Stay away from the burial mound."

I could almost hear the blues floating across these old fields. Sounded like pain and dying and suffering to me. But I didn't know what to do at this point. I had no ritual, no routine and no idea of what was supposed to happen, so I waited in the center of the crossroads. The only light came from the traffic signals where Highway 61 met Highway 49, but there were no cars and trucks coming and going this time of night. The signals changed from green to yellow to red despite the lack of traffic, throwing faint shadows through the fields. Painting me in red and green, over and over again. In a way, each red light felt like a sunset, each green like another thunderstorm, and each yellow like a new day to suffer through, because I felt that way without Katy at my side. Every time the light changed it felt like another twenty-four hours had passed since I'd let her down. Since nothing seemed to be happening, I walked north a ways, shuffling my feet, venturing farther into the darkness. Off in the fields the ground moved. I could hear it. A *shhh*, like a finger to lips. I continued to pace as the light went from green to yellow to red.

Fingers of mist rose from the flooded fields and warm asphalt. Something halfway between steam and fog. The Barbee Cemetery sat on a small rise, one of the only ones around for as far as I could see, which made it feel kind of unnatural. Like a burial mound. Like the one Ray said to stay away from. Tall tombstones stuck out like broken teeth and one old tree grew behind a wrought iron sign. A small dead tree waited a little farther up the hill. Faded Confederate flags popped out of the ground here and there and all around orbs of faint yellow light rose from the swamp. Not fireflies—this light shone much duller, more like the impression of light than anything else. The orbs hung in the air like day-old balloons. I'd never seen foxfire before.

I heard music and turned to look for the car and the crossroads. Both waited nearly a half-mile back. Too far to be the source of the guitar I heard. Peepers called from new puddles. Far away lightning arched across the green sky, turning black clouds white then a lingering gray. It reflected off the vast pools that formed in the low fields. Like the lights that flash in your head when you get punched. There was never any thunder anymore, making the storm seem real far away. But it felt close. Close enough to keep me away from trees and that wrought iron. Close enough that I could smell ozone.

The peepers peeped so loud I couldn't focus on much else. I turned to make sure I had the traffic signal in my sight. "Green means go."

My feet sank into the wet turf as I walked. It didn't feel like earth beneath the roots because it took a long time springing back after I lifted my foot. Out of the corner of my eye I saw movement. A warm breeze tried to blow the weeds at the edge of the mud, but the heavy wind contained more water than air. Toads crawled through the long grass to escape the flood. I went to the top of the hill to escape them.

Blue and green bottles of all shapes and sizes had been jammed over the limbs of the small dead tree at all kinds of angles. Whiskey bottles and beer bottles and pill bottles reflected the distant traffic lights like sad little galaxies. The yellow lights rising from the swamp circled individual bottles for a second, like water around a drain, before rising into the night.

Out in the forest I heard a twang, a scratchy whine, an untuned guitar spitting out talkin' blues. I followed the sounds over an old wrought iron fence, jagged like broken glass, along a raised ridge to an old barn. Like the road that had been built to always sit above the flood. In the night's half-light I saw part of the barn's roof had collapsed. At the far end of a scrubby field a row of white columns held up nothing. Behind them sat the remnants of an old mansion. Dead kudzu covered everything.

A voice in the dark said, "Surprise, surprise."

My knees buckled and I tripped backward. I heard movement. Steps working their way toward me.

"Another guitar player looking for Robert Johnson's ghost."

My heart sped up like when I tasted Jack Daniels for the first time. I steadied myself on the fence.

"If that ain't the most unoriginal thing I ever seen."

A man walked out of the trees carrying an old Gibson arch-top by its neck. He wore a faded denim jacket and a Houston Astros ball cap. One with the old logo, like the one Nolan Ryan wore back in the day. He smelled like cologne from a five-and-dime. I had to say something to convince myself I wasn't terrified, but could only come up with, "You him?"

"You him?" he said, mocking me. He had a long and narrow face, not like any pic of Robert Johnson I ever saw. "You must not know shit. Don't even matter which *him* you're referring to. Ask another stupid-ass question and see what kind of fool answer you get."

"Sorry, man. Just thought..." I tried to shrink back into the darkness. Tried to disappear completely.

"There's your problem—you just thought. I know why you're here, though. You got woes, right? Yeah, I'm sure times is real hard for y'all. God bless you, son. I didn't know."

"Man..." His tone left me a little too stunned to reply. I rubbed my eyes with the back of my hand. "I hoped we could talk."

"We all got them hard times right? Some of us even got it so bad we step on down to the crossroads to see if Old Scratch is really going to show up and make everything better for a little song and dance. I know all about it. That's why I'm here." He shook his head and licked his lower lip as he stared into the fields. I almost thought he'd finished, but he said, "He stole that story from me, you know. Look it up. Robert Johnson don't know shit about no crossroads hoodoo. Far as I know, Robert Johnson wouldn't know that li'l ole funny boy from a bullfrog."

"Well, how could I know?" I crossed my arms and took a step back. "I'm real sorry."

"All everybody ever talks about is Robert Johnson." He stabbed the air with his finger when he talked. "But I'm the only one you see hanging 'round here tonight. Yes sir, Tommy Johnson's here for all eternity because Tommy Johnson did the dirt. Meanwhile old Robert Johnson gets to walk away with all them stories about him."

"Well, Robert died at twenty-seven, right?" I said, trying to throw a little optimism on the subject. "Poisoned, or something?"

"Don't matter. Everlasting life wasn't part of the deal, no sir. Not for this son of man anyhow. But then again, that li'l ole funny boy ain't one to play fair."

"I said I was sorry, man." This felt like one of those moments when I had an opportunity to be proactive as long as I stayed smart about it and kept control of the conversation's tone. For the most part trying to change fate hadn't worked out well for me so far. Pauly ended up with a limp and Stu ended up in a grave because I figured nobody'd notice me trying to manipulate the future. But I knew of no cosmic law written anywhere saying I couldn't try again. After all, I survived. Adopting a more forceful voice, I said, "I'm not here because my car won't start. My girl disappeared last night. Some fucking Bible-thumpers nabbed her at a truck stop and I know I don't have a lot of time to get her back. Like, I know these first few days are crucial."

My attitude pulled him out of his faraway gaze.

"Ooh. So you do got it bad, then? How you know she didn't up and leave you?" he said without sarcasm. He set his guitar on his knee and started to pick. "Coming home at midnight and your girl's home at one. Yeah, you creepin' in at midnight, and you're girl's home at one. You getting ready for some loving, and your girl, she just got done."

"Look—"

He cut me off, practically spitting out the words he said, "You want to know about chains? Then you got to be chained. You got to feel that cold steel cut into your wrists and you got to know how hope looks when it's nothing but a tiny little light in the very pit of your ever-loving soul. You want to sing about hounds? Then you got to know how it feels when them hounds are breathing down your neck, and how a hound'd rather die than beg off a trail. Ain't a man on earth can call them dogs off."

I turned and clenched a fist. Didn't know what else to do with my anger.

Resting his guitar on his toe, he said, "You going to sing about loss? You got to lose something."

"Lose something?" I exploded. "I lost everything."

He maintained his demeanor, which frustrated me even more. "No. You ain't never had nothing. No mama. No family. Big difference between losing and never had. If you ain't never had to pick a sack of cotton then you ain't ever going to know how many pounds it takes to keep food in your baby brother's belly. You may have been to hell and back, but you ain't been to hell and done stayed put there. Trust me, you sit down there long enough, hurting and thinking on all those woes, thinking about the deal you made with that li'l ole funny boy, then you come back knowing all about them blues."

I tried to find the whites of his eyes, but he kept them shut. I wanted to see if he was taking a piss at my expense or if he meant it. "How the fuck do you know what I got going on with me?"

"I don't know shit. But this son of a man knows the blues. It's like a spell on you and your heart hurts and your head spins like a whirlybird falling from a tree." He put his hand on my shoulder. A peace offering. "I know if you don't do something about it, you going to fall down a path you never come back up from."

"So what am I supposed to do? Give up?"

"They say the good Lord sent sunshine and the devil, well, he sent the rain. But that ain't always the case. Back in them olden days, relations between gods and folks like me and you was simple." He pulled me close and started talking real low, like he didn't want anybody else to hear. "But the church wants to control how you talk to the gods. Folks forget that we didn't need a priest for rituals. The church wanted us to forget that we had the ways and means to communicate with them all by ourselves. Some of my people though, they still doing things the old way. Same as some of your people. Using methods that involve a little less church and a lot more getting your hands dirty. My momma had an altar in the kitchen right next to the old potbelly stove. She put on her hat and went to church every Sunday from the day they baptized her to the day she died. But she didn't need church to talk to God. She talked whenever she'd make johnny cakes or cook up a pot of beans. Sometime He even talk back."

He took his hand from my shoulder and stepped back. "You need help from the other side, all you got to do is ask."

While he talked I found that little light of hope that had been buried down deep in my soul. Like finding Katy had just been a matter of asking the right questions, and I itched to get looking. "I appreciate your time."

By now I only half-listened. My mind ran about a half-hour ahead of the rest of me. Had me in the car on my way back to Alabama.

"Son," he said, taking my wrist in his dry hand. His skin felt smooth and warm. "You stopped listening right when I'm about to get to telling you what you need to hear."

I forced my attention back to him. At this point everything distracted me.

"You talk to them gods yourself. You didn't have to ride all the way out here to learn that. Understand this, next time you come out here, part of you ain't coming back. And that's why I'm here. You got to know that playing with this kind of fire burns you every time. Talking to Old Scratch in a bar or in bed's a lot different than talking out here. You come out here to do business—real business—and you got to understand that, son. You stand out there on them crossroads like you was tonight and that li'l ole funny boy's going to take something you can't live without. Then you know a whole new kind of blues and it ain't them talkin' blues or them travellin' riverside blues. Them are the blues you don't come back from. You're going to feel them chains and you're going to feel them dogs breathing on your neck."

"Like those hellhounds I got on my trail now?"

"Ain't no hellhounds. It's a gimmick, son. That's it. The li'l ole funny boy don't work like that. Everybody's got to die a little sometime." He sat against the fence, propped the guitar on his knee and strummed. "The lucky ones die all at once. Don't forget that. Some of us die more than once. Some of us die a little every day. What's left over is who we really are. You're going to have to die a little to get her back, you know that, right? But you have to die before you can be born again anyway. We can't all be butterflies, you know. Picking and choosing our time."

"Can I ask you something?" I shook his hand and held it, trying to feel for a pulse. That his skin felt warmer than my own confused me. "Please don't be offended."

"Just get on with it."

"Well, are you real?" I took a deep breath. "I mean you're not dead, like John Lennon and Joe Strummer when they talk to me."

He laughed. "Ain't no real or dead. There's alive or dead, then there's real or imagined. You knew somebody exactly like me though, a woman neither dead nor imagined. I can smell that fallen angel all over you."

"I understand." I knew exactly who he meant.

"Look it. You got something bigger than a soul. You got potential and you got love. Keep your soul and give it what it really wants." He said, "And make sure you write it all down—everything you hear and see, especially any visions you may have. That's what a prophet does."

"Thank you." I backed toward the cemetery trying to remember as much of what he said as I possibly could. "I mean it."

"You got a lot of miles between you and your girl. You better get moving along now. Don't you come back without that git box."

Behind him I could see the sky getting lighter to the east. A greyness where there had been a violet blackness earlier. Like the wide South was flat enough to let a little early light creep in from the Atlantic.

He said, "Don't you stop 'til you get back in that car, then get the hell out of here. Don't linger out there on the crossroads none either."

Nodding, I turned and left. A chorus of peepers and the lonely sound of a single untuned guitar played me out. In the slight farther off, birds shook sleep out of their feathers with soft songs. Waking up songs. Like being born again after a long night alone.

In the distance the traffic signal flashed red to green to yellow over and over again. Counting out an excruciatingly slow 4/4 tempo to help me pick my way through the tombstones.

The blue and green bottles on the branches of the old graveyard tree shivered as the waxy morning light grew. Trembling, as if an earthquake shook the whole thing.

I stopped to look.

They reflected the tiniest bit of dawn, making it seem like each contained a small sphere of distilled morning. I tapped one of the bottles. A faint globe of light bounced against the glass like a fly against a dirty window.

In the grass all around me toads hopped over each other, an exodus of amphibians pushing their way down the hill. I stepped carefully, picking my way to the road, not wanting to step on any. Faded Confederate flags drooped in fog.

The concrete strip that lead back to the crossroads didn't reflect any light at all. Like it'd been covered with velvet since I last came through. The toads crawled and half-hopped toward the road with great urgency.

"Holy shit." I pulled my foot back like I'd almost stepped in lava.

The surface crawled with a carpet of tiny red spiders, each about the size of a dime. They swirled and moved like snowflakes blown by the wind, oblivious to the feasting toads. I stopped, and tried to look for another way back to the car without cutting through the swamp. *Better the scary you can see than the one you can't*, I thought.

As soon as my toe touched the asphalt a loud crack blasted through the air. A wave of successive echoes split the morning as a multitude of crows took to the sky. They squawked and chirped and flew tightening circles above me. I took another step forward, the birds landing on the road one-by-one to feast on the spiders. Hundreds settling in a black, hopping, bobbing mass.

More toads poured out of the tall grass bordering the swamp and fell upon the road like garbage from a toppled trash-can. They flung themselves onto any vacant bit of roadway. Now annoyed, the crows pecked and jabbed the amphibians with their beaks, but the toads ignored them. They croaked and gorged themselves, their skin reddening as I watched. The smell, something like swamp mud mixed with chicken shit, made me gag.

I took another step, careful not to get anything beneath my heel. Birds took wing as I neared and settled down just as fast behind me.

I thought about what Tommy said about lingering on the crossroad and started running.

Another boom rang through the sky. I refused to even turn around and ran with my head down, careful not to slip, ignoring the occasional squish beneath my heel.

Ray watched me through his window. He yelled, "Where's the fucking fire, dude?"

He was on the verge of cracking open another beer but couldn't focus with me blazing down the highway like Jerry Reed.

Vance stared at me like I'd sprouted another eye in the center of my forehead. He popped open a new beer, tried to chug it real fast, and ended up spilling a good bit of it down his shirt. "You came running out of there faster than a bird dog after a limp chicken."

"Put the rest in the trunk," I said, careful not to look over my shoulder. "And I'm driving. All I need tonight is to get pulled over with two semi-intoxicated minors and a half a case of beer at six in the morning."

While I got settled and adjusted the mirrors and fooled with the radio they chugged. Then they each cracked open another beer. "C'mon. Finish it and let's go."

They finished and tossed their empties into the field, then pissed into the mud. As soon as they got settled we drifted into the dark Mississippi morning, windows down to blackbirds singing. Barns and homes and shacks emerged from the murky black horizon. I kept my foot on the pedal and an eye out for cops. The kids fell asleep and the bulk of the Mississippi miles—up to Senatobia, over to Holly Springs, at least— went by fast.

Just outside Corinth, Mississippi, we hit a truck stop to freshen up. While I waited for the boys to join me back at the car I got my first text of the day. Ben telling me how Jamie and Rachael were headed down.

Right before I could text him back "I'm Only Sleeping" streamed out of the shitty aluminum speakers hanging over each of the pumps. And I didn't think it was weird because it was the first Beatles song I'd heard in a long time. It felt weird because it was a weird Beatles song to hear anywhere. It was one of the songs I worked on with a voice coach right before we first went into the studio. My favorite part of the song was when John yawns right before the reprisal of the first verse. Like a little bit of the real John slipped through George Martin's creative grasp. Whispering in my ear. And right then and there I decided to do something I hadn't done in almost a year.

I texted him.

<Any advice?>

For a long time I stood there waiting for the phone to buzz to life in my hand. It almost scared me that it didn't. Like, if I waited long enough I'd have my answer one way or another, and once I knew, I could never go back to not knowing. I'd learn that Pauly'd been right and all the shit that happened last year happened in my head. Like all that shit in *Pink Floyd – The Wall*. So when the boys came back with a fistful of beef jerky and a few Red Bulls, I didn't make a big fuss. I just got in the car and drove as fast as I could while they goofed off. I decided I didn't want to know if it all existed in my head. I decided it was okay if I'd been a little off my rocker, because I felt a whole lot better now.

Once we hit the Alabama border the day got warmer, the sun higher. The radio stations grew more distant except for the ones with the 24/7 preachers squawking. Almost as soon as I put it out of my mind the phone vibrated. I hated to admit it, but the validation gave me a little rush of adrenaline. With an eye on the road I scrolled through my messages. My heart pounded in anticipation. I knew I'd been vindicated, and I knew not to tell Pauly or anybody this time. I'd never make that mistake again.

Except it was Ben. <Rachael knows how to find Katy, but you ain't going to like it. Get your ass back here.>

I nodded, grateful for the reality check, but didn't text him back. Grateful I had guys like Pauly and Ben to keep me grounded, especially since Katy let me fly as high as I wanted. When the sun fully hit my eyes the tears finally flowed. The weight of her disappearance hit me all at once. I couldn't bear the thought of losing her. But I pulled the visor down and cupped a hand above my eyebrows to let the boys think it the bright light made me tear up. *My reality is an ugly reality.*

I didn't know what I'd do without her. When I met her last winter I thought I'd started living the life I'd been meant to live. I thought I could finally grow up. But she loved me exactly as I was. She didn't expect me to change.

My phone buzzed again and I knew it was Ben scolding me for taking too long getting back to him. Without really looking, I hit reply and started to type.

But the number wasn't his.

The text came from John.

<Better the devil you know> was all that it said.

CHAPTER FIVE

Road shoulder sidewalk, drinking water from a jar.
Clothes in a trash bag, his knees are both scarred,
From the roadside prayers that get him through the day.
But while he looks for answers, more problems roll his way.

"Asphalt" Music and Lyrics by Preston Black

As soon as I got to the hotel I panicked about all the things that I still had to take care of, like calling the label and the studio and explaining everything that had happened with Katy. Meant to hold off calling the venue in Atlanta until the last possible moment because knowing that we had a gig was the only thing keeping my head right. But Pauly'd already taken care of all that stuff. Basically, he acted as our manager and followed up on the missing person reports and contacted newspapers and news media outlets in Huntsville, Birmingham, Atlanta and Nashville. He showed me all the notes from the lawyer he and Ben had talked with and where he'd been vigilantly updating Facebook and Twitter. I hugged him and for a second he just stood there, not totally sure what to do. After a pause, he put his keys into his pocket and held me.

"We'll find her, brother."

I took a quick shower and changed clothes since mine were muddy and smelled like swamp. So I pulled the dry cleaning bag out of the closet and tossed everything in. Pauly and Ben had packed everything else, including Katy's stuff, even though I liked seeing her things, which made it seem like she wasn't gone. But I could still smell her in the room. Before I shut the door I thought of my last morning in bed with her and the way she looked in the gauzy sunlight.

Pauly tooted the horn from the other side of the lot. He leaned out of the door of a new white rental van, squinting into the bright sunlight. He gave me a, "c'mon," and stamped out a cigarette with his boot. The redbuds and magnolias that ran along the highway had begun to bloom. The air didn't smell so much like winter this morning. I wondered if the change meant anything.

"Where's Ben?" I asked as I got into the van.

As soon as I shut the door he pulled forward.

"On his way to Versailles. My buddy lives there. A guy from driving school. I see him whenever I'm down this way." Pauly waited for traffic to clear. "There's breakfast."

A grease-spotted brown paper bag sat in the center console. "Chicken and biscuits?"

"Yeah, but don't be looking at them all pie-eyed like that. One of them's mine." He reached for it as he pulled onto the street. "Andre's going to set us up for a while. Said we can use his house as a base of operations."

"How well do you know this guy? Like, can we totally trust him?"

"You tell me, Preston. He's a pastor at a neighborhood church and he's been to more A.A. meetings with me than you. I spent last Christmas down here with him and his family. When you were up in West Virginia running them mountains Andre and his old man took me fishing with them down in Mobile." He jammed on the gas mercilessly. "We can trust him, man. Don't you worry."

"Sorry, I didn't know."

"It's fine. Shouldn't have barked like that. But you need to accept that we're doing our best. Ain't me or Ben ever dealt with anything like this, but Ben has a plan. Sat up all night talking with Rachael and writing everything down. Said you could explain it to me if you felt like it. And I know you haven't dealt with anything like this either and I know it's hard to share control of a situation like this. But Andre's all right. Lives with his wife and her mom."

So I didn't ask him about it anymore. I ate my sandwich then tried to nap, but had no luck falling asleep. Staring out the window took a lot less energy anyway. Nothing to see but low Alabama hills covered with scattered pines that occasionally parted to give glimpses of the wide Tennessee River. Pauly gave me control of the radio, which let me know it was okay not to talk about it anymore. When the hills started to look like miniature versions of the mountains back home, I asked, "What did Ben say, exactly?"

"That Rachael said you had to talk to somebody who'd know, but finding her was only going to be a little easier than finding Katy." He took a deep breath, held it, then slowly let it out. "Said it would be scary and you weren't going to like it. Said it would hurt. Ben asked if he could be the one, and Rachael said it had to be you."

I tried to take everything in. I knew Rachael hadn't been as cryptic with Ben as Ben had been with Pauly. It seemed like the only piece of the puzzle missing was who exactly she wanted me to talk to, so I asked.

Pauly shrugged. "Somebody named Jane. Henry's sister."

I dozed off right before we hit Versailles and a change in speed and direction woke me up just as fast. I stretched as the mountains speeding past my grimy window got a little taller. As farms gave way to a small town. Strip malls and stoplights and churches. Methodist churches. Baptist churches. A.M.E. churches. A Piggly Wiggly instead of a Kroger's. Pauly navigated side streets until the tiny town turned into rows of houses in too much disarray to be called neighborhoods. Everything looked like it had been built in the forties and renovated in the seventies. Shotgun shacks rubbed elbows in the shade of old sycamore trees, and every corner had its own bar. The sidewalk had been heaved up in many places where the trees decided to crack their knuckles. Kids shot hoops into rims with no nets. Old tennis shoes had been slung over power lines by their laces. Dogs sat next to the trees they'd been tied to, their upended bowls the only things emptier than their bellies. Old Ford Thunderbirds and Lincoln Continentals as long as railcars sat on blocks in front of boarded-up storefronts.

I saw Ben's Jeep in front of a small double-barrel shotgun shack wearing a coat of fresh white paint, which made it stand out a little from all the other houses on the street. In the front yard there stood a dead tree, about chest high, that had all its branches trimmed down to nubs. Each nub held an upturned glass bottle—blue or green—just like the tree at the cemetery last night. Ben was nowhere to be seen.

Right next door a man with skin the color of coffee with too much cream stood on a patch of mud between a juke joint called "Creole Royale" and the sidewalk. He lathered sauce onto random chicken parts cooking on a big steel drum that had been split right down the middle. The juke joint behind him, that looked a little like an old service station, had a corrugated steel roof, whitewashed wooden siding which had faded to grey long ago, and neon beer ads in the windows. A pair of little white signs hanging next to the door said "Beer and Soda for Sale" and "All sandwiches served with Coke and fry" in bright red letters.

"Pres, there's the blues guy I told you about."

"You never said nothing about a blues guy. I would've remembered."

"That's right. Meant to tell you about it last night, but you already done run-off into the wilds of Mississippi." Pauly got out of the van and waved. "Simoneaux. How you doing?"

Simoneaux raised a pair of tongs into the grey sky and waggled them. "You eating?"

"No, Nadhima's making lunch. Maybe tonight?"

"Who you got there with you?" He sounded like the Cajun folks we heard in NOLA when we passed through last fall.

I turned and waved. He cupped a hand over his dark eyes like somehow that'd help him see me more clearly.

Pauly said, "My brother. The guitar player."

"Tell him I'm a father of five, can drink a six-pack by seven. That my mama gave birth to me and raised me in crawdad heaven, but all this red clay up in here didn't make me no redneck." He swatted smoke away from his face as he said it.

Pauly looked at me. "You get all that?"

I smiled and gave him a big wave.

"I don't see no git box. Tell him come over tonight and listen to some real good music." He continued talking like I'd stayed in the van. "Elmore James played here in 1955. Lots of magic still left up in this joint."

"You giving him a free pass because he's my brother?" Pauly came around the van and hopped onto the sidewalk.

"No. He gets a pass because he's a guitar player."

I laughed to put him at ease.

Pauly pointed at the house. A gesture meant to get me inside before things could drag on. His friend waited for us on the porch. Pauly said, "Andre, this is my brother, Preston."

I shook his hand as he said, "Andre Betters."

"Nice to meet you," I said. "Appreciate your hospitality. Don't want to put you out."

"Ain't the first time we played host to invaders from the North, probably ain't going to be the last. I'm sure we'll survive." With a smile, he stuck his hand into the pocket of his blue coveralls. The little bit of grey at his temples indicated he had more years on him than Pauly and me.

"Let's meet the rest of them," he said, gesturing for us to step on inside.

His pad looked only a little bigger than the first apartment Pauly and I had shared back in Morgantown. It smelled of new paint and incense. A flat-screen TV stood against the wall where a fireplace should've been. The comfortable little living room gave way to a long hallway filled with the rich smells of a cooking lunch. A little bit of fat, a little bit of spice and a few things that made me hungry without needing to know what they were. Before everybody got settled I meant to ask Pauly if it'd be impolite to get a hotel room. I didn't like inconveniencing these people any more than I liked not being able to be alone with my feelings about this whole fucked-up situation.

Andre drifted toward the hallway and introduced me before I could get Pauly away. "Preston, I'd love for you to meet my wife, Sabra."

She looked like Jasmine from *Aladdin*, with skin a few shades paler than Andre's and wide, dark eyes. She wore jeans and a pale blue button-down shirt accessorized with a stethoscope like she'd just gotten home from work at the hospital. I smiled, and started to introduce myself, when she cut me off with a quiet, "I'm sorry," and anything else I would've said after suddenly sounded ridiculous. She hugged me, then led me by the hand. "Pauly's always talking about his brother. Figured it was high time we met you."

I said, "Wish it'd been under better circumstances."

Before I even got all the way into the kitchen, Sabra said, "Mom, this is Preston. Pauly's brother."

The thin woman washing dishes at the sink looked a few years older—but not many—than Sabra. She had smooth skin and bright eyes, and her hair was pulled back into a bright red scarf. She wore a long white dress with tight sleeves that went down to her wrist. "Nice to meet you," she said with an accent more Caribbean than Southern, and held her wet palms up apologetically. "Don't be a *manouche*. Sit."

"Thank you all for your hospitality. Sorry to inconvenience you like this." I took a seat at the small table next to the black-eyed peas and fried okra, and couldn't help focusing on a tiny, makeshift altar between the stove and the fridge. A Jesus statue stood on a swatch of sparkly purple cloth, about to ascend into heaven. Next to him sat a Mason jar filled with brown seeds or spice and a wooden cross that had several strings of beads draped over it. A bowl of fresh cut redbud blooms and a bowl of cherries rested at the Son of God's feet.

When Sabra kissed Pauly's cheek, she caught me looking at the altar. I turned my head.

Pauly set a box of chocolates on the counter near the altar. "Thanks for cooking, Nadhima. Really appreciate it."

"Can I help?" I said.

"Just enjoy lunch, because something tells me you may not like dessert so much." Nadhima turned to Sabra and said, "Go get the boys. Tell them it's ready."

Nadhima wiped her hands on a towel and sat at the table across from Pauly and me. "Preston," she said, taking my hand into her own. "You the kind of man who makes it rain by screaming for rain?"

I didn't know what she meant, whether she spoke metaphorically or not. Far as I could tell I had no control over anything. I looked away to avoid answering.

"For this to work, you're going to have to be. Hate to see anything happen to that poor girl." She set a plate of cornbread in front of me and tsked as an expression of pity. As she spooned okra onto my plate, she went on, "Leviticus says 'a woman that hath a familiar spirit shall surely be put to death,' so don't expect them to suffer a witch to live. Not for a second. Those folks don't play."

I pushed my plate away from me. Not as a sign of protest or rudeness, but I couldn't eat. Not now.

"Put food into your belly to clear your head." Nadhima laced her fingers together, permitting me to see the remains of a fading henna tattoo on her wrist. She said, "I know you don't have an appetite. If it makes you feel better, none of us do."

I almost asked her to clarify, but she cut me off. "That's something the angry boy digging the grave ought to explain to you."

I looked at Pauly. He just said, "This is all Rachael. What she said to do."

"Everybody quiet now." Nadhima bowed her head and took my hand again. "Oh, Father, lord of Heaven and Earth, we pray to thee, extend your right hand and bless all elements in the earth and in the sea and in the sky, and all the creatures—your children—and hallow them in thy name. Grant that this meal make for health of body and this water for health of soul, and let us prepare for the return of our lost little girl. In the name of the Father, and the Son, and the Holy Ghost."

Amen.

The okra tasted a little like a home I'd never known, but I couldn't enjoy it. So I stuck with the cornbread. Letting the butter melt down before plopping it into my mouth became a kind of meditation. I didn't have to listen to the wall clock or the ticks of the cooling oven while I waited for butter to melt. Pauly kept my sweet tea topped off.

Ben came to the back door with a man I didn't know. Andre's dad, I figured. Ben's jeans and work boots were muddy. He didn't come all the way into the kitchen. I stood as the door swung shut behind them. Ben said, "As soon as you're ready."

"Ready for what?"

"Best not to talk about it if you ask me. You don't want to know what you're in for." He turned and went back outside.

I stood as Andre's old man came over to shake my hand. Andre and Pauly stood, too.

"Good morning, Reverend Betters," Pauly said.

He shook my hand. "George Betters. Nice to meet you."

"Preston Black. Thanks for—"

"Don't thank me yet." Without sitting, he heaped a mound of peas onto a slab of cornbread and began to eat. Turning to Pauly, he said, "I love you like a son, but I ain't comfortable with all this," and waved his fork over the table like he disapproved of lunch rather than the circumstances of our visit.

Pauly said, "I know, George. I'm sorry."

"Don't pay him no mind. He's still bitter about Alabama passing on Sylvester Croom. Tomorrow it'll be something else," Andre said. "No need for the reprimand, Pop. You know Pauly's taken good care of me and letting him use my yard for whatever he wants is the least I can do."

"Dhima, this is delicious. Thank you kindly. My boy's lucky to have you." George cleaned his plate with a few big bites and served himself seconds. "Son, I mean no disrespect. But you've got to know what I seen in my time to make me believe what I do. Staring at topographical maps for twelve hours a day didn't get me out of Khe Sanh—getting saved did. I never preached to you, but I have a right to testify."

"Yes, sir, you do," Andre cut him off. "I know what you're going to say next. You're going to quote the New Testament—John—something about charity, right? Maybe, '…if a man closes his heart to a brother in need, then God's love can't abide in him?' But we don't need them to believe. Just need to be there for them."

Figuring it was my time to speak up, I jumped in. "I spent enough time with Katy's people up in them mountains to know the kind of things that can happen when faith is strong enough. It can change the weather, pull fire from a wound." I stood and wiped my hands on my pants. "So, let's see how this goes down. Hate to say it, but I'm a little curious myself."

"C'mon, sit down now. Banana pudding is cooling." Nadhima stood when I did.

But the back-and-forth irritated me. Figured talk wouldn't get Katy back. I didn't even hold the door open when I left the house. Ben sat in the grass, wiping his face on his shirt. When he saw me, trailed by Pauly and the rest, he stood, jammed the shovel into the fresh earth and tucked his shirt into his waistband. He said, "Pauly, you were supposed to blindfold him."

I said, "Well, that ain't happening."

The hole rested in a grove of twisted trees shrouded in kudzu down the slope from the back door. The leaves were just little green nubs but were dense enough to make it feel nice and secure. A pair of headstones sat tangled in ivy at the edge of a greenbrier thicket, an old door rested against a chain-link fence. I could smell the river, and when I stood on tip-toe I could see it through the trees.

"What's the hole for, Benjamin?" I asked.

"Ain't for sticking your dick in, that's for sure. Said you weren't going to like it, but Rachael says this is how we find Katy. That should be enough for you. You have to trust me." He tucked his dog tags into his T-shirt.

"I'd feel a little better about it if Rachael was here herself."

"No time for that. Cops ain't doing anything. News ain't reporting it. She's gone, bro. Rachael wants her back. I want her back and I know you want her back. This is how we do it before there's no longer a Katy left to save." Ben pointed at my feet. "Start by taking off your shoes and emptying your pockets."

I handed Pauly my phone, Katy's phone, and my wallet.

"George, let's start that water."

The old man nodded and went back up to the house.

Andre had his hands in his pocket and kept shaking his head. "This ain't right."

Ben said, "Your shirt and jacket."

I hung my jacket on the old fence next to Ben's tan, grey and green camo-patterned field jacket. As I lifted my T-shirt over my head, water spurted out of the end of a green garden hose. Without a word, Nadhima put her palm on my forehead, then pulled me forward so she could drape several strands of colorful beads around my neck. Strands of black and green and yellow and red sparkled in the dull grey light. Ben held his phone and dialed. Sabra set a small first aid kit on a lawn chair. She opened it and took out a CPR pocket mask. She stuck a valve into it and wiped it with alcohol.

Just then I realized why she had the stethoscope. "What the fuck is this?"

Nadhima spread an old blanket out in the grass next to the hole.

Ben handed me his ringing phone.

Pauly and Andre took the old door from the fence and stood it up next to the grave. I stood at eye level with the small square window. The broken glass had all been cleared away. "Hello?"

"Hey, Sweetie." I heard Rachael's voice and got choked up. "This is going to happen pretty fast, so you have to listen really well. We're on our way down now. Be there tonight or first thing tomorrow, okay?"

No 'how you holding up' or anything. My hand shook. *Fuck me.*

"Remember that you are in control. You have to end it. Ben and Pauly can't help you and it's important to remember that you end it." She spoke a calm and forceful tone. "Find Jane and talk to her then get out. Understand?"

Down by the river I heard the scream of a thousand birds taking to the air. "I think."

"No, Preston. Listen to me. You have to make certain you get out of there. Remember that Katy is waiting for you. I know you can do this." She sniffled. "You have to find my little girl, okay?"

I took a deep breath. "I promise."

"Don't lose track of time because…" She sniffed and talked to somebody in the background. "Jamie wants to talk to you."

Pauly put his arm around me while I listened to Jamie. In the background I heard Chloey's voice.

"There's a reason you're going and not Ben or Rachael. You know that, right? Ain't many folks out there to walk away from what you walked away from last winter. This is going to hurt but I know you can be strong. Mom and Pap are home thinking about you."

"No pressure." My dry mouth released a couple of low clicks. Blackbirds circled above the little grove.

"I've been talking to Nadhima and know you're in good hands. But you have to have faith. We all love you, Preston. You familiar with the *Tibetan Book of the Dead*?"

"No."

"Okay, well, 'Tomorrow Never Knows' then. Think about John's words. You need to remember that this is not dying. Got it? You got to get yourself out of there as soon as you talk to her, understand?"

"I do." *I didn't.*

"Now let me talk to Ben."

I handed Ben the phone.

Pauly looked at me, but didn't say anything.

"I know, man."

"What the fuck is this, bro?" His eyes studied my eyes, my mouth.

Nadhima pulled a small sack made of red flannel from her purse. "Black cat bone and Angelica root," she said, dangling the bag in front of my eyes. She shoved it into my front pocket.

Ben watched, still talking with Jamie.

Nadhima handed me a small silver barrette. "This belonged to your beloved?"

I recognized it. "Yeah."

She kissed it, then shoved it into my other pocket. "Get on down there now."

Ben set the phone on the lawn chair next to the CPR mask and my wallet and phone. I watched Sabra write Jane's name on an old tombstone with chalk. She turned, Nadhima nodded. Sabra crossed out Jane's name and wrote mine just above.

Pauly said, "You end it. Remember what they told you, all right?"

I looked at Pauly, then to Ben and Sabra. Not a single one of them looked too happy about what was going down. George had his back turned and his arms crossed.

"George, you should know by now I can pull mojo out of the air like plucking peaches from a tree." Nadhima slipped off her shoes and hiked her dress up to her thighs. "This here isn't my first black baptism. But you can pray if you'd like."

The cold water rose easily past my knees. Bits of leaves and grass circled endless in the red clay-stained water. Small clumps fell from the side of the grave and circled before sinking. Blackbirds flocked to the bare branches over my head, blocking out much of the grey light.

"Don't think, man. Just do it." Ben held the old wooden door, and I could see that it was a little narrower than the hole. "You have to go on your own."

Pauly stood on the other side of the hole and held onto the old wooden door. Through the small opening I watched grey clouds move past tiny patches of blue sky. My hands were shaking. "I'm scared. I don't know if I can do this."

"Katy needs you, bro." Ben forced me into the hole by gently guiding the door. "Rachael wants you to bring her little girl back."

I got on my knees but fought to keep that little patch of sky above me. Blackbirds crowded my view. Water flowed over the lip of the grave. "What if—"

Nadhima stood in the water circling me, chanting something. When she at last came face-to-face with me, she made three crosses on my forehead with her thumb then climbed out of the hole.

"No doubt," Pauly said. "You got this. Don't let that doubt in your head."

"Don't think," Ben said.

I leaned back. My jeans felt really cold and for a second I tried to think if I had any clean clothes left after this, but they pushed the door right onto me and I sought a reprieve from the sky directly above. The clouds had covered it all. I looked for Pauly. His eyes were red. I looked for Ben. He forced a confident nod.

The cold snapped me out of the moment and my legs jerked out to the side to keep myself from sinking lower and I tried to grab the sides of the grave. The mud and clay gave way in my hands. I grabbed the door. Splinters of paint and old wood dug into the soft skin beneath my fingernails. The pain lasted only for a second before the cold took over.

My lungs burned. I fought to push my face through the small opening. The tiny window that let friends in and kept strangers out. I kicked at the clay walls and tried to force my lips into the sky above but the patch of light seemed very far away. My lungs burned. Pain worse than the pain in your legs after gym class. I remembered what Rachael said about ending it. By forcing my arm through the window I tried to end it with everything I had in me. A pair of hands grabbed my wrist and pushed it right back down.

My toes hurt from trying to kick at the door. My chest felt tired from holding my breath, like I had a black mass locked away in my ribs. A tumor pushing the air out. Not pain. A feeling like an ending. A feeling like my line stopped right there. A feeling that my forever, which had been a certainty since I met Katy, had been taken from me. And I remembered all I had to do was breathe. That the pain in my lungs faded meant I was dying. My brain wrestled with what it felt and what it knew, but only the fading pain was real.

Johnny Cash said the water'd wash my sins away, but so far it had only made me wet.

So I let it. Because it seemed easier. I wanted the pain to end.

Turn off my mind.

Water filled my mouth and throat and I knew I'd made a mistake because Katy's face was the only thing I could see and I jammed my hand back through the opening. But my hand blocked the light and I knew, man, I knew I didn't want to be in the dark. Not now. I never wanted to be in the dark again. Mud colored the water, making my little patch of sky a red smear. I'd never been so far from the light in my whole life. But she waited somewhere else, in the hands of people who wanted to hurt her.

I can't help her if I'm dead.

My light wasn't the moon or Venus. She was a little star. Anonymous. And I'd never been away from her for so long since the day we played that first show together. Those few songs that changed my life forever.

Relax.

My faint little light.

Fading little light.

No stars in this dark sky.

Her face had been lost to me. Those big blue eyes, which I'd woken up to every morning. And I couldn't remember them.

Everything is dark.

At the end we are only alone.

Float downstream.

In a river of black static, falling away from myself.

Noise like songs, my songs, my brain trying to hold on to life. He knew he was dying.

A river of memory.

It is not dying.

Every moment of my entire existence, in my head and accessible at this very moment. Knowing everything I'd ever know. Every taste. Every scent. I saw my mother's face in the half-light of the winter of my birth. I saw my father on the day he left.

Every fistfight.

Every kiss.

I saw everybody that'd gone before me.

I felt no more pain. No more seconds flying past my head like shooting stars.

No light except for the light he remembered in his head.

Even when talking to himself, the words seemed far away. Talking to himself to keep a foot on the ground. Talking to himself, in his head, because he didn't know what else to do. And he knew he could stop the words whenever he wanted to.

Just stop the words. Let them trail off.

He'd never known darkness like this. He'd never really known alone, until this.

But he wasn't alone.

He heard the others shuffling out ahead of him.

A rushing noise built in my ears, like wind over a mountain. A voice boomed with heavy echo from both sides of my head. The words weren't English. Small lights off to the side steered me away from the darkness. I just knew to follow the ones in front of me.

It is believing.

The voice got louder and my instinct told me to back away from it, but doing so would've meant leaving them. They weren't my friends, but their presence meant I wasn't alone. They drifted toward a little light that grew on the very edge of a stiff horizon. Like a fog in a forest. Like sunrise in a city. They moved faster and the voice came back. Fading in, I heard it say

…it is not dying.

I heard my voice.

But the noise all around me sounded totally different. Like the static from a TV station after sign-off. Flashes of white and black light. A faint hiss and specks of color—but not color—each existing for only a moment.

I turned to see where it came from.

Metallic warbles emerged from the noise. "Yes, sir... Let's hear it for Rose Maddux." It came from all over.

I spun, still looking for the man who said it.

"That's the kind of singing they like down in Houston. Sings like her motor's still running, don't she?"

Whistles and hoots came from the crowd. The light got brighter, and came from all directions. I held my hand over my eyes. Sweat formed on my temples. Straight lines and movement emerged from the dark blur. Noise and words attacked me from all sides. So many I couldn't make sense out of them.

On the edge of the stage, the announcer wiped his forehead with a handkerchief, and said, "Got a big show for you yet, so don't you go running off."

Electricity streaked through my arms and legs as Johnny walked past. He stood a little shorter than I anticipated, wearing that white jacket with the black piping. Behind me a little Fender Pro breathed steam into the old civic center. A wall of heat and hum that knocked people back into their seats. I pulled on my necktie to loosen it, and for the first time all night I could breathe.

I fixated on a large illuminated clock behind the stage right curtain. A white face with black block numbers. Seemed like the only thing that truly made sense to me.

Then Johnny nodded, giving me the signal to go.

The second I set my pick to that string the crowd stood. That Fender Esquire sounded like an angry dog barking at a freight train. Girls in pale pastel dresses with hair twisted and sprayed into beehives watched Johnny swagger up to the mic. Guys in suits and skinny ties—now that they were being ignored by their girls—watched my fingers work through the first few notes as the announcer rushed to finish his introduction. He said, "America's greatest folk music star—Johnny Cash!"

The kids sat back down, and before that old square could even get his ass off the stage Johnny hovered over the mic banging out the chords to "Big River." I looked over at Marshall plucking that big old upright bass's strings. He just smiled away as he counted out that old 'one, two, one, two...' with his hair pushed straight back from his forehead by a gob of grease. Marshall Grant was a good old boy, all right. He smiled and bounced to the beat, kicking his leg out and slapping those strings like he was swatting a bee.

With my eyes closed it felt like a train rolling down a mountain without brakes. A warm calmness enveloped me. A feeling that crept beneath my clothes, like only my skin was drunk. That feeling told my mind to stop fighting. *I'm home.*

My mind couldn't keep up with my fingers. Only the clock mattered. The second hand ran backward like an egg timer. *7:59 PM.*

Row after row of kids bobbed their heads. Some of the girls wore little white gloves. Some had handbags to match their sleeveless dresses. It felt hot. And I was nervous. My mouth felt like it was stuffed with cotton.

And my head ached like nicotine withdrawl on top of a hangover. The notes sounded right in my ears, but they didn't sound like the notes I picked. It felt like in a dream when a door opens into the wrong room. On the edge of the crowd I saw a girl I thought I knew from school. I could've sworn I saw Abby Fincher. She died in a car crash my senior year, and I wondered how she got all the way down here in Texas.

I rushed the beat. Probably because any time we'd ever played this Stu jacked the pace up. I watched Marshall for the tempo and picked out my rhythm and flashed my cheesy grin for that Texas crowd. When I tried to stretch out my solo Johnny turned and gave me a look.

Marshall clicked to get my attention.

"Huh?" I said, upset that he'd pulled me out of the moment. I muted the strings with my palm.

He pointed at Johnny.

And I only knew the song ended when they applauded. Embarrassed, I stared at my shoes as he thanked the Houston crowd for being so dang polite. His way of saying they needed to make a little more noise.

In a way I felt like I should have gone over and talked to him before he got into the next tune, but just thinking about it scared me. My feet wouldn't move. Keeping my head in "Big River" had taken all my energy.

Marshall leaned over to me and said, "You see her yet?"

"Who?" I said.

"Don't play coy, Preston." Marshall chewed his gum so hard it made my jaw hurt to look at him.

"Before we play our next number I'm going to tell you who we brought with us." Johnny turned and gave Marshall a scolding look for his chit-chat. When he returned to the mic, he said, "We call these boys the Tennessee Two. He's from West Virginia and he's from Mississippi."

While the crowd laughed, Johnny turned and gave me a wink. My body glowed, like I'd been touched by the hand of Jesus Christ himself. My tongue got real dry and the butterflies came back big time.

Johnny said, "We ain't had the heart to tell Preston, but he's been dead for a year."

I knew Johnny meant Luther Perkins, not me. I knew this because I had this concert on my laptop. I listened to it all the time. *Luther's been dead a year. Not me.*

It didn't matter though. Maybe seeing June off to the side of the stage helped me relax. Helped me realize I belonged here. I knew Johnny'd get the joke right next time.

Johnny stepped off stage to get a glass of water.

I looked for the clock. *7:25 PM.* I didn't want to think of what happened when it counted all the way down, and said to myself, *Maybe this wasn't heaven after all.*

Maybe hell would be losing these feelings again, over and over, for an eternity. Knowing that I was always, truly alone. Like my lifetime spent practicing disappointment would finally pay off. I could almost see Katy if I focused my thoughts.

A metallic hum broke my concentration and I lost the image. Anger blew up in my throat like water boiling over from a pot. The intense rage convinced me I was still alive.

I needed to sort this out and decided to talk to Johnny. He'd disappeared into the heavy curtain, and I dove in right after him. Thick waves of velvet engulfed me, buried me in darkness. I spun and called for him. "Johnny."

I paused to listen, but only heard murmurs from the audience. "John!"

Somebody in the audience screamed. A girl. Then I heard another cry.

"John."

Then I heard a thousand more.

The screams expanded and I tumbled forward in the dark, almost like I'd been shoved. Over my shoulder somebody laughed. Shadows moved on the floor by my feet. I pushed toward them.

A multitude of small lights like exploding stars appeared as I emerged. Noise grew like a jet that never passed. It only ever got closer and closer. Like I was being reborn into a whole other universe. Lights flashed behind us. Above us. My eyes followed the flashes around a complete circle. High above, a great silver dome reflected it all back down. A large box hung from the ceiling. A scoreboard. Without any warning at all, I heard John Lennon say, "One, two…" and the rest disappeared into the static of screams.

The game clock on the scoreboard counted down.

5:59.

In my head I knew we were standing in the very spot where Sidney Crosby slapped the wrist shot that should have let the Pens clinch the series with Ottawa. Instead the game went into three overtimes. Stu wanted to drive to Pittsburgh that night and drink on South Side.

I banged out the "Twist and Shout" chords and turned to watched John Lennon at the mic, squinting, shoulders hunched forward in attack mode. He was blind as a bat without those glasses on. Even though I needed to talk to him, I took my place at the other mic, harmonizing with Paul on the backup parts.

The music fell over me like sunlight, and I laughed. I hit every note, every vocal cue with a smile. When I looked into the darkness and waved a torrent of screams bounced back at me. I heard my voice pouring out of the PA, not George Harrison's. The notes were my notes. The words were my words.

We wore the grey suits with the skinny black collars. John's tie hung loose and he wore his black fisherman's cap. His voice cut right through the screams, backed by a wave of guitar noise that pushed across the stage like an offensive line. But the crowd didn't let up. Thousands of tiny vocal chords screamed for the slightest look or nod from one of us. I couldn't even hear drums. The only way I could tell where we were in the song was to watch John's hands. I backed up to his Vox amp and let his music infiltrate me directly. Soaking in every note. Every wavelength. The volume felt like life itself. The noise—that's all it was to some people—that noise sounded like heaven to me.

The music became a meditation. It let my mind clear for a moment. Made me wonder what I was even doing here in the Pittsburgh Civic Arena. A building that they ripped apart and demolished back in 2010. In the dim house lights I saw the Foodland ads on the boards near the goal at the far end. And the WDVE ad. The Thrift Drug ad. In the dark corners I saw The National Record Mart ad on the boards in front of the bench. The arena looked just like it did in the videos from the 1991 Stanley Cup Finals. I watched that clip of Lemieux taking Phil Bourque's pass and threading between those Minnesota defenders a thousand times, at least. When I realized I didn't know why I was here, my heart raced.

In the audience I looked for faces I knew. The only way to see them as people instead of as a flock was to look at their eyes. In the very front row I saw a slight girl with fair skin and dark hair wearing a little black dress. Her hair was pulled back with a silver barrette that flashed like a mirror reflecting sunlight. I smiled, but she didn't. I waved to get her attention, but she watched John. I recognized those eyes, and crept toward her, getting as close to the edge of the stage as I dared, but she wouldn't look up.

"Thank you, thank you," Paul said. His voice never seemed to come from one specific place. Instead it came from all around, like no matter where I turned he stood behind me. After a long moment, he added, "Ooh. It's a bit loud, isn't it?"

John turned his back, and went into his little cripple act. He goofed like that to get a rise out of Brian Epstein, our manager. I tried not to let Brian see me laughing and seized the opportunity to move closer to John—close enough to smell the amber and wood in his British Sterling.

Nobody in the sea of bodies looked like a stranger to me. It felt like playing to a roomful of old acquaintances. A pair of kids from school who got killed senior year. Drowned in the Cheat River after a night of drinking and jumping off Jenkinsburg Bridge. I saw an eighteen-year-old version of Pauly's grandma in a little knit dress. My own mother stood close to the front. Her blond hair was pulled back by a white headband and she wore a tiny black sweater with short sleeves. She looked so proud and clapped enthusiastically. So I stood taller for her. As soon as I could, I grabbed John and said, "There's my mom."

"Yer mum?" John mocked me.

"My mom." In order to relate to him I said, "She died when I was a kid, you know. Just like your mom. Except I was a baby. Somebody else raised me. Just like your Aunt Mimi raised you. My aunt was really Pauly's mom. No relation."

But instead of giving me the nod and the pat on the back I expected, he said, "Your mum's dead? What's she doing here then?"

I couldn't really know what he'd meant for certain and couldn't find the words to reply. I spent a long time thinking of the right thing to say.

"Better yet," he said, interrupting my concentration. "What're you doing here?"

"I'm not sure." I put my hand over the mic and raised my voice, "It feels like this is exactly where I'm supposed to be."

"I don't know, my friend." He took off his cap and wiped the sweat off his brow with his sleeve. Without thinking he looked at Brian, who waved a handkerchief at him. "Seems like the kind of thing you'd know before leaving home without knowing, isn't it?"

Seeing my mom and knowing that I'd made her proud left me feeling like all the nights sleeping in another family's house were worth it. The notes that I'd played for her came directly from heaven. I knew the set didn't last long and knew that I wanted to etch every moment of it into my memory forever. I stared at her so I would know which parts of me were from her. Her smile, which I'd never seen in a photograph, looked like my smile. I didn't want to leave.

John grabbed my arm. His appearance changed—he looked like he did on *Double Fantasy*. Much older, calmer. He wore a leather jacket, jeans, and white sneakers. "You have to find a way out. Pull the plug, brother. I'd show you the door, but I can't."

But I wanted to talk to my mom. Just hear her voice one time so I'd know what she sounded like forever. I wanted to see her up close and put my hand into her hand. And I knew not to look up because I didn't want to see the clock. And I didn't want to see so many forgotten faces, fragments of my past there in front of me like reminders of what waited for all of us at the end.

I closed my eyes because I didn't want to lose my mom all over again. The thought of losing Katy, or Pauly, or Mick, or Jamie filled me with emptiness and sorrow. And closing my eyes didn't change any of that.

In the dark hallways of my mind I saw a cemetery waiting for all the world's dead to be buried. I read the names on the graves and knew that time, no matter what name it took, delivered us all to the same end.

I saw my own grave—the grave where Sabra wrote my name before I lowered myself into the water—plain as day.

Then I saw the small cemetery behind Katy's pap's house. The only name I recognized was her cousin, Jane's. But the images existed only in my head. They were lies.

I opened my eyes to face the truth.

The room smelled a little like sweat, a little like weed. Speakers stacked from floor-to-ceiling made a wall of sound and a fuzzy vibration that made the hair on my arms stand up. I followed Joe Strummer to the stage. I'd follow him to the end of the planet if he'd ask me to.

Armed with the white Les Paul, I spread my legs and waited for the lights to come up. The Les Paul weighed much more than the Esquire and the Gretsch. I waited for the drums to start. Waited for my turn to bring destruction—to split skulls with a power chord and a little sweat. I knew as long I kept the pick pinched between my fingers, nothing could hurt me.

I could see Joe Strummer slumped against the dim light from the lobby. The audience whistled and shouted. They knew we were up here.

In the back of the room, in the glow of the mixing board, I saw a small clock. A reminder that this all ended somehow. An orange light let me see the minutes count down so fast they may as well have been seconds. Pauly's mom had the same clock in her room. I remembered because we weren't allowed to be up until seven on Christmas morning and Pauly and me would watch that clock for hours. It wasn't digital. Little metal numbers flipped over. One per minute.

4:36.

Joe Strummer didn't start us off with a count. He just banged his Tele like he was beating on a drunk in a parking lot after the pubs closed. The lights bloomed in an explosion of wattage that knocked me back a step. I had no choice but to pick up everything Joe dropped. Hammering away at those two chords. London wasn't calling. Joe was. I did all this for him.

4:30.

He bounced and jerked his fist. Twitching in perpetual agitation. He spit and held the mic like he'd choke every last breath out of it. He lunged at the audience. Screamed at them while the drums pulled me into the air, bouncing me higher and higher. I knew this was heaven. And I knew all I had to do was keep playing this guitar forever. I knew I stopped breathing when they ran that hose and drowned me in that fucking grave in that fucking backyard in fucking Alabama. And I looked for my mom, but she left. And I looked for John, but as far as I knew he'd left me too. For a second I thought this show was from The Clash's stand at Bonds Casino based on what Joe wore. Which made this 1981.

John Lennon should've been dead and buried by now.

But there he stood, arms crossed, looking pissed-off. Right at the end of the second row near the fire exit. Just beyond a big stack of speaker cabinets.

He shook his head, disapprovingly.

I ignored him and sidled up to Joe Strummer, but he never once looked back at me. I wanted him to know how much his songs meant to me. How he'd saved me. So I played my leads, letting electric fuzz fill my head like a lifetime of lies and Strummer never once turned around and acknowledged me. And I knew it wasn't because he was a bad guy, or self-centered. I knew he had his own dragons to slay. He believed he could change the world. I never once made that mistake. I tried to get close to him the way I got close to John but he was in his zone. Philosophizing for the kids out there. The ones who paid to be here.

But he'd forgotten that I paid to be here, too. That I was one of those kids, and just because I was on this stage instead of in front of it didn't mean that I wasn't worth his time.

3:42.

So I played to get his attention, pounding those strings with fury. I stood next to him and hammered that Les Paul as loud and hard as I could. But he never noticed. And I knew it wasn't because he was cold or unkind. His agenda didn't include me.

I had my own agenda.

So I looked for friends in the audience. I saw Mike Davis. A kid who went to school with me. Smashed his Toyota into a stone wall one night a few years back. Never should've happened. His funeral made me think about my own death for the first time. His kids were there. Two little boys who didn't have a clue. And I found Sylvester Knox in the audience. Hit by a car walking across a highway the year I started working at Mick's. Never should've happened. Not at their ages.

Stu stood in the center of a group of guys, bouncing to the beat. He jumped, fists in the air. I knew why he was here. I knew I was supposed to keep him from going back into the Army, but I couldn't change his mind. Stu was my drummer, not Topper Headon, or Ringo Starr. He was my heartbeat. My backbone. My lifeline. For the biggest part of my life, time didn't matter unless Stu counted the seconds off. I was supposed to be with him down there. Not up here.

Stu was my friend. Not Joe Strummer.

I rested the guitar on the stage, sat down on the edge, then stepped into the crowd. They didn't part like they were supposed to. Like they did in movies. They fixated as Strummer preached—a punk prophet for kids without degrees.

I locked eyes with Stu, my other brother. We lived for music, man. Lived for those quarter notes and half notes. Lived for lyrics that may or may not have meant shit to anyone else. It seemed unfair that I still had choices and he didn't, all because he gave his life for something greater.

"But we're both here now though, aren't we?" he said, responding to my thought.

I nodded.

"We both had choices to make, didn't we?"

I said, "Music should've let us live forever. I'm sorry that serving a purpose higher than the one I served put you into an early grave."

My hands started to sweat. Joe caught his breath at the mic, and gave a little speech about his politics. And they listened. They hung on everything he said and I felt like a fool. I said, "Like I'd ever save a fucking life with a guitar."

"Who's to say my higher good is better than your higher good? Who says serving a government is better than serving the kids who love what you're playing? Where the fuck is it written down? What about the kids at your shows? The kids who want to be you? Do they deserve another set? What about Katy"

I nodded. I didn't know what to say because I'd never thought of it that way.

Stu wouldn't look away and it made me real uncomfortable. Here I was, dreaming my own dreams instead of the dreams they taught me in school. Instead of the dreams the TV wanted me to dream. Instead of the shit FM radio dreams. And I just wanted to figure out how I could get Katy back. Dreams were only shadows in a world without her.

Stu had his arm around a girl. A young girl, with a sweet face and blue eyes. Just like my Katy. She didn't move to the music. She didn't mouth the words.

"Jane," I said.

Stu said, "Remember what you came for. And remember that you have to put on the brakes." Then he turned and got lost in the crowd.

I didn't know what to say to her, so I waited for her to act.

She looked so much like Katy and her cousin, Henry. Pale blue eyes, surrounded by black eyeliner, and dark hair streaked with red, shaved on both sides. In her hair, she wore Katy's silver barrette. She watched Joe Strummer even as I stood right in front of her. Her skin was pale beyond fair. It glowed in the lights from the stage, letting me see her red lips and slight shoulders. Her arms were crossed. She had on a real short skirt and fishnet stockings and high black Doc Martens. She wore a denim jacket with the sleeves hacked off. Pinned to the jacket were all sorts of patches. And she'd taken a Sharpie and written verse all over. Lyrics and lines from poems.

Written over her heart, I saw the first song I'd ever written for Katy.

Hey, hey little bluebird, why don't you stay?

I thought I heard you singing, I thought I heard you say,

That you loved me...

The band launched into its next song. Should've been "Safe European Home" but they ended up playing "Janie Jones" instead, like an affirmation that this night, for whatever reason, wasn't going to end up like I thought it would when it'd begun.

"Jane?" I said.

"C'mon." She turned and pushed through guys in leather and girls with safety pins through their earlobes. Red Mohawks. Black eye makeup and face paint.

"Fucking bitch," I heard more than once. I wanted to stay and fight each of them, but knew I had to stick with Jane. I knew that she was important, even if I didn't know why.

"Jane," I shouted, even though we left most of the noise behind us when we entered the lobby. I lowered my voice, and said, "So what do I have to do?"

"You want to get Katy back?" She stopped so fast I nearly knocked her over. "You're going to have to call her. Just pick up the phone and call her."

"Call who? Katy?"

"Not Katy." She walked toward the box office. "You're running out of time. Hear that?"

"Jane, wait!"

She walked into the chilly London night as a massive bell rang a few miles away. The sign on the post said Queen Caroline Street. An elevated highway flew above us. Big red busses drifted out of the metro station down the block near a sign for the Underground. I wondered if this was the Hammersmith Odeon or the Lyceum. Couldn't figure out why I thought it was Bond's. I guessed right about the Cash show and The Beatles' show. Being wrong about this one confused me.

"Jane, please. You have to help me."

She turned. Green and red from the traffic signals cast her pale skin in otherworldly hues. "It's too late. You waited too long."

"Don't say that, please." I panicked.

"Aunt Rachael told you exactly what to do. This is her little girl we're talking about. My cousin!"

People waiting for the bus turned around and watched the commotion.

"Don't be like that. She's tough—"

"And do you know why she's tough? Because she never let herself fall for guys like you. Guys who didn't care she graduated at the top of her class." She put her hand on her hip and came at me. "Everywhere Katy goes, she's either climbing a mountain or coming down off one and the minute her dad left she knew she'd never rely on anybody ever again. So consider yourself lucky to be loved by her. She doesn't play loose with her affection. You must have earned it somehow."

"So help me find her." I tried to take her hand, but she backed toward the curb.

"I can help you find her." She watched me process. Like she knew what I thought. "But you're going to have to make the call. Katy doesn't have much time."

"I will. Call who?"

"You know who. You don't want to say it and I don't want to say it." She cupped her hand to her ear. In the distance a great bell chimed louder and faster. "Hear it? Big Ben?"

She stood in the small sphere of light created by a dim street lamp, but cast no shadow. She shivered a little in her short skirt and high black boots.

All around windows rattled as waves of sound rolled through the streets. Lampposts swayed from the growing energy of the bell's thunder.

"Call your fallen angel. It's going to hurt, and you're going to have to give something up. But she is the only one who can help you get Katy before they kill her."

"That'll make things so much worse." It scared me to think about it. I tried everything to forget about her, but every day she found a way into my thoughts.

Jane shouted over the ringing. "Katy won't be mad if you tell her, 'Every girl needs a boy like she needs candy and an extra hole in the head.' Katy'll know what that means."

Jane pushed in front of a middle-aged couple waiting for a cab. They cursed as she shut the door. The black cab pulled into traffic and disappeared into the dark. The last thing I saw was the plate number—3485.

"Calling her is a mistake!" I yelled and the people laughed, even though I couldn't hear them over the deafening noise from Big Ben.

I turned back to the theater's main door, but it was locked. I kicked it, but the chains had already been pulled tight. I kicked again. Behind me people shouted stuff like, "asshole" and "tosser" but I kept kicking the wooden doors. The last place I remembered having a friend was inside.

The door splintered.

At this point I didn't even care if I got in. I grew angry. And I released it the only way I knew how. I wanted blood, but I knew that wouldn't fly in the real world. I wanted heads on spits and hearts beneath my boot.

I wanted a river of tears.

A universe of blood for my Katy.

I kicked until I felt certain I'd broken the bones in my foot. I wanted Katy in my arms. I wanted to feel her warm, soft cheek against mine. I kicked the door off its hinges. Wooden shards disappeared beneath my boot.

My Katy deserved better than the superficial beliefs these fuckers were dishing out.

My Katy deserved a bed of violets and a halo of cherry blossoms and a warm breeze and people speaking in the kindest of tones.

My Katy deserved a thousand years without pain, a thousand songs in her honor. A thousand kind words in every breath. I kicked for her, because my love had been taken. Because my love was cold and hungry and alone. I kicked because somewhere, out there, my girl needed me.

Hands reached through a crack in the door and pulled my jacket. My face hit the wood and warmed with the flush of blood rushing to the bruise. I twisted and jerked, but couldn't get away from the door. They grasped at my face and elbows. I tried to bite whatever I could.

Hands pulled me onto cold, dry earth. Sound hit my eardrums and died in muffled whispers that needed deciphering, half words I struggled to hear. And above me I saw a light. A grey light. An uncommitted sphere of hope.

Somewhere behind me Joe and the guys started into "Clampdown."

Somewhere behind me John worked on "Tomorrow Never Knows."

Somewhere over my shoulder Johnny invited June onto the stage for the first time.

I coughed and an ocean of water splashed forth onto the earth. I tried to turn, but a thousand hands held me fast to the ground. I tried to sit up, but the army above had other ideas. They covered my face and a cold wind blew through me. Shivers crept through my body. They held my head to the ground as I got pummeled with the hurricane, the cold breath of a god I thought I knew.

I heard my name. I looked for the man who'd spoken it.

Maybe it was John or Joe.

I knew the voice though, and I looked, but could only see the dull light of the real world. The muddy sunlight of northern Alabama.

"Preston…"

Water rushed into my throat. My first instinct was to inhale and let the air fill my lungs, but there wasn't room for air. My eyes rolled back and I coughed. My chest got tight as my lungs exploded with violent contractions meant to force the water out. I tried to roll over, but they were holding me down. I wanted to tell them to let me go, but couldn't get the words into my throat. I arched my back and kicked again.

"Pres…" It was Pauly.

I tried to find him with my eyes. I wanted to see his face. I knew as soon as he looked into my eyes he'd know it was okay to let me go. I struggled for air.

Somebody pushed me onto my knees. My view went from dull light to dark shapes. Silhouettes of trees. Outlines of faces. A splintered door. I spit water out of my mouth. Water that tasted like garden hose.

"Push him forward."

When I coughed water trickled out of my mouth and down my chin. I wanted to wipe it away but could only choke and gasp. Like drowning on dry land was my punishment for taking so long. I pushed myself forward and tried to get to my feet.

Ben and Pauly helped, but my balance faded and I fell. An ice cream headache raged through my skull like spiders with black needle feet. I pushed my hands against my eyes.

Pauly caught me. "Got you, man. You're good."

I looked for faces. Ben and Pauly. Pauly's friend and his family. I held up my hand. "Good," I whispered. "I'm good."

Sabra wrapped a blanket around me. George rubbed his chin in disbelief.

But nobody said anything while I tried to get my legs beneath me. Nobody said anything while I fought to get my words. They were waiting. They needed something from me. "Jane…" I said.

"What'd she say?" Ben asked. For the first time since he showed up here he looked hopeful. "About Katy?"

And I couldn't remember the words. I couldn't remember the conversation or her face. I couldn't recall the circumstances or the players. I had a feeling, and nothing else. I had a sense that something happened, but nothing concrete. I had ideas, but no words. I didn't want to have to apologize again. I didn't want to be the one who ultimately failed Katy, the girl I loved. If I couldn't prove it by helping to find her, I couldn't prove it at all. Words didn't come. Only an apology. Something Ben didn't want—or need—to hear.

"She said…" I could only see the cab disappearing into the darkness.

I fell back onto the blanket and put my hand over my eyes. My breath, which should've been so sweet, burned my lungs. My breath…

I'd rather it had been a noose.

"She said…"

Lies came to me. Possibilities. Half-truths. I knew they wouldn't know. I knew I'd die with the secret of what really happened.

"She said that Katy—"

My phone rang. Katy's beeped immediately after. Pauly picked it up and read the texts. I tried to reach for it. To slap it out of his hand.

He stared at the screen. "No message. Just a phone number. Maybe from like another country or something. Look."

I looked at Katy's phone and tried to make sense of what I saw on the display. But the numbers looked random. Meaningless. Definitely not a phone number. *<34.924610, -85.675317>*

Ben took the phone. He studied the message for a few long moments. Then he smiled and showed Andre and George.

"This'll work." Ben smiled.

George said, "That's real close."

"What?" I asked. I tried to sit up.

"Map coordinates." George held up the phone and smiled. "This is where we're going to find her."

Once George saw the spot on the map, he suggested we travel up the Tennessee River by boat, and into a mile-long backwater known as Long Island Cove. He felt we could make our way up the seven-hundred foot high bluff and if we got into trouble, there'd be no fast way for anyone to pursue us by water. But Ben wanted to keep his own mode of transportation at hand, so Pauly and Andre worked out a compromise to have the boat on the river, with Andre and George engaging in a little overnight fishing expedition while we went in from the road.

We all exchanged phone numbers. Last thing George said was, "If things go to crap meet us under the Hogjaw Valley Road Bridge, *tout suite*." He repeated it so many times that all I could think of as I climbed into the car was, *Hogjaw Valley Road Bridge. Hogjaw Valley Road Bridge…*

My hair was still wet when we split. I let Pauly sit up front and navigate because he knew roads a heck of a lot better than I did. Nadhima and Sabra had packed us a lunch—cornbread and sliced ham and a few cans of Grapico.

As soon as we got on the highway I got a text from Joe. <sorry for the cold shoulder mate but you wasn't bloody getting it>

We followed the Tennessee River north out of Versailles. The low hills never let us see much more than some sad, lonely farms and the river, which looked more like a long, mud-filled lake. We finally crossed over it on a tiny steel bridge. Just two little lanes and a lot of water below. I said, "You think Andre will be there? This is a long trip by boat."

"Preston… What're you thinking? Have some faith."

"Yeah. I know."

"We're fine," Ben said. "This is going to be a quick in and out. Like fucking a prostitute."

As soon as we hit dry land on the other side I knew we were getting closer. The highway crept through the trees and up the bluff on the river's eastern side. The same hill George showed us on the map. The steep terrain dissolved my expectations about what kind of operation this would end up being. Thick woods and a steep hillside were a far cry from the flat South I'd seen yesterday and this morning. And as much as I knew I should've kept my mouth shut, I knew I couldn't keep my mouth shut. "You scared?"

Neither of them spoke up. Like they were playing some kind of game to see who had the biggest balls. "Whatever."

"Yeah, man. I'm scared. That what you want to hear? You want to spend the next twenty minutes peeing our pants and blowing our noses? She's my cousin, man." Ben punched the dashboard when he said it. "Course I got the butterflies in my belly, but talking about being scared ain't going to get Katy Bear back. So you got to learn to control that fear, Preston Black, or I'll slap you to sleep and dare you to snore."

Anger made my face hot, but I bit my lip even though it didn't make me feel any better. "Well, I never learned to control my fear. I don't know what you know and I didn't see the shit you saw and I know you buried friends. And I'm scared shitless. I'm afraid of closing my eyes for too long for fear they'll forget what she looks like. So if you think I'm a pussy, or whatever, sorry to disappoint you. I just want her back."

I had more to say, but knew better than to say it. Instead I watched northern Alabama roll by, trying to figure out a way to make the impossible happen.

Ben reached behind the seat and put his hand on my knee. He patted it a few times.

The gesture fell way short of putting my mind at ease, but that simple act of consideration calmed me down. Made me feel secure. Let me know I could trust him. "It's all good, man."

"What the fuck're you talking about?" Ben said, flipping his palm up and beckoning with his fingers. "I want food. Can't take my meds on an empty belly."

"Get the fuck out." I gave Pauly the bag and Ben laughed. I said, "You know what? I'd appreciate a little respect for the way I feel."

"I know you would. That's why I ain't going to give it to you." Ben shoved his hand into the bag and pulled out a can of pop. "This is a lesson for you. That you can't dwell on this shit. You have to trust me."

I nodded.

"What's that?" Ben said, trying to find me in the rearview mirror.

I kept my mouth shut while Pauly pointed out our left onto County Road 97. Ben's hazing routine got old fast. As soon as we picked up a little speed, I said, "Yup."

"Look, Pres. Rachael knows we're bringing her back. Bet you twenty bucks we're back at Andre's before Rachael and Chloey and my old man come rolling in to check on their Miss Katy. And I bet you another twenty Katy's going to be ready to play in the ATL on Friday."

"He's right bro," Pauly said. "Be positive. I barely know this guy and I'd follow him just about anywhere."

"You barely know him and that's the problem," I said. "So what's the plan?"

"Plan?" Ben jammed the rest of a big slice of cornbread into his mouth. "Shoot first, that's always step one. We'll figure out the rest when we get there."

"Is that official Army protocol?"

"You ain't going to find that in the Army FM 21-50. That's in my field manual. The Ben Collins 01-01." He held his breath like he intended to riff on the theme a little longer, but I cut him off.

"What if shooting first isn't the way to go with this? What if—"

"Jesus, Preston. We got to take a look first. You think I'm making this up as I go? Have to know what we're dealing with, man. Then we'll make a plan—"

Pauly cut Ben off. "Yinz both need to shut the fuck up. Bitching like a pair of nanas with their babushkas in a bundle ain't doing squat right now. You want to know how it's going to go down today? There's your sign."

Along the side of the road a small white cross had been planted next to a row of rusted-out mailboxes. None of us had anything to say as we passed by.

Ben said, "Tell me we ain't dealing with the same Westboro Baptist fucks that protested at X and Kenny's funeral."

All around, kudzu grew up into the trees and around old fences. But the cross had been cleared recently.

"No, man," I said. "Different fucks."

Written across its white face were four words in large black letters—*JESUS WON THE BATTLE.*

"Shit just got real," Ben said, rolling down his window. "Stay sharp."

About a quarter mile ahead we saw the next sign on the left—a junked car wrapped in barbed wire, the word *REPENT* written on the side. A large white cross made of two-by-sixes with *Hypocrite you will DIE!* painted in large black letters sprung from a rusted-out hole in the roof. Across the hood they wrote *SEX. READ REV. 21-8.*

"You shitting me?" My face got hot and I made a fist. "Tell me this ain't the first place cops should've looked."

I almost kept going, but we rounded the bend to the sight of thousands of crosses of various size, constructed of different material, planted on both sides of the road for as far as any of us could see. Ben slowed and shook his head. Barbed wire had been strung throughout, draped over some of the crosses like a never-ending crown of thorns. In some places they wound new galvanized wire over top of rusted wire. Crosses went up and over red clay mounds and on rocky alcoves that looked like they'd been bulldozed out of the hills for the very purpose of displaying crosses. A large cross at the top had *NO ICE WATER IN HELL FIRE* painted across it. The one next to it said *Everyone in Hell from SEX USED WRONG WAY!*

Ben laughed as he read some of his favorites out loud to us.

The crosses popped up in groups of three and four. Big ones crowned hilltops like cross shepherds watching over flocks of white baby crosses. Ancient washing machines and refrigerators and cars had been incorporated into the setting. One rusty dryer sported the message *You will DIE!* in hand-painted block letters. An old burn barrel next to a natural gas well had been painted white so the artist could write *Hell is HOT HOT HOT!*

And nobody said anything because none of us knew quite what to say.

Ben said, "Look here—*The devil will put your soul in hell, burn it forever.*"

"Well…" I said. "Better the devil you know."

Ben laughed even though he couldn't ever have known why I found this so ironic.

Pauly said, "In a hundred years I could never come up with something like this in my head."

"Look!" Ben said, totally cutting Pauly off. He pointed to a small square sign propped against a pair of whitewashed cinder blocks that read *All FOR SALE! Five million CASH or best offer!*

"What the fuck?"

"'What the fuck' is right." He slowed down as we approached a big gate made out of chain-link fence and barbed wire. Hand-painted signs—one on each gate—said, *DON'T BRING THE DEVIL IN THIS HOUSE* and *LEAVE THE DEVIL OUTSIDE.*

Without warning he sped up. The crosses disappeared behind us. Trees crowded the road, casting us once again in shadow. After a few minutes we were back in unspoiled woodlands. Ben spotted a small turnoff littered with beer cans and rubbers.

"Listen," Ben said as he turned the key. Without the engine noise we could hear birds in the trees and wind washing through the leaves. He rolled his window down. "I'm going to turkey peek around and find a way in."

"Why'd you drag us out here if you're just going to go in yourself?"

"Calm down and listen. I'm going to get the lay of the land. The three of us are going to be too slow. C'mon back here." He got out of the Jeep and stretched.

"Yeah." I got out, stretched and followed him around back.

Ben had the hatch up and his Army duffle sitting on the bumper. "I know this ain't easy for you, but you got to trust me. This is going to go one of two ways. Either how we planned it, or to shit. I'm trying to make sure this don't go to shit. Here…"

He lifted a tarp and showed me a big pile of heavy chains. "When I need you in there you to have to pull that gate off. Keep it in the granny gear and get it clean off its hinges the second I say 'go.' I'm going to call every fifteen or twenty minutes with updates. I'll let you all know how the road looks and what to expect once we get in. I'm not excluding you, man. And I know you love her and I know she loves you. This is the best way to get her back." He put his hand on my shoulder. "We can't all be bogged down together in there if things get bad."

"I know." I rubbed my forehead. "You're totally right. I'm a guitar player. Just had visions of my face being the first one she saw, I guess."

"Yeah," he said, like I should prepare myself for some sort of big speech or something. But that was it. All he said.

Stripping the cellophane off a new pack of Newport Lights, Pauly said, "So just wait for you to call? That's it?"

"Well, that's the dynamic truth," Ben said. "I'll keep you updated. Let you know what's going on. And the second I see that she's okay I'll call and let you know. I promise. Grab me one of those Klonopins out of the glove box, please."

I sat in the driver's seat and found the bottle, then tapped one of the little blue pills into my hand. While I waited he jammed his pistol into a shoulder holster. He slid his compound bow and a quiver of arrows out from beneath the tarp. He put his phone into his front pocket, tucked a Bowie knife into his belt, and shut the hatch.

"Every fifteen minutes, right?" I said and dropped his Klonopin into his upturned palm.

"Or twenty." He popped the pill into his mouth then squeezed my shoulder a few times. "Don't get too agitated if I ain't checking in like I'm taking your baby girl out on a first date. Okay?"

"Yeah, I get it."

He put a pair of ammunition clips into his front pocket, a Leatherman multi-tool into his back, then bent over to tighten his bootlaces. "You'll be sharing a bed tonight. Maybe even eating a little barbeque or whatever the hell the neighbor's got cooking."

Ben banged on the hood with his fist and gave Pauly a wave. When Pauly nodded back, Ben blew him a little kiss. "*Marsalama*, boys."

He looked both ways, crossed the road, then disappeared over a small knuckle into the forest. I stood by the door and stretched. Pauly opened his door, spit into the sandy earth, and lit a cigarette.

"What do you think, bro?" I asked.

"It's all good. That's what I think. Have faith." Pauly stood up and walked out to the road. "Look at what you've been doing for the last seven months—getting paid to make music. I'll admit, shit like this with Katy ain't typical, and it's probably a result of your music that we're even out here right now. Like, maybe being in the spotlight put a target on your back?"

He took a long drag on his cigarette and held it. "But don't go thinking the universe is out to get you. There are guys we went to school with digging coal right now. Collecting disability because their backs are shot. This ain't the universe out to get you. This is people. Maybe it ain't even personal, I don't know. But they don't represent Christians everywhere. They don't represent the South and they sure as hell don't represent what I believe."

"I'll let you in on a little secret. What if I said it was personal?" I scratched the stubble on my chin. "I know Hicks too. Saw him in Morgantown twice. The first time was the night Mikey asked me to play the show at The Stink on Valentine's Day. He was at The Met with her. The second time was at The Stink. She brought him with her."

"Her?" Pauly just watched me from the road.

"Yep." I took my phone out of my pocket, made sure to turn the ringer on, and set it on the dashboard.

Pauly turned his back while he finished his cigarette. He widened his stance like he was on a surfboard, and stuck his hands into his back pockets. Every so often a small cloud of white smoke rose over his head. He calmly crushed his first cigarette out and lit another.

The phone rang. Pauly turned as soon as he heard it.

"Hello?" I answered. I put it on speaker so Pauly could hear. He leaned into the Jeep's open window.

"Told you I'd call, right? Real quick," Ben said, "The whole place is surrounded by electric fence—barbed wire and chain-link. Had to crawl up a stream bed to get under it. Lots of buildings—like an old church camp. Two rows of little white cabins facing a big building. Showers and shitters I'm guessing. Then there's a huge tent like a mess tent in the middle of a field. A bunch of guys packing it up now. Lots of pickup trucks. Long buildings with shit painted on the sides just like those crosses out front. Wooden shutters over all the windows. No motorcycles. Don't see any guns yet either. So far so good."

"Yeah."

"Check this out—they got this altar at the end of a field. A low mound with three big—tall—crosses on it. Like, crucifixion crosses or some shit. These are some sick bastards. Lots of natural cover, though, natural gas wells all over. Somebody's getting rich off this little patch of ground. The road is rutted out real bad. Your best bet is going to be to stay high in the right side and plow through the weeds. The road ends right at the field. They got pickup trucks and a bunch of vans out front. I'm going to try to slash tires."

"You saying we should head on down?" Adrenaline pumped through my arms and legs. I got real jumpy all of a sudden.

"No, you hold tight for a while."

"So, no sign of Katy?"

"Not yet. I'll call back in a few."

I hung up and set the phone back on the dash. I looked over at Pauly and shook my head. He turned to get back into the Jeep, but his eyes spotted something down the lane. "Shit," he said, and stood up real straight.

My phone vibrated again. I had a text.

From John Lennon.

<Heads up, boys.>

"No shit," I said.

A dingy white police cruiser with black doors and bald tires crept through the little patches of sunlight like a snake toward a birdhouse. An outline of the old department's emblem remained on the door. Black stick-on letters like the ones you put on mailboxes spelled out *New Zion Tabernacle* on the front quarter panel. The cruiser's light bar flashed at almost the exact moment the voice came through the PA. "Step out of the car. Place your hands on the hood."

Pauly looked at me, his eyes opened wide with disbelief. "Have to be shitting me."

I stepped out, jumpier than a long-tailed cat in a room full of rocking chairs. The air suddenly got hot. I reached for my ID.

The PA hissed to life, "Hands where we can see them. Real slow."

I spread my legs, leaned over the hood, and whispered, "They ain't even real cops, are they?"

They parked the car so that it blocked the Jeep's path to the road. The driver strolled around the front of his car with a shotgun cradled in his arms. He wore a black hoodie and an old Alabama hat with the elephant logo on it. Greasy hair covered his ears and his wrists were scarred with the same type of contusions that the protestors at the shows in Louisville and Nashville had. My heart kicked into high gear.

The second one stood directly behind me "This property's private, you know."

"We didn't, officer," Pauly said, forcing a very polite tone. "Didn't see any signs."

"Signs don't make a property private," the guy in the 'Bama hat said as he cuffed

Pauly. He stood about the same height as me but looked about seventy-five pounds heavier. He breathed through his mouth and smelled like fried food.

"That's not what I was implying," Pauly said, still playing along. His voice cracked with a nervous edge.

"Which one of you belongs to the shake and bake?" The one behind me threw a plastic grocery bag onto the ground in front of the Jeep. A two-liter soda bottle wrapped with duct tape and plastic tubing rolled out. "This is what y'all are out here looking for, right?"

"Officer," Pauly said, "I'm a recovering alcoholic. Been sober for a year. Meth isn't something I'd ever fool with."

"Right away you knew what it was though," the man behind me said as he cuffed me. "Ain't it, Herlin?"

The adrenaline made me more defiant than I had any right to be. "You going to read us our rights, or what?"

"Shut your mouth or I'll shut it for you," the one behind me said. "You gave up your rights when you set foot out here."

After collecting our wallets, our phones, the keys to the Jeep, the man who cuffed me pushed me into the back of the cruiser next to a box of little green Gideon Bibles. He wore work boots and a camouflage jacket and he smelled like asshole. I knew better than to resist.

As soon as Pauly joined me in the back seat, I directed his attention to the crucifix hanging from the rearview mirror. "Look."

"Whatever," Pauly said. "They got the guns."

They searched Ben's Jeep while we sat there. They had the hatch up and rooted under the seats and floor mats. Herlin called somebody on his handheld radio.

"You see their wrists?" I said. "All bruised up. Thought it was from shooting up, like my dad. But it looks different. The marks are all in pairs."

"Just be quiet, man. Running your mouth ain't going to get us out of here."

"Yeah, well sitting and waiting feels the same as letting Katy die." I said, "Maybe we should head for the trees and find Ben?"

"Giving them an excuse to shoot us in the back? And blowing Ben's cover? Preston, just shut the fuck up."

"You boys are a long way from West Virginia, ain't you?" Herlin yelled over from the Jeep. "You going to tell me what you all are doing out here?"

I said, "Looking for ginseng."

"Ginseng." Herlin's partner laughed as he slammed the hatch shut. "Boy, you must be as stupid as you are dumb."

"How much time you think they're going to give you for cooking meth?" He waved his shotgun at me when he said it. "You know, Raney?"

"My sister's beau down in Magnolia Springs got life in prison for running a little operation out of his bedroom closet," Raney said as he sat down in the cruiser. "So life, I guess."

Herlin rested the shotgun on the floor next to his feet after he sat down, did a four-point turn and headed back down the road toward the gate of the church camp. A few crimped wires stuck out of the dash where the radio should've been. A pair of handhelds jammed between the seats and the center console took its place.

I said, "This is flat out bullshit and you both fucking know it."

Raney said, "You got the right to remain silent, and if you ain't going to exercise that right I'm going to silence you. Hear me? Boy, I'll slap you so hard you both'll feel it."

"You know a lawyer's going to walk right through this shit."

"Where is he, son?" Raney twisted around in his seat. "You ain't going to find a lawyer in this corner of Alabama going to come against us. Ain't nothing can come against the truth, and the word of God is the only truth you need to worry about. There ain't going to be a trial and there ain't going to be no jury. Only God can judge."

We drove past the rows and rows of white crosses and washing machines and burnt out cars on our way back toward the main road. Even when I closed my eyes I saw the white crosses in my head. But about a half-mile before we would've hit the main highway, Herlin turned into the trees at a right-of-way where a bunch of power lines crossed. The old gravel road snaked beneath the towers for a quarter mile before curving back into the wood. We bounced along that worn-out stretch of road for five slow minutes. The sky opened up as we crossed beneath another power line right-of-way. At the clearing I could see the river in the distance, and on the other side, an old power plant spitting white smoke into the sky.

We slowed to a stop, and Raney got out and unlocked a large gate. As we passed through he closed it. We continued down the road for another half mile, where it ended at an old gas well. Right next to it sat a cinderblock shed with a flat corrugated tin roof. I could barely make out *Dixie Drilling* on a rusty tin sign bolted to the steel door. Just above the sign was a small opening covered with a metal grate.

All I could think about was how people'd been telling me it was time to be a man, time to grow-up. Making a move right here and now was the only way to make good. "No way," I said.

Both back doors flew open at about the same time and me and Pauly were yanked from the car by our wrists. I got onto my knees while Herlin unlocked the shed's door.

Pauly went in first. He turned, and Herlin uncuffed him. Pauly rubbed his wrists and moved to the back wall.

As soon as Herlin unlocked my right hand I spun and lunged at him. I wrapped my arms around him and pushed him to the ground. I knew my attack wouldn't last very long. But I had to make it look worse than it really was. I hit him in the gut once. A weak punch.

Almost immediately, Raney grabbed a fistful of my hair and pulled me off Herlin. My hand ripped his hoodie pocket as I tried to hang on. Raney backhanded me and threw me into the ground.

When I got myself out of the dirt, I turned and looked for Raney. As soon as I found him I raised my fists.

"Pres..." Pauly said. "They're going to put a hurting on you."

Herlin got me from behind. He grabbed my throat and shoved me into the concrete block wall so hard I saw a bright light.

And getting off the ground didn't come so easy this time. I sniffed blood back into my nose as I caught my breath.

"Pres. Stop it." He helped me up and said, "Better the devil you know, right?"

As I got my feet beneath me, I replied, "That's what I said."

"We had enough of you." Herlin straightened his hat. "How about a bullet through the brain pan?"

"I'm done." I wiped blood off my face and stepped inside.

Herlin slammed the door shut and locked it. I coughed as I caught my breath. Raney got into the car first. Herlin watched for a minute before finally getting in himself.

As soon as they disappeared around a crook in the road I showed Pauly my phone. "Got it from Herlin's pocket."

"They're going to be back for it." Pauly said, "Who you going to call that's going to be able to do a damn thing?"

I scrolled through my numbers as Pauly watched. He figured I was about to do something stupid. He didn't know what I knew.

"You'll be lucky to get service out here—" He stopped himself when he heard the car coming back.

I found a number I hadn't called in a long time. And the phone rang, and rang, and rang. She didn't pick up, which I half-expected. But it didn't matter. The call was made.

Raney jumped out before the car even came to a full stop. Herlin parked it, got out, and leveled the shotgun at me.

I pushed the phone through the metal wire and lied. "No service."

"Well, no shit. Y'all going to order pizza? No thirty minutes or less out here, tell you that right now." Raney took the phone.

"There's a Chinese take-out up in Tennessee." Raney held the phone to his ear. "Ching-chong, ching-chong."

"You're all alone. Once you see them bright stars looking down on you tonight, and tomorrow night and the next, you're going to realize that," Herlin said. "Dumb shit Yank."

Raney nodded at Herlin, then sat down in the car. Herlin raised the gun at me.

I fell away from the door as he pulled the trigger. The crack of gunpowder and the immediate snap of a thousand metal pellets hitting steel filled my head. Even as Pauly told me I was okay and patted my cheek, my brain swam in a soup of reverberating sound.

Slowly the hiss of trauma left. Herlin laughed. Pauly sat me up and pushed me onto my knees. I stood in the little opening to catch my breath.

"It's coming down, man," I said. In the distance the sound of faintly calling birds and crickets rang in my ears. The cries of peepers drifted up from the water below. "It's going to hit you like a bag of fucking hammers."

As the sun flew higher it got hotter than a ninth-grade boy at his big sister's dance recital in that concrete box. Never experienced anything like it in my life. Science is science no matter where on earth you ended up, but this heat defied anything I'd ever felt. Whenever I stood up from the wall my back left a wet patch that took a half hour to dry. Right after they left I took off my button-down shirt to wipe my forehead. Didn't take long for it to become completely soaked through. I took off my T-shirt, rolled it into a ball around my other shirt and used it as a pillow.

We took turns at the window doing our best to suck up a little of the breeze. The only problem with standing in the door was how the bright light hit you right in the face. Me and Pauly ran out of stuff to talk about real fast.

We'd spent most of the afternoon trying to kick the door and hoist each other toward the high ceiling. Probably wouldn't have gotten so sweaty if we'd relaxed and waited for whatever would happen next. The only good thing to come out of it was thinking if somebody had to save Katy, I'd have rather it been Ben than me.

Just admitting that felt like a punch in my gut. All that stuff I said to Katy earlier about keeping her safe and protecting her was talk. Bullshit musician talk.

Fantasy. Not that I ever fantasized about shit like this. Still, always figured I was more Han Solo than C-3PO.

"Somebody's coming," Pauly said.

I stood and pushed my face into the little opening. Into the sunlight. I could see the shape of individual trees if I squinted, but I couldn't see the vehicle. I said, "It ain't the cops coming back."

"How do you know?"

"Diesel engine." I knew who it was because I made the call. I just didn't want Pauly to know yet.

The silver car rolled to a stop right in front of the door, shiny paint reflecting light right into my face. I held my hand up to shield my eyes. A door slammed shut and I heard the crunch of feet on gravel. Pauly pushed his face into the opening next to mine.

"Like two little rabbits in a cardboard box," she said.

"What the fuck, Pres?" Pauly released me and backed away from the door, but not so far that he couldn't see.

"Sorry, man. I called the only fallen angel I could think of."

As she stepped closer I could see her. Wearing a plain grey dress with a black belt and sleeves down to her elbows, she examined my face through the grate. "It's been such a long time." She place her fingers through the grate and stroked my forearm. Her touch felt hotter than the day. "I always knew this time would come."

"Hello, Danicka."

"Why so formal?" When she spoke I felt her hot breath on my cheek. The sensation calmed me. "It is because you need something, I suppose."

Trying to keep my head straight, I said, "For a while I couldn't cross the street without thinking about you. Spent a lot of time watching my back."

"What the fuck's wrong with you?" Pauly said, "Don't even talk to her."

"To think I'd devote so much time and energy is arrogant, even for you. To think so much of yourself—that I must sit around with only you on my mind." She didn't blink when she talked. Her eyes never left my face. "In a way it is very, very sad."

I listened for her accent, and the way she phrased her sentences. Like a guitar player, almost, choosing notes for more than one meaning. Now that I knew how she operated, I figured the playing field had grown more even than it had been last year. I said, "So you had something better going on tonight?"

Pauly chanted. A low mumbling whisper.

"As a matter of fact, I'm on my way to church now," she shot back with a slight smile. "Do you know what they would say about this? They would say, '…the greatest of these is love.' See? Not charity. I can still love you without helping you."

Over my shoulder, Pauly mumbled, "Hail Mary, full of grace, the Lord is with thee…"

"Just get us the fuck out of here, Dani. What's that worth to you?"

"You know how it works." She smiled. "Or do you? I'm not sure I benefitted from our time together quite as much as you."

"Bullshit. I fought for everything and earned it outright. I wrote those songs. I busted my ass getting here." I pounded the door when I spoke.

"Perhaps." She closed her eyes and rested her cheek against the door. She exhaled deeply. "Maybe I did like you a little, Preston. Maybe I thought I could manipulate you. You must admit that you are quite easy to push around. But now you know what you know. The price, the result, and the consequences are no longer secrets."

"Just tell me what you want, Danicka."

"Maybe a girl dies tonight. They're either going to stone her or drown her, you know. But what's it to me? Not a thing. Like that…" She cupped a hand to her ear, letting the sounds of distant peepers drift over the engine noise. "That's what she is to me. That's how much I care. But I liked you, Preston. Otherwise I wouldn't be here."

"So you'll help me at the cost of me never being able to be with her again?"

"Your words. But they sound fair. Let the punishment fit the crime, yes?"

"What if I say forget it? Get out of here?"

"You invited me, Preston. I accepted. For that alone, you already owe me." She waved her hand across the door. "This is negotiations and details. Interest rates and amendments."

Pauly said, "What is wrong with you, man?"

Ignoring him, I said, "How do I know you're not bullshitting me?"

"The old man at the cemetery said you were going to have to lose something. Perhaps this is what he meant? You can't always get what you want."

I said, pleading, "What about the assholes that took Katy? You should take them. Why can't they be enough—"

"They are already lost souls. They don't know it yet."

For the longest time I couldn't say what I felt in my heart. Because I knew she was right. The words never quite came how I wanted them to. Katy would've nailed it on her first try. But she wasn't here. So I finally spit out, "Once this is over Katy is safe forever, right? No accidents, no sickness…"

"Preston!" Pauly pushed me away from the door. "What the fuck, man? What're you doing?"

"She's right, man. So what if I can't have her. If she dies tonight I won't have her anyway."

"Give Ben a chance to find us. What the fuck did you even have to call her for?" He clenched his fists.

"Little brother trying to defend his big brother. I like it. Let me tell you this— in the name of fairness. People underestimate the power of hubris. Benjamin is not coming for you. This was a job for three people, at least. Not one."

Pauly pushed me away from the door and pressed himself into the window. "Leave Pres alone. Take me."

"See," Dani said as a smile formed on her lips. "Hubris."

"Shut the fuck up, Pauly."

"Let him talk, Preston. He knows what he wants while you sit on the fence, praying for something when you don't even believe. Paul prays yet still gives in to the greater evil. But he doesn't interest me as much as you do."

"Preston is easy." Pauly spoke fast, his voice thick with panic. "He drinks. He's lazy and he's vain. He's at least three or four more deadly sins into the list than I am."

"Pauly…" I tried to pull him away and could feel him trembling. He pushed me across the room.

"I ain't doing this for you, bro. I'm doing it for Katy." Pauly laced his fingers into the wire covering the opening. "I'm a practicing Catholic and I've been sober for a year."

I grabbed Pauly's arm. He shoved me. Snapping like a dog on a chain, he said, "Sit the fuck down, Preston!"

His cheeks reddened, his words fell to the floor quickly, like dead leaves. "I got nothing. You got the girl, so you got everything to lose. Call it an early wedding gift. And in return I get a little respect. That's all I want from you, Pres. Just a little respect."

I shook my head. "Pauly, fucking stop it."

But he'd turned back to the window. Dani whispered into his ear, and Pauly nodded over and over again.

Pauly said, "I understand," when she backed toward her car.

I felt sick. Like I'd have rather been dead a hundred times over.

Pauly folded his arms and retreated into the other corner.

"Danicka," I said, anger pulsed through me. "You got something, now get us out!"

"Paul," Dani opened her car door and stopped. "Tell your brother that you are safer here."

With that, she got in, turned the key, and backed down the road.

"What the fuck did you do, man?" I grabbed his arm, shook it, then let it go. "I had this under control."

It had been years since I'd been this angry and scared. I knew what I could handle. I knew what being in this situation with her felt like. I grabbed Pauly's shirt and shook him. "What the fuck, Pauly! Why?"

I pulled him as close to me as I ever had. I hated myself for letting this happen.

But he wouldn't speak to me. I turned toward the window and watched the sun slowly tumble down from high. The sky was so clear you could cut yourself on it.

"I don't know, Preston." Pauly finally broke his silence.

I turned and he rested his head back on his knees. "Tell me what the fuck I just did."

I shook my head, and wanted to tell him to be positive. That I'd gotten through and we'd figure out how to get him through. But a tremendous explosion from the top of the hill took my breath, shook the metal roof. A wave of light rolled into the distance.

My hearing came back slowly.

A second explosion hit. This one more distant.

Pauly mouthed, "Ben?"

"No, man." I shook my head. "This is Danicka. This is what you paid for."

THE REVELATIONS
OF KATY STEFANIC

CHAPTER SIX

As an artist you get used to immersing yourself. Descending into endless seas of thought. Letting ideas come and go. Hanging on to a few. Letting the rest sink.

Every so often you tempt fate. You let yourself think. You hold your breath until the surface is so far out of reach only the shadow of an idea remains.

You get brave and try to touch the bottom. Surrounded by darkness. Blanketed with your blackest thoughts, your gravest fear. The longer you stay down, the less likely you are to make it back alive.

When you break through the surface again, kicking and screaming for air, you see that you've pushed everything away. Friends. Family. You didn't mean to.

But you did.

It's selfish—the idea of creating, airing your dirty laundry to entertain people.

With Preston, I knew I'd never be alone again. I knew he'd be waiting for me when I surfaced. Together we made our own little bubble out in the dead center of that endless sea of thought.

Having Preston meant I never had to return to shore.

Preston's proposal seemed like a nice move at the time, particularly since he'd presented it so sincerely. The way he'd said it told me he'd really meant it. Sometimes, when he fibbed, his lip twitched like he was trying to hide a smile. He was all business back at the canyon though. No fibbing whatsoever. My gram always told me that boy had rocks in his head. It would've broken her heart to have found out it was probably all the weed.

The first time I went to look for the bathroom I walked right past it. A rack of travel mugs and pork rinds basking in bright fluorescent light was the first sign that I'd gone too far. I turned back to the old diner and saw the lady's room door hidden behind a cigarette vending machine—the kind with the pull knobs.

Preston loved stuff like that—things that created nostalgia for a childhood he'd never lived. It never occurred to him that I'd spent far too much time in truck stops and bars begging my dad to come home to feel the same way. Don't know why mom ever wanted him back anyway. Maybe she thought she could fix him, but he just beat on her and ran her down. He was the reason I couldn't generate an ounce of sympathy for the "redneck pride" crowd. If it wasn't for Preston, I'd never set foot in one of these places ever again.

Both stalls were locked, but I didn't want to go back into the truck stop. Two pairs of shoes beneath the two doors confirmed that they were occupied. I coughed to get a reaction, shuffled my feet over the old linoleum to the hand dryers, then leaned over the sink to get a closer look in the mirror. Redness stuck to the corner of my eyes like old mascara. *At least he had sense not to point out that I was crying, or ask what was wrong.*

"Maybe I can get in real quick?" I said. "If y'all are finished."

Y'all had been something I always said back home. Somewhere south of Clarksburg was true *y'all* territory, so I grew up half saying it, half being told not to. But my roommates up in Bennett Hall freshman year were from Richmond and Charleston, and I reacquired it in a big way without thinking too much about it. *Y'all* made me feel like I belonged down here. Even though the word sounded out of place at The Beacon and The Trocadaro, the crowds liked it because of the authentic images the word generated. That was why New Yorkers liked New York so much. They didn't have to ever leave. The world came to them. Circuses. Authors. Art exhibits. Mountain folk, like me.

But once we hit D.C. and Charlotte, *y'all* felt more like a secret handshake. *Y'all* presented the audience with an assumed familiarity. *Y'all* felt like a mask you could wear whenever it was most convenient. It could make you that much cuter, more sarcastic, more earnest. Or you could say it to fit in. Or to exclude somebody else. Preston tried using it in Asheville and I told him during the set break that he needed to drop it. That they knew it didn't feel the same coming from him. As soon as he returned to his *yinz* they relaxed.

"C'mon, ladies. I've been holding it for an hour." I tapped my foot.

Neither of them acknowledged me in any way.

"Southern hospitality, my ass."

I pushed the door open with a bang, The waitresses paid no mind to my commotion. They went about filling salt shakers and ketchup bottles like their lives depended on it. Preston only half-looked up from his phone. In a way I wanted him to see me. I'd smile, and let him know that everything really was fine with me. But he texted or Tweeted, or pretended like he was checking email even though I know he never got any. As far as I knew, he didn't even have an email address.

The bright lights of the gas station mini-mart pulled me out of the diner, like a daisy to sunlight. Wandering through aisles of atlases and books on tape led me to the other rest room. The one with the bright fluorescent lights and wall-mounted tampon dispensers. Through all the wandering around, I reminded myself that I didn't really have to pee. I'd left to make a point.

When it happened, it happened so fast I couldn't really yell or scream. Thoughts of Preston, all alone and waiting for me, filled my head as I kicked and twisted. But the hands gripped me like steel traps. I yelled, "Help!" but it came out more like a muffled whelp.

Always thought I'd be tougher.

Biting and pulling, I kicked an entire row of motor oil off a low shelf. The plastic bottles only made half the commotion I thought they would. I jerked and tore at the people who held me. They wrapped my hands with tape. There were at least three of them.

Surely, I thought as I kicked and twisted, *somebody is calling the police right now.*

As soon as I tried to scream again one of them jammed a washcloth into my mouth. I bit as ferociously as I could until I tasted blood. Somebody hit me, then put a sack over my head. Flour went into my sinuses, choking me.

I lost a shoe in the parking lot. My bare foot dragged on the cold, wet pavement. Music from a country radio station faded as they pulled me farther and farther from the truck stop. They lifted me into a vehicle and slammed the metal door shut behind me.

Don't stop fighting. That's what they want.

Unless they hurt you.

Don't let them hurt you.

When the vehicle accelerated the force rolled me right into the back door. Kicking the floor with my heel made a God-awful racket. The noise hurt my head, but it felt like I was accomplishing something.

Make them react.

Force them to change their tactics.

"You best stop that," a woman said. "Or we'll restrain you further."

Don't let them hurt you.

Be stronger.

Working my jaw loosened the gag. I pushed it out with my tongue, and shouted at full volume, "You shall judge nothing before the appointed time; you shall wait till the Lord comes."

Always strong. Never ever weak.

Sudden loneliness fell upon me at hearing my own voice. My face got hot and the tears welled-up. I swallowed and swallowed to push them back down. *Never weak.*

My breath came in big gasps, and before I could even catch it fully, I said. "Corinthians. You all ain't the only ones been to Sunday school."

A woman began to speak, but quickly stifled herself. The next voice I heard belonged to a man. "A spiritual man judges all things—he himself is not judged. You speak with the devil's tongue. You try to twist the words of the Good Book, but nothing can come against the truth."

"Elijah Clay Hicks, I know you, and I know what kind of devil you are. I know you are not a Christian and you are not doing God's work. I saw your face in Louisville, and the feds are looking for you after that bomb threat in Nashville." Vigorous squirming had worn me out, but getting myself into a sitting position gave me a sense of control. I said, "The Lord is good to all, and his tender mercies are all over his works."

I couldn't see anything. I couldn't even make out any light for the sack over my head.

I said, "You get tired of stalking me in Morgantown, loser? I suppose if rape is a woman's fault then 'no means no' means nothing to you. Suppose all these woman you got hanging around don't mind your old school way of thinking."

I heard steps, which made me believe we were in a van or on a bus. Heavy steps that ended right where I sat. When Hicks spoke again his voice was right next to my ear. He said, "The Lord sayeth I will dash them against one another, even the fathers and sons and brothers and sisters together."

He grabbed my throat and squeezed. "I will not pity."

My lungs pulled with all their might, but could not draw a breath.

"I will not spare. I will not have mercy."

He released me and I cried out with the rush of air into my lungs.

"I will destroy."

The women—maybe two or more—called out an "Amen!"

Hicks said, "I will prevail, for I have faith in the power of the Holy Spirit. You tremble before the Lord. I hear it in your voice."

I tried to speak, but he grabbed a fistful of my hair through the sack and pulled my face toward his. "The Lord is a man of war. The Lord is his name. What say you now?"

Still gasping, I said, "Now the God of peace be with you all. Amen."

There was a pause. A regrouping.

He said, "In the Book of Malachi, Elijah appears right before the awesome and terrible day the Lord God himself returns to earth. The harbinger of the coming Messiah? That's me." He pulled me forward again by my hair. A quick jerk that left me breathless. "I have raised the dead by breathing new life into these women, and before I save your soul by forcing you to submit to the Word, I'm going to bring down fire from the sky. Mark my word."

He pushed me to the floor with his palm and forced all his weight on my temple, trying to shatter my skull like a crystal bowl. The pain felt worse than a migraine. I tried to twist away, but he pushed even harder. He took his time, using slow, deliberate words, to say, "She that blasphemeth the name of the Lord shall surely be put to death, and the whole congregation shall stone her."

Then all at once he disappeared, leaving me with my tears on the cold floor.

Like a paper coffee cup blowing across a parking lot.

It wasn't the loneliness so much—being alone used to be something I kind of liked. It was being without Preston. Since last February we hadn't spent more than twelve hours apart. He helped my grandpap and uncles at the farm, bailing hay and chopping firewood, all so he didn't have to go back to Morgantown by himself. Eventually he moved into an extra room at my grandparents' house because nobody would approve of him living with me at my mom's place.

Instead of going to dinner or a movie on a date, we'd walk along the Blackwater or to the top of Cabin Mountain and watch Venus. We'd hold hands and look for ginseng or blueberries. In that way, on those days, we were reborn as a couple.

When we went back to Morgantown in the fall everything looked different. The guys were all too young, too self-absorbed. Girls talked to me differently, complementing my hair or my nails or a piece of jewelry. Like my involvement with Preston had taken me off the market and placed me in a different, less threatening category. I enjoyed being treated like a woman instead of a girl. For once, the things I said had weight because they weren't coming from the lips of a sugary teenager. My mom listened to me instead of always talking, and for the first time, we became friends. My relationship with Preston facilitated that change. It let me be reborn in a way too. I went from being a little girl trying too hard to grow up, trying to be taken seriously, to the little girl I'd always wanted to be.

Now that I was alone, and empty and very, very far away from Preston, I was curious to see which version of me would materialize.

In a feeble last attempt to break through Hicks's circle of contradictions, I said, "And he that killeth any man shall surely be put to death."

Hicks had an immediate comeback, like I knew he would. From the front of the vehicle, he shouted, "The Lord God of Israel said to put every man his sword by his side, and slay every man his brother, his companion, and his neighbor."

"Whatever." I got the last word. Always did. Under my breath I said, "And Elijah was taken up in a whirlwind of fire."

After a long drive on smooth highways—maybe an hour or more—I heard the crunch of gravel under the wheel wells, then felt the deeply rutted dirt roads that shook the springs beneath my resting head. We slowed to a stop. I heard more voices. The back door opened. They dragged me into the gravel.

When they pulled the bag off my head I saw fog parting to reveal a few cold, blue stars. They didn't blink back at me, and I knew that I was alone. Water dripped from wet leaves. My feet got cold in the dewy grass. In the black distance I heard peepers.

Hicks handed me off to two men who pulled me past an old swimming pool and through a large clearing. Hicks and some of the women followed. Pale light from two rows of little white summer camp cabins illuminated a trio of crosses built on a small mound at the far end of the field. There were various vehicles scattered about. Pickup trucks and white church vans and old hatchbacks. One of the vans had a "Living Waters Pentecost" decal running beneath the side windows. The other said, "New Life Tabernacle."

They led me toward the biggest building I could see. A long white structure with milk crates and cardboard boxes stacked near a screen door. When I looked at the sky one last time before they pushed me into an old produce freezer, an urge to ask for help, to ask that Preston be kept safe, washed over me. One of the men cut through the tape wrapped around my wrists with a penknife.

"I'll send Truly for you in the morning." Hicks spun me, so that I faced him. He pushed his finger against my sternum, backing me into the freezer. "Ain't got so much to say now, do you?"

"You don't know me well enough to make that kind of statement," I said, forcing my chin up. "Hatred feeds hatred. It never eliminates it. Only love can eliminate hate. This is the way of the universe."

Hicks jerked to a stop, turned and pointed his finger. His lips parted as he scoured his memory for the translation, the book and verse. But it wouldn't come to him as easily as the others had.

"It's not from the Bible." I saw my chance to end the day with a bit of a win, and

113

took it. "It's from the Lord Buddha. That's why you don't know it."

He slammed the door shut and locked it without another word.

And I let that be my bedtime prayer.

Rule number one is to stay alive.

If I get hurt, or worse, nothing else will matter.

Rule number one is to stay alive.

Eat what you are fed. Ask for bathroom privileges with a 'please,' always.

Somebody will come. Preston has already called the police and my family. The label and our fans will help. They are already out looking. I have to stay alive until they find me.

Rule number two is don't provoke.

Stop it with the attitude. Don't engage Hicks. Don't look at him the wrong way. Be compliant. Stop showing off. Who cares that you went to Sunday school? Hicks doesn't. He thinks you're a witch and is going to stone you or beat you or drown you the first chance he gets. Hicks is insane. Hicks isn't motivated by logic. Hicks has an agenda, and I am part of it no matter what I do, so don't provoke him. If you break rule number two, you're going to break rule number one.

Rule number three is don't run. Don't think about running. Don't look for escape routes. You don't even know where you are so you may as well be Belle in Beast's castle. Rule number three is a provocation. Breaking rule number three means breaking rules one and two. You won't get away. You'll be caught, and hurt.

Rule number four…

"What is rule number four?" My head ached after last night. I shivered for twelve straight hours. I didn't sleep at all.

Rule number four is to prepare for a long stay. Mentally prepare yourself to be here for weeks. Or a year. Remember that Preston and Ben and Pauly and Jamie and Mom and Chloey will look for you as long as they think you are alive. Be a prisoner, a hostage, whatever they want. Don't be a corpse. Don't break rule number four—or three, or two—because they all end with breaking rule number one. Don't ever, ever, ever break rule number one.

I wrote the rules in the dust on the old wood floor with my finger as they came into my head.

Rule number five is to make a friend. Doesn't matter who it is. Get one person to recognize that you are a human being. That you love and can be loved. That you have a soul. You don't have to stay in touch and meet for lunch, but you have to make one of these people like you.

Rule number six...

Rule number six made me very sad to even think it.

Don't ever give up. If you are locked away in this room twenty years from now you do not give up. You never, never, never forget that there is a light that shines for you out there. You do not cry. You do not feel sorry for yourself. Hope is the only thing you have that they cannot take from you. Don't give it to them. Nurture it like you would nurture a kitten. If you forget that, you're dead.

My belly rumbled.

Rule number one is to stay alive...

The sun had climbed well into the sky before somebody came to get me. My little cell grew warmer as the hours wore on. The smell of old dairy rose from the dry wood. Too faint to be nauseating, the sweet smell of old protein, almost like ice cream that had dried in a paper cup, reminded me of days on my pap's farm. I had my jacket rolled into a little ball while I wrapped myself in Preston's coat. If I stuck my nose right against his collar I could still smell him.

I tried to nap, but couldn't. People came and went outside, singing and talking. Kids and men and women. Sounded mostly like kids and women. I sang to myself to drown them out.

The click of the cooler door brought me to my feet. Hicks's girl, Truly, waited there with a crown of thorns tattoo peeking from beneath her jet black bangs. Bright red ink meant to look like blood dripped from the sharp black spines that jutted from beneath her hairline. I only noticed because I thought she was bleeding at first, although it did surprise me. Otherwise, she looked quite beautiful. When she extended her arm I saw the same contusions on her wrists and forearms that Hicks had. Black and blue blotches, like she shot up every few days, at least. When she gestured for me to get up I saw a tattoo complimentary to the one on her forehead splattered across on her palm. A long iron nail exiting the tattered flesh of a bloody hole. She saw me roll my eyes.

"You know what Leviticus says—" I remembered my rules and stopped myself.

She handed me the shoe I thought I'd lost last night as I stood and stretched. She gestured for me to step outside, still without saying anything. Once I'd finished yawning, she brushed grass and leaves off my back and shoulders. My belly rumbled, and she gestured for me to walk.

I knew girls like her back home. Holier than holy. Singing with praise bands, organizing protests at Planned Parenthood. Using their love of Christ as a justification to tattoo their foreheads, never mind that the Old Testament strictly forbade it. Girls whose pencil skirts and high collars came off the first time a pretty pastor like Elijah Clay Hicks came a witnessing.

Morning had turned into afternoon during my sleepless night on the plywood floor of my little cell. Birds squawked and chittered in the tall pines, swooping down every now and then to grab a drowsy fly. Rows of little white buildings reminded me of summer camps I'd never been to. Summer camps were for city kids, or kids in movies. Wire mesh over the windows broke the illusion though. Crude wooden crosses had been nailed over windows and doors, to roofs. Bible verses and meaningless commands had been painted on the white wooden siding. Some of the words were large, like they'd been painted on with a brush. In between the larger words were longer passages written with a black marker. I didn't see anybody else. But I heard singing, disjointed spirituals that sounded too much like hypocrisy to my ears.

She led me up the steps into the old dining hall. It smelled of food already eaten. Maybe a breakfast, because I smelled bacon. Or maybe a breakfast and a lunch. Crumbs and straw papers littered the tables. When I sat down at a bowl of instant grits I knew my patience and complacency last night had been a mistake. *I should've fought harder at the truck stop.*

Truly stood across the table from me. As she sat, she said, "Reverend Hicks said I should let you know about this place. It's an old prison camp. The closest road is miles away. We had the fence electrified to keep people out but it works just fine keeping people in."

I pushed the bowl back across the table.

By the way she spoke I could tell she lacked smarts. Her words didn't possess confidence or the force of wit. If anything, her demeanor was a vulnerability—a trait I could exploit later. At least now I knew why Hicks kept her around. I knew where she sat in his chain of command. Just below him. On her knees.

"He said you'd try to leave, and that I was supposed to say something to you. Give you my testimonial, you know? He believes my story can help you come to Jesus." She sat across from me, and tried to take my hands into hers. "You know, I used to be a lot like you. Hanging out with bands and bikers, drinking and drugging."

"You are nothing like me." I banged my fist on the table. "You like being led around by the nose. That's where the differences start. I will not waste time listing the rest."

"No," she rebutted, forcing calmness into her voice as a sign of control and authority. "I just learned how to hear the voice of God for myself instead of waiting to hear a prophecy from someone else. That's what people like you do."

Basking in the importance of her own voice, she closed her eyes. "I can pray for an hour or more, alternating between tongues and English the whole time. Then, I sit and listen for his voice. Just listen. At first I could only hear a couple of words, but now I hear longer sentences. You know, God wants to talk to us and Elijah is only trying to teach people how to listen. I have been slain by the Spirit in Elijah's presence and he tells me I'll be able to do it on my own before too long. All you need is desire to seek Him, and you can feel that too."

"You hear what you want to hear and tell yourself it's divinity. Grow a spine and take responsibility for your life and your actions." Even as I said it I knew I'd broken at least two of my rules. Three, if I could've been making friends with her. "You like being with Elijah because he's as close to a rock star as you're ever going to get."

She began to rebut, but I cut her off. "The reason I'm telling you this is because when you speak, it sounds like recitation. You can take offense if you'd like, but I'm telling you what I hear in your voice."

Truly glared at me, but could not hide her anger.

"It's called doubt. You speak it like a second language. While you're thinking about that, maybe I can have one of those apples." I pointed to a large bowl of fruit on the end of a stainless steel counter. She watched me walk across the room, ready to yell or pounce the moment I broke for the door.

"Would you like one?" I asked, even though I knew she wouldn't reply. I could almost feel her relax as I made my way back to the table.

Rabbits run when they are scared. I'm not afraid yet.

"Truly, what are you meant to say to me that's going to make me see what parents and grandparents and eighteen years in both a Catholic and Protestant church haven't made me see?" I took a bite of the apple, and chewed slowly while she thought. "You've observed that I know scripture as well as Elijah Clay Hicks, which is more than you can say."

I set the apple on a napkin and took her hand. "It's okay though. Your beliefs are your beliefs. I'm not going to tell you they are wrong, or try to change you."

She traced small figure eights on the tabletop with her fingernail. I'd hit a nerve.

"It's not my business. I can accept you as you are. Tell me how you ended up with Elijah. We can talk."

For the longest time she sat there, thinking, and I worried that I'd lose this game if I was the only player. I finished my apple and wrapped the core in a napkin, then sat quietly for a long time.

Without any type of prodding, Truly took a deep breath and spoke. "He pulled me off the street. I'd been picked up for solicitation, but the judge offered rehab and a reduced sentence if I got clean. Supposed to be at the treatment center on a Wednesday morning, but Elijah found me Tuesday night. On my way to have a little fun. You know, get a little something in my blood to make the detox worthwhile? Can't remember the exact details, because I was already pretty wasted. I know I had the needle in my arm though."

The more she talked the older she got, like telling the story had sped up her metabolic clock. Her eyes yellowed, and looked more tired than they had just a minute ago. Small crow's feet appeared at the corners. If she looked twenty-five when I first saw her, she looked at least forty or forty-five now. "Elijah saved me though. He took me and talked and talked."

"He took you—a lot less violently than he took me, I might add. That's the key part of what you said. How is that humane or acceptable? How is it Christ-like?"

"Doesn't matter anymore. All that matters is Elijah did for me what I couldn't quite do for myself." She stood, and pushed herself away from the table. "I wanted more than anything to belong to something, and that's why I whored, you know? Because they liked me when I was facedown on a bed. But I belong here. *This* is my family. Elijah saved me, in the truest sense of the word."

"If I'm not mistaken, Jesus saves. Not Elijah." I tapped my nails on the table and shook my head, scolding myself for my arrogance. "Hicks has a thing for collecting dirty tricks. Sounds to me like he releases his frustration by dominating women he desires but can't be with."

Somebody came up the wooden steps onto the porch.

Truly distanced herself from the table as Hicks bounded into the room. "My God has created another amazing day, hasn't he, Miss Katy?"

The fact that he'd called me that made me burn with anger. Jamie called me that at bluegrass festivals, but it was a family nickname. Even Preston never called me that.

Truly rested her hand on his knee as he took a seat across from me. Annoyed, he waved her away, and waited until she retreated.

Truly flatly said, "Amen," and turned a cold shoulder as she stepped toward a window.

"Any day a soul finds its way to the Lord is a beautiful day, ain't it?" He smiled a made-for-TV smile. "Did y'all get something good to eat? Want something else?"

"No, thank you," I said. "I wasn't very hungry."

"Sorry about all that," Hicks said it like he was a manager at a Hampton Inn listening to a noise complaint. "You know, Sister Odelia told me all about you and your kin before she defiled my daddy's church up in Alpena. I suppose what you and your folks did up there in them hills can be taken as a sacrifice or retribution, if y'all believe in that sort of thing. I suppose I owe you a small debt of gratitude, and that's why I'm going to help you find the Lord. It ain't going to be so hard as you might think to turn your back on your evil, witching, ways."

My blood boiled at the reminder of what happened with the Lewises up in West Virginia last summer. Add in the indignity of Hicks's assumption that we somehow instigated and it took everything I had in me to stay seated on that long wooden bench. "I took a bullet last summer, just so you know."

Hicks smirked, and I pulled my shirt down over my left clavicle to show him.

"Whoa, girl. Keep your clothes on. We ain't there yet." Hicks smiled and waved his hands like he was refusing old sushi. "They tell me I have a way with the ladies, but I ain't never had somebody move this fast."

Don't provoke.

Don't provoke.

Don't provoke.

I took a deep breath. "I would like to use a bathroom and get cleaned up," and even though it almost killed me to say it, I added, "…please."

"Sure thing. Truly, would you like to show Miss Katy the facilities."

Truly turned and looked at me for a long second. "She won't run."

Hicks's smile grew. I could even see it in his wide pupils, which explored me for a sign it was true. Truly must've seen it in his eyes too.

Hicks said, "You do not know how happy that makes me. We'll wait right here for you then. I see you got your shoe back?"

I stood. "Thank you."

"You are most welcome." He watched me stand and turn. Being able to turn away from his gaze made me happy.

I noticed the deadbolt as soon as I shut the bathroom door. The temptation to twist the knob washed over me like the eighth deadly sin, but I knew better. They'd hear the click. I remembered my rules, and turned to the mirror and scolded myself for my seemingly endless inability to humble myself. "Stupid," I whispered. "Stupid. Stupid."

I pounded my thigh with my fist at each syllable. I looked at myself in the mirror and saw the fear in my eyes. Until now, I'd only suspected it. Seeing was believing.

"Keep him on your side," I whispered.

They're coming. I pushed my hair out of my face and leaned toward the mirror, almost nodding at my decision to redouble my focus. "Preston will find you."

I ran the hot water to wash, but couldn't take my mind off the window. Beneath it sat a patch of grass and a clear shot to the wide open wilderness of wherever we were. Women in long skirts with hair piled atop their heads shuffled past. I wasn't worried about them at all and wondered if I should've been. I stayed close to the stainless countertop, as if physicality alone would keep temptation out of my head. *Rule number one...*

"Rule number one." I let the hot water wash temptation away.

When I opened the door Hicks and Truly waited outside. Hicks gave Truly a look, and even though I couldn't be certain, I could've sworn he shrugged, as if he'd just lost a bet. With an insincere laugh, he said, "You remember to wash your hands?"

"Shy bladder," I said.

He gestured for me to head to the door. As I walked on, he said, "The best explanation for God's gift of tongues to the early Church lies in the necessity of teaching newly converted Christians to pray with their heart rather than their mouths. That's all Truly's trying to impress upon you, she meant no malice by it."

"Aside from the maliciousness of kidnapping me?"

Hicks ignored me.

In keeping with my rules, I almost apologized, but Hicks went on.

"The Church knows a deeper way to educate the heart—you cultivate the inner man." He smiled, as if anticipating seeing me express a change of heart. "Or woman. Dead churches have forgotten how to pray in the spirit without losing control of the spirit. I want to teach you how."

Hicks led me back outside, his hand lingering right above my hip, brushing my back every now and then. I didn't turn my head or react to his touch. Truly, who had been walking right alongside us, fell a few steps behind. We moved between the rows of white cabins toward the field where they'd brought me in last night. Some of the shacks had drapes, tulips and daffodils sprouting from the grey earth, or other, tiny touches of domesticity. Potted flowers. Wreathes on the door. But what didn't differ from cabin to cabin was the scrawl of black letters, Bible verses and other warnings. Old Testament, fire and brimstone-type stuff.

Below the one cabin's window I read *A tithe of everything, whether grain from the earth or fruit from the orchard, belongs to the LORD; it is holy to the LORD!* The same phrase had been written several times on other parts of the house.

Above the door of another was *The life of a creature is in the blood, and I have given the blood to you to make atonement for yourselves on the altar; it is the blood that makes atonement for one's life.* I tried not to get caught looking.

People moved toward the clearing from all over. Some emerged from the various buildings, some from the trees themselves. The mass of bodies pushed toward a giant tent in the center of the field, like an Army field hospital from *M.A.S.H.*, except the sides were tied open to the late afternoon. I didn't remember seeing it last night. At the near end of the tent, surrounded by rows and rows of hay bales sat a crude brush arbor like the lay pastors of old built in fields before a proper church could be constructed. Pine boughs formed a rudimentary roof over four pairs of vertical ten-foot posts.

The remainder of the meadow served as a parking lot for RVs and pop-up campers, vans and trucks and station wagons and SUVs. A hundred vehicles, at least, surrounded the glowing tent like drones around a queen bee. Hound dogs had been tied to pickup truck tailgates with sagging ropes. I heard motorcycles, but did not see them. From beneath the tent people already squealed and applauded to the sounds of a fuzzy, high voice coming through a cheap PA. Sounded like an auctioneer at the county fair. Except that it was a child speaking.

The air smelled like spring. Wet, with the slightest whiff of organic matter, like chlorophyll rushing into young leaves and flowers. But when we got closer to the men and women with kids, drug store perfume and body odor washed away the only good thing I'd found refuge in. Hicks pushed through the throng, past an old natural gas well, around people who wanted to shake his hand or get something, even if just a nod, of acknowledgement from him. Old men carrying instrument cases or fine wooden boxes with brass corners and hinges smiled as we passed. Most of the older women wore their hair in high, tight buns. They covered their arms and wore skirts or dresses down to their ankles. The young girls dressed more or less the same, except their skirts were denim as often as not. Sometimes the only way to tell the young ones from the old ones was by the shoes they wore. Some of the younger girls wore tennis shoes.

The people were working folks, and if they'd have been wearing WVU ball caps instead of Crimson Tide hats, I could've easily been back home. None of them looked like the kind of people who'd endorse an abduction. Hicks didn't stop for any of them. With his hand on my back, he continued to push, holding me close, like he meant to protect me. Off to the far right I saw the bikers from the show in Nashville pushing toward us, and I wondered if Hicks meant to avoid them. He jerked me into forceful changes of direction, like he was suddenly angry. My heart raced with his new mood. A moment ago I felt confident I'd see tomorrow. But the way he shoved me into folks, through couples and children, made me believe different. The way he clenched his jaw told me he'd grown angry.

"Hicks!"

I turned to see who shouted. The biker from Nashville pushed through parishioners.

Hicks made for the tent, and sat me on a metal folding chair next to a drum riser. Two other men helped him wrap my hands and ankles with duct tape. The biker with the tattoos on his face pushed into the tent. "Hicks, I told you I wanted her."

"Boggs," Hicks said, retreating a bit. "How about we sort this out tomorrow, okay? Maybe this is something we don't want to discuss here."

"Discuss what?" I said.

But they ignored me. I looked for acknowledgement from the people seated in the first row of chairs. They looked confused, nervous. I shouted, "Hicks abducted me from a truck stop in Alabama last night! Call the police, please—"

A few turned when I called out. The rest remained fixated on the blue-eyed child preacher shouting nonsense from the brush arbor pulpit. The few rows of bare bulbs strung from the tent made it difficult to see faces beyond the first rows.

Hicks and Boggs moved in at the same time. Hicks clapped his hand over my mouth as one of his guys peeled off another strip of duct tape. "You asked for this," he said, taping my mouth shut.

I kicked my feet, which had already been bound to the chair. The chair rocked forward a bit. Hicks jumped back in surprise, but steadied himself with a hand on my knee.

"Boggs." Hicks stood, and ran a finger down my cheek. "Let's try to do the Lord's work tonight. How about it? If it don't work out like we'd hoped, you can have her tomorrow."

Boggs turned and left without answering.

"You see? God has blessed you with a choice." Hicks lowered himself and whispered into my ear, "God reserves the right to withhold judgment. I'm here to lead you to the font, to let you be born again in his holy waters. Some of the girls survived it. Like Truly over there. God decided she was fit to live and be born again. So we pulled her out of the water and for a long time she didn't even move. But then that Holy Spirit came down into her and she coughed that water out and now she's here to tell her story. Maybe you'll float and tell your story, Miss Katy. You want me to take this off your mouth?"

I nodded.

He pulled it slowly away from my lips, and said, "Maybe you'll sink. You're going to have to decide first though. Whether you even want to be saved or not."

He gestured to the group that gathered within earshot. "Ain't that right?"

They provided him with an immediate "Amen."

"So what, Hicks. You save me. Then what? I'm another trophy? Like Truly? You pull her off the street and pump her up with 'Jesus loves you' and now she's saved?"

"You want the tape again?" He stood and smiled. "I'm trying to be reasonable, here."

"The dirtier the better. Right, Hicks? Truly's a junkie. You think I'm a witch. You probably got an adulterer and a prostitute hanging around too."

Hicks clenched his teeth and smiled. "Look at this kid, will you?"

"You are a monster—"

"Shut your mouth." Hicks grabbed my jaw, forcing me to watch the child preacher. "Or I'll let Boggs shut it. Your choice."

The little boy stomped across the pulpit, wiping his face with a towel like he must've seen Hicks do a thousand times. The boy stopped, loosened his tie and slapped his hand on the big black Bible that sat on the miniature podium somebody must've made special for him. "Hallelujah."

Hicks stood at my shoulder.

The boy flipped through the Bible like he was looking for a particular passage. People in the congregation murmured. Somebody in the back shouted a loud, clear, "Hallelujah."

The kid wiped his face again—a child actor, not a preacher—and I looked at Hicks. He stood there, arms folded, smiling and nodding his head.

The kid said, "I'm going to preach about…" He sighed and paused dramatically. The noise from the congregation grew.

"Tonight, I'm preaching about…" His young voice couldn't articulate each consonant. It sounded like baby talk.

"Praise Jesus!" A woman shouted from the back. Hicks clapped his hands, a gesture that inspired more of the same from the group. The kid smiled, letting the roar build, which had the effect of generating more anticipation. More buzz. The kid said, "Tonight I'm preaching about the one true God!"

Screams of praise erupted from the tent. If it'd been any louder, we all would've spilled into the grass like feathers from a burst pillow.

"The red hot revival!" He shouted and jumped a little. He landed with his fist on the Bible and said, "Made whole by the power of God."

And the crowd bought it. Grown men and women with their hands in the air and eyes closed.

"Be made whole by the Holy Spirit!" He jumped in the air two, three, four times. "The Holy Spirit is coming down into this church tonight to make us whole."

Gibberish. Catchphrases. Not a single word of substance. I could only shake my head.

Hicks got real close to me. Close enough to smell the fake apple in his cheap cologne. "You going to be saved tonight, girl," he said, letting his finger slide down my breastbone. "Or you're going to wish you were. You only get one shot to deny Christ. The second time, we're going to try you as a witch."

He drifted over to the child preacher, clapping and pumping his fist. He grabbed the guitar player's mic out of its stand and said, "Thank you, Grayden! And praise Jesus."

Truly took Hicks's place as my personal attendant. She watched him stoically drop to his knees and hug the kid. I couldn't tell if she looked more angry or hurt. At this point, I didn't know if I could tell the difference. Somebody in the crowd spoke in tongues.

Grayden's mom waited at the far side of the tent. She stood next to a tall man with dark eyes and hair. The man may have been Grayden's daddy, but he sure as hell wasn't his father. Only one man in the room had hair blond enough and eyes blue enough. And he was about to speak.

The drone of electric guitars hammered out dissonant chords over the drummer's straight 4/4 time, drowning out chattering voices. Hicks closed his eyes to the beat. He waved a hand, and the playing got a lot quieter. Just a whispered taptap of the drum and palm-muted chords. Hicks held the mic to his lips. "How 'bout a little intercession?"

The crowd noise grew. Somebody right near me in the front row spoke in tongues. "Eehee keykee mongobah chur chongo un too peek tickakaan…"

"They say I've got God, Jesus and the Holy Spirit itself in my bones from the time I was born," Hicks whispered into the mic. "I ain't educated, but I'm a smart man and I got the degree that keeps the light on for these people. They come to me with questions science and government can't answer, and the response flows through me, like a river. You'll see tonight. Because you are but a dark stain on the face of this earth. But by the time you're done here, by God, you'll either be saved or dead."

He was talking to me.

"My spirit talks to their spirits, and together we have a conversation with God through the Holy Spirit. He tells me it's coming, and that I need to get the people ready." The sizzle of the ride cymbal went into my ears like a Holstein to clover. My head pounded, but all I could do was angle it away from the drum kit. It gave me a little relief, but I still felt a migraine coming on.

At once the drums stopped. A wave of hushes flew through the congregation. Women stood on tiptoes, fanning themselves with paper fans as they strained to find Hicks's baby blue eyes. I felt hot breath on my neck and tried to jerk forward. The drummer put his hand on my shoulder and said, "You need to get your eyes on Jesus. Everything Elijah says is scriptural. It's God's word—not the words of them unholy spirits filling your head. Search your heart and make sure you got your house in order, because He's coming soon and you best prepare yourself for the day of his glorious return."

He placed his hand on my head. I could smell Skoal on his fingertips. "I'll pray for you."

Truly watched.

Hicks paused with the mic at his lips and toweled himself off. Just like Grayden did. He smiled, a blond Elvis, shaking souls instead of hips. He quietly spoke into the mic, "How y'all doing?"

A chorus of responses, and an early "Amen" here and there came back from the congregation. New rounds of voices exploded in tongues. "…deev ell a potom cert ho vzal prayeehan."

"Little hot out here tonight. Sorry about that." Hicks walked to the far end of the tent, spun on his heels and returned to the center. He clasped the mic between his fingers and dropped his head like he was in deep thought. After a moment, he put the mic back to his mouth, and said, "Bet you it's a little hotter in hell right now."

A roar built in the crowd as people jumped to their feet. Behind me, the drummer counted off a real quick four count and banged out that same elementary beat he'd been pounding out since we'd arrived. The guitarist and bass player riffed on a simple I-IV-V chord pattern as the people of the congregation hooted and kicked. Folding chairs were passed to the edge of the tent, handed from person to person, letting more of those on the outside squeeze themselves in. The steady clang of tambourines came from all around me.

Hicks shouted into the mic, "The congregation of God is a living breathing temple and each person in that temple is a stone! This is a spiritual temple where the people worship God in spirit and in truth. It is not a church building—a dead church where sinners follow pedophile priests. In this church… In this spiritual temple, every believer is a priest. God now dwells in and among his people." He toweled himself again and turned his back to the congregation.

Men and women lifted their palms to the sky, eyes closed, murmuring prayers. Together they sounded like summer cicadas. Hicks watched, smiling. When he saw me looking he rushed over to me. He grabbed my jaw and turned me to face a girl in the front row. He shouted into my ear, "This young lady is getting the Holy Ghost!"

To make sure the show never stopped he held the mic up to his mouth so the congregation could hear. "She is baptized in Jesus's name for the remission of her sins! Now she has a new life in Jesus Christ!"

He left me to return to his flock. A thousand hands in the air. Men and women on their knees. A group of people way off to my right pushed toward an old lady wearing a knit cap and speaking in tongues. Their hands waved, fingers in the air, eyes closed. Their eyes were always closed. The music built in pulsating waves. I turned and saw a pair of banjo pickers and another guitarist surrounding the mic stands. They'd abandoned the I-IV-V and hammered away at the same chord over and over again. A pulsing, droning tune that created empty space above the congregation for the prayers of the church. The drone put them into the trance that let Hicks have his way with them.

"Sert nikdy nespi hakkaleena sert veede viljdi k sertupray…"

My mind tricked me into believing the syllables radiating from the congregation made sense. I knew all about matrixing, and finding order in chaos. But I heard the same things over and over, like standing on the beach and seeing only the tops of waves until just before they broke. I tried to keep the syllables straight in my head, and they spoke to me through the noise. My heart raced. For a fragment of a second, I wanted to believe. I wanted to be back at Mass with my grandma on Sunday morning.

"But y'all are not here only to listen. No, sir, y'all ain't. You came to test your faith. You came to show God that his laws supersede local laws. State laws. Federal laws. Man's laws are fine… For some folks. The state don't want us out here, meeting like this." He waved his hands to get the attention of somebody at the back of the tent.

"The state has its laws, and we have ours. Y'all know which I'm talking about, right?"

Men approached the pulpit from all sides of the tent. Three from the back. Two from behind me. Some from behind Hicks. Emerging from the cold humidity itself.

"We got the Commandments, handed down to Moses from God himself."

The men carried wooden boxes of various shapes and sizes. Some had a series of holes drilled into the top and sides. Some had wire mesh tacked to the wood. Like little cages. I tried to see inside, but could only see burlap. Didn't matter. I knew.

At that moment I wanted to feel the communion wafer on my tongue, and to

believe it had become the body of Christ. For a moment, I wanted to belong. I wanted the warmth of my grandma's church.

"The Lord works with mystery, and challenges us to seek out guidance. His Word extends beyond the Commandments, and He challenges us to find answers elsewhere in His Book if we are to test our faith. I'm talking about Mark, chapter sixteen, verse eighteen. Y'all know that one?"

The crowd pushed toward the altar. Hicks held them back with a wave of his hand.

The sound of tongues grew. "Okalla sert nikdy prayay nespi…"

I knew what was coming, because I'd cracked the code. Only thing left to do was verify it.

"Mishkash dapel nespi moor!"

The drummer tripped over the beat and fumbled the turn around. So with all the grace of a stop sign, he hiccuped toward a faster tempo.

"Unkuprayay sertu kalalagod…"

Tongues streamed forth from every corner of the tent now. Dissonant voices spitting out syllables—to break the code I had to listen real close. Women ululated to the stream-of-consciousness voices in their heads. Some bounced like punks. Men kicked their legs up. Some fell to the ground, spasms popping in time with the beat. I fought to keep track of the syllables.

"Holy Spirit, be with us tonight!"

"An dev eel kee sonnitprayayay where kanlal…"

The wooden boxes were laid at Hicks's feet. He kicked the lid back with his toe. When Hicks rolled up his sleeve, I saw the markings that we'd mistaken for needle tracks back in Louisville outside the club. The black and blue bruises that dotted his atrophied and misshapen forearm looked like bad tattoos. But I knew exactly what they were.

"Tumal godkan malee tola billbilled…"

It all made sense at that moment. The syllables.

The devil prays wherever God builds a church.

I rocked the chair as hard as I could. Truly and a man from the congregation held me steady. I screamed, but the noise got lost in the crowd. *The devil prays wherever God builds a church.* That was what they were saying.

Hicks spoke over them. "These 'seminary preachers' don't know a lick about what happens in the world of men and women with bills to pay and babies to feed. One Lord! One house!"

A chorus of tambourines ran wild through the uneven tempo. Children ran through the crowd, screaming, swinging their arms. Old men openly wept. Young men jumped as high as they could, their heads appeared at unbalanced intervals above the crowd. The screams and expression I saw were sexual—orgasmic. Women balled their fists and pulled their hair. They screamed in ecstasy, longing for a touch they'd never feel.

Hicks reached into the wooden crate and wrapped his hand around a magnificent viper. A lazy rattler as thick as his forearm. He held it over his head and danced wild circles like an Indian brave from an old cowboy movie. He kicked his legs out in front of him and spun with his arms out to his side, the mic in his right hand countering the snake in his left. He shouted, "They shall pick up serpents with their bare hands!" And his voice boomed through the PA system.

He shook the snake, agitating it but not hurting it. The lazy rattles shivered, hissing like steam from a pot on a gas stove. He waved it over the people in the audience, shaking it. One of his girls took the mic from him, looking more like a magician's assistant than a parishioner. She held it up to his mouth long enough for him to shout, "And it shall not hurt him!" Feedback screamed out of the cheap PA.

Hicks held his forearm up to the snake's flicking tongue. The snake pulled away, but Hicks persisted, taunting the snake with the warmth of his shriveled arm.

When the snake struck I didn't see it. That was how fast it hit. Only Hicks's reaction, a moment of panic, like he couldn't be entirely sure that this one wouldn't be different, gave way to the smug satisfaction that his God had saved him yet again. The snake clung to his arm, pumping its jaw, working venom into his blood. But Hicks smiled and held the serpent high above his head. Whipping the congregation into ecstasy.

He grabbed the mic and ran at me, stopping inches from my nose. He whispered into the mic, "What say you now?"

"I know what Jesus said." I pulled away from the snake. "Jesus said, 'You know not what manner of spirit they are of. The Son of man is not come to destroy men's lives, but to save them.'"

The drowsy rattler twisted in Hicks's hand, having spent all its energy defending itself. Still, when Hicks shoved it at me my heart raced and sweat formed on my palms. Its yellow cat eyes glimmered in the amber glow of the overhead bulbs.

"The faithful have nothing to fear," he said.

"A drowsy snake…" I should've bit my tongue, but couldn't. "It's not even spring so for all I know it could've been hibernating. Maybe it's well-fed. Or a venomoid. My mom's cousins had snakes with venom glands removed by a vet."

"Miss Katy, I'm going to pray for you." He licked his lips.

"Don't waste—"

Hicks shoved the snake at me. Searing pain, like hot needles ripped into my bicep. Like hornets. Like fire. Like stepping on a nail in the old spring house.

But none came close to the pain of having my muscle split by those fangs. My breath left me. I gasped for mercy, for words, but couldn't find any that would let me talk my way out of it. Hicks pulsed the snake's head with his index finger, driving the fangs deep into the muscle. The rattlesnake twisted, a living thing, defending itself. I turned my head to see, but Hicks pushed my face away with his other hand.

"Please…"

"You asking me? Or God?"

I bit my lip and tried to relax. I tried to tell myself that bites weren't always fatal. I tried to tell myself that some people are allergic to venom, and those were the people that really got hurt. In my head I tried to think of people I knew who survived snake bites. I thought of guys from high school. Relatives. Surely Jamie'd talked about it at dinner. When I thought I'd never see him or Chloey or my mom again my chest ached. I felt like I couldn't win.

There were words I could say, but without ash or silver, they'd only be words. Without faith, they lacked the power to be more than just noise. I didn't want those old ways to be part of who I was ever again. Every time I went down that path, a part of me died. But I needed to do something, or there'd be nothing left for tomorrow. *Rule number one…*

I wanted to see Preston again, even if it meant using the old ways.

I mumbled, "Crotalus horridus, Agkistrodon contortrix, Crotalus adamanteus, Agkistrodon piscivorus, like water to me. Like water to me."

Without silver and ash, I didn't know if it would work. Those words had been passed down generation to generation. The words didn't make the bite any less painful.

"Crotalus horridus, Agkistrodon contortrix, Crotalus adamanteus, Agkistrodon piscivorus, like water to me…"

Hicks pulled the snake off me. The fangs ripped my skin, the spent snake withered in Hicks's grasp. He passed it off to a handler. Warm blood trickled down to my elbow.

"Crotalus horridus, Agkistrodon contortrix, Crotalus adamanteus, Agkistrodon piscivorus, like water to me. Like water to me." I said so he could hear.

"Don't worry, little lamb, I prayed for you just now, like I pray for your salvation. I have faith enough for the both of us." He rested his palm on my forehead, trying to comfort me.

I pulled away from his touch as best I could.

"It's fine. I didn't do it for your thanks." He waved Truly closer. "Lock her up. By this time tomorrow she'll have made a choice. Saved or stoned, Miss Katy."

"Are you okay?" Truly held a clean white cloth to my bites as one of the men from the crowd took the duct tape off me. "I'm so sorry."

I watched the blood spread through the cotton and waited for Truly to lift her hand, trying to see whether or not I'd been invenomated. She took care with me, helping me stand when I couldn't stand on my own. As she led me away from the glow of the tent, waves of relief brought tears to my eyes. I had to follow rule number one no matter what. Truly stopped and turned, and placed her hand on my shoulder. Two men from the congregation trailed a few yards behind.

"Faith saved you tonight," Truly said as we walked.

And I didn't have the will to disagree.

"When you tried to make me out as a doubter today? I didn't appreciate that. But faith is the only reason you're here right now."

I nodded.

In that moment I thought about my rules, thought about what I needed to do to get out of here. So I sniffled a big sniffle, laid my head on her shoulder and forced a shudder.

Truly froze.

I forced more tears and let myself collapse.

When Truly completed the embrace, I forced all the color out of my voice and said, "Please don't let him hurt me anymore."

She pushed the hair out of my face and wiped away a tear with her thumb. When she released me I sniffled, dried my eyes, and let her lead me back to the old freezer. While she fumbled with the latch I waited patiently.

Before she shut the door, I said, "Thank you for being so kind."

Without a reply she shut the door behind me. I heard the latch click but did not hear her footsteps go back off into the dark. So I waited.

Truly said, "I'll be back in a few minutes with pillows and a blanket, okay?"

"Okay," I said, knowing she couldn't see the little smile I let slip. "That is very charitable of you."

In my dream, Preston and I wandered through Cordoba. Or Barcelona. The dream lacked the specificity of a memory, which, I supposed, was kind of the point. But it

felt hot, and the air felt dry, and I didn't hear the Castilian accent I'd grown so tired of hearing in Barcelona. As soon as I figured out we were in Cordoba, I felt a cool breeze from the Guadalquivir and saw the Roman Bridge, which reminded me a little of the Charles Bridge in Prague. Preston wore a white Oxford and khaki shorts and I wore clothes like a Spaniard. A soft violet dress, and strappy sandals and a necklace like I'd seen the women in Barcelona wearing. My hair looked darker, and my high school Spanish sounded perfect. Preston understood me, but continued to speak English.

That was how I remembered where we were. I'd regretted not getting one of the long necklaces I'd seen the women in Barcelona wearing, and Preston told me not to worry, because we'd see something and it would be more meaningful because we weren't looking for it. The one I'd been wanting had a long strand of thick string, like sisal or hemp, embellished with a clunky stone ornament. Almost like a fairy stone my mom had when I was little. But I couldn't recall seeing the fairy stone in years. When my dad was at his worst—coming home from work, drunk, and pulling her out of bed to fight—she clutched that little fairy stone like nothing in the world could ever harm her. And I supposed she was right. Because as much as he beat on her and ran her down, he never managed to once leave a mark on her.

A tap on the door woke me up. The noise pulled me from sleep and I fought to keep the dream fresh in my mind. Even as the door opened my mind raced to see the dream through to its end, replaying the few things I could remember over and over so as to not lose them too.

"Katy," a woman whispered. Lights from the kitchen window above let me see her outline in the doorway.

Breakfast? So I knew it had to be seven in the morning, at least.

But I didn't answer her, because I knew speaking meant I'd fully awoken, and the contents of the dream would be lost to me forever.

"Sorry," she said. "I have to get the blanket and pillows before Elijah finds out."

Early morning birds called from deep in the forest. Their songs trickled through the vegetation, calling flies and gnats to join them for breakfast. "Okay," I said, already shivering from the cold.

I sat up and pushed the blanket toward her with my feet.

"I'm sorry."

No, you're not.

"I brought something for your arm too." She clicked on a little flashlight and showed me a tube of Neosporin. "I don't want it to get infected. Does it still hurt?"

I didn't want to speak to her.

"I can't leave it for you. It can get infected."

I took a deep breath and let the final fragments of my dream slip away. I pulled my jacket down off my shoulder and let her see the small, purple puncture wounds.

She dabbed the ointment on the bite, and said, "He prayed for you, you know. That's why you aren't hurt. He wanted to show you the power of God's word."

Anger flooded into my head, but I knew I couldn't lose control and risk cutting the time I had left to fight in half. It killed me to do it, but I redirected that anger and let it boil. I let my head ache with it and thought of my demise, and never seeing Preston or Mom or Chloey again. I let the tears come and put my head into my hands. Through sniffles I said, "Why does he hate me?"

Truly retreated a bit, like for a fleeting moment she could see the trap.

"Please don't leave me. Stay with me a little longer."

Truly clicked the flashlight off and slipped it into her coat pocket. She got down on her knees and put her hand onto my forearm.

The second she dropped her guard I pounced. It would've been easy enough to have run through the door. But to what end? Hounds chasing me right to the electric fence.

No, I let my muscles soften and fell into her. I let the tears fall, and perhaps even encouraged them by letting my mind run wild with the worst of all possible scenarios. Preston's face upon hearing word that my body had been found. Pap and Gram and Jamie crying over another casket, and for them, the realization that the Lewises had been the least of our problems if, in fact, we were cursed.

Tears streamed down my cheeks. Each, I believed, was more potent than hot bird shot from the end of a shotgun if Truly had any humanity at all left in her.

She put her arm around me and pulled my head to her chest. The thought of the tattoos on the palms of her hands made my skin crawl. A physical manifestation of everything that was wrong with what they believed. But I forced myself to stay in character.

Without a word, she stood, leaving me by myself on the floor. I sniffled and folded my arms.

"Just do what he says, Katy. Even if you don't mean it, do what he says."

She shut the door, and flipped the latch shut.

And I smiled.

The morning wore on like a long, long stretch of highway when I found myself unable to fall back to sleep. Without Preston, or a book or an InStyle magazine, or my phone, the morning felt like a week. As soon as the first streaks of golden sunlight fell through the little window I backed myself right up to the door. The amount of real warmth was negligible, but as a placebo, it worked perfectly. I closed my eyes and saw the wide blue sky running hot with sunlight. I closed my eyes and saw golden light streaming from the tall green trees. And that, at least, brought back a little bit of this morning's dream.

I passed the time by singing. At first I sang Preston's songs. That his words could find me here, in this sad place, brought me hope. With his words on my lips I knew I wasn't alone. I would never pray again, not like these people prayed, not ever. But the little lines of verse Preston had pulled out of the sky served the same purpose, for me at least. His words comforted me. His words gave thanks and praise to something greater than the both of us, whether it be love or music or family. If prayers were constructions of man, then Preston's words, or John Lennon's, or Emmylou Harris's, should be no different. If I chose to praise God without the help of a pastor or a pew, and continued to live as the kindest possible person I could be, then it should make no difference to Hicks or his people.

I didn't come down here telling them how to pray or live.

They took me. With the intense desire to change how I lived my life.

And that's why, I reminded myself, *I will feel nothing when Preston comes for me, and brings all this down right on their heads.*

I went right back to singing.

When the door latch clicked I stood, ready for a late lunch. Ready to see Truly, even if I had to pretend like nothing happened this morning. So I stood, and turned. I put on my shoes and buttoned my coat and ran my fingers through my hair. I had to pee and looked forward to a chance to stretch my legs and see the trees and the sky and pretend, if only for a minute, I was back in West Virginia feeling the chill from the last of the melting snow. Hearing the rush of the Blackwater as it passed behind Hellbender Burritos in Davis. I needed to see the green, if only to be reminded that this world was not all grey in its thousands of different shades. I needed it because even though it had only been a day and a half, I'd started to lose hope.

I needed hope if I wanted to survive.

I stepped away from the door as it swung open.

The woman said, "Into the corner. Move."

She spoke with an uneven cadence and an accent I couldn't place. It was subtle, but not southern. And it wasn't Spanish.

"Where's Truly?"

133

"Elijah said that you spoke to her with a devil's tongue, and that she could not be permitted near you. He beat her at breakfast in front of the entire congregation." She spoke every word forcefully, without hesitation or doubt. "All because of your coldness. Sit down."

I didn't see this woman yesterday. I would've noticed her. Her skin was fair, perhaps a shade or two darker than mine. Her almond-shaped eyes were brown. Almost green. Almost yellow. Even without makeup, with her hair pulled back into a loose ponytail, I found myself unable to look away. Her lips formed a natural pout, even as she scowled orders at me. She wore a simple grey dress, belted at the waist. Her shoes were plain black flats. She didn't wear any jewelry, and smelled a little like ginger or clove, which made my mouth water and my stomach growl.

I wanted her to touch me, to push me to the floor. I wanted her to make me sit down.

She swept into the room, pulling the door shut behind her. I planted my feet, waiting to be slapped or shoved. But she folded her arms, holding the apple she'd brought with her just out of reach. A tease.

"Could I please use the bathroom?" I lied. "I really have to go."

"No, you don't." Her reply came immediately. "Truly would've allowed it. But she isn't a strong person, and you knew that. Didn't you?"

I folded my arms and leaned against the wall in the corner. "So it's game on?"

She smiled as if suddenly surprised. "Yes, I suppose it is game on. If this is only a game to you, that is."

"You know it isn't." Her comeback threw me, and my thoughts reeled a bit. "You know that I'm being held against my will. Where in the Bible—"

"Yes, maybe I do know. What of it? Your station stays the same whether I know it or not. I come and go, not you. You would trade me for your own salvation, given an opportunity—which I will not provide. You were two short steps away from having Truly drive up to this room and escort you out like a chauffeur. In a way it makes you no better than Hicks. I expected better from a little bluebird like you." She tapped her blood-red nails against the apple's firm green skin, drawing my eyes right to it. My mouth watered.

"You must be hungry." She held the apple out, but made no movement toward me. She wanted me to come to her. She wanted me to submit.

I crossed my arms and looked past her, to the bright afternoon. I decided to let the sunlight nourish me instead.

She took a bite, smiling as she chewed. I could smell the sugar in the white flesh.

When I didn't say anything, she said, "Turns out I'm not hungry either."

She set the apple on the floor and stepped on it. Juice sprayed out, the dry plywood soaked it right up. She ground the shape right out of it with her heel. Scent filled the room and I resented my stomach for not sticking to my plan of resistance.

"Game on, bluebird."

I felt sick, like when adrenaline starts to enter the body. Despite the warmth of the afternoon, I had goose bumps all up and down my arms. Even my hair felt like it'd been standing on end. Somehow I knew that I knew her.

Or knew the feeling.

Like when Princess Jasmine figures out the Prince Ali is really Aladdin.

Bluebird.

I made a fist and bared my teeth. "Stay away from Preston!"

"You do not understand. I've waited more than one hundred years for this moment to arrive. I most certainly will not stay away from Preston."

"You leave him alone." I closed my eyes. It burned me up inside to picture him running through scenarios only to arrive at this conclusion because he believed it was the only remaining option.

"You have greater concerns, do you not? Hicks wants to baptize you and fuck you. Boggs wants to stone you to death. I am not so certain that you should worry about Preston. If it's any consolation he has not contacted me yet."

"Why are you here then?"

"The world really is quite small. Elijah Clay Hicks wanted to be a great and righteous prophet. Like his namesake."

"And you're here to help him?"

"Perhaps, if a lie can help. But Hicks is nothing to me. He can not do for me what Preston can." She smiled. "It must hurt very badly to be away from him for so long."

Her expression suddenly softened, her words slowed. "I do not need to see either of you suffer. It makes no difference to me. Maybe you think I'm incapable of love? That I am a soulless husk? It's easy to see why. I can only imagine the things he must have told you about me. Some are true, depending on what he said, exactly. But I loved him, you know. I thought he would be the one to help me free myself."

She turned to the little window and squinted at the bright sunlight. "Saying that I need a resolution means something different than what you think it means. You can't begin to understand. Or maybe you can, I don't know. But I had an agreement. An ugly agreement that caused me more suffering and heartache than you could possibly imagine. No matter how bad it gets for you, you have the luxury of knowing it will one day end.

When I made this agreement I was young and I didn't understand forever could be a real thing. When you are a girl, forever could be a week, if that is how long you have to wait until you can see a lover. As it turns out, in my case, forever meant forever."

I refused to feel for her. I listened, but only as a means of keeping my head in the game.

"Preston will help me, whether he wants to or not. He'll help me terminate my agreement. Contract. Covenant." She rested her palm against her cheek, and closed her eyes. "I can only imagine what my life would be like if he hadn't met you. Do I believe that I could've been happy with Preston? Of course I do. But it hurts too much to think of things that will never be. Like wishing on stars, or pennies in fountains. Or praying."

She folded her arms across her chest and stared at the floor. For the first time, I wondered who she really was.

"But there can be no negotiation with only one party."

I waited for her to continue, but her demeanor changed. She regained the anger in her voice. "Whether he likes it or not, Preston has the means and the motivation to make it so. Or he soon will."

She turned and left, locking the door behind her.

"Leave him alone!" My face felt hot. "Come back here!" My legs weakened, and I slipped to the floor. It hurt my chest to breathe. My heart ran like water down a barn roof. My breath felt hot. Regaining my composure, I stood and pressed my face into the little opening and yelled, "Come back here!"

She took it all from me. In one interaction, I'd lost everything I'd spent a day fighting for. She'd weakened me. She'd distracted me and tempted me with something I thought they could never take from me. The moment I realized she'd see Preston before I did, I knew that I'd lost. She did what Hicks and a thousand followers couldn't do.

I slid to the floor and buried my face in my arms. When I let go of the courageous role I'd been playing everything else went with it. With each sob I lost a little dignity. Every time I wiped snot from my nose I pulled down one of the bricks I'd so carefully placed in my wall.

The time for planning and rules passed without me even realizing. My devotion to my inability to be wrong screwed me. I could've run this morning, when I had Truly's trust. I could've found a way through the fence. Found a phone. Called for help. Flagged down a car. I spent the afternoon thinking of everything that could've been different if I'd have only been more proactive.

Stop it.

One by one my rules came back to me. Just like they had yesterday morning. But they were no different than a prayer. Just words to keep the real fear out of my head. Words to keep my mind from drifting to worst-case scenarios. Words that couldn't protect me from snakebite any more than they could promise eternal salvation. Once I stopped with the words, the fears rushed back at me.

Preston won't ever find me.

I'll die here without ever saying goodbye to him.

More than anything I wanted to believe in some greater good.

Without telling my mom how much I loved her.

And Chloey.

And Ben, Henry, Alex, Jamie, Pap and Gram.

No greater good existed. If nothing else, I learned this before I died.

That when I die, there is no "after."

That once it's over, it's over. Like flipping off a light.

I thought about the punishment they'd threatened me with. In my mind, I saw myself defying them until the very end.

But I won't feel a thing once it's over.

The pain will be temporary. But it will end. And if there is an all-powerful force in the universe, and if it's fair, I won't be alone. If it's fair, I'll see Preston again.

I stopped the thoughts from rushing in after that one. I decided that would be the only one that mattered. That pain, no matter how magnificent, lasted temporarily. They could hold my head under water. They could heave stones at my body. But they couldn't drown me or stone me infinitely.

Footsteps came up the gravel path to the door.

Time to choose.

I never even moved from the sticky juice of the apple she'd brought. A little temptation to seal her deal. When the door opened I fell back into the dirt. They picked me up off the ground and pulled me toward the three crosses at the far end of the field, dragging me roughly through the gravel and high grass. The revival tent and brush arbor from last night had since been dismantled and packed away.

I fought to get my feet beneath me. "I can walk," I said, trying to twist from a grasp that felt much stronger than Hicks's had been.

A set of thick, callused, hands pushed me forward. I stumbled, but did not fall. When I regained my composure I saw two of the bikers from the Nashville show. I saw the scrawl of Corinthians and Romans and Deuteronomy over their necks and forearms and bare heads.

"You..." was all that I could say. I twisted and kicked, but they were too strong.

"Ashby! Stop what you're doing." From the far end of the field Hicks appeared, trailed by a small part of his flock. Mostly women and a few children and one or two men, all wearing white baptismal gowns. Truly stood near the back. She didn't walk out with the rest. Her face looked bruised.

Hicks yelled, "Where's Boggs? Why isn't he out here?" and the bikers stopped. Hicks ran through the grass, tucking in his shirt as he went.

"Boggs says you lost focus. Says you stopped playing the game when you started looking for a wife." When the hands released me they didn't only let go. They shoved me, forcing me into the ground hard enough to knock the wind from me.

I laid there with my face in the warm grass and got my head together. The first stars appeared in the sky. And Venus. A sight I wanted to share with Preston once again.

Rule number one...

As soon as I got my feet beneath me I ran. And I never looked back.

I put my head down and broke for the ticking gas well in the center of the field, hoping to make it past the large pile of stone where the three tall crosses stood, to the trees beyond. The air smelled faintly of natural gas. A chorus of shouts told me they'd reorganized and redirected their efforts. I heard the heavy footfalls at my heel, telling me this race would be a short one. And that I'd lose.

Expecting to be shoved again, I leaned forward to roll with the momentum, but a jerk pulled me back like a dog at the end of his leash. My feet flew from beneath me. My failure and near miss escalated my emotions. I knew right then and there that my biggest mistake was following the stupid, silly rules I'd invented as a way to prolong the ordeal. Should've listened to my pap. He would've said to make hay while the sun shined.

A. G. Ashby dragged me toward the crosses as Hicks sprinted across the field. Hounds barked from the other side of the cabins.

Hicks shouted, "Ashby, you have no right. She belongs to me."

Ashby shouted, "Boggs reckons you're more interested in sleeping with her than saving her."

"Go get Boggs," Hicks barked the order to the twenty people closest to him. "This is my camp."

"And because of us you don't have to get your hands dirty," the other one said with a slight Jersey accident.

A hot wind blew from the river. It brought a new scent with it. It made me uneasy.

"Like tormenting these young girls is such difficult work that you should complain about the difficulty of the work?" Danicka's voice came from the midst of the group and from the forest at the same time. Even Hicks seemed stunned at the defiant tone.

"You are not welcome here!" Hicks shouted. "We're through. I don't owe you a thing."

The group backed away from the woman in grey. They should've run. They didn't know what I knew. They didn't know they were about to be tested. Really tested. Hicks knew though. He was the only one who looked scared.

"How dare you rush to judge this girl without a demonstration of your own faith? You hide behind a microphone and exhort your congregation to do *His* work while you lead a life which requires no test of faith whatsoever. You make and break rules as it pleases you, Reverend Elijah Clay Hicks. You act as if recitation of scripture is enough to get a pass at all this." Her voice boomed, as if amplified. Her tone, angry.

Danicka moved to the space between Hicks and the bikers, filling it with her presence. Her defense of me filled me with an unforgivable sense of warmth. A calmness. I could see why Preston loved her and found myself able to forgive him for that. Over and over I had to remind myself what she was. As she came forward, a whoosh emerged from the forest, like a soft breeze gently lifting leaves one by one. I could only hear it between my own breaths.

Ashby and his companion yanked me up by my arm and dragged me to the dirt mound. Up to the wooden crosses that sprung from the rich red clay like some kind of sick billboard. The farthest cross had quotes from Deuteronomy about stoning for worshipping other gods. The center had verses from Leviticus and John about stoning for blasphemy and one from Numbers about breaking the Sabbath.

My captor shoved me toward the cross on the left. The one that read, *Any witch shall be stoned to death, and only upon their hands shall their blood be. Leviticus 20:27.*

I twisted and struggled, but they were too strong. *Be patient...*

They spun me and pushed me against the cross. My arms were pulled back sharply, sending waves of pain through my neck and shoulders. They meant to bind my elbows together. From this vantage I could see the grass at the edge of the field flutter, as if an invisible hand were passing over it. The grass dipped and sprang back in waves.

Hicks saw it too, and used Boggs's absence as an excuse to leave. "Boggs! Come on out here and put an end to this."

A new scent came in on the breeze. *Cucumber*. Jamie always talked about it, and Henry did too after last summer. Until now, I'd never experienced anything like it.

"Hicks," Danicka said. "Demonstrate your faith to these people. Lead them by example." She picked up a slender, brown serpent and brushed its head against her cheek. She passed it off to a woman standing near her, then bent down to pick up several more. "Behold, I give unto you power to tread on serpents and scorpions, and over your enemy. Nothing shall hurt you."

The first shout of fear came from a woman at the very back of the crowd. A scream when the mass of water moccasins and copperheads moved past her feet. I could see them swarming from the forest. Scales and venom on the move.

"This is the word of your God. These words are not mine. Your God demands this of you. Not me." With several vipers writhing in each hand, Danicka ranted, looking each parishioner dead in the eye in turn as she spoke. "Do not judge this girl without first demonstrating your own faith. You have forced this test upon yourselves."

"Leave them!" Hicks yelled. "This woman is testing you with her evil, evil ways. I know her, and know that her soul is as black as the night. She is pure evil and you all need to stay away from her."

She passed the serpents in her right hand off to the man standing closest to her. Others bent to pick up vipers, as they'd done in services a hundred times. But these snakes weren't well-fed, and they didn't come from refrigerated rooms where they were frequently handled.

"It is not my choice to see harm come to you," Danicka said. "But I would not ask you to follow my words without action and I will let no harm come to this woman without an equal test of faith. Hicks has given me no choice. Hicks has put you into this situation, not God. Certainly not me."

"Do not listen to her! Every word she speaks is a lie," Hicks screamed, his face reddened. He'd lost his swagger. He sounded like he felt genuinely afraid. "I know her."

But one of his people responded to Danicka with an "Amen!"

Hicks went on. "This is real—not a demonstration. You do not understand what this is. She is temptation! Sin!"

Danicka smiled. "Do as I do, not as I say, Elijah Clay Hicks."

"A false prophet, maybe even the devil herself. She doesn't know your names or how you got here. Listen to your hearts, to what you know is right. If it is your will to show Miss Katy some mercy, then so be it." Hicks scrambled to make things right.

"This is faith." Danicka teased a copperhead with her thumb. She smiled when it sank its fangs into her. The snake coiled itself tightly around her arm, like a bracelet.

She let a second snake, a cottonmouth, do the same thing on her right arm. She bent down to pick up a third. "This is living without fear."

Something exploded in the distance. A loud boom that we all felt as much as heard. Through the trees I saw a tall pillar of light.

Some of the people whooped. Some shouted, "Amen!"

"Reverend!" Danicka yelled. "Don't leave this flock without a shepherd."

I could smell death in the breath of the newly awakened serpents. Thousands of them from all directions. The flock huddled, pushing closer, with smaller children in the center.

"They shall take up serpents," Danicka said forcefully.

Hicks paused and turned, coming past the gas well to issue an edict to his people. "Do not listen to her. She is evil incarnate."

A teenage girl screamed. She clutched a wiry cottonmouth. It wriggled and twisted as the girl's mother tried to pull it off.

"Would she have cast the first stone? I want to assure this girl," she pointed at me, "that she only be judged by the faithful and the righteous."

"Stop it!" I yelled.

Another explosion shook us from the north. Bright light followed by a wall of sound.

A man closed his eyes and slowly dropped to his knees. I remembered him from last night. The guitar player. Hicks had used his mic. The man picked up a serpent in each hand and lifted them over his head as he'd done a thousand times before. The snakes spiraled and twisted their golden bodies around his wrists, twisting to lash out at the man's skin with wet fangs. He cried, whether for the pain of the venom or the pain of being forsaken, I'll never know.

"Return with me… We'll bring Katy and minister to her as Jesus did." Hicks stuttered, seemingly torn between his fear of being revealed as a fake and genuine compassion for the people that had followed him for so long. He backed toward the camp. Nobody followed.

As more cries of help and screams of pain rained down from the victims, Hicks had to shout louder and louder to be heard from across the field.

"Please, leave them be," I protested, but my voice didn't carry very far.

Hicks spoke, but a shrieking hiss emanating from the gas well drowned out his words. Hicks turned, but had no time to react to the explosion that followed. White light and a thunderous crack echoed off the trees that edged the forest. A rush of heat followed. I turned my head and twisted away from my captors, who shielded their own faces from the light and warmth.

The noise drew the remainder of the congregation from their cabins. A hundred or so, in various states of dress, watching the pillar of flame that rose hundreds of feet into the air. They had no idea that Elijah Clay Hicks had been on the receiving end.

Danicka turned to me and tearfully said, "And it came to pass, as he walked and talked, that a horse and chariot of fire appeared, parting him asunder, and Elijah went up by a whirlwind to heaven."

I practically choked on the scent of death that drifted through the air. By now the others had been shaken from the shock of Hicks's death and the appearance of the thousands of serpents that surrounded their brothers and sisters. Led by Boggs himself, they broke toward me. They looked mad.

"We're done here," Danicka said. "I'd run."

And the congregation swept past the pillar of fire like it was invisible. They swarmed to the rock pile and took up cobbles by the armful.

I turned and flung myself toward the trees. I pumped my fists and kept telling myself that no matter how much it hurt, I could always push myself to move faster. Rocks whooshed through the leaves. Rocks bounced off tree trunks with thuds. Heavy rocks rolled past my feet after hitting the ground short of me. Branches swatted my face with glossy leaves, so I put my arms up to shield myself. Within seconds, I came upon the electrified fence.

It looked exactly like the one on my pap's farm, except that it hung too low to crawl beneath. So I made a sharp left and ran along the clearing between the barbed wire and the forest. The dry air burned my throat and lungs. After a minute or two I heard a set of footsteps echoing my own. I never once turned and looked. Instead I broke hard left again to a greenbrier thicket. I stayed low to avoid the worst of the jaggers, just like Bruh Rabbit. I based my strategy on the assumption that my pursuers would be larger and wouldn't fare as well in the thorns.

Somebody barked my name. "Katy!"

I heard it loud and clear but did not stop. Bruh Rabbit knew better than to stop in the briar patch. My run had turned into a scramble. I spent more than half of it on my hands and knees.

"Katy Bear!" I knew better than to be deceived by familiarity.

Somebody crashed through the thicket with me, totally disregarding the thorns. I stood and put my arms across my face and broke into a full on sprint again. The jaggers caught my jacket and jeans, tangling me in their wiry brambles but my legs never stopped pumping. I rolled and twisted away from one thorny bush to another. When my hair got caught I jerked away. When the skin on my hands and ankles got pinched I closed my eyes and kept running. I welcomed the tiny stings of a hundred little cuts as an alternative to whatever they had planned for me back up the hill. As each jagger ripped away a little bit of skin I reminded myself that I still had my skin, and as long as I breathed, I'd find a way out.

"Katy, please." I heard something in his voice, but knew better.

A hand brushed my back and I found the speed I knew I could muster before they caught me again. At the end of the briar patch I dashed forward, but my pursuer hadn't been slowed one bit by my tactics. About twenty yards ahead I saw where a tree had fallen across the fence. I focused every ounce of life on that break. I envisioned myself on the other side. As soon as I jumped through I scanned the ground for rocks. He sounded close, and would catch me. But I'd find a rock, turn, and smash his head open.

"Please…" The voice came from right over my shoulder. Just like Freeze Tag in Pap's fields.

I saw a power line right-of-way that paralleled the fence and bolted for it. In the distance I saw a river, I didn't know which. Loose field stone had been piled up at the edges of the clearing. Over and over I told myself to swing until I saw blood. Swing until I saw blood.

My new rule number one.

Swing until I saw blood. Then keep swinging until he stopped moving. I saw my stone and lunged for it.

It felt cold, and fit into my hand like a baby doll head. When I rolled over he ran a step behind me. He fell to his knees. I raised the rock over my head.

"Katy! Hey, hey… It's okay." He grabbed my hand the moment I hesitated.

I looked at his face for a long time, but couldn't make sense of it.

"I saw the explosion."

It wasn't Preston or Pauly or anybody else I ever expected to see out here.

"You okay?"

"Ben?" *More deception?*

"Preston was all over it and he called me right after he called the police." Ben overloaded me with information to calm me. "Rachael and Jamie are on their way down. We got a way out of here."

He stood, pulling me off the ground. Then he took the rock from my hand. "Ain't you cuter than a sack of puppies?"

"Ben?" A wave of relief washed over me. I fought to control my emotions. I hugged my cousin, and rested my head against his cheek. He squeezed me and held me for what felt like forever.

Just before I could ask him about Preston a rumble grew from back at the camp.

"Motorcycles," he said, as he picked up his compound bow from the ground. "Have to move."

"Where is Preston?"

A chorus of hounds joined the pursuit.

"Got picked up by these guys."

"Well, where is he?"

"Don't know. We'll find him. Found you, didn't I?"

"How do you know he got picked up?"

"Tried to call him and heard his phone ring from a fake cop car back by the tent. They got Pauly too." Ben pulled Preston's phone out of his front pocket. "You got a little run left in you?"

I nodded, but he was already pulling me ahead. We worked our way along the edge of the power line right-of-way because the going was much faster than blundering through the forest. The terrain looked fairly level for a few hundred yards. Rocky, but level. Dirt bike paths that crisscrossed the right-of-way made the going a lot easier. But it brought the sounds of Boggs and his guys closer that much faster. Little by little the noise grew louder in the forest behind us. The leaves could no longer muffle the rumble of those tailpipes. In the distance I saw the tall stacks of an old power plant. *The real world.*

"We need to stay in the trees." Ben pulled me in a new direction. "Was there any sign of Preston and Pauly back at the camp?"

"Not that I saw. But I didn't see much. They had me in the revival tent last night. There were a lot of people there," I said, trying to keep up. "But there weren't that many structures, unless I didn't see everything."

"No, there wasn't much to see. I followed that police car back out a dirt road this way. Between the camp and the river."

"How'd you guys come in?"

"Main road. Parked in the trees on the other side. I want to find that dirt road though. That's the only place I have left to look."

Through the trees behind me I heard pickup trucks—at least two, maybe three—bouncing away from camp.

He said, "Trust me."

"How are we all going to make it back to the car if it's on the other side of the camp?"

"We're not leaving the way we came in."

Ben pushed me to the ground as two of the chrome-covered street bikes sputtered through the forest below. Not Boggs. Ashby and another one.

"That the road?"

"Stay low," Ben said as he walked ahead, answering my question.

The guys got off their bikes and walked toward a small, concrete shed. Ben handed me his bow, took a pistol out of his holster and broke into a sprint.

As soon as I figured Ben was right about Preston and Pauly waves of relief washed over me. I followed as fast as I could, quietly, as he halved the distance between himself and the little block building. Ashby still hadn't seen him.

Ben managed to get within ten yards without raising suspicion. He lifted his pistol and brought it down onto Ashby's hairless head. With one blow, the man dropped into the dirt. I ran toward the shed.

The other man shouted into his radio and raised an arm to defend himself. "The shed! They're at the shed!"

Ben hit him and the radio skittered across the gravel. Ben kicked him mercilessly until he no longer moved.

I arrived as Ben shot the lock off the door, covering my ears perhaps a moment too late. Pauly and Preston stood at the back of the tiny building, sweating and shirtless. I dropped Ben's bow, and ran past him to Preston.

He picked me up and kissed my neck and cheeks.

"Katy!" I hadn't seen him cry since the night Stu died.

I knew it was really him by the way his skin smelled. My eyes couldn't be trusted.

"Let's go," Ben said, handing Pauly his phone. "Call Andre. We got company."

"How'd you get this back?" Pauly asked as he dialed.

"Tried to call your sorry ass once I found Katy and I heard it ringing in that cop car. You couldn't tell they weren't real cops?"

"We could tell they had guns." Pauly followed Ben down the hill.

The trucks got closer. Another wave of motorcycles came with them.

I grabbed Preston's hand, holding him back for a second longer. I said, "Why did you call her?"

He looked at me, and without preparing an excuse, said, "Jane told me to. I'm sorry."

"What did she take, Preston? Tell me now because I don't want to find out later that all this was for nothing."

"What are you talking about?" Ben asked as he turned. "We ain't got time for this."

"Nothing. Preston didn't give her anything. I got you covered." Pauly held the phone up to his ear. "Andre? We're coming in hot. Keep an eye out for us."

I couldn't tear my eyes away from Pauly. Preston turned his back to me.

"Damn it, Preston. What did you do?" I pushed him away from me.

But he couldn't say anything.

"Yalla, yalla, kids. Let's move." Ben turned and started jogging again.

I walked past Preston and followed Ben down the hill.

"I'll fix everything, Katy. I promise I will." Preston let me walk ahead a few steps.

But there was always a price to pay. Nothing in the world was ever free. I knew that. Ben knew that. Preston should've known better.

"Let's pick it up?" Ben pointed at the hill where we'd crossed beneath the power lines.

Headlights cast long shadows through the forest. They swept from left to right as the lead pickup negotiated a sharp turn. The sun had set almost fully below the horizon. Enough light remained to see our footing, but it faded fast.

"Where are we going?"

"The river," Ben said. "Pauly's buddy is waiting."

I looked over my shoulder. Pauly and Preston were running side-by-side, a few yards back.

Ben said, "Take it easy on him, Katy. He almost died for you. He may not want to talk about it, so I will. He let us drown him this morning. That's what your mom said to do, so he did it. Without hesitation."

I slowed down, because I didn't want to talk to Ben anymore either.

When Preston caught up to me, I took his hand. I could feel the change in his touch as he recovered from the sting of what I'd said back at the shed. Pauly ran ahead a bit, so I called for him to slow down.

He turned, and I grabbed his hand too. The three of us followed Ben down the hill.

At once, from the forest all around, the sound of engines grew. Motorcycles and pickup trucks. Headlights swept the forest from left to right then from right to left just as quickly. Hounds came at us from the direction of the field. The three groups were converging right on us.

"Move it, boys and girl!" Ben yelled from farther down the slope. Through the trees ahead of him I could see the night sky reflecting off water. A placid, silvery pool undisturbed by wind or current. Peepers and bullfrogs called from dark nooks. The water returned their calls to the night.

The crack of a hunting rifle cut through it all.

"Oscar Mike!" Ben yelled. And after a moment or two, the peepers resumed calling as if nothing had happened. "Let's go."

Off to the far left I saw one of the trucks drift to water's edge. Headlights illuminated the entire pond. People disembarked from the bed of the truck as a second pickup pulled up behind the first. We followed Ben into black mud thick as tar.

A glow appeared over the water ahead of us. A dim blue light like a pilot light in a gas stove. "Fairy fire," I said, but nobody listened.

Ben leapt into the water first. "Stay in the shadows," he said. "Don't drift away from the bank. Pauly, call Andre and find out where him and his old man are."

"Are there alligators?" I said, pausing at the water's edge. More fairy fire appeared to our right like runway lights, leading us to safer waters.

"No, now get in."

Pauly let go of my hand and dug for his phone. I paused to wait for him in the cold water. My feet sank into the soft mud. The next step I took pulled my shoe off my right foot. The smell of decay rose from the bottom. Old mud. Rot.

Ben said, "But there are snapping turtles big enough to take your foot off. And giant catfish."

I looked back and saw the people from the church following us into the water. We had a good forty yards on them. Headlights shone through the thin, white baptismal gowns they wore, creating silhouetted arms and legs. The shapeless men and women swept across the water like some kind of foggy wave. "Oh, shit."

Preston and Pauly looked at the same time. From the earpiece of Pauly's phone I heard a man's voice. *Pauly, what's going on there?*

But Pauly couldn't speak. Neither could Preston. Not while Danicka took her place at the head of the pursuit. It wasn't so much that she'd come to lead them. It was how she led them.

"Fucking go," Preston said, pulling me ahead.

In a way, I wanted them to verify what I saw. That Danicka walked on the water ahead of what remained of Hicks's church. As the men and women stumbled over submerged logs and tree roots, Danicka glided. Like she was on ice skates. Preston's and Pauly's reactions made it very real. Preston pulled me into deeper water. The chill made my breath catch in my throat.

"Paul." Her voice came from everywhere, almost as if from the air itself. I released Preston's hand to cover my ears.

Pauly stopped.

"Get him!" Ben yelled. He shined a small headlamp into the water ahead of us. Waving it back and forth over the black surface. In the darkness I heard the buzz of a small motor, like a dirtbike.

Preston retreated a few steps and grabbed Pauly's arm. "C'mon, brother."

But Pauly could not look away from Danicka.

The water got warmer as she moved closer. My chill had been replaced by warm comfort.

A crash of branches and limbs grew from the trees along the shore. Small yellow beams from a pair of flashlights cut through the distance in a way the people in the water couldn't. Boggs yelled, "I'll come at you where you sleep, girl."

"Pauly!" I yelled.

Their flashlights skimmed the surface, looking for us. The beams stopped when they found us, and Boggs squeezed off three quick shots. Once Boggs realized he hadn't drawn any blood, he resumed his pursuit.

"Saint Paul told us not to act out of self-centered motivation or vain arrogance. He said to humbly put the concerns of others before your own." The serpents Danicka held in her hands danced spiral shadows in the white glare of the cold headlights. As the rest of the church closed the distance between us, I could see that they, too, carried serpents. But instead of the writing masses Danicka held, the people bore vipers with fangs buried deep into the flesh of their wrists and forearms.

I heard a sharp hiss and turned in time to see Ben nocking an arrow into his old bow. A tinkle of glass accompanied the darkening of a pickup truck's headlight, unbalancing the long shadows cast by our pursuers.

"Shoot the rest!" I said, without quite meaning too.

"Katy," Ben said. "I got this. Head to the boat."

Preston pulled me and Pauly past Ben, deeper into the darkness. From the shoreline Boggs thrashed through the trees.

Ben let loose another arrow, but missed. He ran to catch up to us. The sloshing made it difficult to hear anything else. He held his light up, shining it ahead of us.

Something moved past my calf and I screamed. "Sorry," I said as I spun, looking for movement in the water around me. And I saw it in the dusky half-light. Slender fins slicing the pearlescent surface. Backwater fish frantically swimming away from Danicka and the warming water. A flurry of frogs and turtles and snakes threw themselves onto the shoreline. Muskrats and other rodents fumbled through the darkness, scurrying to get onto land.

"Andre!" Ben yelled, waving the light over his head.

Shots rang out from Boggs's position on the right bank. Stray rounds ripped through fresh green leaves. Random, inaccurate, splashes formed in the water near us.

Once again Pauly stopped. Preston ran back to grab his arm and pull him ahead.

"Preston!" Ben and I yelled at the same time.

Pauly twisted free of Preston's grip and stepped backward, away from us.

"Ben, help me," Preston said. His voice quivered with fear.

Ben handed me his bow as his rushed back to get Pauly. Ahead, I could see a johnboat drifting through the channel. The beam from a dim flashlight washed over me. I waved my arms.

"Paul, finding you is an absolute inevitability." Danicka moved faster now, leaving the church behind. "It's time to embrace the suffering. Suffering is the root of hope, and you, Paul Pallini, are going to need all the hope you can muster."

Ben pulled his pistol from the shoulder holster and fired round after round into the people from the church. Every time one dropped into the water more light streamed across the pond from the trucks parked on shore. Ben emptied the clip and ejected it into the water. He pulled another from a pocket and slapped it into his weapon. "Pauly, we ain't leaving you, no matter what this bitch says."

A flow of vocalization came from the remaining members of the church. Fifty tongues, maybe more, flapping to the stream of consciousness in their heads. But these sounds were unlike the nonsensical tongues I heard last night.

Ben fired at the lights in the trees. I covered my ears as the rapid-fire shots turned into one long ringing sound in my head.

"Pauly," I yelled.

But he'd begun retreating from Preston and Ben. I wanted to run ahead with them to bring Pauly back, but a voice from behind me instructed me to, "Get into the boat."

The tongues that our pursuers spoke came in unison. Every man, woman, and child said the exact same thing at the exact same time. "A potom cert ho vzal..." over and over.

I yelled, "Ben, shoot her!"

"Who the fuck you think I'm shooting at?"

"Just get on the boat," Pauly said, walking toward Danicka.

"You boys get over here now," the other man on the boat called out. "Come on now, girl. You're first."

Hands tugged Ben's bow out of my hands. The water felt like lukewarm tea.

"Katy, get in!" Preston said, handing me our phones.

"Not without you."

Ben said, "We're coming, but somebody has to be first."

With the boat sitting out there in the water like that, Boggs now had a bigger target. The shots came closer. One punched through the thin aluminum hull as they pulled me in.

The man with his hand on the outboard motor's tiller turned the boat away from Preston and Ben.

"Go and get them!" I yelled.

The old man at the bow said, "So they can kill us all?"

"Are you okay with them only killing one of us? Because that's what's going to happen if we don't go up there and get them."

But he wouldn't turn the boat.

"Ben! Shoot into the trees. We're coming to pick you up."

The old man got low in the bow. "She's right. I'll lay down some cover." He handed me the flashlight. "Navigate."

From beneath a bench he pulled out an oilcloth sack. He quickly unzipped it and removed an old, well-cared for, sawed-off double barrel. "Most of the time we pull in catfish or the occasional carp. Every now and then you get a redneck cracker at the end of your line. They listen better when you got one of these in your hands."

He threw two shells in and fired immediately. Bits of leaves drifted down to the water.

Boggs yelled, "Kill those lights," and continued to fire random shots in our direction.

The old man flicked the spent shells into the water and reloaded. The boat sped toward Preston and Pauly. The old man fired again, but I noticed he couldn't take his eyes off Danicka.

"Watch where you're shooting there, George," Ben said. "Don't pay her no mind, okay?"

The old man reloaded.

"Ben, right here." I reached out for him as we drifted past. He handed me his bag.

"Don't be afraid to use this," Ben said as handed me his pistol. "Preston, grab his arm."

Pauly tried to twist away from Preston's grasp. He lunged forward, but Ben caught him by the wrist.

"Let me go! Motherfucker let me go! I want to deal with this."

George said, "Get in the boat, son. Nadhima'll help y'all take care of this. Let us get you home now."

"Fucking stop it!" Pauly yelled. Spit came from his mouth when he said it. His eyes looked crazy. Didn't look anything at all like Pauly.

George fired two more rounds into the trees. The only shots returned came from the beach were the trucks were.

Danicka said, "For everything there is a season. Paul, this is yours."

Instead of reloading George leaned over to help pull Pauly into the boat.

As Pauly struggled, Ben grabbed his pistol and unloaded the rest of the clip into Danicka, now only a few yards away. I'd seen him shoot crows with a BB gun from a hundred yards out and I know he never missed. He tossed the pistol to me and went underwater. When he came back up he had Pauly by the knees, pushing him right into the boat. He coughed as he yelled, "Hold him down."

Ben followed him in. As he turned to grab Preston, he shouted, "Go, Andre! Go!"

Pauly kicked and squirmed from the floor between the benches. He cussed and bit. George said, "It's over now, son. Y'all need to calm yourself."

Preston took his hand and said, "We can do this, man. I promisepromisepromise I will take care of this. Please believe me, brother."

"I am not your fucking brother. And don't you ever make that mistake again." He sat up and pushed Preston away. "I'm a dead man walking. You should've let me end it because you ain't the ones suffering. I'm the one who ain't going to be able to sleep and I'm the one who's going to spend the rest of his life looking over his shoulder. So fuck you for saving me and fuck you for thinking I give a shit about waking up tomorrow morning."

Weighted down with all these people, the boat moved slowly through the twisted backwater channels that crawled toward the main flow of water. The breeze made me shiver, and Preston sat close to keep me warm. Nobody said anything once we were in the clear. This most certainly didn't feel like a win.

Andre steered cautiously through the backwater to keep from hitting stumps. Ben and George took turns at the bow, shouted out directions. But as we got closer to the river the wind picked up, and bright lights from a power plant, like the one upriver from Morgantown, comforted me after two days of darkness. I basked in the distantly warm glow as we passed. The sound of the outboard drowned out the noise from the peepers calling out from the shoreline. I would've preferred that sound to the sound of nobody speaking to each other.

After we passed the power plant the sky grew darker. Spring constellations, like Gemini and Leo hung low in the sky. Venus dipped beneath the tree tops shortly after we reached our top speed. I saw one shooting star and one satellite.

Then, as we approached a bridge I saw headlights, cars travelling to and from dark destinations in the low hills beyond the riverbanks. They reminded me that people lived here without wishing harm to others. They only wanted to work and cash their checks and go to sleep in a house where the roof didn't leak. I tried to let these thoughts be the ones I'd take to bed with me when I finally closed my eyes in a warm room.

And they would've been good thoughts.

But the motorcycles that sparked to life as we passed, with their four headlights shining down on us, stole that from me. When I closed my eyes, knowing that this was far from over, those were the only lights I saw.

THE SECOND REVELATION
OF PRESTON BLACK

CHAPTER SEVEN

You don't know shit about hard times,
With your hand-me-down Volvo and prep school rhymes.
You can't go back to nickels when you've been living on dimes.
No, you don't know shit about hard times.

"Hard Times" Music and Lyrics by Preston Black

John Lennon said, "Are you bloody mad?"

The phone only had a chance to ring once. I knew the calls and texts were going to start when Dani showed up. Just didn't expect them to start at sunrise.

"Have you learned nothing? Even stoned out of me head I've never mucked it up like this. I blame meself for thinking you'd grow up. But you're thicker now than you were a year ago. Like you got a head full of pudding." Lennon spoke with more of a fatherly tone than I remembered. Didn't sound at all like the John I knew.

And because I didn't want Katy to wake up, I didn't say a thing to defend myself.

"Look, man. You're halfy-halfy in a pickle now, aren't you? Stop with the whinging. The world isn't analog anymore. Why do you insist on acting like it is?"

I bit my tongue while I made my way to the front door, past the kitchen and pool table and bar. Simoneaux raised his hand in a good morning salute. I snaked between the tables and chairs, past the drum kit that slept on a small riser next to an oversized PA system. I noticed a dim neon cross hanging above the drum kit, and I realized at that very moment that this juke joint transformed into Andre's church come Sunday morning. Light rain tapped the corrugated tin roof and the blue and green glass on Simoneaux's front yard bottle tree. When I opened the door to step onto the porch, the breeze that greeted me felt like the first air I ever breathed. Since the door would lock if I let it shut behind me, I kept a foot inside on that old hardwood. As soon as I figured

154

I had my privacy I said, "Look, man. How could I know what to do? I asked Ben and he asked Katy's mum and she told me what to do. I didn't invent all this."

The door opened and Simoneaux looked at me. I held my hand over the phone to ask him to give me a minute.

"Can't protect you out here." He grabbed my shirt and pulled me back through the door, waggling his finger with his other hand. "Best stay inside, son."

Through the earpiece, John Lennon said, "Look, if you're planning on tiptoeing through life with your head up your bum I don't have a whole lot left to say to you anyway."

"Don't be like that, please." But he'd hung up already. "Fuck."

"Watch your mouth, all right? I don't mind the language when I'm pouring, but I ain't going to tolerate it at seven in the morning." Simoneaux walked across the swamp ash dance floor and back into the kitchen. "Come on now, give me a hand."

I looked at my phone thinking maybe I didn't blow it with John. But I knew his temper. When he finished, he finished. I scrolled through the rest of the texts I got last night. Strummer. Two texts from Lennon. One from Cliff Burton and one from Jerry Garcia. There were three from a number I didn't recognize. I opened the first of them and saw, <Baybrah, looks like it's high time we pow-wow...> but Simoneaux's impatience kept me from reading the rest.

A bunch of black-and-white photos hung on the wall that led back to the kitchen and office. Simoneaux at varying ages with all kinds of musicians. Old black guys with Gibson Les Pauls and ES-355s. The only man I recognized besides Simoneaux was Son House. The rest looked almost as important though. I meant to ask him about them, but as soon as I came through the swinging kitchen door he handed me a pint glass and pointed to a mound of white dough he'd rolled out on the countertop. He said, "Biscuits."

The proper technique eluded me, so he clasped my hand in his and slammed the rim of the glass into the dough, showing me how to make perfect little moons. "Don't skimp on the butter."

He watched as I twisted the glass and pulled out a perfect little baby biscuit. He smiled as I slathered melted butter all over before setting it on the baking sheet. He turned, and after a weird silence I figured I'd ask him about the Son House picture. But as soon as I opened my mouth he cut me off. "Going to tell you a bit about this Hoodoo now, so you can wrap your head around it. You keep on listening while you cut those."

I nodded, even though he'd turned his back.

"About sixty—fifty years ago I ended up in the old 'colored' jail down in Thibodaux. Manager of Rouse's says he saw me putting cigarettes into my pocket, 'cept when the police showed up my pockets was empty. Maybe it happened sixty years ago. Anyway, my mama's sitting outside the jail and this Hoodoo stumbles up the street. He looks at her and says, 'Your boy's about to become a scapegoat for every unsolved crime in Lafourche Parish, you know that?' Course she knows. Why the hell else she be sitting out there?"

Simoneaux wiped his hands on an old rag and brought another pint glass over to the dough. He started cutting biscuits right along with me as he went on. "Says to my mama he'd get me out for fifty dollars. Fifty may as well be a thousand, right? But she goes into town and pawns a silver cross her daddy hid away for hard times. She figured times weren't going to get no harder than this. She gave that old Hoodoo the money and next thing I know this mojo bag come right through the window of my cell. He hollered at me, telling me to tie that coin 'round my ankle and chew on those hawthorn leaves and ginger root like a rat in the cane. He told me to spit that juice all along the cell door and in the corners, and I chewed until my jaw wouldn't move no more and hid that sack down round my nuts so them guards couldn't find it come pat-down. When trial came I went to face charges on ten or eleven different offences. I prayed to Saint Valérie and Saint Vitalis that morning to be safe. Let me tell you, that jury was full of some of the reddest necks you ever saw. Real Sons of the Confederacy types. They had me convicted as soon as they seen me walk in. But you know what?"

He stopped.

"I'm listening."

"A spirit appeared in that courtroom as soon as them proceedings started. A murder victim. Said one of the jurors beat him to death in the cane then burned the fields. Lead the sheriff right to the remains."

I nodded.

"Don't play no games with me, son."

"I'm not. I totally believe you. I know what it feels like."

"It appeared in the *Daily Comet* if you think I'm shitting you. You want to hear the best part?"

"What's that?"

"It happened April 28—Saint Valérie's feast day." He grabbed a bottle of rye whiskey from a shelf above the sink, flipped his pint glass over and poured a generous four fingers into it. "Who got that Hoodoo now?"

"You do?"

"That's right I do. That's why you're here. The way some folks see it, you fucked up by going down to that particular intersection. But I know men who'd done a lot worse for love. Ain't a thing wrong with that. You listen to me and I'll keep you and your girl safe." Simoneaux pulled a yellow legal pad out of a drawer and started scribbling.

"What about my brother?"

He wrote for a few minutes while I waited for an acknowledgement. Finally, he looked up at me and said, "Well, a lot of that depends on him."

He put the list on the counter and left. I read it—*1. wash dishes 2. marinate pork tenderloin 3. start a pot of red beans cooking.* He'd scribbled out a recipe below. Not a single item on his list had anything to do with keeping me or Katy or Pauly safe. But I didn't mind. Being told what to do was a hell of a lot easier than making mistakes on your own.

Katy came in as I finished the dishes and asked what I needed help with. I told her exactly what Simoneaux told me. Her hair was pulled back in a ponytail and she wore jeans and a little grey Uniontown Red Raiders T-shirt she found in my closet the day I moved out of my apartment. The girl who'd left it was a featured twirler the year WVU won the Orange Bowl, but Katy never asked where it came from.

When she tied an apron around her waist, I saw that the bite marks on her arm had purpled a bit, but looked like they were healing.

She soaked the beans in a stock pot, then started the sausage and ham hocks in another big pot. I watched her chop onions and a bell pepper. "Katy?"

"Preston?" she replied, without ever looking up from the cutting board.

Instead of asking what I wanted to ask, I said, "How you feeling?"

"Good." She slid part of the onion into her hand and dropped it into the pot. "And scared. But mostly good."

"About all this…" I said, not really sure how I wanted to follow up. "You know, I never wanted to be alone. I saw Pauly and my mom pray and I prayed too, not because I believed, but because I wanted to believe and be part of something. Part of me had to know there was more out there than only what I saw with my own eyes, and part of me had to know I'd see my mother again. But praying did make my life better. It didn't calm me or make me feel closer to God—it forced me to rely on Pauly and my friends because it left me feeling so empty. I still hope there's something out there, but these people—the ones that took you—I hope they ain't right about what it is."

I slid my hands around her waist and kissed her neck and cheek. At first all her muscles tensed up. As soon as I felt that, I pulled away, but she grabbed my hand and pulled it around her waist. I said, "This never should've happened."

I could feel her smile. So I spun her toward me and kissed her. She set the knife on the counter behind her and put her hands around my neck. I could smell the onion on her fingertips, but didn't care. She said, "This summer we'll run away. We'll go to Outer Banks and get a house and write songs all night long. I'll get that wine you like and we'll eat hush puppies and crab cakes and gain twenty pounds. We'll get nice and brown in the sun and sleep in. And everybody will say all our new songs are weak because we didn't suffer enough and we'll just laugh. Right?"

"Sounds like a plan." I went in for another kiss.

She turned her head, giving me her cheek instead of her lips. "Doesn't it? You say it like you don't really mean it."

"No, I mean it. And I'm ready. I want to focus on what we got in front of us, okay? Like getting you home."

"What do you mean?"

"We need to get out of here. Your mom and Jamie are coming down to help us sort everything out and take us back."

"Why? Because I spent a day at the Reverend Hicks's Camp for Wayward Girls? We haven't cancelled a show yet and we aren't about to start cancelling shows now."

"Katy…"

"What, Preston?" She clenched a fist and held it against her hip. "You start running now and you know what you're going to end up with? Sore feet. That's it. You said you'd do anything for me, right?"

I laughed. "You want to cash that one in right now?"

"By my accounts it's a lifetime supply. There ain't no 'that one' about it. It's time to put your dukes up, boy."

Pauly's Uncle Louie used to say that to me when I was little. He was the biggest man I'd ever know until I saw him on a hospital bed after open heart surgery. "I know. I already have a plan."

She clasped her hands behind my neck and rested her head against my chest. "When were you planning on telling me about this plan?"

I took a deep breath because I knew of only one way to clear Pauly's slate and free everybody from Dani's tangled words in one fell swoop. *And that it would hurt.* "Never."

I kissed Katy's forehead and cupped my hand beneath her chin.

She kissed me back, and then pulled away.

I said, "What?"

"You need to take care of your brothers." She wiped her hands on her apron and grabbed two pint glasses from a rack above the big stainless dishwasher.

"Water. Lots and lots of water. And don't let either one of them leave. Especially Pauly. Mr. Simoneaux said tie him down if you have to, but don't let him out of this building." She pointed to a plastic pitcher by the sink. "And tell Ben that the West Virginia contingency will be here soon."

I filled the pitcher with tap water and backed into the hall. As the door swung the other way, Katy added, "Ibuprofen's in my purse."

In the rear of Simoneaux's juke joint, across from the office where Katy and I slept, sat a storeroom. Through the little window I could see cans of beans and cases of beer and booze. I flipped the light switch, stepped inside, and waved off the acidy/sweet stench of whiskey puke.

Ben's bedroll leaned against a shelf, unrolled, next to his PTSD drugs—Zoloft, Klonopin, Paxil. He slept on the floor beneath it, curled up into a little ball. Pauly slept farther back, sprawled out like he'd been shot. His shoes were off, one arm covered his face, and his foot rested on Ben's hand. Between them sat a bottle of Jack, half-full with the lid screwed on. When I prodded Ben with my toe, I saw the second bottle— the empty one—beneath Pauly's head like a pillow. "Up and at 'em, sunbeams."

"You feel froggy? Then jump." Ben covered his face with his arm. "Or get out."

"You do whatever you want. I just need Pauly."

"Well, I'm taking care of him," Ben said. "Gave him a Klonopin."

"Thanks. I can see that. You didn't literally push him off the wagon, did you?"

"I hopped. I couldn't think of any other way to wrap my brain around what happened last night. If I stop to think about it I'm gone, going to totally lose it, man," Pauly growled from beneath his arm. "So I'm going to hop again. All day long. Like I'm in a fucking bounce castle."

"A puke-scented bounce castle?" I slid the vomit-filled trash-can out into the hall with my foot. "Like a redneck Kennywood. You supposed to mix antidepressants with alcohol?"

"Who made you den mother anyway?" Ben sat up real slow and rested his face in his palms. "Correct me if I'm wrong, but the other day it was you on the floor, right?"

"Yeah, I know. But I'm trying to make it right. You don't have to help, but you ain't got to stand in my way either. Besides, your dad and Rachael are on their way and we all have to give statements. Coffee's on in the kitchen and I'll keep running water back to you guys."

Ben shook his head, dismissing me just like that.

"What?" I said. "We got Katy, which was supposed to be the hard part. Right? Getting her out seemed like a virtual impossibility but we got her. And now she's out there in the kitchen making beans. You did that. With Pauly and me. We got her, man."

Ben said, "Then why does this all feel like ten pounds of shit in a five pound bag?"

Pauly watched, like he hoped I had the answers he needed too.

"Because we got loose ends to tie up. We're going to spend a lot of time answering questions. They found your Jeep already, so they been to the camp."

"Okay. Give me a few minutes."

"Pauly?"

"Yeah, man. But stop being such a fucking jag off. Let me go back to bed, okay? Been a while since I felt like this and the body don't recover like it used to."

"You ain't going to go running off or anything?"

"Stop being so nebby, Grandma. I'm going to sleep, think about how I ain't got a fucking thing to look forward to. Later I'll call my sponsor and tell him I made a deal with the devil."

I thought about the plan I'd put together in my head, a way to end all this in one shot, and said, "You may want to hold off on that, man."

"Why's that?"

Ben stood, stretched, and walked into the hall. "He ain't going to do nothing stupid, Pres. Just let him work this out in his head, will you?"

"We got this, Pauly. Okay? I took care of this once and I can do it again. As far as I know I'm the only person who can and I'm telling you I'll take care of this. Trust me."

He put his arm back over his face. "Hit the light, please."

I flipped the switch and shut the door. When I turned, the sight of Ben still standing there gave me a bit of a start. "Jesus, man."

He pushed me down the hall. "He talked in his sleep all night. About dead people. Must've woke him up from nightmares six or seven times." He grabbed my arm as I walked away. "What the hell is Pauly talking about? Is this real?"

I shrugged and tried to pull away. Ben wouldn't let go of my arm.

"Maybe your dad can explain it to you. I spent a year talking about this to anybody who'd listen and him and Katy are the only ones who believed me." I put my head down and went back toward the kitchen. "Until now."

Simoneaux had said that, "Cuttin' your own switch is the price of forgettin' your manners" before he went outside to greet Jamie and Rachael and Chloey.

Which I knew, because Pauly's grandma raised us the same way. No matter how you chose you ended up black and blue.

Lesson learned.

We watched their arrival from behind the buzzing blue and red neon tubes of the "Dixie Beer 45" sign that hung in the big front window. Our punishment kept us confined to the relative safety of Simoneaux's juke joint. Grounded against temptation.

But Rachael didn't spend much time outside. She burst through the door and greeted Katy with a long embrace. Katy's little sister, Chloey, came in on Rachael's heels and the three of them held each other for a long time. I still stunk of shame, and ducked into the kitchen like I hadn't heard Rachael ask where I was.

"Preston!" Chloey shouted. "Get out here, scaredy cat."

With my head hanging down I went back out, even though I felt like I didn't belong in that unit. Felt like it'd been my responsibility to keep Katy safe, and that I'd failed. And when Rachael pulled me into the circle with her girls a wave of guilt hit me.

Chloey said, "Does somebody need his belly rubbed?"

I relaxed as Rachael held me tighter. She smelled like home, like she'd accidentally brought a bit of the mountain spring down in her coat and scarf. Rushing water and lonely winter birds. When she finally let me go, she said, "Elaine packed biscuits and elderberry jam if you kids want any."

I shook my head.

"Mom's cousin, Elaine Collins? From Boone?" Katy exhaled slowly.

I still didn't follow.

"Jesus, Preston, we stayed with her after that workshop at Appalachian State? She had that cat that ate pizza and spaghetti?"

"Oh, yeah. My head still ain't right." Through the side window I watched Jamie nod while Simoneaux showed him the bottle tree out front, pointing to the blue bottles specifically.

"Going to take a lot more than a bottle tree to stop what's coming," Katy said, before leading her mom and sister to the back to get freshened up.

"You think?" I said, still watching, wondering if it could get worse before it got better. I knew it could always get worse.

While Katy got back to chopping onions and garlic in the kitchen, with Chloey at her hip, yapping, Simoneaux told me and Ben to stack the tables and chairs on the stage. Then, before stepping back out to help Jamie carry stuff in from the car, Simoneaux added, "Put a real quick shine on that floor while you're at it. Dust mop's in the closet."

"That's all you," Ben said, before disappearing behind the bar as soon as Simoneaux left. He grabbed a bottle of something brown and drifted toward the hallway.

Thinking that he kept Pauly from sobering up ate at me, especially since I felt like Pauly needed something more right now. "Ben. That all for you?"

"Half of it is." He turned toward the door.

"I thought we agreed to let him sober up?"

"Don't you go getting your gussies up. Besides, I don't remember agreeing to that." He pushed the door open and drifted back to the storeroom as Katy came through carrying a big tray of clean highball glasses.

"Your cousin's starting to piss me off." I walked over to the closet and grabbed the dust mop.

"Tell him about it." She stacked the glasses onto a shelf beneath the bar.

"For real? That's your answer?"

"Yup. He's pouting and Pauly's scared. And drinking is better than fighting, which you know is what Ben wants. He came home less than six months before Jane died, then all that with the Lewises happened, so my guess is that a big part of him never left Jalalabad. He pops those antidepressants and anti-anxiety meds like they're Gummy Bears. There's a thin line between PTSD and addiction." She walked to the end of the bar, sliding the tray along the top as she went. "But his attitude is going to come in real handy over the next few days."

I met her at the end.

"Listen," she said, laying her head on my chest. "Right now Ben is taking care of Pauly, and by extension, of himself. That's where I want them both. Out of our hair. I'll tell them when they need to be on their toes. And you'll help me make sure they are."

"I don't want trouble with Ben."

"Then don't give any. You look at him, and say, 'Ben, give me a hand with this.' Don't order him and don't ask him."

"And when he ignores me?"

"Then you can say 'please.' It's up to you. This is the kind of stuff I deal with all the time. Club owners and drink tabs. Insurance on the rentals. Deposits on the gear. Look at it as a promotion." She patted my shoulder.

"Well, if you're giving me your old job what are you going to be doing?"

"Preston..." She crossed her arms. "I'm doing my best to make sure everybody leaves here in one piece. That's why I want Ben and Pauly in the back—drinking, if need be—and you watching everything Jamie and Simoneaux do. Tonight's going to be a long one. You're going to be front and center for all of it."

"You really think they're going to find us here?"

"I think the fact that you asked me that shows how important it is you stick with Jamie and Simoneaux. Mom and Chloey are going to babysit Pauly and Ben tonight."

"And what about you?"

"I'm going to be wherever you are. I'm never leaving you again."

"I'm sorry, Katy. I really am." I pulled her head back to my shoulder.

She resisted a bit before closing her eyes and giving in. Her tears warmed my shirt. I rested my cheek on her head. The thought of her being violated sparked something dark in me. I did my best to hide my rage, but the way she grabbed my fist, and slid her fingers into mine, told me I hadn't done such a great job.

"He's dead, babe. I saw him blown into heaven with my own eyes." She sniffled.

"He wasn't the only one. Boggs?"

"They don't matter right now. They're ants and we're about to have a lion problem."

And before I could say anything else, Simoneaux came through the front door with my Tele and the road case with our mics in it. He pointed at the beer taps and said, "Darling, would you be so kind to pass that big box of kosher over to your man?"

"Sure thing, Mr. Simoneaux." She handed it to me with a smirk. "See? A promotion."

"Just Simoneaux, Miss Stefanic. After Preston cleans the floor like I asked him to, he's going to pour a little pile of salt in each corner, then wait for me before doing anything else." Simoneaux wiped his brow in exaggerated frustration. "Think he can do that?"

"Want me to ask?" Katy smiled. "Can you manage, my love?"

"Yeah. Clean the floor. Then pour salt all over it."

And when I finished doing what Simoneaux'd asked, he went into the dead center of the dance floor and poured the rest of the salt into a neat little mound. He said, "Preston, go on into the back and get me four cans of lye from the storage room."

Since avoiding the storage room had been part of my plan, especially with Ben holed up in there, I dragged my feet down the hall before stopping and listening at the door. When I didn't hear anything, I flipped the light on and pushed the door open.

"Damn it, Ben..."

The floor was empty. Ben's shit had been removed. The office, where Katy and I'd spent the night, was unoccupied too. I whipped around, rushed back up the hall, and busted through the kitchen door.

First thing I saw was Pauly with his head in his hand sitting behind a ginormous plate of biscuits and gravy. Ben sat next to him, his mouth full. Chloey stood right over Ben, chirping about the pictures in her phone. Ben looked up at me. Pauly didn't.

"What's wrong, honey?" Rachael asked from behind the wall of steam that rose from a pot. Smelled like cayenne and garlic.

But I felt guilty for assuming they'd run off and said, "What the hell's lye?"

"They use it for hominy and a bunch of other stuff. Probably comes in a can." Katy pushed through the door. "C'mon."

Ben watched as I backed out of the kitchen, eyeing me suspiciously as he sopped his plate with a biscuit. As the door swung shut, he said, "Don't let it hit you where the good Lord split you."

Katy grabbed my arm and pulled me down the hall. "Preston, he's blowing off steam, okay?" She opened the door, found the lye and held a can up for inspection.

"Get the hell out of here."

"Yep." She said, "Red Devil Lye," and went back to the kitchen.

When I got to the front Simoneaux was placing another armload of our gear on the stage. Jamie came in from the cold with Katy's fiddle and a few mic booms.

"What's all this?" I asked.

"Don't you worry about that." Simoneaux took the lye from me. "We'll get to the music as soon as we finish 'evil-proofing' the house."

"'Evil-proofing?'"

"Yup," he said, passing the lye off to Andre.

After that, everything happened a lot faster. Jamie went into the yard with Andre to bury a Red Devil can in each corner, labels facing inward, for protection. Simoneaux took a wooden crate filled with tall blue bottles out to an old tree on the corner and placed them on the dead limbs, making a second bottle tree. Rachael worked at the back door, scrawling inscriptions into the lintel with chalk and coal ash and prepping the storeroom and office with witch balls and bundles of ash twigs.

Since I couldn't leave, I sat on the edge of the stage and watched Nadhima out on the dance floor, as she connected my piles of salt with chalk lines. She had all kind of accoutrements in a circle around the mound of salt in the center: a red candle, a green candle, and a black one, a silver cross with some kind of vine or root bound to it with twist ties, a string of rattlesnake vertebra with the rattle still attached at the end, a skull from a small rodent, like an opossum or groundhog, and two sachets of scented powders—one that smelled like rose petals and one that smelled like feet. While I watched, she opened the sachets, bent down, and sprinkled a bit of powder from each onto the floor at her feet. Before standing she made a cross in the powder with her pinkie finger. When she caught me watching, she called me over with a wave of her long finger.

"Put this into your pocket, hear me? Don't take it out and don't let it go through the wash, neither."

I stuffed the rough patch of snake-skin into my front pocket.

"And this here's your hot foot powder and goofer dust," she said, passing me a sachet. "Go on over to the door and make a big old 'X' there too. Just like this one. That'll trick 'em real good."

So I did exactly what Nadhima asked as she lit the candles and spilled more powder across the floor. Just before heading back to the center of the room, I helped Jamie get my Fender Twin through the door and over to the stage. Jamie said, "Go ahead and start setting up. Like you're playing a show. I want to watch Ms. Nadhima."

"Why am I setting up?"

"Because Simoneaux says you're playing a show." He patted my shoulder and commandeered my old spot at the edge of the stage.

When Nadhima threw powder into the candles, green sparks rose from the flames.

I choked on the smoke as I looked for a power outlet. The smell hit me as I plugged in, and I gagged a little. It smelled like old laundry. And by "old laundry" I mean mostly dirty socks and underwear. Jamie sat there watching everything. I swore he didn't blink once the whole time. Simoneaux came back in, pulled the blinds down and flipped the light switches, transforming the juke joint into one of those places where time never crawled forward ever again. He gave Nadhima a wide berth while she worked.

I miked my amp and Pauly's and set up the vocal mics and the mic for Katy's fiddle. When I finished, I sat on the edge of the small stage with Jamie. Figured he'd tell me when the time came to get out of the way. It had gotten a lot warmer in the place since we woke up. And I grew more tired. And bored.

As the noise and pyrotechnics drew down, Simoneaux asked if I'd intended to eat.

"Didn't plan on it."

"Don't know when you're going to eat again. When we get back I'm open for dinner. I want y'all up on that stage."

"Playing for the dinner crowd? Not sure they're going to like our kind of music."

"Your kind of music?" he said, as he grabbed my wrist. "What kind is that?"

He twisted my hand palm up and placed an old silver dime into it.

He said, "Only one kind of music. I ain't never heard a disc jockey say 'shut your radio off because this song is only for a certain kind of people.'"

"Yeah, I didn't mean that."

"Just busting your balls. Put that into your pocket and don't take it out. That there's a Mercury leap year, okay? You want to bet on a slow horse you better have the odds in your favor, right?"

I studied it for a second and put it into my pocket, right next to the snakeskin.

"Tell that cousin of yours to set the tables and chairs back up out here. Tell him don't pay those lines no mind." Before I could reply, he said, "Me and your uncle are going to finish Dhima's Drivin' Away Spell by dropping some of her things off over at the cemetery. You kids get ready to play. My nephew, Calvin, works the bar, so y'all don't have to worry about none of that. George lends a hand sometimes, but felt his time would be best spent at home tonight, praying. And Sissy and her brother, Marcus, come in at five to work the kitchen. All I want you kids doing is making music, hear me? Get 'em dancing. Music is power and it's the only defense you got. When I get back I'll join y'all. Going to be a long night."

"That's what I keep hearing."

"Make no mistake."

So I ate some of the pork with red beans and rice, washed up and changed clothes then ate a little more. When I came back out to the front of the house I saw people at the tables. Not my crowd. For the first time in a long time the idea of picking up my Tele scared me. Calvin saw me standing there, waiting, and gave me a nod.

I took a seat at the bar next to Andre and a guy wearing a Crimson Tide basketball jersey over a grey T-shirt. He drank Tanqueray.

"Jameson?"

Calvin shook his head. He looked a little like Simoneaux, but much thicker, like he spent all his time off lifting weights.

"Bourbon, then," I said as I scanned the labels. "Whatever."

"This mean you're about to get up there?" He set a pint glass in front of me and poured three fingers into it. "Uncle Simon said not to let you sit on your ass all night."

The stage bathed in the golden glow of several recessed spotlights. Nothing big or fancy. Just a riser and a bunch of instruments and a dim cross made out of glass tubes. One older lady in the crowd wore a fancy hat with a peacock feather in the band. Two older men in suits had their porkpie hats respectfully perched on the back of their chairs. Younger, less distinctively dressed people filled out the rest of the place. Cigarette smoke drifted toward the stage lights.

"I'm supposed to remind you that you have a job to do. My uncle said he didn't ask for this 'shit-storm'—his words, not mine. He said you got to start working that mojo."

"One more," I said, before finishing my drink. "Andre, would you mind seeing where Katy and Pauly are at?"

Calvin poured as I stood. On my way to the stage I ran through lyrics and chords, trying to think of songs they might want to hear. As soon as I set foot on the riser the air got thick, like everybody in the joint stopped eating and drinking at once. I flipped my amp on and slung the guitar over my shoulder, but didn't turn around. When I hit the PA's power switch my mic started to feedback, forcing me to spin, grab it, and push the mic stand to the edge of the stage. Now facing the audience, I said, "Check. Mic check."

Andre gave me a thumbs-up as he backed into the hallway. It felt like the Delts all over again. I said, "Um, yeah…"

Somebody in the back said, "Just play something."

I squinted, and saw a guy with long blonde hair and sideburns wearing shades— the only white guy in the room beside me. I grabbed the neck and chugged along. A slow steady chick-chick-chick-chick on that D minor seventh.

Then it hit me—*That's Duane, man. He came, like he said he would.*

In my head I cursed myself. My brain searched for words to go with the chords. Stalling.

With a laugh, I whispered, "Shoot me."

Strumming. Slowing the tempo, noticeably, but in a controlled way. Nodding my head and closing my eyes. Slowed by a third. By half. *Steady now.*

A fixed tapping on that D minor seventh until the words came. *Come Together.*

Some of the audience nodded to the beat. Duane Allman smiled and tipped his glass to me. The rest went back to their biscuits and beans. But I closed my eyes and leaned into it. Maybe it didn't matter what those folks needed. If my hand wouldn't have instinctively grabbed that D minor seventh, I wouldn't have been able to say the song wasn't exactly what I needed. A return to what I knew after days of not knowing a goddamned thing. A taste of familiar in my mouth after days of eating the bitterness of losing fight after fight.

And when I closed my eyes, I did it as much to block them out as I did to lock myself into the song. I sang all the way to "shoeshine" with my eyes closed, my head bobbing to that unmistakable groove. The slow slink of a single guitar with nothing to hide. The last time I played alone on a stage like this...

Was when I played for Stu the night before he left.

The same day I met Dani at the record store.

I shook the thought out of my head and added a premature 'shoot me' at the recollection of my dead friend. And the memory of seeing Danicka fall from the Westover Bridge. Watching her disappear into the darkness. Whether the reminiscence of "back then" or thinking about yesterday made me feel this way, I didn't know. But the last time I played on any stage, my girl played with me and we were on our way to taking over the world. Now I was holed up in an Alabama juke joint worried about what would come busting through that door if all this belief and superstition turned out to be a lot more than belief and superstition. And because I was into the song, I didn't hear the other amp crackle to life.

When the sound of Pauly's E string buzzing against the frets hit me, I stood straight up but did not turn around. Not because I didn't care. I didn't turn around, because I knew if I did, I'd see somebody other than my brother back there. Right then and there I knew I had to make it real. I knew I had to turn water into wine. So I stopped playing.

But those low bass notes stuck to my teeth like black Twizzlers. I nodded in time to the beat. When I stepped up to the mic Pauly joined me.

Last verse.

Our words fought for space in the PA. They elbowed and pushed each other as they streamed out of the speakers. His breath smelled like bourbon. Stunk like mine. To see if it was real I let my head fall back. And even though it was faint, I felt it. He leaned over and bumped his head into mine. A small bump. Just a tap. *Such a Pauly thing to do.*

I smiled as I soloed over the outro. A few of them bobbed their heads while they lit smokes and drank. I turned to Pauly and said, "Like John Lennon would, to let us down tonight."

At the end I paused, used to the type of applause paying audiences dished out. And the smattering stung, but it didn't hurt. I looked at Calvin for a few more drinks. He nodded and I turned to Pauly. "Your turn."

"Let's do 'Bluebird,'" he said with a smile.

"No, man. They don't want to hear any of my shit."

He retreated from my blow-off with a flinch. "Fuck it, then. Do whatever you want."

I put my hand on his arm. "Sorry, man. I mean it. I thought you were telling me what you thought I wanted to hear."

Duane shouted, "Freebird!" and laughed with the people at the next table.

"Do whatever you want then."

"Pauly…" I said, hoping to talk it out. But he didn't have any fight left in his eyes. I could feel him trembling. "Let's do it."

His arms remained crossed over his chest for a long, quiet minute. He stepped up to the mic and said, "Katy. Would you mind joining us up here? Please?"

I looked for her amongst the tables, back behind the bar. Pauly said, "Andre, would you mind trying again, please?"

I said, "Want to play something until she gets here?"

"Simoneaux said we all had to be up here. He said a table with two legs can't stand."

So we waited, despite the anxious conversation from the people on the other side of the dance floor. I tried not to look, because I didn't like what I saw out there. They weren't just bored. They were *fucking* bored.

"C'mon, boy!" Duane yelled. "You're making it real hard to keep this buzz going."

"Katy?" I said, into the mic. "Why don't you put your hair up and join us?"

I turned to Pauly. "'Beast of Burden.' She'll pick it up when she gets up here."

"No way, man. That ain't what Simoneaux said to do."

I looked back at the bar and held my palms up. "Andre?"

With a laugh, Andre answered. "She said, 'hold your horses,' and that she ain't 'playing a note without changing clothes first.'"

I turned my back and Andre added, "Don't worry, Preston, these folks ain't going anywhere," and a few of them laughed.

"Yeah, Pres," Duane said, "We ain't going nowhere unless you can get us out of these seats."

"Hell with all this." My face got hot and I knew I'd blushed. Like I wanted Duane Allman to see me make a fool of myself. I mumbled, "Sugarplum fairy, one two three…" and launched right into "Shake Your Hips."

I tried to gain a little cred by not mentioning the Rolling Stones at all. "Here's a little Slim Harpo. For Duane back there."

From the back of the room Duane whooped and raised his glass.

Pauly said, "Here she comes," but I'd already moved into the verse. And before she even made it up to the stage I saw heads bouncing and feet tapping.

Pauly's bass notes floated up to that old corrugated tin roof, shaking it like a giant subwoofer. Katy was still putting her hair up when I sang about meeting a pretty girl in that little country town. She didn't smile when she stepped up to her mic.

But when I heard her little fiddle playing the harmonica fills through the PA I knew it was all good in the hood. This train picked up speed. People weren't on their feet. But they were at the edge of their chairs.

Before anybody—and I meant Katy or Pauly, really—could object, I segued right into Bo Diddley's "Who Do You Love?" Seemed like an appropriate tune for tonight. Made me think of the snake-skin in my front pocket. Folks drank and smoked and laughed more freely. And those who wanted to dance, danced.

Standing there with Katy on one side and Pauly on the other showed me exactly what Simoneaux had meant about a table with two legs. Once we locked into that groove, white hot positive energy flew through me, hit the crowd and flew back magnified a hundred times. At the last verse, Pauly and Katy signaled each other to wrap. I shook my head to keep it going. I knew better than to stop now. Katy put her fiddle on her hip, objecting the only way she could. But she never had to play a frat house. She didn't know what to do with a crowd like this.

Using the same chords and same rhythm, I went right into "Ring of Fire" like the two songs had been separated at birth, which they may as well have been. Cash and Diddley were born three-hundred miles and four years apart. The people on the floor didn't act like they noticed or minded.

When Simoneaux came in with Jamie and heard our music, his head whipped right around. He smiled and raised a finger as he shuffled over to the bar, which took a while because he stopped to talk and shake hands. I figured he'd go get his guitar too. While we worked through an instrumental break he poured himself a drink and made his way up to the stage. The rest of the folks who'd been sitting down stood and shuffled toward the floor in anticipation of Simoneaux's turn in the spotlight.

While Katy took a verse, I watched Simoneaux settle into the stool behind the small drum kit and tug the neon cross's pull-string. A blue glow fell onto us like a gentle snow. The moment he picked up the sticks the room changed, like a rabbit about to run. And when he joined us mid-verse, I felt it too. Never figured him for a drummer.

He worked that simple little kit like he didn't have a weak hand, pounding out that Bo Diddley beat on the snare while that high-hat sizzled like it was frying in hot oil. I couldn't believe my ears, and wanted to turn around and watch. His left hand kept tapping out these weird sequences of threes, fives and sevens that made me forget the rest of "Ring of Fire" completely. I tried to think of Johnny's next line, but for some reason "Junco Partner" kept jumping into my head. And just like that my lips were talking about serving eighty-five years in Angola. I could hear Simoneaux laughing behind me.

We blew through seven or eight more songs without even stopping to drink the drinks Calvin poured for us after "That's How I Got To Memphis." We'd pause after each number and I'd ask Pauly what we knew and before I realized, Simoneaux shouted out a song. I'd tell him I didn't know it, and he'd say 'the hell you don't,' and start playing. And sure enough I didn't stumble over lyrics after that.

After a short break we tried "Statesboro Blues" and I avoided eye contact with Duane the whole time. Simoneaux didn't like how I played it, and yelled, "Where's your bottleneck?" as I sang the last verse.

I didn't want to tell him that it embarrassed me to attempt any slide at all with Duane in the room, so I said, "Didn't feel it. I have to work on it a little. That's all."

"Pres, we got hellhounds all through these hills tonight. Heard 'em myself on our way back from the cemetery. You have to get some of them slide blues working or they're going to eat us right up. Go on, get your bottleneck."

So I dug it out of my case and juiced my Twin a little. Last thing I wanted was for Simoneaux and Duane to see how nervous I was. I said, "Man, I don't know if I got it."

"Ain't nothing to it. You make that guitar moan and wail like the wind through the trees. That's all them old blues guys did. Make it sound like pain. Make the devil think he already been there and got everything worth taking." Simoneaux threw down his bourbon then chased it with a pint glass of ice cold water. The glass left a wet ring on his pants where he'd set it on his knee. He wiped the glass across his brow and said, "Try that 'Little Red Rooster.'"

I stepped up to the mic, but I didn't feel it anymore. Without stepping away, I turned around and said to Simoneaux, "You think this ain't working?"

He shrugged. "Don't feel like it is."

"Okay. Let's try this then." I looked at Pauly and said, "Give me some of that John Paul Jones."

He smiled, his fingers walked that slow, descending progression right down into "Dazed And Confused."

I expected to see a smile from Simoneaux. Instead he rolled his eyes.

"Whatever, man. This is what you wanted." I turned that slide loose on the strings. Letting it squeal like my guitar talked to them hellhounds directly.

The crowd responded with indifference, but I didn't care. I figured if part of this supernatural stuff had anything at all to do with me, I'd play what I wanted to play. During the instrumental breaks I stepped over to Pauly to get some sort of confirmation that he was okay. His playing sounded strong, almost like he'd never put the bass away. But his eyes looked for something in me that I couldn't give him. I think he wanted me to tell him everything would to be okay.

And I couldn't.

When I sang, Katy sidled right on up next to me. I could smell her skin, her hair. As much as I wanted to look at her and smile I couldn't, not after what she'd been through. She was tougher than that, and I knew it. But when all was said and done, I couldn't help but feel bookended by the two people in this world I'd let down the most.

So I put it into my singing. I let the guitar hang in front of me, the hot buzz of deaf pickups vibrating in the speakers. And I put my heart into my words. Blood came out of me, instead of saliva and breath. Because I wanted Danicka Prochazka here with me tonight. I wanted to take all this back to Lula, Mississippi, and figure this shit out once and for all. I screamed into the mic.

"Been down on my knees, woman, since I met you, you made me believe all your lies were true…"

Something in Simoneaux's playing changed. It felt like he encouraged me with his backbeat.

So I let myself get caught up in the moment. "I'm out of your bed, got you out of my head, and now you're coming for my brother instead!"

The people on the floor slowed, shaken from their groove by my change in tactics. But if Simoneaux didn't like the way things were going, he never once let on. I figured I learned a thing or two in my time with Katy and her family looking after me. First thing— shit only works when you believe it will work.

"God damn, woman, I miss those eyes, even if I can't be sure they weren't lies."

Second thing was, for shit to work, you had to kill a little bit of yourself. You had to say goodbye to a little bit of your soul every time you dipped a toe on the other side. And that's why Katy stayed away from all that. She said every time you went over there, part of you stayed. I realized right then and there that she disowned the magic because she wanted to leave me with something.

I knew now I had to return the favor.

I cradled my Tele's neck with my left hand, trying to find the notes with the slide before I played them. And I tried to think of words. I tried to think of a way to bring this to an end. Tried to consider what Pauly needed, and what Katy needed.

I sang, "It didn't work out, girl, but you couldn't let it be, and I got what you want right here, but you'll have to fight your way through me!"

Screams from my amp flooded the room, my strings humming like six serpents in parallel—six copperheads with the taste of their last meal on their tongues. And I stopped thinking about what I should play and the notes poured out of me, making me wonder if it wasn't a side effect of my own little trip to the crossroads the other day. My head fell from side to side with the tempo, which had picked up a few beats per minute since the intro. Katy and Pauly were hanging right in there with me and Simoneaux even if I couldn't hear them for all the noise I made. I wanted to smile, but I knew better. So I danced instead. I let my shoulders fall and enjoyed the music we were making for once. I didn't worry about critics and new songs and how we sounded. I made music for the sake of making music and I felt fine.

In the back of the room Duane pulled on his cigarette and smiled. He had his long legs crossed casually in front of him.

I turned around and held up a finger. "One more time through and we're done," I said as I fell back into the chords.

Simoneaux blew through a flurry of beats and fluttered taps, a drum solo that he drew out to cheers and howls. I smiled because I couldn't do anything else. It made me feel silly to think I'd outshine Simoneaux in his own joint. And I happily deferred.

The folks on the floor ate it up clapping and toasting Simoneaux with whatever they were drinking. Andre pointed at us.

I couldn't hear the question, exactly, but I knew what he asked. "Yeah, man," I said into the mic, "I'll have another."

Pauly waved off another drink.

I wiped my forehead on my sleeve.

Somebody shouted a request from the floor. "Rollin' and Tumblin'."

An old man said, "Goin' Down South."

I turned around to look at Simoneaux, who wasn't smiling.

"What's wrong, man?" I said, still trying to catch my breath.

He set he sticks down and cupped a hand to his ear.

By now the people on the floor simmered and listened too.

"What's wrong?" I said, twisting my Tele's volume knob all the way down.

Katy put her finger to her lips.

Pauly went over to the window as a blast of trumpets shook the walls. As my ears rang I thought for sure it was thunder. People drifted from their tables and the dance floor to the other windows. Somebody pulled the blinds up. Simoneaux left the stage, and went over to the front door. He snapped the deadbolt.

A woman wailed, pulling at her hair with exaggerated anguish. At once the people closest to the windows scrambled past the bar toward the storeroom and back door. The rest followed without pushing each other, although a table got knocked over, spilling drinks to the floor. Somebody left a purse. A man left a jacket and porkpie hat.

Deliberate horns and a steady bass drum made their way up the road, slowly, like a city street sweeper. My mind struggled to find a melody, but the notes weren't coming fast enough. Simoneaux backed over to the bar and plopped himself down on a stool, facing the door. "Ain't nothing good coming in this second line."

I stepped over to the window and pulled the heavy blinds. Outside, a man wearing a top hat and tails and bright white shoes shuffled up the street. He wore white gloves on his hands, and carried a miniature wooden casket in the crook of his left arm. A white paint that reflected oddly in the glow of streetlights covered his face. Draped over his shoulder he wore a sash embroidered in white flowers and ribbons and gold beads that sparkled like baby stars bunched together in the night sky. For every step forward he took one to the right and one to the left. He didn't smile or even blink. He led the way with his right elbow cocked high, arhythmically jerking back and forth, up and down, in time with only every fourth or fifth beat.

"What is it?" Pauly asked.

"Don't know. Hang back with Rachael and Chloey."

Katy stood next to me, watching, her hand clasping mine.

From out of the darkness I saw the band—a few loose rows of men in white shirts with back ties and cylindrical black caps with short visors like the marching band wore back in high school. The trees on both sides of the street shook like a storm was blowing in.

Simoneaux said, "Ain't no beans ever burned because nobody stared at 'em long enough."

"What's that mean?" I said.

"Means get out of that window."

But I couldn't. *Wouldn't.*

The musicians wore sunglasses and white gloves and walked in the same side-to-side shuffle as the parade's Grand Marshal. They blew so hard I could almost see the notes spilling forth into the night. Rows of brass—trumpets, trombones, and tubas—blew young green leaves from their limbs. The falling debris cast twirling shadows as they drifted past the orange sodium vapor lights.

The drum corps followed on their heels, tapping out a slow rhythm that crawled into my head like a king snake. The windows rattled with each thunderous downbeat. Ice clinked in glasses. The ride cymbal on Simoneaux's kit hissed with the residual energy of the percussion. And the leaves that had fallen onto the ground blew ahead of the band on each beat, like a sonic broom pushed them all down the street.

A second line had formed behind the musicians. Folks carrying umbrellas decorated with ribbons and flowers and the name of the deceased spelled out in beads and sequins even though I couldn't read it for the way they were being spun and flipped. The second line consisted of large, dark men in black suits stoically carrying straw hats balanced on their right hands. Women in red and gold dresses wearing white gloves slithered between the men, dancing with their knees high. Some hiked their dresses up to their hips as they bent low and shook their chests. Some wore feathers in their hair. Some had their faces covered with white grease paint. Every three or four beats everybody in the group synched up so their elbows cocked at precisely the same moment. And after the moment passed, they reverted to chaos.

Jamie and Ben stood at the far window with Rachael and Chloey. Katy pulled me away from my vantage to join them. Pauly backed toward the bar and waited with Andre and Calvin.

A horse-drawn hearse came next. White horses huffed steam into the chilly night. The large, black wheels that bore the dark, lacquered carriage wound around slowly. Lilies fell from the top, littering the street with little splashes of white here and there, like a stray blizzard had passed through. A large oval window reflected the red and blue neon from Simoneaux's signs. When it passed, I saw the interior had been filled with white lilies. The coach's drivers each wore a black sash with white lettering. On each of the drivers' sashes, the name could be read easily.

"Pauly."

Katy put her hand over her mouth.

Pauly, thankfully, didn't see. He didn't have to.

"That's it, I hope." I let the blind fall, but not close completely.

The silence that accompanied the procession's passing seemed to confirm it. But I knew better than to believe my ears. Katy drifted back over to the stage and sat down. "Preston," she said. "Get away from the window."

Rachael sat with her. Ben tucked his pistol back into his belt. Jamie sat down and fanned himself with a napkin.

I held up my hand. A pair of headlights made a left onto the street from the far end of the block. As much as I didn't want to say it, I owed it to them to say it, so that they knew what I knew. "Here she comes."

Her little silver car drifted to a stop in the middle of the street. She slammed the door when she got out, and took a second to brush the wrinkles out of the front of her grey dress. An amber amulet that matched her eyes hung from a thin silver chain around her neck.

When she rounded the front of the car the room got hot and I found it hard to get a breath. She stepped onto the sidewalk and a boom like an explosion from the destruction of a skyscraper rattled the windows. We all turned as a spray of glass from Simoneaux's bottle trees peppered the front of his building. Shards flew at the window, forcing tiny spider webs of cracks to form. Fragments stuck to the wooden railings that lead down to the sidewalk. The slivers of glass looked like sapphires in the orange glow of the street lights.

She lit a cigarette, inhaled deeply, and blew the smoke out as she sang. "Pauly, pretty Pauly, do you think I'm a fool?"

It sounded like her take on the traditional song, with the lyrics changed to suit her current needs. I think she used the song as a way to take a jab at me.

"Pauly, pretty Pauly, do you think I'm a fool? You make me a promise, then I have to chase after you."

I couldn't look at him. Even if it was only to tell him I'd make this right, no matter what the cost. He wouldn't buy it anyway. Not after all this.

She pulled a pint of something golden out of a brown paper bag. Like Irish whiskey, except for the way it reflected the streetlight. It glowed, as if illuminated from something inside, like molten gold. "My mind was to love you, 'til the end of my days. My mind was to love you, 'til the end of my days, but you've broken my heart so I'm changing my ways."

She heaved the bottle to the ground where it exploded into a feast of golden light that burned through the blinds and walls. The blast turned night into an amber sunrise falling onto a sandy beach. It reminded me of all those filmstrips of the Trinity test site. The light penetrated even with my eyes closed and my arms across my face. The light filled my head, kept me from telling myself everything would be okay.

Thunder accompanied the light. Loud booms that rattled the windows and walls. Never-ending booms that shook the floor. Bottles fell off the shelves and shattered. Simoneaux's cymbals crashed and crashed and crashed until they finally fell over. Tables toppled. Wood splintered as the walls wobbled. Panes of glass popped out of already cracked windows. I found Katy and pushed her to the ground and fell on top of her to protect her from falling ceiling vents and light fixtures.

Windows burst out of their frames as the angles in the walls and floor changed. The roof rose and fell with a tremendous crash three times. Each time the space between the wall and the ceiling grew. Two feet. Then three. Before it fell the last time I saw low-hanging stars over the river.

When it all came to an abrupt halt nobody said anything. The juke joint had lost all its right angles. The only light came from the back of the house—emergency lighting from the storeroom. Outside, the streetlights slowly came back to life as night returned. I looked out of the window. The car was gone.

My ears rang like after wearing headphones with the volume at ten, and my hearing came back slowly. Katy's lips moved, but I could not hear, so I shushed her.

I heard Ben first. He asked if everybody was okay, but seemed to be mostly concerned with Simoneaux. Everybody regrouped at the bar.

"Preston," Jamie said. "What'd you do to get Old Scratch so riled up this time? She wants to hurt you bad, so she's going to make darn sure she hurts everybody around you worse."

I couldn't answer. But I didn't have to. Simoneaux spoke up.

"That ain't the devil. Evil, sure, but not the devil."

Jamie said, "How do you know that?"

Simoneaux said, "All the powder and spells this afternoon... devil would've walked right through that, that's how I know. We got lucky tonight."

"And tomorrow night?" Katy asked.

"I'd imagine tomorrow night ain't going to be the same as this one."

CHAPTER EIGHT

Walk the line, get a spine.
I know I'm wearing mine.
Yeah, I'll toe the line.
Step up, punk, step the fuck up and get cut up.
Knife fight, life flight.
'Bout time the boy gets it right.

"Drinking Class Hero" Music and Lyrics by Preston Black

The clean-up sapped us of what Dani couldn't.

Fear and tension wormed its way into my head during her visit to the bar last night. But stacking tables and chairs, sweeping up busted bottles, boarding up the broken windows, and restacking cans on Simoneaux's storeroom shelves sucked the life and hope from us. Nobody spoke to each other. Maybe everybody felt like coming through all that unscathed was a win, and knew there was no need to analyze a win.

After we finished most of the clean-up, Andre put up Rachael and Jamie at his place. Chloey joined Katy and me on the floor in the back room. Katy snuggled up in the middle, like a cat, and spent a lot of time talking to Chloey before they fell asleep—long after I was ready to sleep. But I liked hearing the tone of Katy's voice when she talked to her little sister. The inflection changed, like everything Chloey said became instantly more interesting than anything I'd ever said. Guess they talked like girls talk, but it made me feel like Katy couldn't get everything she needed from me.

But Chloey, in her own little way, did a lot to help me understand Katy. The over-protective little sister act showed me how Chloey and Rachael perceived Katy as some sort of fragile little China doll, somebody who lived her life on the verge of cracking, which wasn't at all what I saw in Katy. Chloey had told me stories of how Katy, being the oldest, would have to run into Muttley's or the VFW to find her old man if he ran off on another drunken binge. And Katy always had to be the one to run across the fields to get Jamie or Levon when her old man beat on her mom. Katy never talked much about these things with me. She didn't have to.

They slept, tangled in blankets like they'd both spent the longest part of the night still fighting something. But they fell asleep long before I did even though the wind howled and dogs barked all night long. And I smiled as I watched over them. After all the noise Dani'd created, it made me very happy to see them both at peace. They deserved it.

Just before the sun came up I drifted out to the bar. A cool breeze blew in through the gaps in Simoneaux's busted windows. I walked over to take a peek at the street. The leaves that blew around in lazy circles were the only sign that things had been so crazy here last night. Dim lights above the bar shone down on Simoneaux's incomplete rows of glass bottles. Being unable to figure out if I'd stayed up too late or had gotten up too early made it difficult to figure out what I should be drinking. Besides, I knew I wasn't alone. So I spoke up. "Want anything?"

"Brandy Alexander? Unless that's going to put you out." He wore a floppy tan driving cap and a suit that matched. I think he wore something like that on *The Dick Cavett Show* with Yoko.

"What's in that? Besides brandy?"

"Crème de cacao. But I'm starting to feel as if it's going to be a bother."

"There's no—"

"Make it a Scotch and Coke then. I'll pretend I'm twenty-two." He waved his long finger when he said it.

I mixed it with one part Scotch and one part Coke. I figured it didn't matter, since he was either a figment of my imagination or a ghost.

He said, "You've had a bit of an evening."

"Yeah, man." I poured myself a little Baileys. "Stuff got out of control. Thank God nobody got hurt."

"Do you suppose God really had anything to do with it?" He looked deeply into his drink and swirled it around the bottom of his glass.

"No, man. It's just something to say."

"Well, you've got to talk to someone, I suppose. I know an auntie isn't the same as a mum. Band mates aren't brothers."

"No, and I got along fine without all the above—"

"But a pap, on the other hand. Every boy needs a pap like he needs a dog or a guitar. That's why I'm here, isn't it?" He said it like one word—'Innit.' "You know your Uncle Jamie would gladly be sitting up with you right now, sharing a drink. Or Mick. It's not the same and we both know that, but you have plenty of people hanging around you who'd love it if you came to them with a problem like this."

"I hope you aren't saying 'goodbye?' That's what this is starting to sound like."

He stood, and wouldn't sit back down. "I suppose I am. What else can I say? You know the crossroads bollocks is all a metaphor, right? Time has come to change your fate instead of letting it push you around the block."

"So, grow up and stop making music and get a real job?"

"Is that what I said? Don't be a bastard." He laughed and shook his head. "No good can come from growing up. Growing up is our punishment for following the rules, but loads of adults get paid to make music."

I met him at the end of the bar.

He said, "Take care of business. These people really like you. And they like what you do for their Katy. But she's going to need more. She puts on a good front, but it wears her down. She may want kiddies. She may want consistency. She may not. Either way, she wants to know that you're capable of keeping a lid on when the brew gets too hot. She wants to be taken care of sometimes, Preston. She doesn't want to be the queen. She wants to be the princess. She wants a prince."

I couldn't say anything because I agreed with him. But I wanted to touch him. I wanted a handshake or a hug to let me know everything was okay.

He added, "Before I go, you should know that I think you've done the best you could so far. You've built something, and people like you. That kind of thing didn't come because you had a pap. That all came from who you are, and who you love. Don't forget that."

I wanted some kind of physical contact, but he backed away at a steady pace. "Be careful, brother. The world ain't going to look out for you."

And when he waved goodbye and bounded down the steps I just stood in the doorway and waved back.

Everybody stumbled into the afternoon at their own pace. Tension forced a noticeable quiet into the air, but it freed me to pick up my guitar as a way to kill the rest of the day. It gave me time to think, time to go through chords and scales and exercises as a bit of noisy meditation.

Simoneaux was the first to join me on stage. I didn't know whether it was for my sake or for his own, but I turned to face him all the same. I sat on the edge of my amp and tweaked the volume to match the volume of his kit. I played weird little chord progressions to match his weird little beats. Diatonics and whole note scales and Arabic scales. I tried unusual chords in new ways. Keeping up with him almost felt like some kind of game. Like, as soon as I pulled something new out of my hat he threw something else at me. He kept nodding for me to stop, but whenever I backed out he'd pull me back in, jumping in and out of syncopation, back and forth between twos and threes.

After a while he waved his hand across his throat for the last time. I shook out my hands and stood up. I asked if he wanted a drink.

"Nah, Pres. We need to talk." Wiping sweat off his brow with his forearm, he said, "It's all about the ritual with the types we're dealing with out there. They been doing things a certain way for thousands of years. It ain't up to you to decide when to come in and do something different. You skip a step and the whole deal's off. Kaput. They keep you on the hook for your end of things while they walk off into the night like they was looking for a lost dog. They rely on the way things are said—wording means everything to them. You have to understand this, Preston. The step-by-step is important. Just like putting together a little rhythm, like we did now."

"I don't suppose I'm going to put myself into a position where I'm going to have to worry about that."

"You don't know. Ain't none of us knows what's going to happen. Too easy for a guy like you to lose everything. That's how come you ain't lost everything already."

"Because I didn't follow the proper steps?"

"Maybe. This one's like a tick. You don't pull at it with tweezers because you might not get the head out. You hear?"

"I do. Thanks for looking out for me."

Jamie drifted out to investigate. I waved him over.

Simoneaux said, "That's all we're doing, man. Looking out for you. Remember the ritual. Sign of the Cross, 'body of Christ' and all that. Same thing—ritual and step-by-step. This is a different side of it."

I said, "You know the procedure, don't you? How to make a deal that sticks?"

Jamie brought a chair onto the riser with him.

Simoneaux said, "I know how to bake a cake and you ain't eating cake now, are you?"

Nodding, I said, "I got you."

"So, what do you think she is? You spent a lot of time with her." Jamie looked over his shoulder to make sure nobody else heard. "Is she a maligned spirit or what?"

"Jesus, Jamie." I closed my eyes, but wanted to roll them. "If she's not The Devil or a devil then I don't know what she is."

"Do you remember any strange smells, or sensations from the time you spent with her? Noises or voices in a different language?"

"Like *na zdravi*? Yeah, I heard her speaking other languages. Honestly, even after everything that happened out there and back in Morgantown, I'm still inclined to say she's a woman. I know that ain't an answer you want to hear."

"Preston, I spent a lot of time working on this," Jamie said, his tone making me think he was trying to find a way to put it mildly. "See, there's a Kabbalist mystic belief that all words contain secret syllables. When uttered in the right sequence, they have magical properties. Maybe some songs even work that way—like the one, four, five chord progression? Makes sense, right? So if you could learn her real name, we could figure out what she is and gain a little leverage over her. Does that make sense?"

Ben and Pauly ate at the bar, alone together. Katy and Chloey and Rachael ate by candlelight at a table in the far corner. Andre and Calvin and the rest decided to take the day off. I couldn't blame them.

"It does, but I already told you what I think. And what if she isn't The Devil?"

Simoneaux said, "If she ain't, we're lucky, son. But if all this goes on like a rain that don't stop, it may not matter."

"I understand." I stood as my belly rumbled. "Jamie, part of me is afraid you'll only ever see me as a flaky guitar player, the kind of guy who'll wear the same T-shirt for days in a row if there ain't somebody around to tell him to change it. But I want everybody to be able to go back home okay with the idea that they didn't have to worry about Katy anymore. You all are going to see that I'm capable of being a wall when the time comes."

I put my hand on his shoulder. "I'm going to wipe away the memory of me stealing the guitar from Mick even though I already worked everything out with him. I want you to respect me the way you respect Ben and Henry. I'm going to leave it at that and eat now."

"Now, Preston, that ain't fair…"

I turned and drifted toward the kitchen before he could change my mind or fill me up with patronizing sentiments. On the stove Simoneaux had a pot of cold grits congealing next to a pan of red-eye gravy. In the oven a tray of corn bread warmed. I grabbed it with an oven mitt.

Through the service window I heard Katy and Chloey laugh at something, and smiled as I buttered the sweet, dry cornbread. It smelled like August county fairs. The butter had softened from sitting next to the stove. The knife pushed it deep into the pores, where it turned into liquid that soaked all the way down through to the plate. I put a big spoonful of grits next to the cornbread, then covered them with the red-eye. After thinking about it for a second, I dipped the ladle back into the gravy and dumped it onto the cornbread too.

But one bite was all I got. One taste of the salty butter-soaked cornbread, before I heard the clamor of chairs in the front room.

"Preston," Katy yelled as I ran out of the kitchen.

Jamie and Simoneaux were peering through a gap in the boards of the window closest to the stage. Rachael and Pauly shared the other.

Ben had gotten the baseball bat from behind the bar. He handed it to me and said, "Nobody gets through," as he ran back to the storeroom. I knew he went back for his guns.

The thunder of motorcycles drowned out the rumble of all the pickup trucks and vans. Without walking all the way over to the front door or window, I knew. I put my arm around Katy. She called the police.

"There are so many…" Jamie said.

"They won't send a radio car." Simoneaux said, "Once you give them this address they put you on a waiting list."

"Chloey, Rachael. Why don't you both come on back here?" I said, leading Katy with my hand on the small of her back. "Maybe even head back into the storeroom and lock yourselves in."

Chloey nodded, and the three of them took cover.

I joined Pauly at the window and gave him the bat. "This is for you, man. Take the first shot. You deserve a little payback."

"What about you?"

"Pool cue or mic stand? One is poetic, one is classic. What do you think?"

He gave me a small smile. "Mic stand."

Jamie watched Ben roll out of the back hallway. I couldn't quite read Jamie's expression. Based on the way my own interactions with Ben had been for the last few days, I'd say it troubled him to see his son enjoying this. Ben gave his dad a revolver.

"Listen up," Ben said as he moved to the center of the room. He took his pistol off safety and snapped the slide back to make sure there was a round in the chamber. "I want to give them the door. Keep the lane clear and I'll unload on them as they pop through. Once they hear shots they're going to back off. I guarantee it."

"You saw these guys at the river, man." I said. "They're like zombies. Bullets didn't stop them back there."

"You just worry about yourself, Preston. I got this." He positioned himself at the end of the bar and set two extra clips there in front of him.

"I don't think we should give them the door. Give the cops time to show up," I said. "If anything, we can reinforce the door to buy time."

Jamie added, "Maybe Preston's right. We need to try to keep a lid on this situation for as long as possible."

Ben's face got red and he kicked a stool over. The noise made me jump.

After a long pause, I said, "Jesus, Ben, you do what you want. This is your gig. I'm going to go back and see how everybody's doing. I'm not going to fight you too, man."

I wasn't being sarcastic, and didn't say it with any kind of passive-aggressive tone. "When I come back out I'll do whatever you tell me to do."

He took a deep breath and released it without saying anything.

I said, "We good?"

"We're good," he replied low enough so nobody could hear. "Just trying to keep everybody safe, Pres."

"I know, man."

"If there's something I'm good at—"

A crash from the back cut him off and sent us both running for the storeroom at the same time. Ben yelled, "You guys keep this secure up here," as he passed by the kitchen's service window.

Near the office we could see the orange glow from a sodium vapor light falling across the tile—the first sign the door had been kicked down. A cool breeze blew in from the night. As my eyes adjusted to the change in brightness, Ben raised his pistol. I stopped a few steps behind him.

He said, "I got the storeroom."

I waited for Ben to give a sign. As soon as he pointed at the door I rushed into Simoneaux's office, catching one of the men from the church by surprise. A tall, wiry guy with a bit of a gut lunged at me. I swung the chrome boom from my mic stand and caught his forearm as he tried to shield his head.

He took a step back and I swung again, this time hitting his right temple with a thud. He dropped to his knees and crossed his arms over his face. The purple, hemorrhaged skin on his forearm jiggled like a water balloon. Blood and watery puss dripped out of puncture wounds that skipped, two by two, from his wrist to his elbow. Patches of stiff, black skin on the palms of his hands cracked and bled around the edge.

I swung the metal mic boom as hard as I could and hit his elbow with a snap. He tucked into a ball on the floor. I took a step to the side, lined up my shot and hit him again in the ribs. He held up a palm in surrender as a brown snake slid out of his jacket pocket.

Adrenaline made me bigger than I'd ever been in my whole life. My arms felt huge, like they'd burst through my shirt. My breathing came faster, which scared me. I broke the snake's back with a quick tap from the boom and backed into the hallway to tell Ben how I'd taken care of the man in the office.

The storeroom door hung wide open. I nearly tripped over a woman sprawled out on the tile. Blood ran out of her hairline onto her face. She had the same purple blotches all over her arms and hands as the man in Simoneaux's office. But something else hid there, amidst the blood, and I had to look to see it. Tattoos on her palms. And when I looked at her face again I saw that blood wasn't real. Right below the black ink that represented a spiky crown of thorns.

On the floor near the woman's feet lay a dead rattlesnake. The front third of its body appeared flat and shapeless.

I immediately made eye contact with Katy to see if she was okay. She spoke with somebody on the phone, which didn't really make sense to me.

Ben turned and said, "Hold this while I get the first aid kit from the office."

"Holy shit." I dropped to my knees and held a bloody mass of white paper towels against the skin above Chloey's collarbone—too close to her neck. "Chloey, you okay?"

Rachael, fighting to maintain her calm, handed me another wad of paper towels. "She needs to get to an emergency room."

"I knew her, Preston." Katy looked at the woman on the floor. Her voice sounded a little weak. "She acted like we were friends."

"Did Ben kill her?"

"Ben didn't do shit," Chloey said, with a bit of a smirk. "She came at me with that big old knife and Katy hit her with a can of beans."

"This is an emergency," Katy said with a weak smile meant to keep Chloey calm. She held her hand over the mouthpiece. "The dispatcher says there's a major accident over on I-59. It's going to be a while."

"Bullshit," I said.

"Here," Ben said, cutting me off. He signaled for me to get out of the way. "They got dad and me blocked in with their trucks."

"Listen." I wracked my brain to come up with a plan. "Maybe Andre can get you guys to a hospital. I'll tell Pauly to call him. Just stay on the line with 911, okay?"

"You and me are still going to need to clear a path to the street." Ben said, "Tell Pauly to have Andre come down the alley to the back door. Might be a little better than taking Chloey out the front."

"Go out there and fight those people face-to-face?"

"Maybe," Ben said. "You're going to have to get your hands dirty sooner or later."

I bent down and gave Katy a kiss on the forehead. Chloey watched me with sad eyes, so I bent over and gave her a little kiss on the cheek. "We'll take care of this."

"I know." Katy took my hand when she said it.

Just before splitting I said, "I'll make this right." I turned and looked back at Katy. "Stay on the line. Somebody will have to come, right?"

"I will." She looked at me with her watery blue eyes. "Preston?"

I couldn't make eye contact with her.

"Don't do anything you'll regret."

"I'm making a vow to you right now, with your mom and baby sister as my witnesses that I will fix this." I backed away slowly, taking a last look at the woman on the floor. The sight filled me with anger and disgust. Figured I needed a little extra fuel if I expected to hang with Ben out there. "Were you going to tie her up?"

Katy said, "One thing at a time, Preston."

Ben interrupted, "Tell my dad to come on back. He can help take care of Chloey and watch the door."

Thunder pealed in the distance like a kettle drum boom. Wind blew a moist chill in from the night.

"On it," I said before turning and running to the front.

In the bar nobody spoke. Simoneaux sat on a stool at the window, watching the scene on his sidewalk. Pauly sat at the foot of the stage, bouncing the baseball bat off his toe.

"Jamie, Ben needs your help back there."

He stood and walked toward me. "Everything okay?"

"You'll see." I relaxed my grip on the mic boom and let it fall to my side.

Simoneaux said, "Are the girls okay?"

"Well, I got one of them bastards in your office and the girls got one in the storeroom." I rubbed my eyes, because saying it finally made it real. "But she got Chloey first. Pauly, can you please call Andre and see if he can come around back to pick Chloey up? She needs a hospital."

"Shit." He pulled his phone out of his pocket and dialed immediately. "All over it."

"Tell him back door as fast as possible."

"He can't get back there with all those people," Pauly said while the phone rang.

"I know. Ben wants me to help him clear a path."

"Good luck with that," he said as Andre picked up. Pauly relayed the info to Andre using almost the same phrasing I'd used.

I said, "Anything new out there?"

"No man," Simoneaux said. "Lots of freaks. Lots of snakes. More coming all the time."

"Where's Boggs and his gang?"

"Don't see them," Simoneaux said. "Their rides are still there, but they ain't."

I peeked through a gap in the old two-by-sixes. In the distance the dark sky glowed with the lightning of an oncoming storm.

"I guess we're going to do this then."

"Stay safe, man," Simoneaux said. He gave me a little wave as I went back up the hall to join Ben.

"Ready?" he said, bouncing on his toes a few times.

"I guess. Ain't shot a gun in a while."

"No, no. My old man keeps the gun. In case anybody comes through the door?"

"Yeah," I said, trying to process everything. "That makes sense."

"Hopefully you ain't going to have to shoot anybody any way. But if it makes you feel better, you can have this." He held his pistol out to me.

"No, man." I waved it off.

"Eyes on your six at all times." Ben stepped past the splintered back door. "Stay on my tail, okay?"

I nodded as he dropped down the steps and went left, hugging the building, crouching until he got to the trash-cans and barrels of used peanut oil on the corner. Lightning flashed bright enough to cause the dusk-to-dawn lights to reset. As their glow brightened, thunder cracked. I followed.

He waved his hand. "Four," he said, pointing to the alley around the corner.

"Boggs?"

"Look at the shadows."

I heard the rustling of their leather jackets against brick a yard or two away. Just before I saw the shadows myself. A light rain fell.

Ben held a finger to his lip and took two steps forward.

I lingered, afraid to do something stupid. "Subtle" and "quiet" were two things I hadn't mastered yet.

Ben held a fist up and I stopped.

A cold gust of wind blew loose papers up the alley. I shivered as my shirt grew wetter in the rain.

"Now," Ben said.

I hesitated, waiting a moment to give him space to work. As soon as I took that first step the woman with the tattoos from the storeroom screamed "Zeb!" from the back door. She stomped down the stairs and stumbled into the alley. I lunged for her as she ran past.

Ben bolted ahead. "Stay with me!"

He fired a shot as Boggs closed in. The man Ben shot twisted and fell to the gravel. Boggs swung a metal rod at Ben.

The woman took cover up the alley as Ashby came at me. I swung the mic boom and he ducked, lowering his head and driving me into the dirt.

Unable to get any leverage on him, I swung my elbow at his ear as hard as I could. Ashby lifted his head and I caught him on the shoulder with a short swing that didn't do any real damage.

He pushed off me and hit me in the face—right between my nose and my eye. Cold pain shot through my head as warm blood fell past my lips, over my chin. Twisting and flailing were worthless. I tried to bite his ear but couldn't get close.

"Get off him," Jamie shouted from the back porch. He fired a round into the grass off to my right. Ashby hesitated, then hit me again in the same spot.

Jamie shot again, aiming to miss. "Get up. Now," he said, edging toward us.

Ashby stood and backed toward the alley, taking slow steps to where his companion lay, holding his belly. Blood came through his fingers.

Ashby said, "Get up, Ferlin."

Jamie helped me to my feet, and quickly went up the alley to where Ben had Boggs wrapped up in a chokehold. "Ben—"

"Shoot them!" Ben couldn't get an angle on the retreating bikers himself.

"They're leaving," I said, choking a little on the blood in my throat.

"God damn it, Preston!" he said, furiously. "Do something!"

Boggs gasped for breath, his struggle weakening.

"I can't kill them all," Ben said. A loud crack of thunder split the sky right above us.

"You don't have to kill them, man," I pleaded.

"There's a difference between vigilance and a vigilante. It's time to come home, son. Killing these guys won't bring Kenny and X back." Jamie handed me the revolver and took a knee at Ben's side.

"They're just going to keep coming back. Preston, I told you to get eyes on those fucking Hajjis, and what did you do? They fucking flanked us."

"Son," Jamie said, grabbing Ben's wrist. "Let justice work. He'll serve time for what he's done."

"Ben, we need you, man. Chloey needs you. Andre is on his way. You don't have to kill Boggs. Being locked up for manslaughter ain't worth it. If you go to jail, Chloey and Katy and your mom and dad lose too."

Boggs faded like the light after a hard day. Like the music at the end of a show.

"Hey," I said. "Tomorrow is something different, okay? Tomorrow is breakfast and a bed. Tomorrow is your dad and your cousins and your Aunt Rachael and me and Pauly. Tomorrow is redemption, man. Tomorrow is a clean slate, okay?"

He didn't seem to agree with me. Boggs stopped moving.

I held my breath.

Ben handed his pistol up to his dad. Nodding, he released Boggs. "Okay. We'll get him inside and tie him up."

I pushed Boggs off Ben and held him, even though he offered no struggle.

Pauly came to the back door. "Andre's coming but he can't get through. We got to get these fuckers out of here."

"All right," I said, letting the rain wash the blood off my face. "I'll take care of it."

Brushing the dirt from his back, Ben said, "How we going to clear all those people out of the front if you ain't going to let me shoot any?"

"Just get ready to carry Chloey up to the street."

"Seriously, Preston. Tell me. This is going to happen tomorrow and the next night, you know. They ain't going to stop coming for us."

"I know how to make it stop." I handed him back his gun. "It's time to negotiate, I guess."

I knew the more I thought about it, the harder it'd get to actually do it. "I'm on it."

"Pres," Jamie said. "Why don't you hold up a second?"

But I ran up the steps. When I passed the storeroom they had Chloey in a chair ready to be moved. I gave Katy a weak smile and blew her a little kiss.

"Preston," she said. "Preston, wait…"

But I couldn't hear her. Not now.

I grabbed a handful of napkins from the service window and held it against my nose for a moment. When I saw that didn't do a thing to stop the bleeding I used my sleeve.

From below the bar I took a pint glass and filled it with water. I swished it around my mouth to get the taste of blood out then spit in the sink. I drank more as I walked toward the chanting.

When I got to the window, I heard distant trumpets blaring from the hilltops. Not like the clamor from last night's funeral procession. It sounded disjointed and abrasive. Noise for the sake of noise.

"What the fuck is this, man?" Pauly said. "If it's me they want you should just let me go out there."

"Pauly, that's enough. I told you I'd take care of this, and I'm going to take care of this. Don't know why everybody has such a hard fucking time believing that." I stood with Simoneaux and watched through the window. Men and women bitten and bloodied by days of handling serpents looked up to the sky, praying.

"Do you believe me, Pauly? That I'm going to take care of this?"

He didn't say anything.

"Stringing together a year's worth of success ain't enough to clear last year's slate?"

"It ain't that, man. You had help—"

"So this last year was all because of Katy?"

"That's not what I'm saying. But you've definitely changed since you met her."

"Well, I took care of Danicka Prochazka back then and I can do it again."

"Pres, if you'd have taken care of her she wouldn't be here now."

The rain hitting the old corrugated metal roof grew louder as the storm intensified, banging like the crack of a rimshot each time. Just like a hickory drumstick against steel. Rain dripped into buckets and coffee cans. I walked over to the door and flipped the latch. Dani's silver Mercedes pulled to a stop amidst all the pickup trucks and motorcycles. The people turned and prayed to her.

A wave of hail bounced off the hoods of the vehicles. A stiff wind blew leaves and paper through the empty streets, past empty houses with dark windows. Homes that once meant something to people. Probably just needles and used condoms in there now.

"Y'all lock that door and come on back in," Simoneaux said.

But I couldn't. Not while the sky deepened, like there were thousands of miles between the fog that hung over the roofs and the yellow light pouring in from the cloud tops. A heavy light that pushed all the blue away while it sank. Like wringing water out of a towel. On the wind I tasted anise and mint.

The hail intensified, forcing the people on the street to cover their heads with their coats and jackets. A little kid pushed himself against his mother's hip. She covered his head with one of her arms while still shielding herself with the other. When the hailstones got larger, some of the people cried out in pain. All the while, the yellow faded, leaving a trace of green.

Hail hit the roof so hard now I had to cover my ears. Trees were stripped of their remaining leaves. The ice rolled spring back into winter. Pounded the grass into the mud. All this as a milky jade grew in the sky above. An unearthly shade, one definitely not found in a Crayola box of sixty-four. A strange heat penetrated the blasts of frigid air from the cold front.

Out on the street it looked worse.

Hundreds of birds took shelter beneath the juke joint's eaves. Those that didn't fell out of the trees, dead before they hit the ground. In the dark far off, dogs howled painful cries. Begging to be let off chains. Men and women fell to their knees and crawled under the pickup trucks and into their vans. The water that ran into the storm drain looked like blood in the strange mixture of light from the streetlights and sky. As far as I could tell, no green remained anywhere on earth's surface. It'd all been pulled into the dividing sky. Like the clouds had been split by a streak of clarity. My eyes were drawn up to it. A never-ending thunderclap rattled what remained of the windows. The noise grew like a squadron of jet fighters with freight train engines coming from somewhere beyond the mountains. Beyond the sea. Beyond the heavens themselves.

In the clearing above, a pinpoint of light grew in the darkness where space should've been. Without stars to remind me of my location, the glow looked more like it was rising from a hole than falling into one. Ascending out of an abyss. And earlier, if I thought I should've been scared, it was because I didn't truly know fear until I saw that drop of light double in size every few seconds. Like I'd fallen into it.

"Pauly, come see this." I waved my hand without checking over my shoulder to see if he was even looking at me. "Pauly?"

Simoneaux joined Pauly behind the bar and said, "They call that star *Wormwood*. A third of all the waters became poison when it fell. Thousands of people died from that bitter water."

"You thought you could take care of this?" Pauly said, "I had a hard time believing that dude from *The Goonies* could carry Frodo up that volcano. But this…"

"I know." My phone buzzed to life in my pocket. "It's time to go."

I walked into the rain. Mint and the tingle of alcohol washed over me. My lips burned with a long-forgotten taste. I turned and saw Katy come through the swinging door from the kitchen. She looked at me for a long time. And when she cried, Pauly held her.

I held up the pint glass to the dim street light and saw my water turn milky. Each droplet left a trail of cloudiness. I tilted my head back and watched the star continue to fall.

"From the emptiness where heaven used to sit."

I drank.

And when I'd emptied the glass I let it fill again. Rain mixed with wormwood, mint, and star anise. My phone buzzed in my pocket. I wiped water and alcohol and tears out of my eyes. I licked the saltiness and the burn of the absinthe off my lips. Tasted a lot like those nights in Dani's apartment.

I scrolled through my texts. Hundreds of them. From Kurt Cobain. From Berry Oakley. John Bonham. Jim Morrison.

From Willie Dixon.

MCA sent one that said, <Don't be pulled down by the weight of your own karma, Pres. You can't be in the light when you react with anger. That's how you end up in hell.>

I flipped through a hundred more from Layne Staley and Ronnie Van Zant and Andrew Wood.

From Brian Jones. Elmore James. From Cliff Burton. George Harrison.

Duane Allman sent me a text that said, <Baybrah, there's always another way. Don't leave your girl like this.>

Strummer's said, <don't be daft, mate.>

I downed another glass, this one much stronger than the first. I held my eyes shut, and in that instant, experienced every doubt I'd ever known.

I'm insane, and I imagined all this.

I dropped the pint glass into the grass.

I died on the bridge that night after the show, and this is purgatory.

I looked up at the falling star one last time. It had taken up almost all of my field of view. The dim light fell into my eyes like dust and I tried to blink it away.

I looked at Dani—Danicka—out in the street in her little silver car. A ride I once believed would take me to the end of my dying days, embraced in a passionate love that didn't know work or hunger. When I saw her sitting out there, my heart ached for the way I'd hurt her. The way I lied to her. My stomach knotted, my face burned with the regret of not seeing things through with her.

With Dani.

For all I knew, she was the woman I was supposed to die with.

My phone beeped again. I expected a hundred more texts.

192

But it was a call. Before I even held it up to my ear John pleaded with me. "Brother, go back in and lock the door."

"How do I know you aren't a trick of my mind? Making me weak, when I need to be strong to end this like I said I'd end it?"

"I'll prove I'm not a figment." John said, "Ask me anything. Things you know from the books. Ask me about 'Tomorrow Never Knows' and the rope. Or about the day Geoff Emerick quit because of 'Revolution' and that bloody amplifier."

"But these things that you are telling me are things that are already in my head. So if I ask a question, it's one I already know the answer to."

"Preston, please go back inside and see Katy and Pauly. Nothing is real, and you know that. I'd like to think I taught you something. Let them help you come down from this."

"I hear what you're saying," I walked toward the street. "But the only thing that's different about tonight is the clarity I feel. You know, I ended it all once before."

"That's the illusion! Somebody is pulling your strings." Rage filled his voice. "None of this would be happening otherwise."

"That's what I keep hearing. But I have to try this, I have to show Katy and her people that I can be the hero. That I'm not a fuck-up juvie. If this is my defining moment or if I'm about to go down I have to go down singing, right?"

I'd meant to say "swinging."

"I have to have my chest out and my jaw stiff. Isn't that how you got as far as you did? And you're about the closest I have to a role model. So that's what I'm going to do. It'll be okay. I promise."

I hung up and walked toward the car.

Back in the bar, the phone rang. I turned. Katy stood in the door, wiping tears away. Her face blanked. I couldn't see a hint of anger or sadness in those eyes. Her lips, for once, had nothing to say.

"I love you, Katy."

She turned, and went back inside. Before shutting the door completely she stopped.

I said, "This is all going to end tonight."

Nodding, she said, "I love you, too," and clicked the lock.

I shoved my phone into my front pocket.

The passenger side door to Dani's car popped open. As I got in, little frogs emerged from the storm drains and crawled up over the curb to the naked trees that lined the streets. Their glossy bodies caught the light, reflecting it like a cat's eye reflected the moon.

When I saw her face I wanted to love her all over again. I remembered the way it felt with her head on my lap, her hair splayed out across my legs. I remembered the warmth, the way time seemed to last forever. I remembered the way she looked at me and I wondered if I'd confused compassion for insanity. I remembered the way she tasted. I remembered the way her skin felt in the shower and in bed. And all the bad stuff that happened may as well have happened to somebody else.

Feelings of warmth and excitement bubbled up in me. I wanted her to touch me. I wanted to feel the excitement of something new and dangerous. I'd never know if things would've worked out because our situation didn't last very long. The harsh thoughts I'd harbored for her seemed suddenly meaningless, as if her eyes made it okay to forgive her for being what she was. Like, the way they looked at me made me think that she never really meant to hurt me the way she did. It was all an accident. A misunderstanding.

She drove off, slamming the Mercedes into gear with all the passion I remembered from our nights in her apartment. She sped through the little town, past the liquor stores and boarded up gas stations, out of the projects and past the town hall and strip malls and fast food joints. I watched her every move. Not because I was suspicious of her. But because she excited me. It felt like I'd never left her side. My muddy memory formed an unending chain of earnest events that began that day in Isaac's Records.

Dani and me last winter, staying warm on dark mornings as it snowed outside.

Dani and me last fall, out for a walk in a copper-and-brass-colored canyon, bundled against the stiff mountain wind.

Dani and me last summer, wandering green fields where blueberries grew in such abundance you just had to inhale to taste them.

I saw myself in her eyes. Dark rich forests and a fireplace blazing against the blackest of nights. A wide bed in a room that never saw light. A table set for two with never-ending drink and the sweetest sweets. I saw her coming out of the bathroom, wrapped in a towel, ready to love me again. I saw long conversations about who we'd used to be, and felt the kinship of a girl who knew the trauma of growing up without parents to call her own. I saw the bond that brought us together, the loneliness forged against brothers and sisters who had parents they could hold and kiss. I saw the invisible threads that made us a special pair.

I let my head fall back into the headrest and closed my eyes. In that moment, I felt dry, and warm down to the bone.

Danicka left town on a dark road that twisted through wide bends. She hit the gas on the corners, letting the tires slip on the narrow grey roads. Through cracked speakers shrill violins screeched over staccato piano. The dashboard threw dim green light up at her face. She tapped a pack of Lucky Strikes against the shifter until a single cigarette popped out of the pack. I pulled it out, rolled it back and forth between my finger and thumb, then pushed the lighter in.

When the lighter clicked I held it up to her. She leaned into the electric orange glow and inhaled, lips puckered, then cracked her window to blow the smoke out. As I lit mine, the road slanted down steeply. The car accelerated through curves aided by the mountain's slope. I opened my window to let the moist spring air into the car. I wasn't afraid.

"So," I said, feeling the need to finally say something. "Is this all you?"

"All what?"

"The storm and all that craziness?"

"Preston… That's silly, isn't it?"

"I don't know."

"It is silly. Are you a superstitious twelve-year-old?"

Beyond the glow of headlights I could only see total darkness. And within the glow, only a grey stretch of road that disappeared into velvet blackness ahead of us.

"Well," I said, blowing smoke. "I'm ready to talk,"

She laughed. "I knew you would speak first. But it doesn't change the conversation. Not in the way you think."

"So what do we have to do to take care of all this?" I pushed through the fog in my head by flicking the cigarette out the window. In the glow of the headlights I saw a yellow HOT SPOT sign like the ones we had back home.

I reached up and ran a finger from her temple to her jaw.

She closed her eyes and let her head fall to the side. She inhaled deeply, then her lips formed a pout. "Preston, don't tease me. You hurt me, do you realize?"

"Things didn't turn out the way I'd hoped when I first met you. But things changed, didn't they?" I rested my hand in my lap and turned toward the window. "Besides, you weren't seeing only me."

"Is it fair that I protect myself? If I saw anybody else it was only because I didn't want to get hurt. I didn't love Hicks, or any of them."

"Like you loved me?"

"I did. You were special." She looked at me when she said it.

"Dani, I saw you with Hicks. I know you were seeing other guys. It's fine. It happens."

"So just like that our time is reduced to sentences. Apologies. Those nights when we shared dark bits of our past are only memories. Dates on a calendar like old birthdays."

"I think you know that isn't true. I think deep down you know that I would've dropped everything to be with you if you would've given me half of what I needed." We crossed under I-68, past Listravia Avenue, and where the Sheetz and Burger King in Sabreton should've been. When we passed Fawleys I looked to see if I recognized any of the cars in the parking lot, but Fawleys wasn't there. With a bit of a stutter, I added, "You know that I gave you everything and if I thought for a second you were giving me half as much, I would've been there for you."

I turned away from the window because none of it made sense. It felt like somebody had superimposed 1980 over my mental map of Morgantown. The cars were old Ford Thunderbirds and Pontiacs. Big cars from the early eighties and late seventies. I thought I knew what was happening here and tried to focus on my job. Letting my mind get away from me, like it had with Jane, would've been a typical Preston move.

Time to be new.

The stores in the strip malls were old, hanging on at the very edge of my memory. I knew I'd find the Hills department store over in Star City instead of the Target on the other side of the river. There'd still be a Scotto's Pizza on High Street, but no Black Bear on Pleasant. There'd be coin-operated ponies in front of Kresge's. I knew Mountaineer Mall flourished, with its Pizza Inn and Murphy's Mart, and the Lum's where we'd go for a "fancy dinner" with Pauly's mom because mall employees got a discount. At Murphy's, I'd look for new G.I. Joes in the back while Pauly checked out the fish tanks. I said, mostly to myself, "So, what is all this?"

But my memories drove the car. She didn't. We headed up Greenbag Road, past the old miniature golf course where the whole scene bathed in the glow of reminiscence. Past the trailer park where Stu lived. Past the middle school. Slipping deeper and deeper into a sea of old photos and smells. Deeper and deeper into memories of family events. Old toys. Birthday parties and Christmas parties in elementary school. Embarrassed to exchange gifts because mine came from the dollar store.

I knew the farther I got from Simoneaux's juke joint, the harder it would be to get back to it. So I fought to keep memories of Katy in my head like a trail of breadcrumbs to find my way home, even if I didn't know whether or not she'd still be waiting.

With that thought, Danicka skidded to a stop in the big Mountaineer Mall parking lot. It snowed. I heard the Salvation Army bell from over at Montgomery Ward's. People left the mall with bright plastic bags. Some pushed shopping carts. Some loaded the trunks of their cars. Old ladies with their waitress uniforms sticking out from beneath their winter coats led a pack of mall employees into the rows of Lincolns and Fords. TV salesmen in wrinkled suits. Kids from National Record Mart in leather jackets, laughing. At the tail end of this pack a pair of girls walked arm-in-arm, sharing a cigarette and a Tab. They had big hair and wore acid washed jeans.

I rolled the window down.

My mom and Pauly's mom.

They laughed as a pair of guys in an old Ford Bronco tooted their horn. When my mom opened the back door I heard David Bowie and Bing Crosby's "Little Drummer Boy."

My mom was pregnant.

"So what, Dani? So fucking what?" I figured my dad sat in the Bronco and decided I didn't need to see any more.

Candy canes and snowmen hung from the light posts. Fat Christmas bulbs did little to warm the night or make it seem any more festive than any other day of the year.

"Nothing, Preston. I thought you might like to see."

"Well, I don't. I'm here to resolve things and you're playing head games. And I know it's in my head. I know it's a mash-up of my memory and my imagination and I don't appreciate it." I made a fist and pounded her dash. "Stop it with the fucking games!"

"If you are certain that is really what you want." Dani put the car into reverse and hit the gas. She backed all the way to the end of the row and slid through the wet snow while the National Record Mart gang stared in mock disbelief. She turned the wheel and banged it into first.

I looked for my mom in the side view mirror. For the smallest part of a second, I wanted to tell Dani to turn around and go back, but pride wouldn't let me. She used my emotions to manipulate me, just like she had when we were together. Part of me—the part that wanted to see my mom alive, to see her smile, to see the way she interacted with my adoptive mother—didn't care.

I twisted in my seat and reached for the door handle, but Dani hit the gas and skidded through the icy parking lot.

"Please stop," I said, louder than I wanted to.

She turned out of the parking lot and sped down the hill to Greenbag Road, ignoring stop signs and traffic lights. Drivers honked as she cut them off. She ran the light at the bottom of the hill and raced down University Avenue toward town.

"Slow down," I said.

She drifted into oncoming traffic to go around the row of cars stopped at the Pleasant Street intersection. I grabbed the seatbelt and tightened it.

She hung a sharp left and I fell into the door. When we crossed the Westover Bridge, she said with a smile, "Ever wish you would've jumped too?"

"No. Never." As I thought of all the things she said that night, my mind struggled to find a way to gain control. But the absinthe wore me down, and I didn't feel as sharp as I should've. All I could come up with, "I'm in love with Katy, and I will always remember that day as the day everything changed. That day we were born as a couple. I think that I gained my freedom that day."

She forced a little laugh. "You are not free, Preston. What you call freedom is an illusion, and you will never know otherwise. Never. It is easy to live with your eyes closed, isn't it?"

She pushed the gas pedal all the way to the floor. Street lights and lights from store fronts blurred as they swept past my field of view. The car skidded through turns, and I held on because I knew this wasn't real. Even the transition from pavement to bricks did little to stop this speeding bullet. She had an agenda. A mission. I was just along for the ride.

After a while, I lost track of Westover's twists and turns and tried to find something to orient myself. The river was too far away, so I looked for the Coliseum. Then I looked for the interstate. Then I looked up, into the black sky, and could see no light at all. Only the amber glow of the headlights fading to black. I didn't want to look at Dani, so quietly stared ahead.

She lit another cigarette. I declined another.

Mile after mile of black silence yielded to a glow at the edge of my vision.

Lights finally appeared on the gentle horizon. When the streets narrowed she let the car slow. The roads in this town rarely met at right angles and curved for no particular reason. Old churches that looked like cakes decorated in stained glass and stone and long blocks of apartments stared quietly. She hit the brakes for a big red streetcar that rattled ahead of us on rickety tracks.

Everything around me moved in extravagant motion. Orange-tiled roofs rested next to tall white spires that extended their arms into space. Patches of light and shadow played with alternating patches of red and orange and stark whiteness. Bold columns held up gold curves bursting open with long white pearls. Every building seemed like a palace that could evoke a vision more potent than any fairytale castle could ever dream to. Lavish statues and concrete bows kept even the straightest of lines from being ordinary. After a few minutes of squeezing through the cobbled streets I fought to think of new words to describe it all. *Melodramatic splendor. Anxious. Lavish. Intense.*

"Is this Paris?" I said, figuring if Morgantown, West Virginia, was purgatory, then this must be heaven.

"The Malá Strana," Dani sighed. Pointing to the strange little cars parked along the streets, she added, "And the tireless Trabant."

None of the cars had drivers. The only people I saw were shadows behind thin curtains. Dark shapes preparing for bed, smoking a cigarette. Golden bulbs burning from the end of the heavy iron lampposts perched on the corners created infinite darkness down every side street.

Stanger than the Trabants and the emptiness, were the large military trucks I saw at the ends of some of the long streets. They looked black against the orange glow of the city, and were always surrounded by several grumpy soldiers who talked and smoked. One of them took a piss on the black and white checkered sidewalk as we passed. A small cloud of fog rose from the stream of urine.

On the far side of town, on the other side of a river, an enormous tower rose above the city, like a giant tripod walking across the orange rooftops. Its red lights penetrated the rich blackness.

"Žižkov Tower. It's new," Dani said when she saw me looking. "Fairly new, but the people hate it as if they've hated it for a hundred years. Too much the party and Moscow, they say. Too much like a Soviet rocket. Perhaps to remind us they have something we don't? Some say its only purpose is to jam Radio Free Europe, but I don't believe them."

I nodded, even though I didn't fully understand. "What do you think?"

She ignored me.

"Fuck." A trio of soldiers wearing high black boots that disappeared into long grey coats stepped around the black chains that lined the sidewalk. She slowed to a stop and they surrounded the car.

"Where are we?" I said.

"Quiet." She rolled down her window and reached for her purse.

One of the soldiers shined a flashlight in my eyes.

Dani said something I didn't understand and shoved a wad of American cash at the soldier standing at her door. She whispered, "I told him '*kakoj kurs obmyen*'— what is the rate of exchange?"

He gestured to the one standing on my side of the car and shoved the wad into his front pocket. "*Pasport*?"

Dani said, "Preston, do you have any cash?"

I had the rest of our per diem in my pocket, but I didn't want to give it to her. "No."

"Don't play games." She shoved her palm at me. "You don't have papers. They will arrest you."

"Are you shitting me?" I couldn't make sense of her words. "What the hell are you getting me into?"

The soldier standing to my right tapped my window with the barrel of his assault rifle. His eyes were just slits.

"Preston!"

The soldier motioned for me to roll my window down.

"This is so fucked up, you know that?" I reached into my pocket and gave him all I had with me. About seventy dollars. "Fucking bullshit. Another one of your fucking games."

He counted it then stared at me for a long time. I looked up at him, trying to figure out if he wanted something more from me. My heart raced. He would not look away. So I finally lowered my eyes and stared ahead. With that, he laughed and banged the hood twice. Dani put the car into gear. In the side view mirror I saw the three of them converge in the red glow of her tail lights.

"What the hell? Danicka—"

"An *úplatek*. Like a shakedown." She said it with a casualness that made me embarrassed for even asking. "Ritual is very important to these people. Even for something little, like trying to drive across town."

I watched for another minute to make sure they didn't follow. "Yeah, well if the ritual is so important why am I out seventy bucks?"

"They want you to be submissive and scared, even if it's a bluff. They only have power when you have something to lose. That is the most important thing to remember— not everybody has something to lose." She looked at me very earnestly when she said it. "People with nothing to lose have all the real power. The rest, like us... But they can't come right out and demand the bribe—that defeats the purpose. You have to recognize that you stand beneath them because they have guns. There is always noise and lights and weapons and uniforms, right? Elaborate pomp and music and thunder and fireworks. The party has its flags, the church has its cross. Symbols to help the powerless make a decision."

She slowed to a stop in front of a grand cathedral. White columns topped with green domes and golden crosses stretched a hundred feet into the air. I counted the statues of at least nine different saints perched on the corners that faced the street. Each held a cross or some other ornament made out of gold. Two more saints and a bunch of smaller statues looked down on a pair of red doors.

"That is why the ritual matters. It is part of the system designed by those with the power to keep the powerless from getting exactly what they want. They slap your wrist for skipping a step, for not following procedure. Submission is created by ritual."

A group of children descended the stairs from the church's front doors. All young girls, all wearing grey coats and red scarves. Some held hands. Some of the smaller girls were carried by nuns in heavy black habits. Danicka said, "We always arrived early to pray the Rosary. Always the same pew, always next to *Christ's face is wiped by Veronica.*"

I knew then why she'd brought me here. She wanted me to see her as a person, to realize her motivations were the same as mine. More than anything, I wanted to see her as that person. But the way she spiritually held Pauly captive, the way she'd hurt me, made it hard to not be blinded by her gesture. Her ritualistic game.

None of the young girls looked like Danicka, and for a second I thought she'd meant for me to see something else. The scarves and red cheeks were exactly as she described back in her apartment last year. Small, round faces breathed heavily in the cold air. Danicka smiled as they walked past by the car, one by one. Her eyes followed each one until they passed and just as quickly she looked for the next. If I thought I'd seen her happy back at her little apartment, I was wrong. Here, in the car watching the girls pass, she radiated joy.

"Is this your home? Prague?"

"It is." That I remembered made her smile. "Very beautiful, yes?"

She only turned her head when a young nun passed. Danicka looked for something in the sky far away and did not turn back again until they'd all turned the corner behind us. She said, "A *sestra* is not a suitable mother for a child of the revolution. Sometimes I believe I have lost more love than you could have ever known."

"I never meant to hurt you."

"It's fine. Love is not just like a hat you can change as the seasons change. Maybe it has been much longer than I remembered since I'd been in love. Maybe I didn't love you, Preston, but I thought I could." She put her hand on my knee. "Knowing the dreams I had about you would always only be dreams hurt most of all."

"I'm sorry. I truly am."

"It's fine." She slid a cigarette out of the pack and stared at it for the longest time. Her lips pursed with concentration as the little diesel engine idled into the night. Finally, she slid the cigarette back into the pack and said, "You are free to live as you please."

The words rattled around my head. It took a moment for them to slow to a complete stop. Seeing a shift in her tone, I made a move. "Is Pauly? Can I go back now, and tell him he's free? That he doesn't have to worry about the promise he made under all that stress?"

"Preston," she sighed. "There are rules to follow. Rituals, just like military rituals and church rituals. You can tell him that he is free, that I will pursue him no more, but they are just words." She said all this while continuing to watch the dark corner where the orphans had gone. She looked very sad all of a sudden, then put the car into gear and drove.

"So what do I have to do to clear everything up with Pauly, officially? Surely we can work something out, right?" I tried to hide the excitement in my voice.

But she didn't reply. Her eyes narrowed as she pushed the car through dark alleys toward a rounded arch built into a high, pointed tower. Up in the windows lonely figures stared from dimly lit apartments. This city had too many dark corners, too many dead ends to ever feel like a place I could grow to love, yet seeing it with Danicka made me want to remember every little detail. She made a right onto a lane that curved slowly to the left. Finally, she slowed beneath a patch of naked trees, next to a graffitti-covered wall. "I thought you might like to see this."

I tried to read the spray painted words, but there were too many. Looking for a place to start, my eyes drifted toward the top, and when I saw *All we are saying…* I smiled. His face floated there, right above the lyric. An *Abbey Road*-era John, with the round glasses and long hair, but older.

"Husák hates it. He calls the students that deface the wall with their anti-party protests *Lennonistas*. He says they are all sociopathic drug addicts." She read the slogans and phrases while she spoke. "But this is where the revolution starts, and we will do it our way. No violence. No guns."

"How do you know that?"

"Because it has already happened." Danicka put the car in gear and talked to me like one would talk to a child. "Preston, there are informers all over. In a few weeks one of them will report the *Lennonistas*. Students and *StB* will clash on Charles Bridge. The party does not yet know this, but their days are numbered. I just wanted you to see this before we return."

"Thank you."

She pushed the gas pedal to the floor. "What if you could know everything you'd ever forgotten—every sound, every scent, every little detail about the home where you were born and raised? What would your mind do with so many warm memories of family feasts and laughing with friends every waking second? Think about it, Preston. Everything you'd ever known in your mind at once? How do you think this storm of detail would affect the way you live right now? Do you believe the past would not be as bad as you remembered? Or would you lie awake every night reevaluating every single one of your prejudices and transgressions?"

Once again we were speeding along the narrow streets. She said, "For me, the memory makes it all worse, and every morning upon waking up I stare down the same path I'd struggled down yesterday."

I didn't know how to respond at this point. We were former lovers turned reconciled enemies. So I chose to not reply.

"As a girl I made a promise—a deal—under great duress. Under pretenses that never existed. But it's easy for a young girl to make such a mistake. I let love go when I should've fought to hold onto it. All the crying has made me angry, bitter and very sad. I don't want to be sad anymore, and I want to die with a man who will love me without pretense. But I can't do any of that because I am bound by an agreement I made with a party that refuses to negotiate." She drove faster as the main part of the city fell behind us. "It's a debt I can never repay even though I have money, so to speak."

The buildings got plainer as the road got wider. Instead of curves and waves of gold and plaster, every straight line met at a right angle. Row after row of apartments with windows in straight lines, both up and down, like air holes poked into a cardboard box.

I took a moment to process everything she said, and still none of it made sense to me. After what seemed like an appropriate amount of time, I said, "That doesn't mean you can't let me find a way to repay Pauly's debt to you, right?" I secretly patted myself on the back for staying focused and doing right by him like I'd promised.

"That could be a bit of redemption right there," I added.

"Do you wish to settle debts? Or erase them? Because that is what you are asking. Either way, you must go to the crossroads before dawn on *Voskresenie*—Sunday morning. We will resolve the situation then. For everything there is a ritual, Preston. Can you do this exactly as I tell you?"

I listened very closely, trying to keep an ear open for deception. "I guess. But you sort of said the ritual isn't really necessary?"

"I said it is symbolic! Not unnecessary. Do not confuse the two." She accented each syllable by jabbing the steering wheel with her finger. "Preston, you asked. Do not waste my time if you are not willing to follow my instructions."

I smiled, because for the first time it felt like the more she talked, the more power shifted. "How do I know you'll even show up?"

She smiled. "You want a promise from me? My word?"

"I guess that's what I'm saying. In the past you've left me hanging."

"The ritual binds me," she huffed. "If you do as I will tell you, then I will be compelled. I have no choice."

"Well," I said, dragging it out so I could think. "I'd rather have something as a sign of good faith. Like, I'd rather you wanted to be there than were forced to be there."

"Good faith? Like what, Preston? A wish? Good luck?" She rolled her eyes at my silliness. "My real name?"

My breath caught in my throat.

"Sure," I said, stopping her, then scolding myself for being too eager. My mouth got dry while I waited for her to reply.

She nodded, a pause for drama, maybe.

"Fine." She lit another cigarette. The orange glow cast harsh shadows upon her face, and all of a sudden, she didn't look like somebody I knew. "After you have done exactly as I've told you, I will give you what you want."

When she dropped me off back at the juke joint, the streets were clear. The only cars parked out front were Jamie's and Ben's. The only sign that something apocalyptic had taken place here was the absence of leaves on the trees. I picked up the pint glass I'd dropped in the mud. I didn't know the time, or how long I'd been gone. I tried to tell myself only a few hours had passed, but for all I knew, it could've been a few days. There still weren't any stars in the sky.

The front door clicked open.

I waited.

Katy stepped onto porch. She didn't say anything.

I said, "Where'd everybody go?"

"The people from the church followed you out of here like you said they would. They up and left right after you did."

"Told you I'd fix everything." A little bit of pride welled up in me. "How's Chloey?"

"Good. The cuts were mostly superficial, but she's at the hospital for observation. Got a few stitches. Seven above her collarbone and seven in her hand. The drugs knocked her out." She came down the steps and met me on the sidewalk. "What did you have to do?"

"We talked a lot. Nothing more. She acted like she really didn't care one way or the other about Pauly."

"Doesn't sound like her to just let it go." She tucked her hands into her back pockets.

"But she did. Sunday morning I head back to Mississippi to make it all official."

"How do you do that?" She looked at me skeptically.

"By going back down to those old crossroads one last time."

CHAPTER NINE

Brick walls, bathroom stalls, long dark halls,
Hold your tongue until you get out.
Elbows locked, pushing forward—
A thousand to one.
Stand your ground and we'll knock you over.
A thousand to one and I'll carry your gun.

"My Own Army" Music and Lyrics by Preston Black

I woke up knowing that a new life had descended upon Katy and me. A life where I could be free of Dani's entanglements. A life that represented the clean break we never had. The freedom we always wanted. On Sunday night, when we packed up and headed back to Morgantown, West Virginia, all this would be behind us forever.

I did this because I loved Katy, and knew she deserved better than what I'd given her so far, even though I'd given her everything I could. It took losing her, and being scared, to make me realize that I had a never-ending pool of love and strength for her. It took getting her back, and taking care of things with Danicka to make me see that I lived and breathed for her.

So this morning, when she said she needed time to think, it stung. But I hoped it was just girl talk for "I'm still mad" and figured I'd let it go. And when she said she didn't want to ride to Atlanta with me, and that we needed to take a little breather after the show, I wracked my brain trying to figure out what it meant. When I asked Pauly, he said, "It means she needs some time, bro."

Simoneaux made saying goodbye easy—he assured me he'd see me again one day. He left us with no warnings and no sentiment, whatsoever, and even refused my offer of coming back after the show to help him clean-up. And when Jamie mentioned money Simoneaux got mad. He said, "Friends don't ask for something like that."

205

Pauly, Andre, Sabra and I said our goodbyes over grits with cheddar cheese and biscuits with white gravy at a diner near the interstate. After a quick handshake they went home, and me and Pauly quietly rolled south out of the little Appalachians toward the wide Georgia flats all by ourselves. It took two hours to get to the interstate, and after that life returned to a pace I was used to. Homes and strip malls peeked through gaps in the trees as rolling hills gave way to suburbia. The excitement I felt embarrassed me, and to quench it, I reminded myself that she wasn't here to share it with me.

Atlanta was big. The sun shone brightly on the mountain of concrete and glass that rose from the Piedmont like it had just landed on earth a few nights ago. Cars jockeyed for space on the wide parkway, reminding me that no matter where you went, somebody was always out to get you. Pauly drove aggressively, swearing when he got cut off, then racing ahead to retaliate. I didn't say anything. I didn't care what he did, as long as it made him feel better.

Pauly knew Atlanta, so there were no wrong turns, no need to stop for directions, and we arrived at the theater rather easily. Our arrival felt a little sad after everything that happened this week. Nobody came to greet us. The label didn't send flowers. I didn't dwell on it though.

The venue blew my mind. An old vaudeville theater that had been returned to all its glory by a community restoration effort. A heavy red curtain muffled all but the loudest sounds from beyond the stage. I couldn't even hear cars on the street outside. Gold ribbons and angels in the highest corners reminded me a little of what I'd seen on the church in Prague. A low balcony hung over the rows of red seats. I figured it'd be empty tonight except for the pot smokers. An orchestra pit sat below the stage between a small pair of private boxes. Rachael and Jamie and Chloey would be comfortable in one of those boxes if they came.

A custodian helped us haul our gear into the back, showed us the green room, and hung out, BS-ing with us while we set up. The return to normalcy felt strange. Like he was upset about politics and football and me and Pauly were just happy to be here, mostly unharmed. When we were done, he introduced us to the manager and showed us around. After that we did a quick soundcheck, then left to find the hotel and check in.

Then we waited.

And it was a very lonely, very quiet, wait.

Bo Diddley said every generation's got its own little bag of tricks. Nobody from my generation bothered to tell me what our trick was. Maybe digital was the only thing up our sleeve, even if it made having a hard copy of anything meaningless. I thought about how Pauly's mom had pictures on the walls, photos of weddings and school pictures. She may not have looked at a photo every time she walked past, but the people in the images were always there with her. Looking over her shoulder. Watching TV with her.

Looking at Katy's picture on the little screen of my phone wasn't doing it for me.

Pauly helped me get through it the best way he knew how. He went down to The Varsity after we got back to the theater and bought chili slaw dogs and onion rings and fries while I warmed up. We set our picnic up on the stage, listening to the Allmans while we ate. He got too much food for us to eat ourselves, but Pauly always used to buy for three people so I didn't say anything. We didn't make small talk, or discuss what happened last night, although Pauly did say that he felt as though the weight had been lifted off his shoulders.

I meant to tell him about Prague and all that, and was on the verge of figuring out how to tell him he could stop worrying about Danicka, when a security guard came into the theater to tell us there were a few folks out front who wanted to talk to us. They claimed they knew me.

Pauly shrugged, so I followed the security guard out. As soon as I stepped into the lobby I saw Katy's cousin Henry and his girlfriend Alex. He smiled real big when I stepped forward to hug him. He looked around like he expected to see Katy pop through the door behind me.

After kissing Alex's cheek, I told them the girls were running a little late because I didn't know what else to say. I asked where they were staying, asked what he'd been up to, and all that other chitchat. While he told me about the drive down from West Virginia and the stuff they did all morning I watched a group of protesters on the other side of the street.

My heart fell.

To cover my emotions, I pointed to the door behind me and said, "Henry, we got all kinds of food down there. Pauly will hook you up. I'll be right in."

As soon as the door closed behind them, I walked over to the security guard. "You think they'll be a problem?"

He put his phone into his pocket and answered me with a big old dose of Southern honesty. "Not my problem. I'm off at seven. Y'all have fun though."

"Thanks, man," I said before I went back inside.

As I walked down that long aisle, I ran through all kinds of scenarios in my head. The first involved me asking Henry to play whether or not Katy showed. Figured that was the best way to approach it. I knew he could handle our songs if I made crib notes for him, and made a list of simple I-IV-V tunes he could blast right through. That meant no duets and no two-part harmonies, but it would be easy enough to substitute cover songs. The best way to play it with the crowd would be to let them know we were going to stay on stage until the sun came up tomorrow morning, or until the venue kicked us out, whichever came first—an Allman Brothers at the Fillmore type of thing. And I'd have to talk Pauly into doing a whole set at least. Maybe even go into Pipeline stuff like the old days. Weezer. Guns N' Roses. Foo Fighters. The Clash. Jane's Addiction. Ramones. Social Distortion.

A set of covers wouldn't be the same as a show with Katy, which they'd paid to see, but they'd have to understand after everything that went on this week. I'd tell them that she felt just fine, that she was a little worn out after the ordeal, and that she appreciated all the Tweets and emails.

Hope y'all understand.

I felt like shit for even thinking it, and reminded myself that we probably could've gotten away with cancelling the show altogether.

So I took a deep breath and explained the situation to Henry as he tore into a hot dog and asked if he'd be interested. He looked nervous as hell and I thought for sure he'd decline, but Alex gave him a look that changed his mind.

As soon as he agreed I grabbed Katy's backup violin and my new Martin, and led him down to the green room to practice. I explained how I thought the format would go, and I did my best to tell him the type of things we'd play as I wrote out a set list. Henry told me which of our songs he knew best and where he'd be able to improvise or just play around me. He nodded a lot, and if he was nervous he didn't act like it. We spent a good hour or so running through stuff together and he eventually loosened up. I told him to practice while I left to try to convince Pauly to play.

As I got to the top of the stairs I heard voices on the other side of the curtain. My heart raced, and I suddenly felt very scared and very sad. The other side of the curtain felt like the other side of the planet after everything that happened this week—I couldn't trust what was over there anymore. Pauly knelt in front of my cabinet, taping cables to the floor. He didn't see me.

"Hey, man," I said. "You feel like playing a full set tonight?"

He stood and brushed off his pants. "Ain't played a full set of anything in a year."

"I'm going to need you."

"Man, what are you talking about?" He put his arm around my neck. "She'll be here, okay? How long's it going to take for you to realize that when a girl says she needs space, she needs space. You know her better than that."

"Yeah…" I shook my head because he was right. "Was she mad when I left with Dani?"

"Truthfully, the whole thing with Chloey kept most of us busy. She never said anything to me about it." Pauly checked his shirt pocket for cigarettes. "How do you think she felt when she saw you get into that car?"

"Well, Katy knew I acted in the best interest of the group, and that I love her more than anything. So, me getting into the car with Danicka—who may or may not be the devil or whatever—is just like walking down to Dairy Mart for pepperoni rolls. That's how I think she felt." I tried to smile.

"Well you keep telling yourself that, big brother. And I'll keep pretending you're right." He gave me his best "authority figure" look when he said it. "By the way, there's a pair of kids out there who said to tell you they came to see you. Ray and Vance from Lula?"

"No shit." I walked over to the edge of the curtain and pulled it back. The boys stood right in front of a speaker cabinet talking to a pair of disinterested college girls. Only the first four or five rows were full, but people were streaming in steadily. I didn't want to count heads, but couldn't stomach playing to another half-empty house.

"Look at you guys," I said, kneeling down on the edge of the stage. "It's a long drive, ain't it?"

"About seven hours," Ray said, shaking my hand. I could smell weed on him.

"We partied the whole way out, so it didn't seem that long." Vance spit into a Mountain Dew bottle he carried inside his coat pocket. "We left yesterday."

"Well, last night. Then we hooked up with these guys in Birmingham." Ray pointed to a bunch of dudes in flannel shirts. "They brought those girls with them."

"Yeah," Vance added, "When we told them how we drove you out to them crossroads to talk to the devil, they got real interested."

"You told people that? Shit, Vance. Don't do that. Like I need people thinking I'm insane."

"It's all good. They all got it in their heads that this is going to be a big deal tonight."

"Because of what you told them?"

"I don't know about all that. But being on the news all week helped, I'm sure."

"You saw that, huh?" I stood and tried to see what it looked like in the lobby. "Maybe

I'll catch you after the show. Grab pizza or whatever. Just don't go blabbing to everybody, okay?"

"Word spreads, man," Ray said, smiling. "One way or another people find out."

"Ain't nothing private no more. You should know better." Vance passed his Copenhagen to Ray.

"You'd think," I said with a wave, then left.

When I ducked back behind the curtain, Pauly said, "Sounds like a good Friday night kind of crowd."

I shook out my hands. "Well, we'll see what happens once I plug in."

"Preston."

I turned around to see what he had to say.

"Have a little faith."

"Thanks, baybruh. I will." Saying it didn't help my nerves. I tried curling my toes as a way to calm myself.

Except for Henry sawing on Katy's little fiddle, everything was mostly quiet backstage when I ducked into the bathroom. I pushed the drain stopper down and ran the cold water to shove the ambient noise away. After so much music, I wanted quiet. When the sink had filled, I held my breath and lowered my face into the water. I could still hear Henry getting ready, doing me a solid, but the sound didn't comfort me. His playing had a harsher, more traditional edge to it than Katy's. Sounded more like Jamie. When the music finally came to a halt I figured I needed to go give him a pep talk.

I dried my face off with a clean white towel that smelled a little like the fabric softener Pauly's mom used. I tried to pee, and couldn't. Anything to kill time. But the play clock ticked faster, and I made up my mind to make the best of whatever happened tonight, figuring I could deal with the fallout on Monday. But when I turned the corner I heard a bunch of voices in the green room.

I clenched my fist and slowly drifted toward the end of the hall. That was when I saw Rachael standing in the doorway.

"The Collins clan doesn't do anything quietly," I said, relaxing a bit. "How's everybody doing?"

"We're good. How's Preston doing?" She put her arm around me.

"Better now." I tucked my hands into my back pockets as she let me pass. I said, "Jamie and Ben?"

Rachael gently placed her hand on my elbow and said, "Jamie's at the soundboard."

"And Ben is at the bar," Chloey added.

I looked at her and said, "How're you?"

A bandaged little hand peeked out from behind her jacket's zipper. Her left sleeve hung limply at her side. "It hurts bad."

"I'm sorry to hear that."

She half-shrugged. "I got a prescription for the pain, but Mom's afraid I'll abuse my pills and become a druggie."

"Want me to kiss it and make it better?" I laughed, awkwardly.

She smiled. "I got something you can kiss."

"Chloey," Rachael scolded. "Preston, my little girls were so innocent until they met you."

"Sorry," I said. She probably didn't know how much I'd truly meant it.

She hugged me and held me for a moment. "I can't wait to have you guys back home. What do I have to do to keep you from running all over like this?"

Katy stood in the far corner next to Alex, slipping a tiny white rose into her hair behind her left ear. On the table next to her fiddle sat a bouquet of flowers in a vase, a fruit basket, and a bottle of champagne that the label must've sent over.

But I couldn't take my eyes off her. She had a curl in her hair and cherry red nails and lips. Beneath her eyes she wore just a little more dark eyeliner than usual. She pointed at her fiddle, there on the table.

I defended myself with, "I asked him to sit in on a few songs."

"Is that right?" She turned to her cousin. "Or did he think I wouldn't show?"

Henry answered as diplomatically as possible, which meant he didn't say a thing.

"Thanks, man." I grabbed Katy's little hand and pulled her over to me. She smelled like a plum blossom and looked like an angel. I kissed her. "Where'd you go?"

"Retail therapy. Got my nails did." She rested her head against my cheek and held out her fingers. "Mom bought you a new shirt. She thinks we should start matching, like The Osmonds."

"No, that's not true, is it?"

Katy said, "She's not denying it."

I smiled, but didn't mean it.

The small talk was nice, but I wanted a chance to be with to her in private, and knew that wouldn't happen until we were in bed at the hotel. It frustrated me, not being able to say what I wanted to say because of everybody hanging around. We'd been in this situation a thousand times before, moments when a few words in private could've offset a squabble later. When I felt my stomach ball up, I figured I needed to say what

I had to say no matter what. This was too big to put off until later, when we were both exhausted. I said, "Are you mad?"

"Pres, tonight, baby. Okay? I'm not mad. I'm too tired to talk."

"I understand that. But I have to know what's going on with us. We didn't talk last night when I got back and we didn't talk today. We never even got a chance to talk after the church camp and the boat. All I want to do is talk to you. I miss you, okay? I love you, Katy. Your disappearance scared the shit out of me. You're my best friend, and I want to make sure you're okay. And that we're okay."

By now nobody could say anything. It was so quiet I could hear the rowdy audience on the other side of the curtain. Katy looked at her mom and cousin and baby sister. They all seemed to want to know where she stood as well.

"Honestly?"

"Why not?"

"I want to pick up right where we left off at the truck stop. Pecan pie and butter pecan. I want to finish that conversation before we have this one. I figure if we finish that conversation, this one won't matter." She put her arms around me.

When I held her, I felt invincible. I wondered how this girl could make me feel so safe and strong. When she exhaled I felt her breath on my neck. When she blinked I felt her eyelash against my cheek. When she was with me, every breath felt like a laugh, and every time I opened my eyes it felt like waking up from a dream.

Henry raised a finger to get our attention. "Shhh," he said.

I held my breath.

From the crowd I heard a chant, a familiar cadence. But the curtain muffled it too much to be certain. I said, "Just hang back for a second," and followed Henry toward the stairs.

The voices grew louder, more unified as we got to the top of the stairs. I closed my eyes like that would help me hear more clearly. Then they got to the chorus.

"Katy," I went back down the steps and grabbed her hand.

She crept alongside me, slowly putting one foot in front of the other until she heard it too. Henry handed her fiddle and bow back to her at the top of the stairs. There was no light behind the curtain except for the LEDs on my effects rack until Pauly walked over from the far side of the stage with a little flashlight in his hand. He handed us our IEMs. "You ain't going to believe this shit."

When he signaled for the curtain to be raised the audience didn't react. As the gap between the floor and the golden tassels grew, I could see them, bathed in the house lights. Hundreds of people packed between the seats and aisles, every back turned to us. People in the balcony tried to make sense of what happened on the floor below them. Even though they couldn't see, they still sang. "Preston Black couldn't sleep the whole night through…"

Katy shook her head and smiled.

I couldn't believe it either.

"Preston Black couldn't sleep the whole night through…"

The remainder of Hicks's congregation pushed in from the lobby. With Boggs locked up, A.G. Ashby and the girl with the crown of thorns tattoo led them. Should've figured we hadn't seen the last of her. I'd imagine seeing your beau blown into heaven ain't the kind of thing that dries up and goes away like a zit. Figured she wouldn't be happy until Katy suffered a little more. The rest carried the same old signs we saw in Louisville and Nashville, but freedom of speech only goes so far. And they chanted the same hate-filled rants. But our crowd, a unified mass of otherwise unrelated people, made sure their noise wasn't heard tonight.

"He'd lay in bed 'til the morning came, but the devil'd visit him just the same…"

I walked to the edge and waited. The raw energy coming from the unaccompanied singing made me woozy. My knees wobbled. I wished my mom could've been here to see something like this. And I couldn't have that thought without thinking about what John had told me back at the bar, so I looked for Jamie, back at the soundboard. His look of shocked disbelief said it all.

Then I looked for Ben, at eye level in the box to our right. He smiled, and toasted me with his PBR as Rachael, Chloey and Alex joined him.

I looked for Pauly. He stood in the dark with his arms crossed, watching just like me.

When I turned to Katy for acknowledgement, I heard the squeal of fiddle through the PA. At once the crowd rose in a gigantic roar. They turned to the stage where a single spot lit Katy at her mic. People had their hands over their heads, some were balled into fists. The applause had mass, like a dense fog.

They all stopped singing at the break before the next verse. In their collective silence I heard the *God hates witches* chant from the protestors.

I stepped up to the mic and said, "Y'all know the words…" and they turned around and picked right up where they left off. At the end of the line they whistled and applauded wildly. A long wash of static that left me speechless. Pauly shrugged as he walked out to meet me. "Atlanta P.D. is on its way."

I put the IEM into my ear and joined Katy back at the center of the stage as the crowd sang, "Preston Black went down to the crossroads…"

This whole situation with the crowd and the song felt like the climb right before the Jack Rabbit's double dip at Kennywood, the *click-click-click* like a stopwatch, counting down the seconds until you felt like you were going to fly right off the track. Afraid that any move I'd make would feel anticlimactic, I put my guitar around my neck, but didn't play. Instead, I stepped to the mic and sang right along with them.

The protesters went limp as soon as the cops showed up, dropping to the floor as a passive resistance tactic. Some grabbed chairs or audience members, others tried to disappear into the crowd. Ashby became violent, swinging his retractable baton in a wide arc before being tackled from behind by a couple of skinny guys in black T-shirts. If the bright house lights and awkward silence hurt the mood the crowd had created with their act, then the shouting and shoving and tension buried it.

Almost instinctively, some of the guys in the crowd formed a wall by locking arms, preventing the intruders from escaping into the audience and disappearing. Fans blocked the doors and assisted the incoming police officers by doing whatever they were asked even as they were spit on and cursed at. House security filtered in from their various spots throughout the theater to step in between the protestors and the fans, taking the punches and insults from what remained of Hicks's people as they were laid out on the floor, face down. The crowd cheered.

"Thank you all for your patience and cooperation." I spoke into the microphone. "You sure know how to throw down a welcome."

I backed away while they applauded.

"And you all know how to take care of guests. I want to thank the ladies and gentlemen in blue for coming out and making us feel safe after the week we've had." That line was almost a prerequisite, but I'd meant it. "And as they get all these folks ready for the paddy wagon, I got something I want to say to them."

I ran my hand through my hair because I didn't know where I needed to go with this. "Anything else I have to say after these people are gone, I'm going to say it with my guitar. But this, right now, is for the folks in the back. The ones who saw fit to take Katy, and drag her into a camp in the hills where they could force their beliefs upon her. And I'm going to say it in a way they understand."

I licked my lips and looked for a bottle of water before realizing I'd forgotten to bring any up from the green room with me. So I went on. "You all are really good at telling people what they need because it's what you need. But that doesn't work for me, and I'm not going to pretend to speak for anybody else here tonight, but I'll bet it doesn't work for some of them either. Even the people who worship the same God you do."

I unbuttoned another shirt button and wiped my forehead with my sleeve.

"I listen to 'Layla' and I feel like I'm a part of something bigger, because in my experience, God doesn't only exist in cathedrals or out in outer space or in some other dimension. In my experience you find him wherever you find him. And that's all I want for me and for Katy and for anybody else in here who doesn't believe same as you do—is to be able to stumble upon what we believe where and whenever we'd like."

Rachael watched from their box. I tried to gauge my progress by her expression. But she motioned for me to go on. "When the piano kicks in, and Duane's guitar soars, I can close my eyes and be anywhere on earth. Anywhere. And it's not just the guitar—Mick says a guitar's just a block of wood somebody saw fit to take a saw to—it's the union of guitar, piano, drummer… It's a group of people locked in to each other, making something more beautiful and more perfect than a single man could ever make alone. The piano by itself doesn't go anywhere. It doesn't say anything. It's a chord progression. That's it. Nothing divine there."

I wiped sweat out of my eyes. "And Duane's guitar?"

I waited while a bunch of the guys cheered and smiled. "Man, there's a reason Clapton went looking for him down in Miami. In my opinion, divinity brought them together. Divinity put Duane's slide with Clapton's melody. And I don't need the likes of you all telling me my ideas are wrong. Because I know who came through the darkness and saved me when I was down. I'd close my eyes and ask God to bring my mom back or make my presence less of a burden on Pauly and his mom and pap. And you know who answered?"

They waited in silence.

"Duane Allman, that's who. He coaxed me to sleep night after night with that guitar. I let many a tear dry while I zeroed in on the sound he made with a bottle over his finger. You can call me stupid or whatever, but I thought Duane's guitar sounded like angels singing. Who here is going to tell me otherwise?"

I paused, for drama, but figured I had to keep going even as the cops removed the last of the protestors to the street for processing.

"That's what I thought. But there ain't a single one of you can say that a choir of angels don't sound like Duane's guitar."

People clapped. Responding to the mojo I worked.

"So if I want to keep praying to John Lennon and Joe Strummer and Johnny Cash and Duane Allman, I'm going to, because those guys got me through more shit than any saint or priest ever did."

They liked that line, and let me know it.

"I don't know what heaven's like. Maybe I ain't ever going to see it. But I know what it felt like in the studio when those two got together because I heard it with my own ears. So keep your rattlesnakes and water moccasins. I got this song. And a hundred like it."

I looked over at Pauly. He stood at his amp with his Fender P over his shoulder, cracking his knuckles.

"I do believe in something greater. It's just not what you believe. That is my statement of faith."

The polite applause continued. And I knew I'd talked too long. But it didn't matter. I'd said what I needed to. And now the time had come to move on.

So I turned to Katy, and to Pauly, and said, "Let's give them some of what they came for."

CHAPTER TEN

I watched the stars, but they never moved, that night lasted days,
The devil came down from the mountain and found me straight away
She told me I could trust her, and made a promise with her eyes
I tried to run, but stumbled, and she replaced my dreams with lies.

"Hey, Hey Little Bluebird" Music and Lyrics by Preston Black

The inscription on Duane Allman's grave read, *"I LOVE BEING ALIVE AND I WILL BE THE BEST MAN I POSSIBLY CAN. I WILL TAKE LOVE WHEREVER I FIND IT AND OFFER IT TO EVERYONE WHO WILL TAKE IT... SEEK KNOWLEDGE FROM THOSE WISER... AND TEACH THOSE WHO WISH TO LEARN FROM ME."*

Only Jamie chose to visit the gravesite with me and Katy. And Katy only did it because she wanted to be with me, and I was fine with that. The rest went on to Sardis, Mississippi, to get a hotel and sleep.

I didn't hear any music at his grave. No Les Paul. No slide guitar. The sun shone brightly on the white marble, nearly blinding us. In my head, I couldn't understand that a body rested in the ground. That beneath the marble and dirt lay what remained of Duane Allman. In my head he was always smiling, smoking, riding his motorcycle, playing his Les Paul. Because of all the live recordings and the pictures and the little bit of video, he'd never have to be truly dead to me. In other words, seeing his grave didn't change as much as I thought it would.

I said, "Coast is clear?"

"You're good," Jamie said. Sometimes I think he liked using me as an excuse to trip into deviance.

I grabbed the black metal fence and hoisted myself to the top, then dropped onto the sacred ground between Duane and Berry's final resting places. When I knelt between them I felt a little sting of guilt. "Should I feel bad about this?"

217

"Only if you get caught," Katy said. "So stop screwing around."

"Right. What's first?"

Jamie pulled out the little scrap of paper Simoneaux had written the directions on. He brushed the crease out of it, cleared his throat, then said, "Put thirteen pennies on the headstone, and say, 'Come here, kind spirit, and sell me some of what you got. Please protect me, Katy, Pauly, Jamie, Ben, Rachael, Chloey, Henry and Alex."

"Now?"

"Sure," Jamie said. "Then you walk around the grave three times. Clockwise."

So I put the pennies on the headstone and said the words just as he'd read them. When I finished my laps, Jamie said, "Now you take the dirt from near the head, go down about eight to ten inches. Dig out your thirteen handfuls and say, 'I'm paying you for what I'm taking, and for your protection tonight. In the name of the Lord.' Then you drop the pennies in the hole and bury them."

I took the Jack Daniels bottle from my jacket and unscrewed the lid. I stuck my hand in between the plants and yanked out a big hunk of grass. I dug into the topsoil with the bottle cap, scraping the sides of the hole to loosen the red Georgia clay. Then I scooped it into the bottle a handful at a time.

The dry clay consisted mostly of dust that coated the inside of the bottle, and it didn't go in as easy as I thought it would. I broke up bigger clumps the best I could and shoved them into the neck. When I finished, I had red clay stuck beneath my fingernails. I turned and passed the bottle through the fence to Jamie. Before I could climb back over, Jamie said, "Preston, would you do me the honor?"

He held his hand through the fence and turned his palm up. I took the two guitar picks, one for Duane's grave, one for Berry's, and placed them. As I turned, he nodded. "Thank you."

The crossroads, and Barbee Cemetery, just south of Lula, Mississippi, were right where I'd left them. But the hundreds of cars lining the road were new. Kids tailgated next to hatchbacks, middle-aged guys wearing Atlanta Braves caps and Arkansas Razorback hats and New Orleans Saints jerseys sat on the hoods of their Navigators and Land Cruisers. Guys walked up and down both sides of the highway making moves on the girls sitting in the front seats of their Focuses and Civics, texting. There were high school kids straight-up blazing right out there in the open. I could smell their skunk weed as we drove past.

"Hundreds," I said.

The flat landscape went on for miles. Every now and then a row of trees hinted that there was more to this place than fields to be plowed, crops to be tended to.

"Thousands," Katy corrected me.

Pauly said, "You got to be shitting me."

When we got to the intersection of 49 and 61, I could see them stretched out to the north and south as well, with their blinkers flashing and parking lights on.

"This is my life," I said. "My problem. What do these people need to see?"

"Who told them about all this?" Katy asked. It came off as more of a scolding, really.

"I told Ray we were headed back to where it all started, that's all. I kind of assumed he'd think it was metaphorical."

Pauly said, "You assumed that kid had a head for metaphor?"

"Okay, everybody calm down," Jamie said. "No matter what happens they're going to see what they choose to see."

"Yeah, but if nothing happens I'm the one that looks like an asshole. If nothing happens, all these people are going to run home and say I'm a fraud and I'm full of shit."

"If nothing happens, Preston, then we have nothing to worry about." Katy put her hand on my knee. She wore my green Army jacket over top of her other jacket. I didn't want to say anything, but it was pretty much what she wore the night they abducted her.

She said, "If nothing happens, we go home and sleep in and eat Sirianni's and write songs—or not write if that's what we want. Then Easter Sunday we can eat ham and pierogi until we can't move. Grandma's making halupki special for you. You can sleep until April if you want. But let's get this straight—if nothing happens tonight, we win."

"Okay." I pulled her over to me and kissed the top of her head.

"Pull right over here?" Jamie slowed to stop in the median.

"Looks as good as anyplace else." I turned to take it all in. "Surprised the cops ain't showed up. Kind of wish they would."

We drifted into the soft grass between the divided lanes of Highway 61. The rest of the gang pulled in right behind us. Ben got out of the other car first. He couldn't believe it either. "Preston, you ready to embrace the suck if this all goes south?"

I ignored him as I buttoned my denim jacket up over my hoodie. "What time is it?"

"About ten 'til twelve. What're you supposed to do?" I could see Katy's breath when she talked.

"I don't know, for sure." Over my shoulder somebody tooted their horn. From the other direction I heard a loud car stereo playing techno. The whole scene pissed me off. *This ain't fucking Bonnaroo, people.*

Jamie popped the trunk and I grabbed my guitar. "Danicka said be here before midnight with my guitar, a silver coin, and the grave dust. She said I go to the middle and get started."

Katy said, "Just like that, huh?"

"I don't know. I have to read something too." I gulped down the rest of my coffee and set the cup on the hood. "You think this is a waste of time?"

"We'll see. What do you do with the coin and grave dust?"

"She said they're for protection."

Ben said, "From her?"

"I don't know."

Katy stood there, expecting a little more from me.

I shrugged. "Maybe this will all be over tonight."

"Maybe?" She kissed my cheek and I set my guitar in the grass.

"Well, I don't know what you all are going to see." I crossed my arms. "I think it's going to be a discussion. Like a negotiation."

"Preston," Rachael said my name like it was a placeholder to hold the conversation until she could take a sip of hot tea. "Don't you have to give something up in a negotiation?"

I took a deep breath as she went on. "What will you put on the bargaining table? Considering how much everybody has already lost."

Nobody said a word. Except me.

I replied, "I don't know if you all know how much Katy, and by extension, all of you, have done for me. Pauly knows, because he's known me his whole life. Jamie knows. He saw what happened with Ernie Currence down at his farm, and he knows Mick, so he probably has some backstory that you all don't."

I couldn't exactly turn and look Rachael in the eye, but I tried my best. I said, "Maybe you don't remember the first time I met you, but I sure do. We played Scrabble at your mom and dad's house. That night I found out about Stu's death and Pauly's accident within minutes of each other. A monumental night. If there's a bigger word for that kind of night, I don't know it. And the major difference between my life then and my life now is Katy. The show at The Stink doesn't matter if I'm on stage by myself. And therefore, nothing matters if I'm by myself. The best thing about the life we have, for me, isn't about the music at all. It's about waking up with Katy and sharing quiet moments with Katy and going to McDonalds' drive-thru in our pajamas on a Sunday morning. It's about the surprise of feeling her hand in mine when I don't expect it. It's about having somebody ask you if everything's okay when you wake up with a nightmare at four in the morning."

In a way I felt like I'd gotten too far ahead of myself. But in a way, it didn't matter. "So what am I going to put on the table if I have to put something on the table to get things back to the way they were? To make sure Pauly can live the life he wants?"

Everybody waited.

"I'm going to give Danicka back her music. I'm going to tell her to shove it. I'll work construction if I have to, but I'll still be able to make Katy happy. Because I believe I make her happy. This thing we got—making music as a couple—is a rare thing. It doesn't bother me that interviewers always ask about being in a relationship even though there are things we'd both rather talk about. I don't see us as Johnny and June for a lot of reasons, although there are a lot of similarities there, too. But it comes down to being able to wake up with her every day."

I knew nobody would be able to say anything after all that. So I just left it out there to the stars. Katy slid her hand into mine.

I knew if I stopped to think about what I'd said it would really get to me and bring me down. So I didn't, and it took a lot of effort to keep the things I said out of my head.

Thank God Pauly was there to put everything right back in.

"You'd give all this up for me?" He dumped out his coffee and lit a cigarette. "Then you are fucking stupid."

I pulled Katy closer to me. She took a deep breath and leaned against me. I kissed her, then said, "Do you think this is stupid?"

"No, Preston." She kissed me back and I closed my eyes. She let go of my hand before backing away.

When I walked into the intersection, a fuss washed through the people lined up along the sides of the road. The noise went out along the highways, like ripples from a stone thrown into a pond. And when I strummed, the crowd plopped down into the grass in the median, on car hoods and in truck beds. The alternating yellow, red, and green light barely broke through the darkness.

For a second I thought I should say something, maybe apologize in advance to the people who came out tonight. When I looked at the Post-it notes stuck to the top of my guitar I figured Katy was right—I didn't owe anybody. Dani never said if I had to read while I played or if it even mattered, so I strummed lightly. Over and over I told myself

221

you don't owe them. "I'm going to recite a little bit of the one hundred and thirty-sixth Psalm here. So bear with me for a bit."

I cleared my throat, and said, "Give thanks unto the Lord, for he is good, for his mercy endureth forever."

Strumming made it feel natural to want to give the verse cadence, like a song. I fought the urge. I didn't want this to be anything at all like the music I loved. "Give thanks unto the God of gods, for his mercy endureth forever."

Saying the line made me think that it provided a clue to the state of the heavens. "God of gods" meant that there had to be more than one, making me question everything else I ever learned in catechism.

Or it meant I'm about to come toe-to-toe with a lesser god.

And the possibility of seeing Danicka for what she really was scared me.

"Give thanks to the Lord of lords, for his mercy endureth forever."

I shook my head and tried to turn my back, but they'd surrounded me. They were everywhere, watching. These last few days made me realize that all I ever wanted to do was be free to write and play my music and here I was, on display, showing the world my fears and weaknesses. Public therapy. Katy would say I already did that in my songs. Put too much of myself into them. And I figured no matter what happened tonight, I'd lose.

If the devil didn't show, they'd call me a fraud.

And if the devil did show…

"To him who alone doeth great wonders, for his mercy endureth forever." I kept my voice low because I didn't want to end up hoarse.

"To him that by wisdom made the heavens—"

Off in the distance I heard a commotion. The noise came from afar, but to me it sounded like people talking in the back of a quiet theater. Just inaudible whispers at first, but the warnings being yelled down the road got progressively louder.

"Heads up!"

I changed chords and slowed the tempo so I could hear.

"Watch your feet."

I held my breath.

"Off the road, there."

I softly plucked the low E.

"Holy shit—"

Katy and the rest turned. I figured it was Danicka, and prepared to step aside.

People pressed themselves in between the vehicles along the berm, clearing the highway for something dark and slow. Like a shadow.

Something that shook the ground, like a steady pounding on a bass drum. I didn't see headlights. I didn't hear the tap of her old diesel engine.

The surprise on the faces of the last few rows of people made it impossible to know what to expect. Those who stood farther off craned their necks. Flashes of white light lit the night as people took pictures. Little red LEDs glowed as people videoed with their phones.

Because I couldn't move, I was the last one to see the magnificent black bull stride beneath the traffic signal as the people parted. Yellow light splashed across the pavement as the bull walked right up to me. The light turned red as the animal circled.

I could smell the sweat and manure on its hide. I felt its hot breath on my hands as it sniffed me. It lifted its head and its snout came to just below my chin. I took a step backward as it snorted and blew mucus into the night.

It stared at me for a long moment. Then, as quietly as it came, the bull turned and resumed its tour.

People at the other end of the intersection cleared a path, same as when the animal arrived. A tense silence lingered after it crept back into the darkness.

I looked at Katy and shrugged.

After an anxious moment I heard whistles and howls coming from the darkness. A wash of applause that lasted a minute too long considering what was about to go down tonight. I looked at Katy. "What time?"

She said, "Midnight exactly," as the applause diminished.

My hands were shaking.

"Preston?" Jamie said, getting my attention as he strummed an imaginary guitar.

I continued. "To him that stretched out the earth above the waters, for his mercy endureth forever."

The verse went on and on until the words meant nothing to me. My eyes got tired from reading in the dim light. My hands got sore.

I looked for stars. Looked at the people who came out to see something they might not even be able to fully describe later. Nothing changed but the words.

"The sun to rule by day…"

In the distance I heard cars starting and saw the sweep of headlights as people got bored and decided to head home.

"The moon and stars to rule by night…"

223

There were new faces in the first few rows. I turned slowly as I read, completing one revolution per verse, more or less.

"Oh, give thanks unto the God of heaven, for his mercy endureth forever."

Over and over and over and over, counting second after second for the next hour with each word I read, until Katy finally said, "Five 'til."

I continued, quieter now, with an ear open for whatever came next. "His mercy endureth…"

And right on schedule a murmur came from up the road. Once again the crowd cleared a path. Their collective tone came off sounding a little less surprised this time.

I heard the click-clack of claws before I saw the large black dog trot around the legs of the folks closest to the intersection. It ran a wide circle, stopping to sniff the ground and coffee cups and fast food wrappers. Nobody reached out or called to it.

Then, just like the bull, it headed off to the north.

This time they didn't applaud. People returned to their Monster Energy Drinks and their iPhones. Texting and playing Words With Friends as I went back through the verse.

"With a strong hand, and with a stretched out arm…"

Katy leaned against Pauly. Rachael and Chloey were wrapped up in a big old Mexican blanket from the back of Ben's Jeep.

"And slew famous kings…"

I yawned. In the distance I heard birds. Aside from me and my guitar they made the only other noise.

"And brought out Israel from among them…"

Off to the west lightning flashed from a distant cloud. Faint blue bursts without sound seeped through the blackness. I watched it for the better part of forty minutes while my fingers blistered and bled. When they hurt too bad to play, I tuned my guitar to an open E and pulled the bottleneck slide out of my coat pocket. I didn't like the sound it made.

Sounded like an invitation to trouble.

"But overthrew Pharaoh and his host in the Red Sea…"

In the distance red brake lights disappeared into the horizon as more people left.

"Who remembered us in our low estate…"

After what seemed like another hour, I expected somebody to tell me the time had come to head back to the hotel. To call it quits. Maybe I would've even welcomed it. Maybe I'd gotten in over my head, and figured I could pull out before I embarrassed myself. Or worse.

But a black horse coming across the muddy field changed my mind. I didn't react as it passed. And as it returned to the night, I found it easy to get lost in the meditation.

"For his mercy endureth forever."

At three a.m. a black lamb bolted out of the field from over by the cemetery. By now most of the people had gone. A few dozen stragglers sat in truck beds and on car hoods on the medians and shoulders. It didn't feel like a party anymore.

It finally felt like a ritual.

"For his mercy endureth forever."

At four, a black rooster strutted onto the pavement. It lingered for a long time, scratching the blacktop and walking small circles. Crows gathered in the trees at the edge of the fields. I could hear them cry between verses. I kept expecting the rooster to respond, but it left quietly, without paying anybody any mind at all.

"For his mercy endureth forever."

At five a black cat fell onto its back at my feet. It rolled in the grit, bathing in the dust. The birds grew louder.

"For his mercy endureth forever."

At six, a crow landed on the traffic signal and cawed. It hopped along the metal support, flicking its tail and flapping. As it yapped, its cries were answered by others, off in the blackness. They approached the intersection, flying circles around the crowd like the souls of the departed fleeing this plane at Rapture. They formed a high dome, a swirling black cup that forced my voice and guitar right back down to me, creating an amphitheater in which the fantastic could happen. The air warmed. The caws seemed superficially loud, like they were in my head. And when that wave of birds landed, another surged in from the blackness.

Some of the kids tried to video with their phones, but there was nothing to see above the glow created by the traffic lights. It was as if the night itself transformed into a mass of black feathers. The cawing grew as birds flew tighter circles around me. Their shadows caused the light from the signals to be reflected in all directions. I could see faces in the crowd. Some looked like they regretted coming out tonight.

In the space between the birds I saw the faintest trace of pink appear in the sky to the east. Katy wouldn't look.

Hundreds and hundreds of them descended upon us, their wings creating a superficial breeze that made the air heavier as they flew tighter circles around the intersection.

So I didn't see the car come in from the west. I only saw the shadows created by her headlights grow down the highway ahead of me. Then I heard a pair of thunderous booms. Just like the night I met Tommy over in the cemetery.

Everybody turned and looked.

The crows didn't fly off at the noise. So I didn't actually hear Danicka get out of the car and shut the door behind her over their clamor. But I could smell clove and citrus. Like clementines at Christmas. Beneath it all I caught the faintest scent of wood ash. She wore a short grey wool jacket over a black dress. Her hair was pulled back in a silver hair band.

She said, "So you saw the dog and the bull and the rest?"

"Just like you said. Followed the steps down to the letter. No shortcuts." I let my guitar hang on its strap and shook out my hands. Pins and needles shot through my fingers, up to my shoulders. Bursting with confidence, I said, "Let's get to it."

"Preston, we don't talk." She set her fingers lightly on my arm. "I'm sorry."

And like that, she shattered my resolve. I could barely find words to express my disappointment. "But you said—"

Katy and the rest were on their feet, ready to act if needed.

"Preston, be quiet. Please." She spoke without her normal poise. Her reply was quick and frail. "Do you have the items I asked you to bring?"

When I tapped my toe she bent down and picked up the Jack Daniels bottle.

She shook it hard, breaking up the little clumps of clay. Then she walked a few feet due east and sprinkled a spot of dirt onto the road. She did it again to the north, to the west, and to the south. There was still a good bit of dirt in the bottle by the time she'd finished, and she used some of it to connect the dots to make a circle.

"Lift up your foot," she said. "Quickly."

She scattered half of what remained under my left boot.

"Put your foot down, and do not move it." She'd moved fast, methodically. "Now the other."

She poured the rest beneath my right boot. When the bottle was empty I planted my foot, and did not move it.

"Silver coin?"

I found it in my pocket.

"Put it on your tongue. And whatever happens, do not speak. Do you hear? Don't say anything. In your head, think 'Body of Christ' over and over, nothing else."

"Dani—"

"You cannot speak, Preston. This is a warning." She put her hand over my mouth as she turned to look over her shoulder.

"I misled you—we have nothing to discuss tonight. Maybe you will never believe me, but it was not easy to have used you like this." She looked very sad, distracted. "I didn't know any other way. Surely you must think I'm horrible, which I do not deny, not anymore. I have acted selfishly, and am very sorry to have involved you. And I am not evil in the way you think."

She took a bit of chalk and wrote crazy letters I didn't recognize on the blacktop.

"In my apartment, when we were eating sushi, I said to let everybody write what she wants, and I meant it very sincerely. Do you remember?" She stopped writing long enough to look up at me. "I said that nothing matters until it is written. If it is not written, it never happened. Do you remember?"

I looked for Katy. It hurt a bit to see Ben holding her. Protecting her. Pauly had his face buried in his hands.

"Well, I have nothing with your name written on it. And I have nothing with your brother's name written on it. I am the only one here bound by an inscription."

From the east I heard a rumble and tried to turn, but was too scared to move my feet.

Danicka said, "For one hundred and fifty years I have tried to renegotiate my destiny. But the biggest part of my agreement specifically forbade that."

I bit my lower lip and glared at her. *That's where I come in.*

"And I am sorry to have deceived you. So very, very sorry. Perhaps, I recognized that a part of you would harbor compassion for me even though I'd hurt you so badly. But I couldn't rely on that. Not tonight. The price that I paid was the price of never being able to love or trust." She sniffed back tears.

"With everybody I touch recoiling from me..." Her eyes searched the sky for something. A word maybe, or an intervention. "Every time I share a kind word with a man, he learns to abhor me. Two lifetimes of accumulated hatred. Enough rejection and coldness for ten women."

She pointed at Katy. "You can find love and die knowing you are loved, but I can't. Because I can never love, even if that is what my heart wants more than anything. But until I have loved, I am the same stupid girl I was one hundred and fifty years ago. It's my shame, to have agreed to something I now see is a lie. A tremendous lie and a curse."

She put her hand over my mouth again. "Remember not to speak and do not move."

A cold wind blew down from the salmon-colored sky. I heard a commotion from the cars. Somebody shuffling their feet.

Danicka yelled, "No!" and I twisted to see.

Ben and Rachael both yelled, "Katy!"

But it was too late. She broke Ben's grip and ran into the intersection, past Dani and into the circle. She put her feet right next to mine and wrapped her arms around me.

"I'm not doing this anymore, Preston. If we're together…" she cried.

I lifted my arm and held her against me while my guitar slid to my back.

"She is stupid. Stupid. What does she think—" Danicka reached into her pocket. She held up a silver coin like a priest holding up the Eucharist. "You do not need to be here, only Preston! Put this on your tongue and do not speak."

As Katy closed her lips my body shook, like electrodes had been clamped to my shoulders. My back and neck jerked and my legs wobbled. My ankles felt like they'd been replaced with marbles.

"I needed only Preston because I am forbidden from performing this ritual. You must understand that I could not simply ask him to do it as a favor to me." Danicka stumbled as the ground shook. She took Katy's hand and looked into her eyes. "You must not say anything."

I held Katy and fought gravity to keep the grave dust beneath my boots. All along the intersection people fell to their knees.

"Get back." Danicka yelled, "Stay off the road."

An electrical sensation rose from the pavement. My shoulders jerked up to my neck as my head rolled forward with each pulse. My fingers curled as current throbbed through them. Katy and I kept each other from falling over. Danicka toppled toward the edge of the circle she'd made. I grabbed her wrist with my free hand.

A flash of light appeared on the horizon, like from distant fireworks. Another boom hit so hard the traffic lights shook. Our shadows swayed back and forth in front of us like pendulums. The energy traveled through my knees and hips as people ran to their cars.

Then everything was quiet.

As my mind tried to anticipate what came next, a figure emerged from the light on the broken white line of Highway 49. Down where the white lines met the horizon I could barely perceive movement. But it closed the miles fast.

"Stay off the road!" Danicka yelled. "Everybody!"

Like an animal, but I couldn't be certain.

Running at full speed.

A clumsy, uneven march. A gallop.

Stumbling over nothing.

Arms flailing out to both sides.

It fell and tumbled forward and pushed itself back up. Danicka pressed herself against me and Katy, holding her arms out to the side like a mother trying to defend her children. She placed her foot between mine, trying to get a little grave dust beneath her own toes. "Don't say anything. You both must remember this."

Short in stature, it ran from one edge of the concrete to the other. Zig-zagging from side to side. Banging car hoods and kicking quarter panels.

People recoiled and hid behind their cars and trucks. Some ran into the trees.

As it got within twenty yards the highway cleared completely. Some got into their vehicles and locked the doors. Some screamed.

Danicka trembled while I fought to stay on my feet. The smell of sulfur and human waste filled my nose. Like the odor of the sewage plant down by the river. The aroma caught in my throat. Made my eyes water.

Unable to take more than two or three steps in a straight line because its legs were two very different lengths, it came into the crossroads, running wide circles. Its clothes were old-fashioned but difficult to place. Black pants torn at the knees. A white collared shirt with buttons and long sleeves, ripped and stained yellow and brown as if from vomit and shit and whatever else. Blond hair stuck out at all angles from his head. Its eyes drifted up to the stop-lights as it spun wide arcs that got closer and closer to the dead center of the crossroads.

Closer to us.

"Do not speak."

It looked like one of the kids from the special classes back in school. Not special, like Billy Clover from second grade. He had art and music with us and all his other classes were in another building.

This boy had eyes that never quite found anything to focus on. His face, neck and arms were covered in dark scabs. The white of his left eye appeared brown and bloody. A lazy half-smile stayed on his crusty lips, his cracked tongue waggled in the cool air. Except for when he spotted my guitar. He stumbled toward me and reached for it with a dirty, curled finger. The stench made me gag. He batted at the strings. His right arm was dramatically longer than his left. Like, fifteen inches longer.

"Don't react to him," Danicka whispered in my ear. "Do not speak."

I put my hands at my side as it tried to pull the guitar away from me. I turned my head and leaned back.

It stamped its feet and the ground shook. A noise like a bray from a hound dog came from deep in its chest. Headlights and tail lights flashed, and horns blared as car alarms were activated.

My ears rang, shooting sharp pain into my head like an ice pick through my eye into the dead center of my brain. Tears streamed down my cheeks. I held Katy's head to my chest, even when she wanted to turn and look at him.

Danicka pleaded, "You must listen, please."

She folded her hands and bowed her head. "You've made your point and I am sorry."

It stood there, swaying on uneasy legs. Its head fell from side to side like a slow metronome.

"Please!" Dani screamed. She sniffed back tears. "I have done everything for you. Even at Leningrad and Srebrenica I did everything you asked."

Its posture stiffened, its arms didn't fall so easily at its sides, like it was swelling.

"You lied to me." She pounded her chest, her tiny little fist accented each syllable. "My family died. Every last one of them. You promised protection."

To the east, the sky grew pinker, inch by inch.

"I've fulfilled my end, don't you—"

It grabbed Dani by the hair and slammed her to the ground. Blood came from her nose and ears. She pulled her knees toward her chest to shield herself from further harm.

"You can't hurt me anymore." Danicka looked up at it and said, "You've taken everything."

It stomped its foot. The force knocked me back to the edge of the circle. Katy fell into me. My guitar hit the blacktop with a crunch. The birds took to the sky in a wash of blackness. Even the wind came to a sudden end.

With the voice of a kid, speaking in multiple, ancient accents, it said, "If you break this seal, I will rape you like the Benjamites raped the Levite's concubine. I will eat the flesh of every last king and general, of every last saint and prophet, in your name. Then to honor your broken promise, I will wash it down with the blood of every last man and woman on earth."

It brushed the grave dust aside with its foot and stepped into the circle. "Then I will cut you into twelve pieces, and I will eat you, and each bite will be like honey in my mouth."

It hovered over Dani, inching closer and closer to me. Its bloody tongue searched for something at the corner of its mouth. "And I'll leave only the children to cleanse the earth's surface with their tears."

"Do not move," Danicka looked up at me through teary eyes. Her voice was frail. She wiped the blood from her nose with the back of her hand.

It walked backward, then slowed.

"And you," it said, looking at Katy and me. "Next time you dial my number, we're going to talk."

It turned and drifted back toward the sunrise before shuffling into a flailing run.

My eyes fell. I didn't see it disappear into the light.

For the longest time I couldn't move. And Katy didn't move. She held me so tight I thought she'd lift us both into the air. I realized I'd been holding my breath. I turned my head and spit the silver coin onto the road.

"Hey," I said.

Off in the distance I heard a car horn. Somebody needing to get through the crossroads on their way to church. That broke the spell.

Rachael and Jamie grabbed Katy, helping her to her feet. Pauly took my hands and lifted me off the asphalt. Some of the people who'd stayed to watch drifted into the crossroads with us. Nobody spoke.

Finally, after giving us both a good once-over, Jamie said, "You kids okay?"

I nodded.

Jamie began to speak, but Katy cut him off. "Nobody saw anything. Hear me? Nothing. Let these people all say what that want. But you didn't see anything."

All I could do was bite my lip.

"Chloey, do you hear me? Mom, tell her."

Rachael said, "She knows."

She looked for Ben, to tell him, but he'd walked right past us and took a knee on the ground next to Dani. With a gentle touch, he wiped blood from her cheek with a blue bandana. "I'm Ben."

He extended his hand, and added, "Collins."

"Danicka Prochazka." She gazed up at him with those big amber eyes and accepted his hand. While she gathered her composure, he bent over and brushed dirt and gravel from her knees.

She turned to me, and said, "Danicka Petráková Prochazka," then waited for some sort of confirmation that I understood.

I acknowledged with a nod.

Ben put his hand around her waist and led her over to her car. He opened the passenger-side door for her. Just before getting in himself, he tossed Henry the keys to his Jeep and gave us all a half-salute.

And as Ben started the silver Mercedes, Jamie reached into his jacket pocket and handed me his own keys.

As Ben completed a three-point turn, Jamie took off his glasses and wiped his eyes.

As Danicka and Ben disappeared into the night, Jamie broke off from the group and headed back to his car. I released Katy, and caught up with him. He slowed when I put my hand on his shoulder.

"He's never coming home, is he?" Jamie's eyes searched my face for honesty.

"He'll be back, Jamie," I said. I didn't know what else to do. "He just finally found a soul that needed saved more than his own."

Jamie hugged me before settling into the backseat.

The rest of them stood there wearing their saddest faces. They held each other for support, keeping that grey cloud over their heads for just a little bit longer. I had to prompt them to follow us back over to the cars.

"What the hell do we do now?" Henry said.

"I don't know, man. I really don't know. We'll figure it out once we get out of here."

I grabbed Katy's hand and kissed it, then I grabbed Pauly and pulled him over to me and gave him a big kiss on the cheek. I looked at Chloey, still nursing her arm. She rested her head on her mom's shoulder.

"Preston..." was all that Katy could say.

"I know," I said. I watched the sky for some sign that this was over, some sign that I'd done the right thing. By now I knew that sign would never come.

Katy sat down and looked at me for an answer, maybe expecting from me the words I wanted from above. But try as I might, the only thing I could come up with was a weak, "I told you I'd take care of everything," before shutting her door.

ACKNOWLEDGEMENTS

The Revelations of Preston Black is not the result of writing to impress. I wrote this book for fun, and I'm extremely grateful for all of the people who have helped to make this process so rewarding and so wildly entertaining: Brad Vetter for the incredible cover design; Joe White and Ayla Nett from Black Bear Burritos' Morgantown location for their infinite generosity and support; Sam McCanna of Skurvy Ink for the awesome T-shirts; Jennifer Barnes, John Edward Lawson and the rest of the Raw Dog Screaming Press gang for the camaraderie and legitimized debauchery; and Michael A. Arnzen for always being the best friend a writer could have.

And Heidi, thank you for needing me as much as I need you.

ABOUT THE AUTHOR

Jason Jack Miller knows it's silly to hold onto the Bohemian ideals of literature, music, and love above all else. But he doesn't care.

His own adventures paddling wild mountain rivers and playing Nirvana covers for less-than-enthusiastic crowds inspired his Murder Ballads and Whiskey series, published by Raw Dog Screaming Press. The next installment, *All Saints*, is due out in 2014. He is a creative writing adjunct at Seton Hill University, where he also mentors in the school's prestigious Writing Popular Fiction MFA program. Jason is a member of the Authors Guild and International Thriller Writers. He lives just outside of Pittsburgh with his wife, Heidi, and a cat. His blog is http://jasonjackmiller.blogspot.com. Tweet him @jasonjackmiller.